USA TODAY bestselling, RITA® Award–nominated and critically acclaimed author **Caitlin Crews** has written more than 130 books and counting. She has a master's and a PhD in English literature, thinks everyone should read more category romance, and is always available to discuss her beloved alpha heroes. Just ask! She lives in the Pacific Northwest with her comic book artist husband, is always planning her next trip, and will never, ever, read all the books in her to-be-read pile. Thank goodness.

Millie Adams is the very dramatic pseudonym of *New York Times* bestselling author Maisey Yates. Happiest surrounded by yarn, her family and the small woodland creatures she calls pets, she lives in a small house on the edge of the woods, which allows her to escape in the way she loves best—in the pages of a book. She loves intense alpha heroes and the women who dare to go toe-to-toe with them.

Also by Caitlin Crews

Her Accidental Spanish Heir
Forbidden Greek Mistress
An Heir for Christmas
Sicilian Devil's Prisoner

Also by Millie Adams

After-Hours Heir
Dragos's Broken Vows
Promoted to Boss's Wife
Heir of Scandal

Discover more at millsandboon.co.uk.

IN THE KING'S BED

CAITLIN CREWS

MILLIE ADAMS

MILLS & BOON

All rights reserved including the right of reproduction in whole or in part in any form. This edition is published by arrangement with Harlequin Enterprises ULC.

This is a work of fiction. Names, characters, places, locations and incidents are purely fictional and bear no relationship to any real life individuals, living or dead, or to any actual places, business establishments, locations, events or incidents. Any resemblance is entirely coincidental.

Without limiting the exclusive rights of any author, contributor or the publisher of this publication, any unauthorised use of this publication to train generative artificial intelligence (AI) technologies is expressly prohibited. HarperCollins also exercise their rights under Article 4(3) of the Digital Single Market Directive 2019/790 and expressly reserve this publication from the text and data mining exception.

® and TM are trademarks owned and used by the trademark owner and/or its licensee. Trademarks marked with ® are registered with the United Kingdom Patent Office and/or the Office for Harmonisation in the Internal Market and in other countries.

First published in Great Britain 2026
by Mills & Boon, an imprint of HarperCollins*Publishers* Ltd,
1 London Bridge Street, London, SE1 9GF

www.harpercollins.co.uk

HarperCollins*Publishers*, Macken House, 39/40 Mayor Street Upper, Dublin 1, D01 C9W8, Ireland

In the King's Bed © 2026 Harlequin Enterprises ULC

King's Heir of Hate © 2026 Caitlin Crews

From Convent to Queen © 2026 Millie Adams

ISBN: 978-0-263-41817-0

02/26

Printed and Bound in the UK using 100% Renewable Electricity at CPI Group (UK) Ltd, Croydon, CR0 4YY

KING'S HEIR OF HATE

CAITLIN CREWS

MILLS & BOON

CHAPTER ONE

His Majesty Xavier Tadeo Santiago did not have to make it all the way up the drive to the remote manor house in the farthest reaches of the royal estate to know that it was far past time to divorce his queen.

The drive itself was a pageant of early spring flowers flung in all directions like a discordant quilt. They were clumped here and festooned there, their bright colors clashing with each other and running all over the place, making a dramatic visual cacophony on both sides of the drive.

He found them offensive at once.

Tadeo was well acquainted with the work of the groundskeeper and his staff. They kept the rest of the royal estate in pristine and orderly condition, as was right and proper, since the royal family served its subjects and was called to present—always—their best foot forward. These grounds belonged to the kingdom. As did the palace, its contents, and indeed, the royal family itself.

Even the king himself was no more or less than the property of the kingdom, or so Tadeo's father had always taught him.

It meant more with the ghost of Tadeo's mother hanging always between them. The spectacle she'd made of herself. The shame and scandal she'd rained down upon the palace and the kingdom. His father had done his best to remain stalwart in the face of her behavior—always an uphill battle.

Now it was Tadeo's duty to take up the mantle that his father had carried until the day of his death five months ago. It had taken him all of this time to feel comfortable in the role that he had been preparing for all his life. It had required all of his focus and commitment to make the transition from his father's reign to his own as seamless as possible. There had been the somber funeral, then the burial, then the typical period of mourning.

But spring was coming. The Kingdom of Bellaza was coming alive after its cold, hard winter.

Tadeo needed to divorce his wife and move on—though, to minimize scandal and disruption, the divorce would have to be civilized. He had already plotted out the messaging with his team, and he had come to do this unpleasant task in person because he felt that was appropriate and a husband owed a wife that much. He assumed that it would be an uncomfortable conversation, perhaps, but a brief one.

After all, he had made it perfectly clear during their widely publicized courtship that this was precisely what would happen once he became king. They would play the part of a royal couple so well-suited to each other that their subjects made up happy endings for them—though there would be precious few public displays as they went about their official duties. Tadeo's family was well known for its adherence to the strictest protocol. They would let the public make whatever meal it liked from perfectly polite and expected touches.

Tadeo had been told there was fan fiction about their

private life all over the internet. He chose not to know what that was.

But this marriage would end. They would never see each other again once they navigated their way through a divorce so amicable it would be applauded. He'd already spent time with his team plotting out the details. Once the divorce was handled, after a suitable period of reflection, Tadeo would find a far more suitable queen and set about making the heir the kingdom required.

He had spent seven years making certain that he saw Esme only when required to for the work they did, never in any private capacity that could lead to complications in his plan in the form of the child he adamantly did not want with her.

Well, a voice in him chided, *you managed it for* almost *all of those seven years, anyway.*

Tadeo did not wish to think about that one slip, five months ago. There were other, more pressing things at the moment, like the fact that the condition of the manor's grounds appalled him. More than that, the sight seemed to dig beneath his skin, as if she—and he knew it was her, if not with her own hands, then at her express direction—had planted all of the flowers in as unorthodox a fashion as possible *specifically* to bother him.

Queen Esme, betrothed to him since the day of her birth, his wife for the past seven years—and for one reckless year across an ocean in a foreign city, his lover—was astoundingly good at bothering him. She had a talent for getting under his skin in a way no one else could. Or ever had.

A reality that he had never come to terms with, though he had learned how to control his reactions to her over the years of their marriage. Tadeo, in truth, did not wish to come to terms with the ways Esme got to him. None of that mattered now.

"It all ends today," he assured himself, his voice a dark spool of sound in the interior of the car.

He was glad he was alone.

Tadeo had driven himself, waving off his usual guards because he did not intend to leave the royal estate. Now, still on the garish drive, he slowed the vintage Rolls-Royce that had been a part of his grandfather's collection and ordered himself to find his center. To remain calm.

Something that was normally not the least bit difficult for him.

Only Esme disrupted his equanimity. Only Esme forced him to confront the distasteful evidence that he truly was his mother's son, made of all the wild, impossible parts of her that had led her to make such a display of herself for all the world to see. He loathed that he possessed such depths inside himself and had spent most of his adult life doing all that he could to keep them locked away.

He could not be the king his country deserved unless and until he removed Esme from his life. He had known this going in, but there had always been so much investment in the fairy-tale notion of the Prince of Bellaza marrying the Princess of Clarebonne from the neighboring kingdom. Not least because the two kingdoms had been one, long ago, and this only added to the fairy-tale mystique. After the scandal his mother had wrought on her marriage and therefore also on Tadeo's father's reign, a fairy tale had seemed like a gift. A gift that could fix what his mother had broken.

But the fairy tale had run its course. Now was the time to act, and Tadeo was ready. He was more than ready.

Their marriage would end quietly. There were no children after seven years of living completely separate lives in private, so there was no claim to the throne to worry about. Esme could go off to make a mess of whatever she wished, wherever she wished to do it, without it having any bearing on him.

Just so long as she left Bellaza and Tadeo never laid eyes on her again, he would be happy.

Because he would finally be able to *breathe*.

He would not let her damned flowers get to him, reminding him of too many things he did not wish to think about. All of them involving Esme and that recklessness only she conjured up in him. He would see to it that her gardening additions were summarily removed as soon as she left the manor house and replaced with a tidy hedge. There would be no sign of Esme's disruptive presence once she left, and that was what mattered. This chapter of his life was finally ending.

And not a moment too soon.

The drive wound around at last to the house itself, which was a fine old Bellazan structure made in the late medieval period, then renovated time and again in the centuries since to suit the whims of a succession of queens. When Tadeo had handed it off to his brand-new queen on their wedding night, it had been a sturdy, quietly elegant monument of the kingdom's history. He had not been here since.

An oversight, clearly.

Tadeo was not certain that he could entirely believe his own eyes as he gazed out at the monstrosity that loomed before him at the top of the drive.

She had…painted it, if that was what it could be called. What she'd done was gaudy. It was an *assault*.

In place of the expected white walls and red-tiled rooftops that nodded toward the kingdom's Spanish neighbors, plus the hint of the nearby French countryside in the sprawling gardens that would not look out of place surrounding a chateau, the Queen's Manor House—once considered the refined jewel of the royal estate—now appeared to have been vomited upon by an intoxicated rainbow.

Tadeo was so aghast at the tasteless horror show in front of him that he almost forgot to step on the brake in the car. He rolled to a stop only centimeters from crashing into the insufferably bright magenta wall before him. He continued to stare out through the windshield, not able to accept that he was truly seeing the ornate, excessive, and expansive palate of too many colors before him.

He wondered if it was possible that he was, in fact, having a stroke.

At least that sensation was familiar.

It was much the way he had felt the morning after his father's death five months ago, when he had woken to find that it wasn't a dream. Not only was his noble and admirable father truly dead, when the old man had always seemed so invincible, but Tadeo had actually gone and done the one thing he'd vowed he would never, ever do.

He had allowed Esme into his bed. Or rather, a couch in his father's study, but it was the same regret either way.

Tadeo knew better.

God help him, did he know better.

He could recall that morning perfectly. How he had lain there on the couch in the study where she'd found him after the funeral, feeling as if he was fracturing into a thousand shards of jagged glass as she curled up at his side. She was so peaceful. She looked like an angel as she slept, the way she always had.

She still fit against his body perfectly.

It seemed impossible, after all those years, and yet there was no denying it.

Tadeo had felt as if his chest was cracked wide open, and she was to blame for it.

Just as she had been the first time, years ago, when they'd finally met each other on the other side of the world. He had been doing his graduate work in the sort of business, economics, and public policy issues that could only serve the kingdom. She had been an undergraduate in the same city. A city that seemed like a long-lost daydream to him now. The Boston of his memories was always covered in towers of snow to mark its bitter winters. There were no mountains to speak of, when Bellaza was ringed with them. More, the wild Atlantic was forever seething about at the end of streets and in the distance, as if keeping watch.

He liked to tell himself that he had been happy to leave that strange, small city—but he still woke up from dreams that smelled like the salt marshes of Cape Cod on a quiet spring morning, or sounded like the rattle of the T, or had him remembering walking along the Charles River on a picture-perfect fall afternoon.

Tadeo exited the car outside the manor house, shutting the driver's door sharply behind him. Then realized that he was standing about because he wasn't used to arriving anywhere and not being immediately greeted by staff. He was quite certain that there was staff at the manor house. What he did not understand was why none of them made themselves known as protocol demanded.

Thoughts of Boston felt like a reprimand, but then, he

had known at the time that those years were an indulgence. That he was permitted to indulge in a kind of freedom there—the independence to walk where he pleased and live a life with far less scrutiny in a country not his own. He had known he never would again.

Still, he found himself shaking off unwanted memories yet again as he started for the main door, painted in a revolting shade of pink. If he was a vindictive man, he might have been tempted to make Esme pay to restore the house to its traditional state before releasing her. But that would only prolong this.

And to Tadeo's way of thinking, their entire relationship had already been entirely too prolonged.

He had known that he was betrothed since he was a child. He was five years older than Esme and had been showed pictures of her over time. She had been raised in Clarebonne, which was even smaller than Bellaza and had always enjoyed favorable relations with it, dating all the way back to the time in antiquity when the kingdoms had been joined. Their betrothal had been speculated about in the press all throughout their teenage years because it was not a formal, legal betrothal in the old style. It was an understanding.

An understanding between two kings was as good as law, in some places, but the two kings in question had been very deliberate about the way they'd handled Esme and Tadeo. The two of them had not met. They were deliberately kept apart, in fact.

No one expects you and Esme to molder on shelves, at least until you meet, Tadeo's father, King Hugo, had always said. *You can enjoy yourself as you wish, as long as you remain* ever-conscious *of your duties and* scrupulous *about your reputation.*

Yes, sir, Tadeo had murmured. He had been all of fourteen and did not wish to think about his duties any more than necessary, given he had already found them crushing. Much less his spotless reputation, though that part he was admittedly more concerned with.

King Alain and I are agreed that you and Princess Esme should meet when she is finished with her studies. What that means, his father had said, perhaps more sternly than before, *is that you may do what you wish, but you should never be linked in public with another woman. Neither one of you must ever be seen in any kind of amorous situation, or in any questionable position that could be interpreted the wrong way. You might find this onerous. But it is excellent practice for your future.* His craggy face, with the blue eyes Tadeo had inherited, had been somber. *I expect there to be no scandals, Tadeo. Not one, not ever. Do you understand?*

Tadeo had always understood.

He had only been eleven when his mother had died, off in a boating accident in Italy with one of her many lovers. Some had claimed that Tadeo was too young to understand what was happening then, but they were mistaken. He had understood completely. And even if he hadn't, he certainly would have heard every sordid detail at school, where his status as crown prince had long since lost its luster.

Even if he'd wished to avoid his mother's exploits, he'd been unable to.

For years at that point, it had been impossible for Tadeo to avoid the sordid details that his mother seemed to have no shame sharing with the whole world. Everybody knew the story of the selfish, unsatisfied Queen of Bellaza who had provided the kingdom with its needed heir and then declared her duties and responsibilities completed.

The rest of my life is mine, cries the Queen! the headlines screamed.

Tadeo had understood completely and totally that he could not, as that queen's son, create that kind of scandal. No matter what.

Even if he hadn't been told exactly that by his father, repeatedly, he would have come to the same conclusion himself. The kingdom prized its calmness. Its peace. Scandals were for other, more volatile nations.

It was Tadeo's duty not to become a scandal. He took that seriously.

He had therefore enjoyed himself, but always with women who understood his position. And who, more to the point, he trusted not to sell him out to the papers. This meant that he was significantly less of a player than many of his boarding school friends, but he would not be the one to put the family's name into the mud again.

He had vowed it after his mother's funeral. It was the first, last, and only time he had ever seen his father cry. Or, more precisely, allow his eyes to look damp. For the smallest moment.

Tadeo had learned over time that there were warning signs when a woman he might have been interested in was the wrong choice. Bright red flags that would indicate when a woman was appropriate for him or not, and it was his duty to look for those flags and react accordingly. He liked the women he dated, very privately, to be circumspect in all things. Modest, practical, and smart enough to think twice when it came to exposing him.

He had never chosen wrong.

If it had been up to him, he would never have chosen Princess Esme.

Tadeo had been the one to initiate their meeting in Boston. He'd been in graduate school across the river in Cambridge and even though he did not go out of his way to keep up with the Princess's every move, he could not avoid knowing that she was attending nearby Wellesley College, a very highly selective women's college with an august reputation.

His palace handlers—now his team—made certain he knew.

They were both far away from the intense press interest that surrounded them in their own countries. They were both still immersed in their studies, so there would be no chance of accelerating the march toward their wedding. Tadeo had thought it would be safe. Easy. A smart move to build a friendship in advance, so that the years they would spend together as husband and wife could only be better for it.

Too well had he understood the point of the stories King Hugo had told about his own courtship of Tadeo's mother. Lady Marisol had not been his family's first choice. She had not been a choice at all. She had been impetuous, bright, and bold. The King had fallen hard and had insisted that he would marry her or he would not marry at all.

But soon enough, Marisol had grown bored of royal life. Just as everyone had warned the King she would.

What had followed had haunted his father for the rest of his life, and now haunted Tadeo too. The ghost of Marisol was what lay beneath every decision and every plan Tadeo made for his life and his reign. He thought about the scenes she had made, the extramarital affairs she had flaunted, the contempt with which she had treated the kingdom in general and his father in particular, and vowed to do whatever was necessary to protect the kingdom from a repeat of such embarrassment.

He had married Esme because their kingdoms were invested in their wedding, a choice he would make again if necessary. Just as he would divorce her now because she could never be an appropriate mother to his heir. She was too difficult. Too…problematic.

Back in Boston, Tadeo had possessed absolutely no desire to repeat history. He'd had no intention of ever allowing the kind of passion that had blindsided his father and made him turn his back on his kingdom for the pleasures of the flesh to level him as well.

He had been completely and totally unprepared for Esme, in other words.

Another familiar feeling he very much wished to banish from his life entirely.

No servants appeared at the door, or responded when he knocked, so he opened it himself and went inside. And in case he'd imagined that the exterior of the building was the only place that his wife had allowed her creativity free reign, he was quickly disabused of that notion.

The color scheme—though that word, *scheme*, suggested some kind of a plan, which Tadeo doubted very much had been used here—continued inside. He walked through, finding that his jaw was tense and that he was grinding his teeth as he looked from one ruined room to the next. There was nothing in the whole of the historic house that she had not changed.

Nothing.

It felt like a metaphor for the way she had laid waste to Tadeo's own principles and self-regard.

Tadeo hated fucking metaphors.

Though as he walked through one atrium that bled into the next, with more floral theatrics at every turn, he knew that he could not lay that solely at her feet. The woman could be as wicked as she liked, but it was the wickedness in him that had met hers.

He was the one at fault. He accepted that.

Now he wished to be done with it. There was no doubt a sweet, unassuming, deeply boring heiress somewhere that he could marry and never think about again. She would do her job and leave him to his. They would have a pleasant, comfortable, smooth sort of life, marked by nothing but the milestones of their children and the peaceful prosperity of the kingdom.

He could almost taste it. All that was needed was the quietly amicable divorce he had planned, with tasteful statements to the press about going their separate ways with no acrimony and the best of wishes for the other's happiness, etcetera, and he could have peace at last.

At last.

On the other side of the ruined house, he stepped outside onto one of the back terraces and surveyed the gardens as they stretched out toward the horizon and the Pyrenees in the distance.

It did not take a degree in landscape architecture to realize that the gardens, too, had been changed.

In seven years, Esme had completely transformed the sophisticated, manicured gardens that previous queens who had lived here—excluding his mother, of course, who had never set foot on this property while the gleaming shores of the Côte d'Azur existed—had enjoyed. They had all taken pride in overseeing the tending of these gardens, always passing the torch along to keep them quiet, contemplative. A fitting place of respite for a queen. A place for meditation and relaxation.

There was nothing the least bit *relaxing* about the gardens greeting him now.

They were a deafening bugle of early spring exuberance.

There were daffodils and crocuses and cherry blossoms, and they were everywhere, bright and bold. Unseemly and overwhelming, Tadeo thought darkly, and he could not understand why he could not find a single, solitary soul to explain to him what was happening here.

He knew that Esme had not gone on a trip of any kind. Her schedule went through his office, for his review. The palace had only just begun taking on their outward-facing duties again as mourning for the late King had only this week come to an official end.

Esme should have been here. Doing whatever it was she did with her time.

Which was, he reflected now, wrecking heritage sites with the wanton application of tawdry colors slapped about with no thought whatsoever for the lines of the garden or its pathways or its internal logic, apparently.

He stood still in the not precisely warm air of the late February morning, generating more than enough heat on his own. The sun was already warm, hinting at the fairer months to come. The chill of winter almost felt like a memory when the sunlight moved over his face.

Tadeo needed her excised from this house, and the kingdom, and his life before another season passed. If he allowed himself the sort of dramatics he felt only when he was in Esme's vicinity, he would be tempted to think his own life depended on it.

"But I do not allow it," he growled out at himself. As

a reminder he should not have needed, yet clearly did. Another reason this long, torturous chapter of his life needed to end.

He thought he heard a sound in the distance and he made himself walk toward it, scowling at the once-orderly flower beds everywhere, now showing no restraint or any evidence of planning. It was all too bright. Too out of control. As if someone had spun around in a circle like a child with bubbles, flinging seeds about.

The image he had then, of Esme doing exactly that, did not help his mood any.

Tadeo battled his way down an overgrown pathway where vines had been encouraged to do as they liked, making his way out toward the far end of the gardens, where a pergola sat between the garden proper and the start of the vineyards that some enterprising queen had insisted be grown here some while back. They did not produce a lot of wine, but every year, the queen's vintners produced a specialized run of limited-edition bottles of the queen's Pinot Noir. It had long been seen as something of a status symbol among certain sets in the kingdom's society.

Tadeo half expected to find the vines torn up and discarded in favor of an amusement park or something equally hideous, but they were still there. Waiting for the summer to ripen into grapes suitable for wine.

He heard voices again and strode toward them, feeling more and more like a storm cloud as he went.

Then he walked up through the vine-laden path to the pergola and found his wife at last.

She was sitting at the long table in the shade there with what appeared to be her own staff members. There was food and drink in platters, but there were also swathes of fabric, and Esme herself seemed to be wearing half of them.

It took him long, heart-pounding moments to realize that he was reacting to two things at once. One, he had no idea what they were doing, and no one seemed to look at his direction or even notice he was there, which was unusual. Two, and more concerning, it was impossible not to notice that Esme looked…well.

Very well.

Glowing, in fact.

And his body, his temple that he preferred to keep completely under his control at all times like a bit of marble that he alone could sculpt, betrayed him yet again.

The way it had from the start where Esme was concerned.

Because every time he laid eyes on this woman, it was like he was burned alive. She was a poison in his blood, a curse upon his soul, and a great lamentation in the cock that he otherwise ruthlessly controlled. If *a great lamentation* was what to call it when he was nothing at all but hard and needy while the woman was doing nothing but sitting in a chair across a table from where he was standing, with very little of her visible aside from her face.

Damn her.

He waited. Esme didn't look up. She was talking animatedly to one of the women dressed in black beside her. They were both moving their fingers over the fabric that was swaddled all over as if they'd been draping it over Esme on purpose, but he couldn't hear what they were saying.

It was possible he had stood there a long while before a different woman altogether looked up, met Tadeo's gaze, and gasped.

"Your Majesty!" she cried.

He watched the ripple effect as it happened. First everyone froze. Then, as if lit by the same flame, all of the servants leaped to their feet—pushing back their chairs so there were loud scraping noises against the tile patio, then dropping into deep, deep curtsies.

His queen, Tadeo noticed—his *wife*, though hopefully not for much longer—did not rise, though it was protocol that she do so. Esme stayed where she was, draped in so many different shades of billowing fabric that he could barely see her body beneath it.

"Leave us," Tadeo told the staff, and did not watch them as they all fluttered off, like so many dark-feathered birds. He kept watching Esme. He studied her maddeningly perfect oval of a face with her dark flashing eyes and that lush, impossible mouth that he absolutely could not feel all over his body, because that was insupportable.

"Have you taken up sewing?" he asked her, not convinced he was entirely in control of his voice. He blamed her for that, too.

The proverbial straw on a camel's back.

"I'm redecorating a room," she replied.

In that same serene voice of hers. Brimming with that same abominable confidence that he found both atrocious and wildly compelling.

Tragically, she also remained the most beautiful woman he'd ever encountered.

This had been true when she was but a sophomore at Wellesley. It was even more true now. It was an outrage on every level, but she still looked like the model of the perfect woman, should he have been asked to draw such a creature.

Should *drawing* be one of his talents.

It was not that she was the most beautiful woman in the world, he supposed. But it was a cruel trick of fate that she managed to hit every single one of the buttons Tadeo had not entirely realized he had until he'd met her. She was elegant. She was graceful in everything, from her smallest gestures to the way she laughed—a sound that came from her belly and transformed her whole face. She had the sort of exquisite manners that were necessary for the circles they moved in, but Esme always made them seem as if they were innate.

As it was not something she was *doing*, but something that was simply a part of *who she was*.

She had been kind to his father, who had been less enticed by the *fairy-tale* argument and had been largely chilly in return. She was always kind to their subjects, no matter what sort of questions they tried to ask her while she was shaking hands and playing her part. It was his cross to bear that she also looked equally as stunning when she was in jeans and flats as she did in a bespoke gown made for ceremony and circumstance.

Today, she had her dark, glossy hair piled casually on the back of her head. It looked like she was wearing a simple T-shirt, which seemed to hug her curves more than usual. And yet she still simply emanated sophistication from every pore.

Only Tadeo knew that there were ways to touch this woman that lit her on fire. Only he knew what she looked like, her dark eyes glazed over with sex and longing, her mouth open while sounds of desire poured out, and how she writhed beneath him, taking more and more until he wasn't certain if either one of them would actually survive—

But that was not the point of this visit.

"My father has been dead for five months," he told her curtly.

"Five months and thirteen days," Esme replied. Oddly specific, to his mind, but she said it so calmly. Her lips curved. "I am aware, Tadeo."

If he could go back in time, he would not have given her access to his family name. By the end, only his father still called him that in person. Most of his friends from school called him variations on his title. Or other nicknames of one sort or another.

The press, of course, used all of his names as they pleased.

He could have had her call him by his proper first name and he often thought that would be easier, because he wouldn't feel this tug of undeserved familiarity. Maybe the name alone would have done it. Maybe then he would never have become familiar with her at all.

But he couldn't go back to that first dinner in a quiet restaurant overlooking the Charles and fix what happened.

He could only do the necessary damage control now.

"I told you long ago that we would remain married only as long as necessary," he told her, no longer caring how dark he sounded. It needed to be done. It didn't matter *how* it was done. "I've come here to let you know that I intend to begin our divorce proceedings. Immediately."

Tadeo didn't know what he expected. For her to cheer, perhaps? Sometimes he convinced himself that she was no more interested in continuing this marriage of theirs than he was. Perhaps he thought she might cry? After all, he hadn't been so far gone that he'd forgotten the things she'd whispered in the night after his father's death.

Sometimes he thought those words haunted him.

But of all the possible responses he'd imagined, it wasn't the way she smiled at him.

Her lips curved gently. Even kindly, he thought.

And then she rose.

The fabric cascaded off her and slid in heaps of shimmering color to either side of her, landing on the tiles at her feet.

But Tadeo forgot all about that. He couldn't take his eyes off her.

Because the Esme he had last seen five months ago had been lean and lithe and in some way resembled the ballet dancer she had once told him she would have liked to have become, in a different life.

She stood, the fabric fell, and she placed her hand on the shelf of the belly—*her belly*—that had swelled up to enormous size. A great deal as if she had a ball beneath her shirt, when, of course, she did not.

It was impossible. It was inconceivable.

It was a disaster of epic proportions and she was *smiling*—

"About that divorce," Esme said, as if they were discussing the weather. Or what to have the staff prepare for a snack. As if she was not very obviously *pregnant*. "I wonder if you might want to rethink."

CHAPTER TWO

ESME COULD ADMIT that she found the look on Tadeo's face deeply satisfying, whatever that might have said about her as a person. She accepted that it likely said nothing good.

And yet there it was, just the same. Pure satisfaction, sweeping through her like a small, personal tsunami.

She had anticipated that this moment would please her when it came—and she'd known it would come eventually—but she had to admit that this far exceeded her expectations. Esme would not go so far as to say it made up for the past five months of self-recrimination, worry, and intense doubt, but it certainly felt like a gesture in that direction.

After all, she'd been expecting him for a long while now.

At first, she'd thought that he might come sooner. Right after that night in the palace, when the passion that he'd been denying for seven years had finally boiled over in that mess of grief and comfort…and what she thought was simply humanity at its most basic. What people did when they were still alive and someone they'd loved was dead.

But he didn't, because he was made of ice when he

wanted to be. So frigid it was a wonder flowers could even grow in this kingdom.

Then she'd been certain that he would make it happen at different times over the past few months. After he got back on his feet in the wake of the funeral. After he soothed the nation with his careful speeches from the iconic Bellazan throne room, promising his rule would be what they'd come to expect from his father—smooth and peaceful. After he figured out every last in and out of his new position, which shouldn't have been *too* overwhelming or taxing for him, all things considered. Since he had been training for it since the day he was born.

It had taken her a long while to accept that he was really going to wait as long as possible to face what had happened that night. To come to the bitter conclusion that he had no intention of addressing it, only of divorcing her.

In the meantime, of course, she'd had other things to think about. More pressing things, as said things were growing inside her.

"How is this possible?" asked the man himself now, after a satisfyingly long while looking *stunned*. The way a cartoon character looked when struck with a shovel, she rather thought. She'd never seen Tadeo look like that before. She would have said it was impossible.

But then, their entire history was studded with impossibilities, one after the next—so what was another one tossed on top?

Esme was distressed to find that he was still as offensively gorgeous as ever. He had not lost all of his hair. He had not shrunk down from his more than six feet. He had not lost that rangy, athletic physique of his that made it seem as if he spent significant hours of his life roaming about playing sports of one kind or another when she knew full well he did not. He was the king now and had previously been a very visible and involved crown prince. He could not be racing about playing football—soccer, when he'd been in the States—the way he had in his youth.

Sadly for her, he still possessed that chiseled male beauty and the most beautiful face she had ever seen on a man in her life. He had those remarkably blue eyes. That thick brown hair that wanted desperately to curl when he wasn't being so stern and austere. That impossibly perfect jaw with a *dimple*, no less, on the rare occasions he smiled.

That dimple had been her undoing.

More than once.

There was no sign of it today. Tadeo was wearing one of his casual outfits, such as it was. Esme was in a soft pair of maternity jeans to hold her precious belly, but His Majesty preferred not to wear jeans at all. He found them *déclassé*.

He had told her that shortly after their wedding as if she couldn't remember him wearing them back in Boston. All the time.

Here in Bellaza he preferred dark trousers. They were actually cargo pants today, and clung lovingly to his unduly powerful thighs. He was wearing what she supposed was technically a sweatshirt, but was of course of such fine construction and made from such intensely exquisite fabric that it fell over his exquisite chest like cashmere.

Esme's whole life would be completely different right now if this man had been even slightly unattractive.

She thought about this all the time.

If she had simply found him pleasant, if the conversation had been stilted that first night. If he hadn't reached over, that wondering sort of smile on his beautiful face with that *dimple* in evidence and that intensity in his blue gaze, then picked up her hand—

They would be different people. She would probably still be here, in this house of exile on the palace grounds, but she imagined she'd be resigned to it. And happier for it. Or they would have committed to one of those dreadfully common marriages of cold convenience, with separate rooms and scheduled copulation for the making of heirs, with a happy retreat into polite if distant companionship thereafter. Not unlike the marriage they'd had, really—except notably devoid of all the seething tension that had always underscored even their most seemingly polite interactions.

Tadeo scowled at her. "Do you intend to answer my question, Esme?"

She ordered herself to stop thinking about *copulation*. And his ruinous dimple. "I beg your pardon. I thought that was facetious at best." She studied him. "How do you think it happened, Tadeo?"

"But…" She had never seen this man flustered. Furious, yes. Cracking at the seams, certainly. Wild with passion, temper, emotion. All the things she had learned since that he deplored. She had seen all of that. But she'd never seen him simply…flustered. Yet today she thought that was exactly what he was. "But back in Boston…"

She thought she could hear his teeth grinding together. No doubt because he was physically allergic to admitting that they had, in fact, been in Boston. Together. Intimately.

"Are you…referencing our secret, scandalous past?" she asked in a very sweet tone that was not all that sweet. "Heaven forfend! Next thing you know, you'll be acknowledging that it actually happened, and then where would we be?"

"You didn't get pregnant then," he gritted out, a flash of something in his gaze that made her think that he was remembering that breathless year, the sheets they'd torn up, the pleasure they'd found—

But Boston was not the issue here. Not today.

"Of course I didn't get pregnant then." She folded her hands over her belly bump and allowed herself to enjoy the little things right here and now. Like this moment that felt a bit like schadenfreude. "Perhaps one of the numerous things you've conveniently forgotten about that time is how much we both wanted—"

"I do not want to discuss the details of those days," he bit out. Confirming that he was indeed remembering the same things she was, she rather thought. "They are like a fever dream I do not wish to revisit now that the worst of the illness is past."

"So you have mentioned," she said, soothingly, as if he was a fractious child. It had the effect she expected it would. He glowered.

But for years, that had been the closest she could get to the passion she remembered. The passion that sometimes woke her in the night to fume in her empty bed.

Or, some years, cry.

She would act the part required of her, poke at him a little, and call it a result when he responded in some way. In any way. And so had seven years gone by, somehow.

Yes, she was enjoying this today. It felt like payback. After all, he was *so* shocked. As if he hadn't been a full and enthusiastic participant in the act that led to this. "Let me set the scene for you. Two people meet and their attraction is overwhelming, outrageous. Life-altering, some might say."

"Esme."

"I know *you* wouldn't say that. Now." He scowled and she kept going. "Yet both of them knew that they had degrees to finish, kingdoms not to disappoint, and so on. They spent their first two weeks together in an agony of extended foreplay—"

"*Esme*. Why must you always do this? I do not wish to wallow in these memories you seem to want to trot out at the slightest provocation—"

"I was on the pill, Tadeo," she told him coolly. "I got on the pill the morning after our first meeting, and it worked. After our wedding, when you informed me that I would be imprisoned in this marriage until the day your father died and then summarily released, I saw no particular reason to continue playing games with my hormones. I went off the pill then. And here we are."

"You knew that you were not using birth control," he said, sounding as if he was being extremely careful with his words, likely because he thought they might detonate. Or he would. "You knew, and yet—"

"Be very careful, Tadeo," Esme advised him then. "You are straying perilously close to blaming me for a night in which both of us were drinking the very same alcohol from the very same bottle, and then made the very same choice. Perhaps you should question yourself."

"I've questioned myself every night since."

"Marvelous." She clasped her hands together. "Then you have already taken yourself to task for not handling the birth control options yourself. Either way, here we are. I am five months and thirteen days pregnant. If you would like to go ahead and divorce me, I won't stop you. That might even be best."

Her clasped hands folded nicely, so she did that and then propped them up on her belly again. Esme made herself smile, as beatifically as possible. Then when all he did was glower in her direction, she kept going. "I've had a lot of time to think about it, and I do think it might be best. I'm happy to divorce. You can continue doing... whatever self-flagellation exercises it is that you prefer. I can have a life. And our child can have the attention of both of its parents without having to worry about living in the ice fjords of the palace here." She considered. "Or at least not full-time."

"You might have had a lot of time to think about this, but I have had not." *Flustered*, she thought again, as he raked his hands through his hair. It made her wonder if he would ever grow it out again the way he had when he was a graduate student in a foreign land. And the other occupant of her bed.

After their affair had ended, he'd cut it all off.

She'd seen it in a tabloid and had cried for days.

"You can have all the time you need," she told him serenely now, as if bestowing upon him a great gift. "That said, there is a ticking clock." She patted her belly. "Like it or not."

Tadeo glared at her for what felt like a very long time. His gaze swept over her, from the top of her head to as much of her as he could see from his side of the table.

Esme could have told him that she'd been sitting out here playing with fabrics, imagining the nursery in this house. She had decided with the help of the staff members here, who had all become her friends, that it would be best to decorate it. To celebrate the baby and her impending motherhood while they all waited for that other shoe to fall.

They had all known that it would. Esme had told them from the start that if they felt it necessary to confess her condition to the King, she would understand. At the end of the day, they worked for him. Everyone in the kingdom did.

Especially her.

But not one of her staff had taken her up on that. Over the years, they'd become close. With the occasional addition of her friends from college, who would sometimes fly in and brighten things up for a while, the staff here were Esme's daily support.

Her parents were only a mountain range away, and supported her in all things, but she never wanted them to think that they'd made a mistake in setting up this marriage. She never wanted to worry them. She still didn't. In fact, she worked hard to convince them that everything in her marriage was fine. Perfectly *fine*—and she assumed her perceptive mother chose to believe her. Because her mother loved her.

We can see about confessions when His Majesty chooses to visit, the housekeeper had said tartly one morning, waiting for Esme outside the bathroom suite in her rooms. The older woman had held out the ginger drink they'd made for her on those early pregnancy mornings when her stomach wanted to separate itself from her body. As violently as possible. *But he would have to come here in order to do that, would he not?*

Esme could tell Tadeo all that. She could tell him what the past seven years had been like, sequestered in this manor house and trotted out only to smile and wave and play her part, all while pretending she felt nothing for him outside of the roles they played. But why start there? That was simply how long they'd been married.

She could go back even further. To having to drag herself through her final year of college utterly heartbroken, a ghost of her former self, because he had dropped her so cruelly. Her friends had rallied. They had done their best, but they didn't understand—and how could she explain?—that the situations with college boys they loved and would forget that they were comparing to her affair with Tadeo were different. Not as intense. Not as all-consuming. Not as *real*.

There was no way to share those things, even though she knew it was true. It would only make her sound delusional.

Esme had become so embarrassed by the fact that she couldn't seem to find her smile again that she'd forced it. She'd figured out how she could always put on a face appropriate to the moment, no matter what she was feeling inside. She'd learned how to play whatever role was needed and expected, with no one the wiser.

This new ability got her through graduation, then off to London for a charity internship that had been plotted out long ago. Princess Esme of Clarebonne had made a few tasteful charity-based headlines that year and at the end of it, she had been certain that she would be left to explain to her parents, her own kingdom—and his—that there would be no fairy-tale betrothal after all. That just because their families had agreed that there would be one, one day, and had even hinted in public at their being betrothed from her birth, it would never happen. She'd been preparing her statement since college.

Esme had been nothing short of flabbergasted when

she'd received formal notice from his kingdom that the royal courtship would begin.

Maybe, finally, she could tell him what it had been like to have to succumb to an extremely public relationship, every moment scripted for the cameras, with the ex who had ripped her heart out of her body and stomped it into dust. Like it was nothing.

But she doubted he wanted to hear any of that.

Now, she watched him turn away from her, looking back over the gardens that she had made her own. They were happy now. Bright explosions of color, basking in their own beauty. She treated the manor house itself the same way. Every time he made her sad, she found something else to brighten. Room by room, wall by wall, she put bright colors in place of the parts of her heart that he'd bruised.

She couldn't say that she regretted it.

"This isn't what I had planned either, you know," she said, addressing his back. His outrageously well-muscled back that, if she let herself think about it too much, she could actually *feel* beneath her fingertips. As if she was wrapped around him, holding him close, her fingers digging into his shoulder blades as he surged deep inside her—

The trouble with being pregnant, she had discovered, was that—contrary to what she'd always believed, given the way people talked about the state—she did not feel at all like that beaming, sexless, goddess mother figure she'd expected would take her over.

All she thought about was sex. Not just any kind of sex. Specifically, sex with Tadeo.

It was a torment.

His being here today didn't exactly help.

He didn't respond to her, so she kept going. "I was looking forward to our divorce. I was going to move back to the States. Do some good work with my time. Help others, perhaps launch a lifestyle cooking show, whatever came to mind. I thought perhaps I would find a chic home in Manhattan like Jackie Onassis and swan about with oversize sunglasses for the rest of my life, refusing interviews. Either way, the world was mine." She blew out a breath. "But somehow I think that's no longer the option that it was."

Her friends had been more and more adamant on every visit over the years. She needed to get the hell out of Bellaza. She had to get as far away as it was possible to get from King Tadeo.

That man has been a shadow over your entire life and has blocked out your sun since you were twenty, her best friend, Hilary, had said matter-of-factly. *It's been too long, Esme. It's time for something new.*

Esme had agreed. And instead, she was pregnant. Not just pregnant the way anyone might be, *she* was pregnant with the baby who would be heir to the kingdom of Bellaza and there was precious little possibility that anyone in the palace or this valley would look kindly on that heir being raised on a separate continent. So that was that.

A full eclipse, I'm afraid, she'd told Hilary.

Tadeo turned back to her and though there was a glittering in his gaze, his face remained unreadable. When there had been a time, long ago now, that she'd been able to read him so easily.

"I will concede we are both to blame for this," he said, sounding darkly formal and so stuffy it made her want to scream. But that would be playing into his narrative about her—so emotional, so immature, so over-the-top, and so on—so she smiled instead. "It is both of our faults."

"I understand that you are getting used to this," she said in the same soothing tone she'd been using, that she hoped he found condescending. "You've had a shock and you'll need some time with it. That's acceptable. But I'm not going to stand around and talk about the child *we made*, who will be coming into this world in not so many months, as something we should be ashamed of. Or call it a fault or a mistake. I just want that very clear."

"I wasn't the one who kept it a secret," he replied with that cold efficiency that had always left her breathless. It was like a knife. "Have you seen a physician?"

"No, I thought that it would be great fun to simply risk everything and see what happened," Esme shot back at him. When his eyes widened slightly, she sighed. "Of course I've seen a physician. The same physician I always see."

"You mean the palace physician." When she nodded, Tadeo looked astonished. "And no report was made to me?"

"I imagine the palace physician was under the impression you already knew," Esme said coolly. "Since you are, in fact, my husband."

"You knew that I did not."

"I saw no reason to tell you." Esme shrugged. "You made your position very clear. You told me to leave the palace and not to return unless and until I was summoned. That you would tell my people when that was and that you did not want to lay eyes on me until that occurred. I listened."

She had not only listened. She had finally accepted,

deep in her poor battered heart, that there would never be the kind of future she wanted with this man.

It had hurt almost as much as losing him the first time, but she'd gotten there. She knew he'd meant it when he'd said he would divorce her. He'd meant it when he'd said it before their wedding and he'd meant it even more when he'd reiterated it the morning after his father's funeral. Esme had mourned that spark of hope she'd carried inside all this while, truly she had. But she had finally started to think about what life might be like *without* this particular shadow blotting out the sun.

And then she'd discovered she was pregnant.

Esme found that empathy for him in this moment felt scarce on the ground.

His gaze went cold. His jaw clenched. "You know perfectly well that I didn't mean you should hide the fact that you were *pregnant*."

Esme lifted her chin. "I don't know that. I only know what you said, Tadeo. Isn't that something that you were at great pains to make me understand years ago? You only wished to discuss what you *said*. Not how your actions might have been received and certainly not how the way you said those things might have made someone else *feel*."

"I do not wish to discuss Boston," he said then, in that low, furious voice of his that reminded her—violently—of that hideous day when he'd told her he was done with her. And had meant it then, too.

It still made her whole body flush. It still *hurt*, and she hated herself for that, but he didn't deserve to see that any longer. So she smiled instead.

Because she was so damned good at smiling.

"Here in the house of exile," she said, with an airiness

that actually hurt, "I talk about whatever I wish. If you would like to direct the conversation, decide what words are used, and determine what eras are worthy of discussion, you can go back to the palace and order everyone about to your heart's content. Your Majesty."

Something flared on his face at that and Esme caught her breath, because for just a moment she could see the Tadeo that she knew. The Tadeo she missed. The hint of him, right there—

But he pulled it back. He hid it away. And then he stepped back as if she'd thrown herself over the table and tried to touch him.

As if she'd be so foolish after all these years.

She really had learned. At last.

"I am not going to process this information in real time with you," he told her, with scathing formality. "Certainly not while you clearly wish to make my doing so as painful as possible. You'll hear from my people soon."

Then he turned sharply, as if he was back in the military service he'd done after graduate school, and marched away.

Esme watched him go. She took in that straight line of his back and the powerful way he moved until he disappeared into a riot of bright yellow daffodils, happy purple crocuses, and reckless sprays of forsythia.

She watched him until he was gone and then, when she was alone again, all of her masks and coping mechanisms tumbled at her feet like so much more slippery fabric for the nursery of a child who deserved better than all this acrimony.

As she sat down in her chair, cradled her head in her arms, and, despite her best intentions to banish the shadows from her life, sobbed.

CHAPTER THREE

THE SUMMONS FROM the palace came the next morning, bright and early.

The housekeeper brought it in with Esme's breakfast, which was happily no longer a few dry crackers and a ginger drink. Her appetite had come roaring back with a vengeance once she made it into the second trimester, and having sorely missed it, she liked to indulge it. Her cook liked to tempt her with various breakfast dishes and today it was some kind of frittata, fluffy and cheesy, and she tucked in with pleasure.

But the heavy envelope from the palace was there the whole time, a baleful presence in her otherwise happy, lovely room. She stared at it, sitting there on its own silver platter, and ignored it while she ate.

It was still a habit to wait to see if her stomach would behave, even though she hadn't had a morning sickness episode in weeks. When she'd first experienced it, she'd thought she had some sort of flu or cold that wouldn't go away. Not unusual during the cold months of the year, and she'd assumed that she was simply run-down. Or that it was her body's reaction to seven years of royal appointments and public engagements, forever playing the part of the perfect queen for an adoring public and having to act like the frozen iceberg beside her when in private with him.

Esme had been fond of the excruciatingly formal and distinctly chilly King Hugo, despite his best attempts to cut her down to size. She would not say that she'd managed to charm the man, but she thought he'd come to accept her—and clearly approved of the separate lives she and Tadeo led on the palace grounds, which only palace denizens knew. She had even come to see that the old man had a certain charm that she'd seen in his son, too, if long ago. She had genuinely mourned his death, but it had still taken her much too long to realize what she was feeling was not simply illness or grief.

Then there had been coming to terms with what it *meant* that she was pregnant. That had taken longer.

Especially because she had finally been at peace with leaving this place, and Tadeo, and starting over.

When her stomach indicated that it intended to stay in place again today, Esme rose from her bed. Still not touching that envelope, she puttered around through her usual morning routine, but when it came time to choose something to wear, she stopped. Blew out a breath. Then accepted the inevitable and picked up the small, square envelope that felt as if it was lined with metal and was actually sealed with wax.

Because here in Bellaza there was a right way and a wrong way to do things, and the right way very often involved archaic rituals.

She cracked open the seal and pulled out the card. And then accepted that she was disappointed when she saw that the message inside was typed. More importantly, it was not in Tadeo's bold, dark hand.

The Queen's presence is requested at the palace, it said. Baldly.

No time. No date. Just a request that was not a request at all. It was an order.

Esme did not pretend that she didn't understand that.

She walked into her dressing room, a large, expansive room with alcove offshoots that featured accessories of all descriptions. Many of the clothes no longer fit. She slid her hand over her belly and found herself feeling sentimental about the press of it into her palm.

Esme had rather given up on the idea of children. Or maybe it was more accurate to say that it was one of the many things she'd put into a deep freeze, because it was that or spend more time sobbing about futures that could never be hers.

She had decided on her chilly—so beautiful, but so personally *cold*—wedding day that she had a choice to make. It was clear to her that nothing would change between her and this brand-new husband of hers who had already smashed her heart into smithereens more times than she could count. It was true that she'd held out hope that he might have had ulterior motives for going through with all this, but that day, she'd known better.

His kingdom had been promised Princess Esme of Clarebonne and Tadeo, by God, would give her to them. Without regard for her feelings or his own, assuming he had any left in there somewhere. For on their wedding day, he had informed her that he planned to shunt her off to a separate house so it would not be necessary for them to lay eyes on each other for any reason but work.

The choice she'd had to make was all too obvious. She could let him hurt her over and over again by simple dint of his insensitivity and coldness and *absolute refusal* to admit what she knew to be true about the things that had happened between them in Boston. Esme had been all too able to envision that future. Forever smashing her head against the brick wall of him. Over and over again, hurting only herself, and to what end?

The other option was the one she'd chosen. She prided herself on playing the perfect princess, now queen. She was kind, warm, unfailingly polite and courteous at all times. The kingdom loved her. Her own kingdom was deeply proud of her. The papers fell all over themselves to praise her quiet elegance and her endless charity. Everyone was in awe of her ability to remember the name of every person she'd ever met, make every person she interacted with feel special, and to always support her husband as well as King Hugo.

She did these things not only because she was good at them, though she was, but because she rather thought that Tadeo expected her to descend into a tantrum and never emerge from it again.

Esme kept her emotions at the manor house. That was the place where she allowed herself any outlets that she liked for the things she couldn't let herself feel anywhere else. Whether it was tantrums on the floor, screaming into her pillows, or experimenting with paint. Or all of the above, on particularly bad days.

It wasn't the life she'd imagined they'd have, all those years ago in Boston when it had seemed miraculous that they were so well-suited when they'd been promised to each other sight unseen, but it worked.

Now all of the rules she'd lived by for seven years seemed out the window. They'd gone straight up in smoke the night of the funeral, when she'd finally touched him again the way she had only when they'd been across an ocean and everything had been different—

She'd had time to regret that. And to…not regret it at all, to an epic degree.

But the trouble was, she knew Tadeo. She knew him better than she wanted to, most of the time. His response to this would not be to finally open up, meet her halfway, and pledge himself to working on making himself a better man, husband, and soon-to-be father. Open, giving, emotionally available.

Esme laughed out loud in her dressing room. "Whatever he has planned is far more likely to involve the palace's medieval dungeons," she said to herself.

Then laughed again, because how would *dungeons* play in the press Tadeo cared so much about? She couldn't wait to find out. How would his team handle *that* messaging?

She turned around in a circle, her eyes narrow as she looked at her image in the mirror, deciding how best to approach a meeting that she assumed would be more of a chess match. She settled on a very simple and casual dress in royal blue that hugged all of her curves—so that there could be no mistake about the state of her body. Then, to forestall any commentary that she might have dressed down in a jersey midi dress in defiance of his beloved protocol, she accessorized with a full face of makeup and chunky jewelry.

The better to send conflicting messages. The Queen was off-duty today, yes—but she was still the Queen.

Esme considered walking to the palace but rejected it, as she didn't wish to appear before Tadeo flushed from exertion. That it would irritate him made it tempting, but she was afraid she would end up feeling too flustered.

That wouldn't do. She called to have a car brought around and drove herself over, trying her best to settle her nerves and her mind. Both were racing, because whatever else might be happening, she was still excited to see him.

It had always been this way. Since the moment she'd met him—and if she was honest, before that, too. She had never minded that she was promised to someone. She had always thought it was romantic, though she doubted she would have felt that way if the man she'd been promised to had been something other than outrageously handsome, with those impossible blue eyes, a jawline to write poetry about, and that body of his that he kept in such peak physical condition—

But that was not a good way to keep herself from coming over all *flushed*.

At the palace, the guards directed her to drive back around to one of the family entrances, which was what they called the secret passageways with covered entries that allowed members of the royal family and any guests or companions they wished to keep secret to come and go as they liked. No photographic evidence. No crowds or watchful eyes.

She pulled up in her car and the King's personal secretary was there to greet her, stiffly. Always stiffly. The proper older man could fade into the wallpaper if he chose, disappearing in plain sight. He had been here forever. He knew everything about everyone, and more.

Esme was even happier that she was wearing a dress that made her condition so clear.

If the old man noticed Esme's pregnancy, she would never know from his demeanor—but she knew that he did. He noticed everything. It was his job.

"How interesting that I need a personal escort today,"

Esme said merrily as she left the car for the staff to move where they liked. "Does the King think that I am likely to foment rebellion on my way to see him?"

"If Your Majesty would watch your step," replied the studiously unbothered Arturo, as he held the door for her.

Esme trailed after him once inside, trying not to let herself become too emotional. It was difficult, but she couldn't blame her hormones entirely. She had been emotional the first time she'd walked into this palace too. It had been before their wedding and she'd still had that reckless core of hope deep inside her—

But that was long gone. She tried to shake the memory off as she followed docilely enough behind Arturo as he led her deep into the palace.

Having grown up in the palace next door—give or take a few mountain ranges—Esme had always thought that the Bellazan palace felt like a fairy tale. It was all about its spires and flourishes, with dramatic details in every direction. Her father's palace was far more utilitarian, more of a civic expression of royalty than an ideal.

She would never admit this to her own people, but she preferred the Bellazan palace to the Clarebonne one. This one was prettier. Airier. It made her want to sing songs and spin about, not that she ever had. It would be frowned upon.

Luckily, she thought as they walked, its inhabitants made up for their lovely fairy-tale palace by being as dour as humanly possible.

Arturo took her on a route that, she couldn't help but notice, avoided all the main thoroughfares of the palace where anyone might see her. Then delivered her into a salon in the family wing where only one person could possibly see her and left her there, with a deep and proper bow as he exited.

She wandered over to the window and gazed out of it, looking at the hills in the distance. The small principality of Andorra was to the south. Her own Clarebonne to the east, Spain to the west, France to the north.

It struck her then that her own world had become quite small these last five months.

"I was nesting," she said under her breath, defending herself. "And sleeping."

And mourning kings and lives lost in more than one way.

Then again, she thought as the door opened behind her and her whole body reacted—indicating at once that Tadeo had entered the room—it was possible that she had been preparing for battle.

She turned to look at him.

Today he'd chosen the typical dark, bespoke suit. His usual fare. And also his armor, she thought. She stood where she was, smiling gently as he let his gaze track all over her—lingering on her belly, of course.

And had the satisfaction of watching his jaw clench.

"I apologize for my emotional outbursts yesterday," he said without any preamble, and he didn't even sound stiff. Though he also didn't sound all that sorrowful. "It won't happen again."

"I should think not," she replied calmly. "That would mean you might actually have to feel things, and we can't have that."

That blue gaze of his went frigid, but he did not reply. Instead, he moved to take one of the seats, gesturing for her to do the same.

Esme thought about resisting, but decided against it

for strategic reasons when there were far bigger things to worry about. She went and sat so she was facing him across an exquisite little table made of glass with dramatic leg flourishes. So cozy. So intimate.

Such bullshit.

She imagined it had taken most of his team to decide on this room. They would have debated it. Would the austerity of his office be the wrong touch? Was the royal glory of the more formal rooms too aspirational? She hoped that he was up half the night concerned with the messaging of this.

Tadeo was always preoccupied with his *messaging*.

"I will confess to you that I did not make any provision for something so unforeseen to occur in this marriage," he continued in the same relatively friendly voice, despite the chill in his gaze.

Esme gazed back at him. "Points for sounding so human, Tadeo. How long did you practice that? You sound sincere and slightly self-deprecating. The faint smile is a nice touch as well."

Said faint smile disappeared immediately. "I'm trying to have a conversation with you."

"No," she replied steadily. "You are not. You are trying to manage me. They are not the same thing."

"I'm not going to have a semantic battle with you, Esme," Tadeo replied, sounding significantly more like himself. Which was to say, a lofty robot.

"I don't think that pointing out the reality of a thing is a battle," Esme said, sitting back in her chair. "Unless, of course, one of the people in this room is overly committed to protecting a reality that does not exist." She patted her belly. "That couldn't be me. Reality is growing inside of me, by the day, whether I like it or not."

"It has always been my intention to divorce you, as you know," he replied, something like steel around his eyes.

"The topic has come up a time or two, yes," Esme agreed, warmly enough that she hoped it covered that spike of *hurt* she wished she didn't feel any longer. Yet did. "But then, you wouldn't be you if you weren't planning your escape before you walked into a room. I do believe that some people refer to that as a trauma response, Tadeo. Have you ever considered—"

"When I want your psychoanalysis, Esme, I will ask for it. You may note that I never have."

She inclined her head. "Please," she said, smiling wider. "Don't let me keep you from opining on the state of our marriage. I do love these chats. They are like quarterly performance reviews. Or better yet, like small, sweet love notes tucked into my life at these delightfully random intervals. I can't tell you how I look forward to them."

Tadeo studied her for a long moment, his face impressively impassive. In the beginning, she'd been able to get a frown out of him. These days she had to content herself with that flexed muscle in his jaw.

This was part of why her performance as the Princess, now Queen, of Bellaza required such a commitment to perfection. The more beautifully she did her part, the more outrageously she could behave in private.

A girl had to have her fun somewhere.

"This ruins my plans," he told her. After some while.

Esme felt an actual flare of temper at that, but she had years of practice batting such things down. "I beg your pardon. Do you mean to say that your child, the heir to your throne, has destroyed the plans you made in your head? That's a strange way indeed to say congratulations, Tadeo. Even for you."

"I like to tell myself that there is a perfect heiress out there." He leaned forward as he said this, his blue gaze heavy on hers, so Esme could make no mistake. He *wanted* her to hear him on this. To well and truly *hear him*. "When I think of her, her features themselves are blurry. Because it doesn't matter. What matters is how she will *act*. She will be quiet. Accepting. Meek in all things. She will not be emotional, or arch, or forever making attempts to be witty."

Esme allowed herself to frown slightly, as if picturing this saint among women. "She sounds deeply boring." She clucked her tongue. "The poor thing. Send her to me and I'll teach her how to live a little. It's necessary when married to an animated plank of wood to make one's own fun, you see."

Tadeo did not react. He continued to list off this made-up heiress's manufactured virtues. "She will be soft-spoken in both public and private. She will never make demands. She will be practical enough and clever enough to understand her place."

"She sounds like *quite* the paragon." If Esme felt these words of his—this description of the perfect wife he insisted on painting—like a small, wickedly sharp dagger to the heart, she kept it to herself. "I wish you every happiness, Tadeo, assuming that is one of the three emotions you allow yourself to feel annually. Does that mean we're going ahead with the divorce?"

"You know perfectly well that we cannot," he retorted. "And so I must give up on this perfect paragon of a queen and make do with you instead."

Esme wanted to scream so she smiled at him instead. "A fate worse than death."

"I struggle with how best to arrange this unforeseen situation to its best advantage," he said after a moment, no longer *spearing her* with that look of his.

"You keep calling it that." Esme shook her head. "I do hope you get that out of your system. I don't think that I will find it amusing if you call our child an *unforeseen circumstance* to its face."

"I understand that this is all a grand joke to you," Tadeo said, and he leaned forward then. And more surprising, he looked...*undone*, somehow. Everything inside Esme thrilled at that, though she knew better than to show it. "But it is not a joke to me."

"If you had to suffer through morning sickness for three solid months, with bits of it thereafter as a little treat when you least expect it, I doubt you would think it was all that funny yourself, Tadeo," she murmured in reply.

He ignored that. "You persist in poking at me whenever you can. You think it's amusing. I do not. I have certain obligations—"

"I am aware of your obligations." Esme rolled her eyes. "This entire speech worked better when I was barely twenty-one, and in case you're laboring under a misconception, I didn't really like it all that much then."

"Things will be different now," he told her, that ruthlessness she sometimes thought only she'd ever seen in him making his voice low and dark. "I will not tolerate these displays of yours that you trot out, presumably for your own entertainment."

Her heart skipped a few beats, then sped up, the way it had when he'd shown her this side of himself the first time. So many years ago, she'd thought she was having a heart attack. She'd wondered if losing him might actually kill her.

Now she knew there were much worse things than dying of a broken heart, and one of them was living with it. Another was marrying the man who'd broken it. Repeatedly.

Survival meant she'd learned how to ignore her heart when it beat like this, so she could soothe it when she was alone.

"And what exactly will you do?" Esme waved a languid hand, the very picture of someone completely unbothered by this. By him. "Will you march your pregnant wife, your queen and the mother of your heir, down into the dank recesses of your dungeon? However will that play in the press, Tadeo? Do you think it's possible that an out-of-control, raging king who's decided a pregnant woman is the enemy might finally be more scandalous than a very boring story about a woman who wanted extramarital—"

"Do not bring up my mother," he growled.

But Esme had long since decided that the much-maligned Queen Marisol was not an off-limits topic. She had decided that Tadeo could not use his mother as an excuse for everything he did and then refuse to hear her mentioned in return. Not that she had found many opportunities to put this decision into practice.

There was no time like the present.

She leaned forward. "Do you think it will work?"

His eyes glittered. It was obvious that he didn't want to answer the question.

"Will what work?" he asked, as if it made his jaw hurt to get the words out. She hoped it did.

"Do you think that your perfect, anodyne heiress will

wash away your mother's grievous sins at last? Or do you just not wish to be reminded of them when you sit in a private room with another woman who dares speak her own mind?"

She didn't expect him to move. Maybe he didn't expect to move himself.

But one moment she was sitting in the seat opposite him, and the next, he was there. He braced himself above her, caging her in place with one arm on either side of her as his hands gripped the arms of the chair.

"How many warnings do you think I am going to give you?" he demanded, his face—his outrageously perfect face—far too close to hers.

"You don't want to feel anything," Esme said, tipping her head back so she could truly look him in the eye. "You take it as a personal failing when you have a stray emotion. I can't help you with that. I don't *want* to help you with that. But I do think, Tadeo, that you might want to consider the fact that fatherhood is not an unemotional state. Your child is not likely to respect your boundaries."

"Not with you to teach him he shouldn't," Tadeo gritted out.

"Do you think the babies you might have with your perfect windup doll of a queen would be any better?" Esme asked and she laughed a little, right there in his face. It had gotten easier over the years—or so she told herself—to ignore how beautiful this man was. But it was not easy now, with his face so close to hers. Not when she could remember kissing him months instead of *years* ago. Putting her hands on his jaw, pressing her lips to his, indulging herself in him the way she hadn't in so very, very long…

"I think everything would be better with the woman

who was less..." He shook his head, eyes glittering. "With a woman who was not you, Esme."

"But the woman you described would never suit you," she said, and she laughed again. He didn't need to know that it felt like glass broken into pieces in her mouth. "I don't know why you're pretending otherwise."

"I think any man dreams of peace, king or not." She could smell the faint hint of that scent he always wore. The scent she had always found maddening, overwhelming, addictive. It was something that reminded her of wood smoke with a brighter note beneath. Pine, perhaps. Rosemary. "You wouldn't understand."

"But I do," Esme said. "It's never going to happen." She lifted a brow, and kept her gaze trained on his. "You like fucking too much for your little saint, my love."

His eyes flared. And she'd used all of those words deliberately. *Fucking*, to get his attention. *My love*, to remind of the thing he wanted to remember least.

She didn't see any reason why he should get to forget the thing she couldn't help but remember, like it or not. Especially when he was the one who took that love they'd shared and shattered it.

How could he have told her he loved her—again and again—and then act as if she'd made that up in her head? She would never know. She only knew that he'd done it.

He'd done it. Brutally. And she had been living with it ever since.

Esme could see the way he sucked in a breath and she leaned forward, her chin high and defiant. "You like to deny yourself like a monk or indulge yourself in me, but I doubt you've admitted the truth to yourself yet. That no matter what, it's not going away. It's still me. It's always going to be me."

She could see the way his hands clenched hard on the chair's arms, and kept going. "You hold yourself back, you capitulate, it's all the same. What you have never known, nor ever will, I fear, is peace. Exchanging me for a more biddable model won't help you. Because I will still exist." She angled herself toward him, letting the intensity between them lead. "So unless you're going to kill me? I'm afraid, Your Royal Majesty, that you're stuck."

"Damn you," he growled at her, but then he made it worse.

Or better, depending, Esme thought in a rush.

Because he crashed his mouth to hers.

CHAPTER FOUR

Esme was a fire in his blood, all bright colors and wild songs in his head.

She tasted the way she always had—too good to believe. An impossible, immediate addiction that he had always felt as keenly as if she was an injection straight into his veins.

Sometimes he thought he hated her for showing him that it was even possible to feel like this.

And he knew he hated her more because she wasn't afraid to turn him inside out and lay out all his weaknesses before him. So he could not continue to tell himself stories that cast him as the hero.

Once upon a time, he knew that he'd found that sharpness of hers, that clear-eyed intensity, refreshing.

She had been so very different from the other women he knew, the *safe* and *careful* women he'd chosen, and Tadeo had been mesmerized.

Kissing her was like coming home to a place he'd long since thought had burned to ash. It was an immediate shock to his system. It was like catapulting himself straight to the heart of a burning inferno and he knew better.

He knew better.

But he deepened the kiss.

Tadeo kept one hand braced on the arm of her chair and used the other to angle her jaw where he wanted it, because there was no simple kiss when it came to this. To them.

Everything with Esme was plunder, possession, and each and every time, it was perfect. She was *perfect*—

That was the word that got stuck in his head. The word that grew until it drowned everything else out, even her.

Or *almost* her.

Tadeo pulled away and found her eyes glazed, dark and starry, and her lips ripe from his. He could feel the way he wanted her like a broken bone. Like a crack and a shattering, a rending apart.

But he was a king now. There had never been any room in his life for this. There wasn't now.

"*This*," he bit out at her, though for a moment he wasn't sure that his mouth wouldn't kiss her of its own accord. That his body wouldn't mount its own rebellion, the way he could feel it wanted to in every cell. "This is the problem."

"It's not a problem," she returned, even though she was breathless. Even though she looked kissed within an inch of her life and she was round with his child but still had *lips* like that, lips that tasted like everything he'd ever wanted. "You just want it to be."

It took a Herculean effort, and he hated that it was so difficult, but Tadeo pushed himself upright and stood back. He knew that she could see exactly what she did to him. His cock was so heavy that it ached and he was certain she could see it clearly as it pressed against his trousers. He could see that greedy look in her luminous eyes. He knew what it meant.

Tadeo could also think of any number of ways that she

could help him with this issue—but that was how they'd gotten into this mess.

Back in Boston. Five months ago. Every time he thought he'd found a measure of self-control, Esme proved him wrong.

Every single time.

"I don't need you to understand this," he managed to grit out, though he had to dig deep. "I don't need your comfort or your help."

"So you have said. Many times."

He hated when she used that voice, so arch and *amused* when he was stretched over quicksand and could lose his footing at any moment. Tadeo ran a hand over his face, though it did nothing to remove the taste of her from his mouth. "What you fail to understand is that I don't *want* to be the kind of man who feels the things that you make me feel, Esme."

That landed. He could see it got to her, though she covered it beautifully in an instant. Sometimes he thought he was the only one who could see behind the masks she wore. Other times he thought that the fact he could was part of this curse she'd laid on him at first sight.

And he had never found a way to stop caring when he hurt her. He never took any pleasure in it.

But it still had to be done.

"I have never wanted it," he told her, very deliberately. "Boston should never have happened. You seem to think that what happened there is the truth of things between us, but surely the past seven years should have proved to you that Boston was the aberration."

"What exactly do you think would have happened if we hadn't met in Boston?" Esme asked. She did not look as wrecked as he felt, or even as wrecked as she'd seemed for a flash a moment ago—but then, she never did. She dabbed at the corner of her mouth with a delicate finger, and shrugged. "What do you suppose it would have been like if we'd met for the first time when you decided to start courting me? How do you think that would have gone?"

He knew exactly how it would have gone. And he understood her point, though he would have preferred it if he had not.

They were conflagrations waiting to happen, the two of them. When they were together, they burst into flame. It was as simple and complicated as that.

It was entirely possible that if he'd met her for the first time on one of those public dinner dates, the whole world would have seen him toss her up against a wall and kiss her wildly, savagely, the way he had after that night in Boston.

Then, too, the whole world would have seen the way they couldn't keep their hands off each other that whole year. They would have known that he'd neglected his duties and his studies so he could spend days in bed with her, unable to do anything if it meant he had to stop touching her.

That he had even imagined himself head over heels in love.

It was the kind of alternate timeline that could keep a man up at night. And Tadeo had already lost enough sleep over this woman.

"I know exactly what would have happened, and so do you," she said, as if she could read his mind. Sometimes he thought she could.

"I'm not debating that. The difference between us is that I know that the relationship we had—and, indeed, still have—was toxic. You seem to think it was a love story."

For the first time, he saw something in her...shake. There was a flash in her dark eyes, but more than that, he thought he saw her tremble.

A direct hit, he supposed, but he couldn't say he felt good about it. She didn't have one of her quick responses ready and he found he didn't like that either.

Esme was sitting in an ancient chair in a room noted widely for its charm and beauty, but she was the only thing he could see. She was the focal point and it was not only because she was so impractically pretty, though she was. It was because there was something about her, some lightning that crackled all over her and drew people to her.

She lit up every room she entered. She took the light with her when she left.

Leaving her was one of the hardest things he'd ever had to do. As was marrying her.

He felt like a starving man, but he took this unexpected moment of quiet between them to let himself just...*look* at her. Her lovely dark eyes that had always contained too much to bear. Too much wisdom, too much love, *too much*. Her dark brows. Those marvelous cheekbones that made her face a true work of art. That gently bowed upper lip that he dreamed about, some nights. The dark hair she wore up in the front and let cascade down behind her, a mass of thick waves.

Tadeo could smell the sweetness of her shampoo from here. The hint of coconut. The touch of spun sugar.

The woman was a menace, and that stretchy, skimpy dress she wore was not helping any.

Her breasts were indeed bigger, rounder—and now

he knew why. And that rounded belly made him feel...
Tadeo told himself it didn't matter what he *felt*. What mattered was how he *handled* this.

That was all that ever mattered.

"You are so afraid of this thing between us," she said, her soft voice breaking into his thoughts like a detonation.

Though he was surprised to find her gaze was directed toward the window, not at him. He thought that she was taking another swing at him, but instead, she turned her head and found him with those too-wise dark eyes once more. He thought he saw something like reproach there. Or maybe it was something deeper than that. Maybe she was simply letting him see it hurt her.

He felt his hands clench and forced himself to straighten out his fingers.

"You're terrified," Esme said, in her devastatingly quiet way, "and so you come up with all of these rules to keep it under wraps. But surely what happened five months ago should make it clear that hiding from something like this only makes it inevitable that it will burst out eventually. And now you are apparently trapped with me."

She threw all of this at him in that way she did, using that outrageous *calm* she could pull out at will—though Tadeo knew she would probably claim that he was the one with armor.

"So what now?" she asked when he said nothing, and her dark brows rose like an indictment. "Do you shove it back down, hide it away in one of your little locked rooms, and hope for the best? Because it's been ten years now, Tadeo. The chemistry between us hasn't gotten any less intense since the day we met. In fact, I'd say it's going in the opposite direction."

He reminded himself—again—that he was the king. He had a duty to his people, one made more complicated by the damage his mother had done to the royal family's reputation. Everything he did was a restoration project, aimed at rehabilitating the family in his people's eyes—up to and including the fairy-tale wedding to the princess from the neighboring kingdom that had already been considered a love story for a quarter of a century by the time they got married.

The divorce he'd planned would have taken all of that into account.

But he wouldn't be any kind of a king—or much of a man—if he couldn't pivot when necessary.

"I've already thought of our problematic chemistry," he said.

"How shocking that you consider it *problematic*."

Tadeo should not have been pleased, somewhere down deep, that she was clearly recovered. "Seeing what you did to the Queen's Manor, a historic site that is meant to be a legacy upheld by every queen lucky enough to live there—"

"It's a house," Esme said. With excessive calm, to his ear. "It doesn't know that it's historic. It doesn't care what color its walls are. It's amazing to me, Tadeo, that for a man so allergic to emotion, you certainly do manage to find it in the strangest places."

He wanted to jump on that. He wanted to argue. But that was what she wanted him to do, he knew that.

Instead, he stood there above her, glowering down at this bane of his existence. He knew that it had been ten years. He'd been there. But it was somehow exposing to hear her say it. Ten years of the problem that was Esme and now she was pregnant.

And he was no more in control of himself in her presence than he ever had been.

Tadeo had thought about a lot of things last night, because he hadn't slept at all. He had worked until he had to accept defeat, because he wasn't processing anything effectively and certainly not at the level he should have been. He'd gone to his private gym and had pushed himself to muscle failure as many times as he could in the hope it would put him to sleep.

But all it had done was make him tired enough that his defenses were down. It didn't do a damn thing but give him more time and space to think about this mess.

"You have spent the past seven years developing a regal persona that is, as I know you are aware, the envy of Europe," he told her now.

She gave him one of her best queenly smiles. "If I must be damned by faint praise, so be it."

He pushed on. "Instead of accepting my decision about how our marriage should operate, or even simply acknowledging that it is what *I* need whether you agree with it or not, you have always mounted this passive-aggressive campaign of yours in private."

"Oh no," Esme said, shaking her head. "I don't think that's a fair characteristic at all. I haven't been the least bit passive."

He ignored that. "What I did not realize until I saw the outrage you have visited upon the manor house is that you are as poisoned with emotion as ever. And, apparently, incapable of finding appropriate outlets—as I have."

She let out a laugh at that. "*As you have*," she repeated. "Do you have *outlets*, Tadeo? Really? Because I rather thought you shut everything off and stormed about like a computer program brought to life and in search of an algorithm."

It was the unerring accuracy that made her so dangerous, Tadeo thought. Against his will. He'd had five months as a brand-new king to consider precisely how he appeared to others—meaning, mostly, his subjects. His father had been stern, but fair.

Tadeo's team had carefully suggested that perhaps he could…*unbend*.

So, naturally, the one person alive who had ever seen him lose control—and more than once—thought he was a robot.

"This is how our marriage will work," he told her, stern himself this time. "You have often commented on the fact you felt I made all the decisions for us whether you agreed with them or not."

"I *have* commented on that," she agreed. "Because you have made all the decisions, whether I agreed with them or not. You knew that I would never back out of a betrothal that meant so much to my father. He still considers it his greatest achievement, aside from marrying my mother." Her dark eyes seemed to see too far into him. "You have shamelessly exploited the emotions you claim to find so distasteful. Is that what we're talking about? Finally?"

Tadeo ignored that aside about her family. Or tried to ignore it, anyway. It was another blow that struck too close to home. It felt a little too *right*. Was he really that shameless?

But he already knew the answer. Of course he was. He would have done anything to present the correct image of himself to his father and the world, and he had. He couldn't regret that now.

He cleared his throat. "Little as I hate to admit it, you're not wrong that pretending for all these years that this chemistry does not exist was always destined to end in an explosion. This explosion has now had consequences."

"I'm making a list now," she told him. "It will be of all the things you call our child in advance that if I hear you call them when they're here will not end well. Just so you know."

"Our lives are now irrevocably altered," he told her, and he could hear how stern and uncompromising he sounded.

Not that Esme seemed to care one bit.

"We can alter them however we see fit," she tossed back at him. Carelessly, he thought. "I know that you like to play these games of yours, where you pretend that your life is perfect, and make it look that way. But it's really not necessary. Maybe the gift you can give your kingdom is showing them that a divorce can be healthy." She shrugged. "Sometimes two people aren't meant to be together, particularly when their marriage takes place in the pressure cooker of a palace. There's nothing wrong with it. It's not shameful. I wish you could see that."

"Divorce with a child is unacceptable," he told her at once, and did not care to examine the tug deep inside him at that. As if his body rejected the very idea. "But I will also never tolerate the things my father did in his marriage."

If he'd slapped her, he doubted she would have reacted more strongly. Esme sat up straighter, her body jerking slightly, as if she really had sustained a blow. He could see color flood her cheeks.

And he didn't understand how he could feel both satisfied by that and disgusted with himself.

"Are you accusing me of something?" she asked, and for the first time in a long while, perhaps since Boston, she did not sound calm at all.

"You are clearly a woman who is ruled by her basic needs," he said. "Are you not? You always seem to be at such pains to show me that you are."

Esme shot to her feet and Tadeo thought, not for the first time, that this would all be so much easier if he wasn't so *affected* by her. Like she was in his *bloodstream*.

It was worse now. He knew that her curves were lusher and that he had done that. That was *his* baby she was carrying. *His* baby that was changing the shape of her.

Even thinking about this made him outrageously hard.

There were many things that were blurry about the night of his father's funeral, but not the way he'd lost himself deep inside Esme. Again and again, tearing them both apart, letting himself enjoy the one indulgence he denied himself above all others.

"Will you be requiring a paternity test, then?" Esme asked sharply, her gaze dark and furious and, if he wasn't mistaken, curt. "By all means. Call in a parade of doctors. Knock yourself out and make this all about data. Maybe then you can process it."

He refused to give her the satisfaction of seeing that land. "Going forward, you will have to choose," he told her, coldly. "We are going to alter the rules of this relationship. You will, of course, take up the mantle of your responsibilities once more."

"Of course. I feel naked without my mantle, don't you?"

Tadeo decided that was simply a bid to get him to

imagine her naked, which was not difficult. Or unusual. Only now he had to imagine this new, succulently *ripe* version of her and he felt himself very nearly break out in a sweat as he fought to think of anything but that.

Literally anything else.

Esme shook her head at him as if she was disappointed in him. "If you want to insult me, Tadeo, you should probably start with things that are actually possible. A slip in perfection on my part is not one of them."

He was letting her distract him, and that was another thing that needed to end. This would be a new start for them. This would, he was certain, solve a great many of their issues and make all of this *tension* dissipate.

In truth, he thought it was a brilliant solution. He expected she would not—but he thought she'd come around.

"In private, you can either run your mouth or you can work it out in my bed," he told her starkly, and had the satisfaction of watching her mouth drop open. It was worth the wait, he thought. "You will no longer live at the manor house. You will be installed in the queen's compartments here in the palace that adjoin my own. If you cannot control your mouth, that is your choice. You will sleep in your own room. If you can manage to keep your jabs and witticisms and little veiled attacks—always delivered so archly and so *sweetly*—to yourself, like a good girl, we will work off some of this friction together."

He studied her. This time he thought the color on her face was for a different reason. "But that comes with a caveat."

"What a shock," she breathed.

"We will not discuss these things again," he told her, like thunder. "The rules are the rules. In private, you can talk all you like, but you may not touch me. Or you can touch me, but you must do so silently."

She blinked. "You can't possibly think this is healthy. This...psychotic compartmentalization. Can you?"

He moved then, responding to that part of himself he tried so hard to keep on ice, and instead of trying to lock himself down—he indulged himself.

Something he almost never did, because this fierce, overwhelming wildness surged up in him immediately. As if it only *waited* for an opportunity to burst free. It threatened to knock him over where he stood.

It was an irresistible riptide, hauling him out to sea whether he liked it or not.

Today—here—he allowed it.

Tadeo didn't fight it. He let it take him, and he closed the space between them to loop a hand around her neck. Tight enough to lift her chin up. Tight enough that he could feel the way her skin heated and her pulse went wild.

And he was close enough that he could see the look in her eyes that he both craved and tried to avoid. All that longing and need. All that glorious passion he had finally decided he could taste—but only if there were rules.

That was what he'd concluded very early this morning, after exhausting himself. He'd stood in the gallery where their wedding portrait hung—so formal and controlled—and he'd finally conceded that what had brought them here was a failure. His failure.

But he would not fail again, and that meant rethinking the boundaries that he'd maintained for the whole of his life.

"What about any of this would you call *healthy*,

Esme?" he demanded, his voice unrecognizable, like a stream of smoke.

Her mouth was so close to his and he had the taste of her on his tongue already. It would be so easy—

But he could not allow it.

Tadeo had to prove to her that he could maintain the boundaries he had set out. He had to prove it to *himself*.

He made himself let go of her.

He made himself step back.

There was a kind of exultation in the pain of it—in forcing himself to do this thing he did not wish to do at all, because it was *right*. He needed the reminder.

"I suggest you take yourself back to the manor house," he told her. "And pack. Or I will instruct my staff to bring over only what I think you need."

She only stared back at him, her gaze dark and glimmering and utterly unreadable. "What a charming invitation."

"It is an order, Your Majesty," he said formally. "But you can call it what you like. Either way you will be fully installed in this palace and under my control by tonight. I suggest you start thinking about how you intend to handle it."

And then he tested himself even further. He didn't wait for her to respond. He didn't give her the opportunity to land another blow.

He turned on his heel, walked out of that salon, and left her there.

Even though every last part of him screamed for him to go back and finish what he started.

As deep and hard as possible.

CHAPTER FIVE

LEAVING THE MANOR house was painful.

Esme found herself close to tears, when really, she should have been celebrating. Steps were being taken, finally. She was moving closer to Tadeo, which was the right direction to be moving in. She knew that it was better for their baby. She hoped it would give them a chance to be…something different from this cold storage of marriage they'd been in all this time.

But it didn't matter what she *knew* or what she *hoped*. It still hurt, because this house of exile and the staff who'd helped her make it a home had been her world for seven long years. She said goodbye to each member of her staff personally. There were many hugs and promises that this would not change a thing, though Esme wasn't sure if any of them believed it.

They all knew better.

The housekeeper walked her out to her car after all the determinations had been made about what would go with Esme and what would remain at the manor house. Esme assumed that the palace would come and restore the house back to its previous elegant austerity, but she could not bear to ask about it.

"You are doing the right thing, of course, Your Majesty," the older woman said as Esme slid behind the wheel, her gaze knowing and kind. "Whether it feels like it today or not."

Esme blew out a breath. "I know that it is right. I know it."

The housekeeper nodded sagely. "At the end of the day, if I may be so bold, His Majesty the King is only a man, my lady. And sometimes they have to be *shown* things that are obvious to anyone else." She smiled. "If you'll pardon my temerity."

Esme found she held that closely to her heart over the course of the next few days. Moving into the palace required nothing of her. All she did was walk into her new bedroom and situate herself there, as part of the palace at last. As promised, her rooms adjoined the King's—but it wasn't as if that afforded them any particular intimacy.

The king's compartments took over the better part of one wing of the palace. The queen's rooms were what was left along that same wing. This was no small thing. Esme had a bedchamber, but the rest of her compartments provided her with more rooms than the manor house had.

She could wander around in them all day and not feel the least bit confined.

What made her feel as if someone had curled a fist around her were the rules. Because there were *so many* rules. Not simply Tadeo's rules, but the general palace rules too. Who could speak to whom first. When certain gestures of obeisance were to be observed, when perhaps all she wished to do was walk through the house she lived in of a morning.

It wasn't that protocol was new to her, but in the manor house, they'd all relaxed into informality. She found that reversing course was harder than expected.

Esme was grateful that moving back into the palace

coincided with the resumption of her official duties. It also happened to take place during Tadeo's absence, as he was touring a new hospital complex in the far side of the country and was staying there for those days. She suspected he'd planned it that way. So that she could ease into the palace, and back into her duties, without having to worry about him in the mix as well.

Though, of course, if he *had* planned it that way, that would suggest a level of emotional intelligence that he professed not to possess.

Esme thought about what her housekeeper had said and tried to focus her energies on more important things. Like concealing her pregnancy, as it had not yet been announced widely. She hadn't even told her parents, something she felt stranger about by the day, but she had wanted to come to terms with it all first. She'd wanted to make sense of the reality of her marriage—and maybe figure out if she'd still have a marriage—before sharing the fact that she was having a child. Only her best friend, Hilary, knew, and as Hilary was a research scientist at one of the world's premier research universities, always neck-deep in her work, Esme was certain that no one else had the faintest idea.

She really had been nesting these last months.

The real truth was that she'd missed her official responsibilities. Esme quite liked the access her position gave her to people and groups that might not have found her otherwise. She liked the shaking of hands and all her interactions with the kingdom's subjects. She accepted their condolences on King Hugo's death and listened to their own stories about their feelings about the late King or their interactions with him over the years. She smiled when they told her of the hopes they held for the new King, having watched him grow up.

It was a way to connect, and Esme hoped she never took it for granted. While she felt certain that Tadeo had not brought her back to the palace to engage in any kind of healing exercise, that was what happened all the same.

And if she found herself at loose ends in the queen's compartments at night—wandering from the well-stocked library to the media room to the separate reading rooms to the salon arranged for a phantom high tea to the five different seating areas nestled here and there to the balcony that overlooked the sweep of the valley that comprised the bulk of the kingdom out toward the mountains in the distance—wondering if she really should have pushed for an escape back to America, she thought about her baby instead. She thought about the fact that whatever her relationship was or would one day become or would never be with Tadeo, it was her child's legacy that she was securing here. This was her child's birthright—this palace and everything in it, not to mention the kingdom that surrounded them. She could no more run away from that than she'd run away from her own duty, back in the day. Some responsibilities outweighed personal considerations. That was what her parents had raised her to believe, and she did.

She still did.

By the time Tadeo returned from the other side of the kingdom, Esme felt settled in. If not *at home*, necessarily, she was comfortable. Better still, she was resolved.

Though it seemed to her that everything in the palace changed when the King was present. When he was finally *in residence* and back home. It was as if the air changed, becoming electrically charged, making everything inside the palace walls seem to *hum*.

Including her.

Even before he called her into his office the afternoon he returned, she felt that shift inside her own body. As if all her flesh and bones ever wanted to do was get ready for him, no matter what *she* might have to say about that. No matter what *she* might think was a better course of action. It was humbling.

It was also dangerous.

His office was in the public part of the palace, and the walk to reach it involved seas of glossy marble, lashings of armored statues, and kingly possessions dating back centuries. The interior of his office was a vast affair, and as stark and unwelcoming as she remembered it from before their wedding. There was the great wide desk that was kept largely empty, because the point of it was its forbidding granite massiveness. It was meant to imply that the King himself was no more tractable than the many-acred expanse of that desk of his. If the desk itself was not enough of a focal point, there were also the pieces of art on the walls, all of them grim-looking kings from throughout Bellaza's history, looking down at their descendants with what always looked like deep dismay to Esme.

Though she kept that observation to herself.

Once she was grandiosely bowed inside by his guards, she found Tadeo already there, applying his official, slashing signature to a selection of documents in front of him. He stopped as she came in, then stood, and she offered him the curtsy that protocol demanded when she saw him for the first time in a day.

Tadeo inclined his head in return.

And then, for what felt like an intense and overlong moment, they stood there and gazed at each other.

"Does this count as mandated silence?" she asked, when the intensity felt as if it might choke her. "Since we're in your office, I assumed that this would be a work-related discussion, not something having to do with our private life. You will have to let me know."

"If it was mandated silence, you would have broken it," Tadeo replied after a simmering moment or two. "As usual."

"If you cannot explain what it is you wish me to do, I'll be forced to assume that you don't know what you wish me to do," Esme said with a shrug. "You set all this up, Tadeo. Once again, we are here in service to your wishes and your demands." Though she did smile as she said it. "I believe the onus is on you."

"You would believe this, of course," he replied in his typically chilly manner, yet always with all that brooding beneath. "As believing it suits the narrative you tell yourself."

"In any case," she said, as calmly as possible, which did not feel particularly calm today, particularly when he said such things to her, "have you given any thought about when and how you would like to make the announcement?"

Tadeo did not exactly frown, though it seemed to suggest itself somewhere in the vicinity of his brow. "I do not think that anyone in the kingdom needs to know our precise living arrangements, Esme. Why do you?"

"I'm referring to the impending birth of your child and heir, Your Majesty," she replied, with scathing courtesy. "There will come a point—and that point will be soon—where even the most ingenious fashion in the world will not be able to hide my belly. I imagine it would be best to get out ahead of speculative articles in the press, don't you?"

His jaw flexed. She took that as a win.

"I will consult with my team and get back to you."

"Naturally," she murmured, in the same tone he'd used when discussing the *narrative* she told herself. "After all, what surely matters most when anticipating a child is the messaging."

Unsurprisingly, it turned out that words he didn't care for spoken to him in his office did indeed count against her. Though Esme found that was not a particular hardship that night, because he'd annoyed her in return.

She did not *tell herself narratives*. She was the one who had to live according to his.

"I hope it was made clear to you that you are not to treat rooms in this palace in the same shocking fashion you did the manor house," he said one evening while they were being transported to an event.

They sat in the back of one of the palace's fleets of vintage cars, each of them dressed magnificently. Her gown flowed over the seats, and while it was impossible for him not to touch the fabric, he was very careful not to touch *her*.

"No garish paint jobs, please," he told her, as if he thought she might mistake his meaning.

"No one has made anything clear to me," Esme replied sweetly. So very sweetly. "In fact, I've been under the impression that it's all been left opaque on purpose. It seems I am to be left to my own devices in all things and it is true that historically, this has indeed involved a few rounds of cheerful paints."

He sighed, and made a meal out of the sound. "Let me

be the one to make certain you understand. The palace is a monument. It is the property of the kingdom as well as its joy and its emblem. Nothing in it is to be moved, renovated, changed, or even reconsidered without a consult with palace staff. Not your palace staff. Mine. Is that understood?"

"I understand perfectly," she said, in what she hoped was a voice so placid it irked him. The look he shot her way suggested that she was successful. "As there is no nursery available in my compartments, I can only hope that the royal heir will be perfectly happy to loll about on the floor. Catching every draft and building a baseline of neglect that will likely color the rest of his or her existence. When this astonishingly hardy child grows up and decides to end the monarchy in retaliation, I'm sure that his or her Spartan beginnings will figure highly in that decision."

Tadeo did not respond to that. Not with words. All he did was turn his head and fix that fulminating glare of his upon her, making it perfectly clear to Esme that if she had any designs on his body that evening, they would be denied. She had not *earned* the right to touch him. Again.

Once more, she rather thought she was glad.

But the trouble was, being irritated with him didn't last.

Too many of their engagements involved them standing too close to each other. Touching each other—whether she took his arm as they walked or allowed him to sweep her into his arms for a dance in the middle of a ballroom.

All theater, she told herself. All smoke and mirrors.

But she was weak, it turned out. It had been easier before, when she could repair to the manor house after nights like these. When she did not have to lie awake at night, knowing that he was *right there*. Right on the same hall, in the bedchamber next to hers. Sleeping beneath the same ornate roof.

And if she could only follow his obnoxious rules, she could have everything she wanted.

Everything she *thought* she wanted, that was.

For the first few weeks, she wasn't entirely certain that she did. Or maybe the real truth was that she'd always imagined that if something changed in their marriage, everything would change. It hadn't occurred to her that it could substantially change in so many respects, yet still leave her feeling as abandoned and alone as ever.

It hadn't occurred to her that there were so many more complicated places to go.

One night, Esme was so busy turning these things over and over in her head that they made it all the way to their night's engagement without her saying a word. She didn't even realize it until they were on the way home again.

It had been a long night of forced gaiety, but it turned out that they were both quite good at that sort of thing. She'd forgotten that, somehow, over the course of the last five months. That for all that Tadeo liked to brood at her, he could turn on his charm when it mattered.

That was what she was thinking about in the car as it slipped through the old city streets and then bumped over the old cobblestones around the palace. How easy it was for him to be charming to everyone else in the world but her.

She almost asked him about it—or, perhaps, bludgeoned him a bit with it, as that was likely to make her feel better—but then she remembered.

Somehow Esme had managed, quite accidentally, to remain quiet in private this entire night.

And beside her, she was certain that she could feel Tadeo getting more and more tense the closer they got to the palace.

It was as if a light bulb went off in her head with a loud *pop*.

Esme could have kicked herself. She'd been so busy thinking about how it *felt* for her that she'd forgotten that there was no way that Tadeo would have put all these strictures into place if he wasn't trying to protect *himself* somehow too.

And now that she'd finally gotten around to thinking this through, she knew exactly how he was protecting himself with this: He didn't think she could do it.

He didn't think that she could ever stay quiet enough to win herself a place in his bed. He might even have thought, and not without reason, that the very idea that she was expected to win her place in his bed would keep her from trying. She was a Wellesley woman, after all.

It made perfect sense. Tadeo could wrap everything in ice when he had his clothes on. He could and he did.

But the moment they touched—and even more so when they were naked—he was as helpless in the face of the wildfire that they became as she was.

How could she have let herself forget this?

The car pulled up to the palace entrance. The courtiers and guards descended upon them as always to guide them inside and relay any pertinent information that could not wait to get the King's ear. But Tadeo looked over at her as they exited the vehicle.

"I want to see you tomorrow," he told her sternly. "In my office. I should like to discuss some of the finer points of protocol that I think the last five months might have erased."

Any other night, or any other time at all, Esme would have responded to that provocation in kind. But tonight she knew exactly what he was doing. And why.

So all she did was smile at him, as demurely as possible. She inclined her head graciously, wordlessly agreeing to his ridiculous demand, as if she had not been raised a princess herself and—unlike him—spent her formative years with her very own comportment instructor as her parents had not wished to send her to any finishing school. The *cheek* of the man.

But Esme said not one word.

He was pulled aside to attend to some matter or other, but Esme headed straight to her rooms. She found she was trembling, slightly, but she knew full well it was excitement. Inside her compartments, she took specific care as she went through her nightly routine. She brushed out her hair and left it to flow like ink down her back. Instead of comfortable pajamas she liked to sleep in these days, she went and dug out a chemise she'd bought before her wedding in excess of hope.

She let the silky fabric shimmer over her body and then laughed when she looked in the mirror and saw the way that her baby belly made the whole thing...shorter. And far more provocative, really.

Perfect for tonight, then.

Esme dabbed a hint of perfume at her wrists and then pressed her wrists behind her ears, because long ago, in Boston, he had once groaned about how wild that scent made him with the proof of his admiration pressed hard against her thigh.

She took a deep breath, and laughed at that too, for she felt as shaky as an untouched virgin on her wedding night. Though she had been nothing of the kind, thanks to him. And this was no wedding night anyway.

Though in a way, she thought as she walked back into her bedroom from the dressing room here that rivaled the one she'd had in the manor house, it was. This was a new beginning for them whether he liked it or not.

Because Esme was quite certain she'd finally cracked the code. Like it or not—and she was quite certain he would not like it at all, at least in theory—she'd figured him out.

She went to the door that joined their bedrooms, took a deep breath, and then pulled it open. But when she walked through, instead of finding herself in his bedchamber she discovered that she was in a small antechamber instead. It was little more than a closet, with a chair and a small table beneath a portrait of a bucolic scene that could have been any mountain slope in the Pyrenees. A door to what was obviously Tadeo's bedroom and also a door to what she assumed was the hall.

Esme knew immediately what this room was. A little waiting area for the ladies, in case the king was otherwise occupied—as she imagined many a king had been over the course of the kingdom's long history. This room allowed His Royal and Rutting Majesty to cycle wives and mistresses in and out as he pleased without any unpleasantness that might put him off his stroke.

It was one of the things she loved about these old buildings. They always told on themselves.

But she did not intend to wait about for the King's pleasure tonight. She knew Tadeo's essential character too well, despite all these years of chilly discord shoved deep beneath their public personas. She not only knew he wouldn't be with another woman, she knew he was regretting the bargain he'd made with her, too.

Yet she also knew he kept his promises, even if that was to what he believed was his detriment.

She went to the other door, half expecting it to be locked against her.

But it opened easily when she turned the knob and she supposed that wasn't a surprise, no matter that it felt like one. Tadeo was a man of his word, good or ill.

Inside, she found herself in the King's bedchamber. It was an imposing, august sort of room. There was a grand four-poster bed on one wall and a capacious hearth with a seating area arranged around it. The rugs on the stone floor were thick and fine.

Over by the windows, bathing in the starlight, stood Tadeo himself.

She knew that he had heard her come in and she also knew, simply at a glance, that he was bracing himself against this intrusion.

He probably wanted her to say something now so that he could send her away again.

Esme would bite her tongue in half before she did anything of the kind.

Besides, she could think of far greater uses of her time. And her poor tongue. She glided across the room toward him and could see herself coming in the window's reflection. So she knew he could see her too.

He turned to face her as she came closer, no longer wearing the majestic suit with all its regalia that he'd worn out tonight. Now he wore a T-shirt and lounging trousers, yet both of them were made of a fabric so exquisite that she could see the way it fell—lovingly and caressingly—against his body from across the room.

It was even better up close. So was he.

"I don't think this is a good idea," he growled at her.

But all she did was smile at him.

Esme went up to him and stopped just before another step would send her catapulting into his body. She could feel the heat he gave off, as if he was a furnace. He smelled like the shower he must have just taken, a fragrant sort of damp that made her feel a bit damp herself.

She took a breath, because she wanted to remember every moment of this. No blurriness, no alcohol, no crushing grief—and the silence that made everything that much better. That made it all so much *hotter*.

That somehow made everything roaring here between them as stark and undeniable as she remembered it from the night they met.

Then, holding Tadeo's gaze, Esme knelt down before him and watched those blue eyes of his burst into flame.

CHAPTER SIX

HIS EYES, SO FULL of fire and need, told her everything she needed to know.

Esme knelt up and slid her palms along his powerful thighs. As she did, she could not mistake the thick impression of his cock or the way it pressed out against the soft fabric of those lounging trousers of his.

He was so big. So hard. He made her mouth water.

Still holding his gaze, she rubbed her cheek against the length of it. And listened to the telltale sign of his breath as it sighed out of him, as if against his will.

But Esme knew the sound of this man's surrender when she heard it.

Just as she knew the way it echoed inside her, making her feel shivery and magical, bright with yearning in every last cell.

She put her mouth on him, through the fabric, and smiled against him when he jerked. Though he did not push her away. She could feel the tension in him, but if anything, he pressed himself toward her mouth, not away from it.

Esme worked her way up until she could peel the waistband of his trousers down and free him at last. Then she used both of her hands to take him out of the trousers, fully. She sighed a little, happily, sitting back on her heels.

She let her hands do what they liked, relearning the shape of him, the heavy weight, the bold heat.

Then she wrapped her hands around him, knelt up high again, and took him in her mouth.

She heard him groan but better yet, she could *feel* it. Then he did it again, the sound even deeper and more raw, like the fire was taking him under.

Like he was already burning alive.

And then his hands were in her hair. He took the thick length in his fists and held her head where he liked it as she licked and sucked and gave herself over to the sheer, dizzying glory of this.

To the sounds he made in the back of his throat and the hint of salt on her tongue as he surged into her mouth.

Esme could feel her whole body respond to the taste of him. To his excitement. To the delicious tension she could feel all through his long, rangy body and the fists in her hair.

She could tell the exact moment he gave himself over to her, completely. When he stopped even pretending to fight, or hold back, or keep himself apart from her in any way. When he stopped doing anything but this.

There was another raw, rough sound and then everything was sensation—so hot, so intense, so *them*—until he flooded her mouth with the essence of him.

Esme tilted her head back, swallowed him all down, and then smiled up at him. She didn't wipe away the tears that had gathered in her eyes and trekked down her cheeks, her body's usual reaction to taking him so deep in her mouth.

She was not at all surprised when his gaze went supernova and he hauled her up, straight off the floor and into his arms.

He carried her over to the bed and she thought he meant to toss her on it, but he clearly remembered that she was pregnant at the last minute. Accordingly, he *placed* her on the coverlet instead.

Esme was just pleased that he was as swept away by all this as she was tonight. More pleased than she wanted to admit, because it felt a lot less like a victory and a lot more like…something softer.

Something much more fraught with peril than beating Tadeo at his own game.

"What is this thing?" he muttered, rubbing his hands over the silk of the chemise and then pulling it up and over her head.

The look on his face when he saw her naked made her eyes go blurry.

Esme didn't know what he told himself. She didn't know how he justified all of these cold and distant years in his own mind. She only knew what he told her, but that always hinged on the official business of their royal marriage. The *messaging*. The *positioning*. The delicate math of appearances and outreach, glamour and approachability, and what the public's experience of these things meant in how they perceived the royal family.

It had all been so dry and cold for so long.

And then, of course, they'd had a wildly bright and blurry night that he had, apparently, decided he could simply write off as a mistake and never look at again before he divorced her—something he had always seemed to think he could do without too much public outcry. The only thing he claimed to care about was what his subjects thought of him and the job he did.

If she hadn't been pregnant, Esme imagined she'd be locked up with the crisis team, working on messaging that elevated the King's desire for a divorce into a *national necessity*.

But tonight had nothing to do with any of that. It had nothing to do with any messaging or crisis management.

This was purely between the two of them. This was a culmination of the same fire that had *been* right here, between them, for a decade already and counting.

She could see it all over him. Like he'd forgotten how to be cold for a moment—just a moment. Just tonight. And instead he was something like starstruck as he took her in.

All of her.

There was a look of sheer wonder on his face as he crawled onto the bed with her and learned the new contours of her body.

The heaviness of her breasts. The new, darker color of her nipples.

The faint line from her navel down over the insistent swell of her belly.

He took the longest time there, smoothing his hands over the place where their child grew and pressing kisses all along the curve. Esme didn't know how she kept from crying.

She thought that if he knew what she could see on his face then, he would have stopped this at once. He would have thrown Esme straight out and ordered her not to return.

But he didn't know. And she wasn't about to tell him.

Instead, she kept silent—as ordered—and somehow that made everything hotter and more intense as he slid down between her legs, spread them wide, then set his mouth to the molten core of her.

Where she discovered she was even more sensitive than before.

So sensitive that she let out a shuddering sort of sound, because she was already *right there*—

Tadeo licked into her, growling the way he always had, as if her taste electrified him. As if he was enjoying himself as much as she was. He had been her first, her only. She had heard all sorts of things about what men liked and didn't like, but Tadeo had never fit into those categories.

There had never been a single part of her, or any possible activity, that he had not thrown himself into the way a person only could when they loved every moment.

Esme knew this, because it was how she felt when she got to explore his marvel of a body and make him shudder beneath her own hands.

Tonight was no different. Tadeo applied himself to the task as if he'd been dying to taste her like this for years. She threw her head back and she arched up against his mouth. She moved her hips and she gave herself over to the slow, insistent, and inexorable build of all that pleasure.

He slid one finger deep inside her, then another. And that made it better. It made everything hotter and wetter and slicker, and when he started to thrust his fingers in and out of her body, Esme simply shattered.

She bucked against him, muffling the sounds she might have made against the back of her hand.

Tadeo climbed back up the bed and lay himself out beside her, then scooped her up so that he could roll her over and arrange her above him. He settled her on her hands and knees, and it seemed the most natural and inevitable thing in the world to sit up, then guide that marvelous length of him deep inside her.

For a moment, when she sank down on him, it was like the whole world stopped spinning.

It was that glorious, that impossibly *right*, that good.

It was the same as it always was. It was perfect.

It was scalding hot and it made her want to sob out the pleasure of it, of him. He filled her completely, then slightly more, so it took her a moment to settle in against him. To let her body adjust that last small bit so that she could truly take all of him.

And this time there wasn't anything the least bit *blurry* about it.

Esme breathed until she felt herself relax internally. Even if she hadn't been able to feel it herself, she would have known by the way his gaze sharpened. Those bright blue flames.

Making her wonder if this was the time he'd cause her to simply *combust*.

After a moment, then, she propped her hands on his chest and began to work herself against him. She rocked herself back and forth. She raised herself up and then slid back down that whole, hard length of him.

He watched her, his hands on her hips to help her and to guide her, that gorgeous face of his filled with passion and command, desire and longing.

She doubted he knew she could see that, too.

Esme bit her lip and every stroke felt like glory. Like them.

Like everything she ever wanted, the way it always had.

The way it always would.

She kept on and on until his head fell back and hers

drooped forward, his hands gripping her while he pounded into her from below, until they both exploded all over again—scattering themselves to every part of the Pyrenees. And the galaxy. And any universe that waited beyond.

Esme collapsed against him and he caught her, then pulled her down on top of him. She lay there, spent and giddy, especially because he didn't toss her aside the way she had assumed he might. He didn't order her to go. He didn't ruin this.

She had been so sure he would cut them back down to size that the fact he didn't made her heart swell inside her chest—until she was terrified that he would hear the way it beat. That he would know how much she loved this sweet heat they'd made and do something to make it cold again.

They lay there in the dark, silent—save for the way their breath sawed out into the dimly lit room.

And she got to drift off to sleep curled up into Tadeo's side, which was—the way it always was, the way it always had been—the best sleep of her life.

Esme wasn't exactly surprised to wake up alone the next morning. Hurt, yes. But not *surprised*.

She sat up, looking around, but she could tell immediately that he was nowhere nearby. That wasn't surprising either.

And when the immediate hurt subsided, she decided that she was perfectly satisfied. She had seen his face. She had held his body close to hers, and held him inside her. And yes, all of those things were true about the night of his father's funeral, too.

She remembered that night entirely too well, despite the alcohol. She had found him in his father's study, down near the offices in one of the more public areas of the palace. He had disappeared after the funeral and she hadn't wanted to just…leave him to his grief.

Maybe it was silly, after all they'd been through over the years, but she couldn't bear to think of him hurting. She'd instinctively headed for the study, not sure if she knew or simply remembered that his father had spent the bulk of his time with his books in his last years.

Sure enough, she'd found Tadeo there. Systematically working himself through a very large bottle of something amber-colored and pungent.

I don't want you here, he'd growled at her when she'd come in, dressed in her fine black clothes.

But he'd gestured to the couch beside him, inviting her to take a seat.

Esme hadn't intended for things to go the way they had. Or she didn't think that was what she'd intended. They hadn't spoken much. He'd passed the bottle to her and they'd traded back and forth like that for far longer than they should have.

When he'd buried his head in his hands, she'd rubbed his back—and then it had seemed like the most natural thing in the world when he'd pulled her close and kissed her.

It had been a savage kind of grief, she thought. She had offered him comfort, because she knew he needed it. Because she'd known and cared about his father. Because despite everything, she cared about him, too.

Maybe that was when she'd understood that she always would.

But it had been followed by that slow-dawning understanding that, once again, he was going to pretend none of it had happened. He was going to pretend it had been a forgettable drunken night.

He was going to carry on exactly as he always had.

Esme had been forced to go through the painful process of finally—finally—accepting that her life with him was over. That there was no future. That no matter how many times he'd once told her he loved her, safe across an ocean from here, or how often she thought that really, he still did, it didn't matter.

He didn't want to. And he would act as if he didn't into the grave.

She'd finally accepted that she really and truly couldn't change him. That this was a doomed enterprise, it was time to cut her losses, and she'd be better off out there without him.

Esme had started imagining what that might look like. She'd been, if not *excited*, ready.

But now, sitting in his bedchamber all alone, Esme understood that she'd been lying to herself. She didn't simply *care* about Tadeo. She hadn't really accepted that he didn't love her the way she wanted him to—she'd simply accepted the fact that it was going to end and there was nothing she could do about it.

She had been head over heels in love with him since the moment she'd laid eyes on him in that Boston restaurant ten years ago.

Nothing had ever changed that love. Not the way he'd ripped her heart out of her chest a year after that first meeting. Not the way he stomped on what was left of it repeatedly during their agonizingly public—and so deeply fake—courtship. Not the way he'd broken the remaining pieces beyond repair at their cold, heartless wedding.

Not the past seven years of cold duty and quiet exile.

Not even her own acceptance that it was far past time to stop pretending that it could ever be something he wouldn't allow it to become.

Not even now, pregnant with his child, naked in his bed, alone.

Esme had loved him all along. She loved him still.

A big breath seemed to come from deep inside her then, not sure if it was a sigh or a sob. She took that as a sign to go. She got up from the bed and looked around for her chemise, but couldn't find it anywhere.

The palace was not the place to be wandering around naked—that was surely against protocol—so she pulled the coverlet from his bed, wrapped it around herself, then made her way back through the antechamber that happily did not contain a mistress and into her own bedroom. It was set up very much like his was, though her four-poster had a canopy and her fireplace had a mantel festooned with lovely objects that she could tell at a glance were priceless.

She went and sat in front of the fire, though it wasn't lit. She stared into the cold hearth.

"I love him," she whispered into the uncaring bedchamber around her that must have heard too many confessions to count. Maybe she'd accepted that she always would, but she wasn't sure if she'd really understood, until this moment, that she had never really intended to divorce him no matter what daydreams she'd let herself have about other lives without him.

Because surely she could have divorced him herself at any time if she'd truly been ready to leave him. In fact, she could have changed the course of their relationship at any time, but she never had.

She could have declined his courtship. Her parents

would not have forced her. Esme liked to bang on about responsibility, pandering to her people, and giving them what they wanted. But was that really what she'd done?

Or was this what she'd wanted all along—to be near him, no matter how?

Because she might not have him the way she wanted him, but she had him just the same.

Esme knew he hadn't touched another woman in the time they'd been married. He'd told her that much, drunkenly, the night of his father's funeral.

Now, all she could think was that it was a shame. All those years of celibacy for both of them, and for what?

When they could have been doing this the whole time. Though he wouldn't want that, she knew. Because Tadeo liked to play his games, but he couldn't keep his distance from her when sex was involved.

He'd proved that back in Boston in that house of his in Beacon Hill.

The truth was that it had never been *sex* between them. It had never been as simple as a *release*, or *a little bit of fun*, or whatever people liked to claim sex was—or should be—these days. These were conversations that made Esme think the people having them had never had the kind of sex that she and Tadeo did.

Life-altering. Earth-shattering. Absolutely catastrophic in all the best ways, and maybe in some not-so-great ways, too.

But there was no pretending that the things they did to each other didn't change them both. Even Tadeo had never denied that. *I love you*, he would whisper while he was deep inside her, his hands in her hair and his mouth against her cheek, her neck, her mouth. *I love you, Esme*, he would murmur as they drifted off to sleep, fused together like some kind of Gordian knot. He had denied he'd said those things, but never the passion that had prompted him to say them. His contention was always that the kind of passion that ignited between them was a liability and he could not allow it to derail his monarchy.

She blew out a breath and pulled that coverlet tight around her. As she did, she accepted another truth she wasn't sure she wanted to sit with.

Esme didn't want to divorce him. She didn't want to raise their baby in this environment of cold distance and responsibility and no love.

She wanted everything. The mess, the passion, the *hurt* of it all. The love that had changed them both so profoundly. The love that they both deserved.

A *husband*, not an officemate.

Her man, not just a king.

And it was also true that she had no idea how she was going to go about getting it, but Esme knew one thing.

Last night had been an excellent start.

CHAPTER SEVEN

AS THE DAYS passed and the nights continued to set them both afire, Tadeo came to the careful, considered conclusion that everything was going well.

Or as well as could be expected.

It had been a bit of a rocky start to this new phase in their marriage, he could admit. Possibly only rocky for him, little as he liked to imagine himself so affected, but the reality was that Esme seemed as unaffected as ever. As if she had only been waiting for the opportunity to have something far closer to a real marriage and was happy to dive straight in.

As if she was less thrown by the uncontrollable wildfire that still burned between them. As if she *liked* it.

He could not allow himself to think about *how much* she liked it when he was attending to his many duties during the day. And yet, too often, he could think of nothing else.

The first night that Esme had come to his room had thrown him. He hadn't expected that she would ever manage to keep her mouth shut. He had never known her to try. The girl he'd met in Boston had been a revelation. She had shared her ideas, her dreams, her theories, her opinions, her questions, her silliness—all seemingly without a shred of concern that she might be judged for these things.

Indeed, Tadeo had not judged her. He'd been too smitten with her.

Esme had burst into his life and shown him all the light and possibility that he'd been raised to abhor, because his father was a man of neither too few nor too many words. King Hugo prided himself on always being concise. Precise.

Pointed.

And he never spoke simply to fill a space.

Tadeo had aspired to be just like him.

Meanwhile, Esme's words could fill rooms and paint them too, in all the vibrant colors she held inside her. Sometimes, in the long years of this cold marriage, he had found himself awake when he ought to have been sleeping—imagining what it looked like inside her head. How bright it must be in there.

How different from this kingdom of icy winters and cool summers, and the deep freeze he kept himself in. Even if it was by choice.

This was why he'd been so certain that the deal he'd made with her favored him. He had never known her to stay quiet for too long. Not even when she should have.

He'd convinced himself she would never manage it. That she would be too busy finding new and clever ways to eviscerate him with her tongue to ever follow the rules that would lead her to his bed. That she might *try* to make it happen, but would fail at the slightest provocation.

That she hadn't made him wonder if he knew her as well as he'd always assumed he did.

She had fallen asleep in his arms and he held her there,

liking the sensation entirely too much. He stared at the ceiling, wondering if he'd made a terrible mistake.

Again.

But as the night went on, he decided that he could handle this. He could handle their chemistry as long as it was confined to the spaces where it belonged and could thus be contained. What he could not allow was it bleeding over into everything else. He was not a graduate student any longer. He could not be so reckless this time. He was a king and he had a whole kingdom to consider. He could not let passion make everything *blur*.

Tadeo decided that he could do it, and more, that this was a natural and reasonable evolution in their marriage—providing he maintained the strictest control outside the bedroom. They were husband and wife. Their marriage looked like the fairy tale they'd crafted it to be to please the outside world. He already knew she was an excellent queen in all the ways that mattered to the kingdom.

There was no reason why she couldn't make him a kind of wife that he wanted, too, sex included. It had been so long since Boston now. It was all less raw.

He knew better than to let his feelings trick his tongue into admissions that might ruin him.

As long as he maintained the strict control of his emotions that he'd held in place since breaking up with her back then—and they were second nature to him now, a part of who he was, as automatic as breathing—Tadeo couldn't see why it would be a problem.

And besides, Esme could not help but be who she was. That meant she could not always control her mouth and some nights, he was quite certain she didn't even bother to try.

"Our presence is requested at the wedding of King Gervais," he told her one afternoon, as they sat in his office discussing their schedules—one of the anodyne diary meetings he insisted upon. Not because he could not have had access to her schedule either way, but because he liked to test himself in her presence.

"King Gervais has been married two times before," Esme pointed out.

"And the heads of all the houses of Europe have been invited every time," Tadeo replied. "This is no different. We will, of course, make our appearance."

Esme studied him. The rules of their arrangement had evolved over the past weeks. If the discussion was purely related to the business of their responsibilities, that did not count against her. It did not mean she lost her chance to find him in the night.

If, however, she got emotional about anything—by his reckoning, not hers—it did.

She kept studying him now and Tadeo felt his pulse pick up, because he knew that look in her dark eyes. It was Esme's version of *devil-may-care*. The point at which he could almost see her throw up her hands and say, *what the hell*, though she would never be *quite* so vulgar.

Or not in front of him, anyway.

"Have you met King Gervais's intended?" Esme asked. Calmly.

Too calmly, by his reckoning. The kind of calm that typically foretold an explosion, if he was not mistaken.

"I have."

"I haven't," Esme murmured, toying with the hem of the sweater she wore over a dress that made her look entirely too pretty and also—through the magic of fashion he could not begin to parse—not particularly pregnant.

"But I am certain I can list the accomplishments that allowed her to rise to King Gervais's notice." If she saw the reproving look on Tadeo's face, she ignored it. "Let me guess, she is significantly younger than him, *spectacularly* more beautiful than him, and, most importantly, sheltered and naive in every possible way."

"She is an heiress of no small means from Brazil," Tadeo said. Carefully. "I believe she was selected because she meets all of the King's needs."

Those needs, in Gervais's case, did not involve dynastic aspirations as his first wife had already provided the throne with its next in line and two spares—along with scathing critiques in the press. Those needs did not involve the old king's much-discussed heart, as he had already made a fool of himself over his second wife, a wholly unsuitable actress, who had left him for her personal trainer.

Gervais had cannily selected a new queen who would give him no trouble at all.

Tadeo dreamed of such a queen.

As if she could read his mind, Esme smiled. Tadeo knew immediately, before she said a word, that he'd won today. Though was it really winning when it meant he would not have access to her tonight? Who was he punishing?

But that was a question for another time.

"You kings and your perfect little heiresses," Esme said, in a perfectly pleasant tone that was at complete odds with that sharp look in her eyes. "It's like a sweet shop, is it not? Shiny, brightly colored, consumable objects for you to eat up and throw away. How lovely for them."

He should have ignored this entire line of conversation. And he should not have felt the least bit as if she'd landed a blow. "What you seem to forget, Esme, is that you were raised to be the same sort of bit of candy."

"Incorrect," she retorted, and he thought she sat a little straighter. More, there seemed to be something almost *condemning* in the way she looked at him. Or maybe it was worse than that. Maybe she looked *disappointed*. "I am my father's heir, as you know perfectly well. It was his dearest wish that I married you so that our neighboring nations could once again unite the way they did long ago in antiquity. If not as one nation, then as the closest of friends and allies. Our first child is meant to rule Bellaza, our second, Clarebonne." Esme tilted her head to one side. "Surely you have not forgotten this."

He had not forgotten it so much as he had never imagined that it would matter, as he'd never intended to touch her again. But something kept him from saying that.

She continued. "I was never intended to be an object on a shelf, sat there to be admired from afar. I am expected to instruct the heir to Clarebonne in the ways of the kingdom in the same manner that I was instructed myself. You know that."

He shifted uncomfortably in his chair and blamed her for it. "I remember your father mentioning that, yes."

In truth, he remembered that her father had spoken for some time about his dreams for grandchildren and the unification of their kingdoms, but Tadeo had not bothered to pay close attention. So sure had he been that such a future would never materialize.

Esme studied him in that same way, and he could not account for how deeply he disliked it. It seemed as if she could see *into* him. "I can only assume that you're trying to be provocative, then. Does it make you feel as if you've won something?"

He disliked *that* even more.

"It's not my fault that you can't either school yourself from your emotional outbursts or simply keep them to yourself," he said, proud that he sounded very nearly disinterested. As if she was a science project he was observing from afar. "Sometimes you can, of course. What that tells me is that you are making a choice. You could choose something else, Esme." He could see it so clearly. They could be models of cool propriety and exquisite protocol by day and keep the rest of it purely in the bedroom. Expressed only and ever that one way. "Everything could change for the better, and for good, if you would only obey."

She leaned in, and he was struck by how much rounder she was now and how well her dress hid it. He found he hated that it was hidden. It continued to surprise him, how beautifully her pregnancy suited her. As if she was made to bear children.

He didn't know what it was about that notion—about her ripeness and her round sweetness—that made him feel as if he was breaking his own rules. As if that was an emotional thing he was feeling rather than a simple observation.

"You would hate it if I obeyed," Esme told him, with a laugh. "You would be bored out of your mind."

Tadeo could not have said why that infuriated him. "I rather doubt that."

"You would calcify in real time, Tadeo, and do you want to know how I know that?" She didn't wait for him to answer. "Because you were a shell of yourself for seven years. And *I* was perfectly fine."

"You were creeping about the manor house like a hysteric in an asylum," he shot back. "Smearing paint on the walls and befriending your servants. I would argue that you were something very far indeed from *fine*."

And the name she called him then—in her cool, crisp, *calm* way—was so outrageous that he decided she'd lost access to him for a week.

He told himself that his reaction was the only possible one to have. That he was doing the right thing and she was testing boundaries that he needed to uphold.

But he also knew that it was the loneliest week he'd had in a long while.

He was happier than he wished to admit when it ended and she managed to bite her tongue in the face of his pointed provocation after a dinner with some ministers, allowing him to glut himself in her once more.

Afterward, they lay together. Tadeo traced patterns against her belly, murmuring to the child inside. A habit he chose not to question himself about overmuch. All he knew was that he no longer thought of the child they were having as a problem, or any of the other things he'd called this pregnancy when he'd first heard of it.

These nights with her, with the baby a very real presence between them and with them, had changed everything for him.

He could not think of the last time he'd thought of this child as anything but that. *His child*.

Something of a marvel, if he was honest. He didn't think that strayed *too* far over the line into maudlin.

"I saw the palace physician again today," she said. He already knew this. But he had not expected her to share it and he found that his chest felt unexpectedly tight when she did—and of her own volition. Another marvel, perhaps. "Do you want me to tell you what we're having? A boy or a girl?"

He knew the answer to that too. But he nodded, to let her tell him.

"A boy," she said softly. Almost shyly, he thought. "And I wondered if one of his names should be Hugo, to honor your father. And the night he was made."

Tadeo felt too many things slam into him then. They all seemed to crash around inside him, when he would have said he was immune. He would have said that he wasn't the sort of man who felt anything, because that was the kind of man he wished to be.

But he felt *this*. He felt all of *this*. Too much of *this* to name.

The trick, he decided, was in not showing it. Ever. In keeping it contained. "I'd like that," he managed to grit out.

Then he kissed her, hot and hard, to forestall any further conversation.

She was six months pregnant now. Time was running out. Soon, their child would be here and Tadeo found that he both couldn't wait—and couldn't imagine what that would be like. His own memories of childhood were divided between the happier, brighter memories from before his mother died—mostly of her laughter, the games she would play with him, and the way they'd sometimes hidden from his father. In those memories, he recalled only shadows and glimpses of his father, as if he was more a monster from a nightmare instead of simply part of a game.

His later memories were sadder and quieter, as he'd learned the truth about all those bright memories of Queen Marisol and how truly noble and good his father had always been in the face of her sins. So there was regret laced through it all too, that he'd been too young and foolish to understand what was happening.

This was not something he shared with anyone. He could still remember—too well—when he'd said something along those lines to Esme in Boston.

They had been wrapped up in each other in his bedroom in the house he'd bought for his studies in the leafy, gaslit, cobblestoned neighborhood that had reminded him of home. *I wish I could have seen my mother for who she was while she was alive*, he'd said in an unguarded moment.

It chilled his blood to remember himself like that. So *open*. So *vulnerable*.

Esme had propped herself up on her elbow and pushed the weight of her hair back from her face. She'd looked at him seriously. Too seriously. *You saw your mother as your mother. Maybe that's a gift.*

Tadeo did not like to think about how often those words came back to him. How they'd haunted him across the years. He hated that he'd allowed that moment to happen, but he'd hated even more that he couldn't let it go.

The next day he found himself in the portrait gallery, studying the formal portrait that hung beside his and Esme's. It was of his parents in their wedding finery and Tadeo wasn't sure why it had never occurred to him that his parents might very well have been as at odds with each other while they'd sat for theirs as he and Esme had been.

That maybe there had never been the happy period he'd liked to think there had been. Maybe that had been a story they told. An act they put on.

He certainly knew how that went.

Tadeo found himself looking at his own wedding portrait. It was so cold, he thought now. They looked like strangers who happened to have found themselves in the same ornate frame, subject to the same brushstrokes with nothing else in common.

Though he would not have described it like that before his father's funeral had turned everything on its head. Back before that fateful night, he would have said that he and Esme looked formal, yes. Perfectly appropriate. She sat in her lovely gown and he stood behind her in the usual pose for a portrait like this.

Two people who looked suitably solemn as they started their life of duty and obligation together, he'd thought.

Now Tadeo thought he looked distant and faintly disapproving. And while Esme looked beautiful, as always, if he was fully honest with himself, she also looked terribly sad.

What he didn't like was that his parents looked much the same to him now.

Tadeo didn't think of his mother as *sad*. Careless, certainly. Reckless and scandalous, but not *sad*.

Somehow, the fact that he was having a son—within a few months—brought this home to him. He found himself thinking about his parents more than he had in a long while, and in ways that felt different to him. He particularly found himself thinking about that expression on his mother's face.

Had she truly been *sad*? And if so, why had his father not done something about it?

That felt disloyal. He hated that he could entertain any notion that did not paint his father in the bright light King Hugo deserved.

"And to what end?" he asked himself during one of

his ferocious workouts on a night that Esme had decided to poke at him, thereby ensuring he would sleep alone.

He lifted weights until he thought his muscles would betray him and then he walked back toward his rooms, not pleased when his mind took him back again to his father.

But not about his mother this time.

What was on Tadeo's mind tonight was his child. His soon-to-be-born baby. He preferred the nights when Esme followed the rules—that he relaxed once she was there, he acknowledged, because they talked in bed now. He preferred sleeping with her, yes, for all the expected reasons and more. But he also liked that he had access to his baby.

He could not conceive of treating his child as anything but the miracle he was. He already liked to feel him kick and roll. The child wasn't here yet and his antics already made Esme laugh and even Tadeo smile in the cocoon of his bed.

He could not imagine how he would take these feelings within him and turn them off. The truth of the matter was that when it came to his son, Tadeo did not feel neutral or icy at all.

What he could not figure out was why—or, crucially, *how*—his father ever had.

CHAPTER EIGHT

THE WEDDING OF King Gervais and his young and starry-eyed heiress took place in the former's kingdom in its iconic cathedral that was mostly famous for having not been bombed in any of the twentieth century's wars.

Esme and Tadeo entered the cathedral with all the rest of Europe's royals and nobles, all of them walking across the grand forecourt in their finery while looking pleasantly sophisticated for the cameras and the crowd.

In many ways, Esme thought as they walked in the sedate procession, this was something of an extended family reunion. The grand crowns of Europe had been intermingling for so many centuries that it was likely more difficult to find two royal families that *weren't* related to some degree. Somewhere in their gilded family trees.

They were directed to their seats, where there was a great deal of nodding and smiling, even between heads of state who would normally consider themselves enemies. Weddings called for better manners. Or at least a competition to see who could pretend better.

Esme knew her ability to seem delighted in her surroundings, no matter what, was top-tier. And despite his penchant for chilliness, Tadeo could do the same.

Still, it was a relief when the ceremony started in all its high pageantry, and the graciousness no longer had to be directed at each other. Everyone could relax and watch an old king marry a young woman as if it was still medieval times.

A sentiment Esme rather thought she could see on almost every face in the cathedral. Especially the faces of Gervais's heirs.

Esme had been to a friend's wedding some while ago on a beach somewhere along the rugged Maine coast. The officiant had gotten certified online. The bride and groom had made up their own vows and the whole thing had been interrupted by some chattering seagulls.

It was amusing to sit in the middle of a spectacle like this one and think about ceremonies like that. So unpretentious. So easily accessible. The entire wedding party and all the guests had fit into one small dining area in a nearby pub. It had been lovely.

This was not that kind of wedding.

After the ceremony, there was another procession out of the cathedral. It was another opportunity for Europe's aristocracy to wave at the cameras and the gathered crowds as they slipped into a sea of waiting Rolls-Royces and were borne back to the palace.

"These weddings are all the same," Esme said when they were settled in their car, her mouth fixed in a cheerful smile as she waved to the crowds outside the window. "It could have been our wedding. The only thing that changes are the coats of arms and the languages."

"It is yet one more way that monarchies remain eternal." From beside her, Tadeo was offering a wave of his own out the opposite window. "How else would anyone know to support us?"

Esme looked over at him. "That sounded suspiciously

like republican sentiment dressed up in sardonic inflection."

"Perish the thought." But he glanced over at her. "Though I will say that it is...*different* to know that I am bringing a child into this world. Into this pressure. I would not change my life in any regard." Esme thought he put a little too much emphasis on the word *any*. Then was surprised when he kept going. "But I can't deny it had its challenges."

Esme rested her hands on the convenient shelf of her baby bump, no longer hidden at all today. It had been decided that they might as well use this opportunity to launch her pregnancy to the world in one go. *Not a moment too soon*, Esme had thought when the team had informed her of this decision, because she couldn't imagine that very many people had been fooled this whole time no matter what games she'd played with shapes and fabric and flow.

Still, back home in their own kingdom, the people would only whisper their suspicions. They would not print them, out of respect.

There was nothing respectful about the broader European tabloid press, and so Tadeo's team had decided that they would use the expected feeding frenzy to their advantage. The thinking was that the tabloids could and would shriek about Esme's Royal Bump or some such thing and then cooler heads from the palace would put out a far more restrained announcement. The kingdom would tut at the intrusiveness of the press and would in fact argue that *were it up to them, they* would not wish to know if the Queen was pregnant until *the day she gave birth*.

Even now, pictures of her in her wedding finery that

had been altered to showcase her belly should likely be appearing on all the usual websites. It was all part of the game, and few people played the game better than Tadeo and his message-obsessed public relations team.

But it also felt like a good thing, Esme thought as the car inched along the ancient streets of this old, storied European city. She might not have wanted her marriage to have been the way it was for those first seven years. She might not have wanted the divorce she knew that Tadeo had been so bent upon, either, though she'd been prepared for it.

She was well aware that this baby was the reason everything had changed. It was possible that there was a part of her that resented it, but it was a vanishingly small part of her. If that. Because she had always wanted Tadeo more than she'd ever wanted to be free.

The reveal of her pregnancy meant that he was accepting their future too. She couldn't hate that.

Esme knew that Tadeo believed that *he* decided whether he got to feel emotion, and hated that she had always forced him to do exactly that and not on his schedule. She didn't know how to tell him that a baby was likely to do the same—babies being babies—but that didn't matter. He would find out soon enough, and anyway, the great thing about their marriage was that there were dynastic implications to the children they had. The only option he'd had to get rid of her was to make sure there was no issue. That was the only way he might have managed to pull off the supposedly amicable split she assumed he'd wanted to sell to his people.

The whole world would have assumed—no matter what they said—that the marriage had ended because she couldn't have children. Whether they thought that was sad or not, they would have accepted that as a fair reason for a king to find a new wife.

Just in case Esme liked to pretend that the world had moved on from the Dark Ages.

Oh well, she thought now. *That won't be happening now.*

But these were not the challenges Tadeo was talking about.

"I think that we are uniquely qualified to mitigate the challenges of this life," she said, her belly warm beneath her palms. "My parents very much wanted me to have more real-world experiences than some other heirs to thrones. I went to grammar school with the public. That was very important to them. I did go to a private school after that, but they insisted that I leave the country for college, so I could see something of the world outside of Clarebonne. They were deeply opposed to those finishing schools so many queens are polished up in. I think they always felt strongly that education was by far the better thing to concentrate on when manners can always be learned."

"I'm not sure that schooling is the issue," Tadeo said.

Esme smiled. "Is it not? Where else will you interact with others who are not of your rank? Who do not share your history? I think schooling is very important. Not just for the education you might receive, but for the social interaction. How else can you get to know your subjects?"

Tadeo looked as close to *bewildered* as she'd ever seen him. "My father had a different view of the situation," he said after a moment. Then he cleared his throat. "He spoke to me of duty, of course. And the responsibilities that would always trump any of my personal concerns, naturally. But when it came to education, he was very traditional." He named the famous boarding school he'd attended that was known to handle the schooling of a great many royal children, not to mention the offspring of celebrities and billionaires of all stripes. "Then Cambridge, of course. Followed by Harvard, as you know. My father considered this a sort of hat trick of an educational pedigree."

"But you already had a pedigree," Esme pointed out softly. "The child I'm carrying does too."

She thought that he looked taken back. Or, again, something like *bewildered*—though he hid it quickly beneath his more typical neutral expression. He aimed his attention out the window again, to continue the smiling and waving that was expected in situations like this.

"These are things I'm sure we can argue about once a child is here," he said, dismissively. But it was like those nights when she was obediently silent and he started poking at her. She had the distinct impression that he was trying to get her temper to flare. He wanted her to fight with him, clearly.

Esme looked out the window again, but she didn't see the crowds pressing in at the barricades. She had a little prickle of awareness that told her that this was an important moment, so she couldn't quite see why. Aside from her inkling that he wanted her to poke back at him, he was perfectly right. They had years to worry about the schooling of their unborn child, not to mention what sort of society the next king might keep.

But somehow it felt as if this was a bruise that she'd unknowingly pressed against.

At the palace there were more cameras, and she could already hear the roars from the paparazzi as Tadeo helped her from the car. He made certain to pause for a moment outside it, as if he needed to adjust his sleeves, with her belly on full display. Then there was the long procession up the palace stairs and in through its grand gates that allowed most of Europe to get a glimpse of the contours of her pregnancy.

Precisely as planned, she knew. Esme couldn't quite put her finger on why it was that she felt so unsettled by the conversation they'd had in the car.

It wasn't his rules. As the weeks passed, they had loosened. Now it was not pure silence that he required. It was pleasantness. Only if he felt attacked, or he felt she was being unreasonable, did he decree that she'd lost access to him.

Though it was never for a week these days and the real truth was, he didn't do that much anymore anyway. It was as if he'd become as addicted to their nights together as she was. Esme suspected that he didn't sleep any better without her than she did without him.

But she didn't dare say that, either.

What she did instead was pour her feelings into everything they did. Whether it was a dance at a ball or the way she held on to him as she found her pleasure, she did anything and everything she could to infuse these moments with the love she felt swimming inside her, as sure as the blood in her veins.

Sometimes she was sure that he could feel it. Sometimes, in those unguarded moments when they were together and naked, and there was nothing in all the world but the fire they built together, she was sure that she glimpsed it. That light in his eyes. When he looked at her, sometimes, that curve in his mouth.

All those things he never said.

Inside the palace, they moved along a gorgeous entry

hall that led into a ballroom. They were announced and then they walked down the stairs and were swallowed up by the crowd. Only then did Esme allow herself to start looking around with purpose.

"Are you expecting to meet someone here?" Tadeo asked, sounding amused.

"My parents." She smiled up at him. "They are the King and Queen of Clarebonne, after all. I feel certain they are on the guest list."

"They didn't tell you?" He looked confused.

"Why would they tell me?" She shook her head at him, though she didn't think he was joking. "Gone are the days when the Clarebonne palace kept me apprised of the King and Queen's movements."

"I thought you said you spoke to your mother every day."

"I do." Esme frowned at him. "We don't talk about work, generally."

Again, Tadeo looked as if he couldn't quite comprehend what she was saying. "Then what do you talk about?"

Esme didn't get a chance to answer him, because he was swept into conversation with some other heads of state. But she couldn't stop thinking about what that question revealed. About what it suggested about his relationships with his parents. With his father, most of all.

Had they ever *not* talked about work?

She moved through the grand ballroom, smiling and clasping hands with many of the people she recognized as she went. And she recognized almost everyone. It was all quite lovely, and in some cases decidedly not lovely—that was part of the fun of these events, she always thought—and either way, she found herself smiling far more genuinely when she saw the people she was looking for standing over near an alcove.

Her mother saw her a few moments later as she drew near, and Queen Luisa's practiced, regal smile turned into something far more personal, wide and happy, at the sight of her daughter.

Then her gaze dropped to Esme's belly and her smile dropped. It became a gasp. Then she tugged on her husband's arm in a complete violation of all known protocol, yanking his attention away from the earnest Dutch minister he was speaking with.

And when Esme finally reached them, they were both talking a mile a minute, hugging her close and already making noises at her baby belly. Then even more noises when she told them it was a boy.

For a while, there was nothing but that. This outpouring of emotion, so pure and so happy, that it took Esme a few extra moments to realize how much she'd missed it.

How inured she'd become to the empty shell of Bellaza. And her less empty, but still decidedly cold husband—

But that made her heart hurt all over again, and she didn't want to *hurt*. Not now. Not while her parents were here and felt like a long dose of sunlight after an endless winter.

"You have been holding out on us," her father, King Alain, said sternly, though his dark eyes danced.

"I have been," Esme confessed.

"I'm sure she had her reasons," said her mother at once, because Queen Luisa never had and never would waste an opportunity to champion her daughter. No matter what.

Tonight, Esme couldn't help but wonder who had ever championed Tadeo.

That made her heart ache too.

When her father's attention was reclaimed by the Dutch minister, Luisa linked her arm through Esme's and hugged her close.

"I'm so happy for you, my darling," she said in her musical way. "But at such a happy time, what I cannot understand is why your eyes are so sad."

Esme felt all her breath go out of her in a rush. She felt both exposed and seen, her mother's specialty. It felt like a kind of nostalgia. Like a perfect hug she knew would end. "Not *sad*," she said after a moment, when she was sure her voice would not sound the least bit rough or choked. "It's more complicated than that."

Queen Luisa studied her daughter for a moment, then turned her attention to the crowd before them. She kept her arm linked with Esme's as her own gaze took on a faraway look.

"You know that Queen Marisol and I were friends, do you not?" But that was not really a question, Esme knew. This was a story. And that she'd invoked the name of the scandalous Marisol, the much-maligned mother of Tadeo, had Esme immediately riveted. "Long before she was the Queen of Bellaza, she was a childhood friend. We grew up together, I suppose you could say, and spent several summers in our youth doing the same circuit of house parties with the sorts of people our parents wanted us to know, outside of the glare of the headlines." Her smile was mysterious, but all she said was, "I got to know her rather well."

"No one speaks of her in the palace," Esme said softly.

Her mother made a low noise. "I am not surprised."

"When she does come up, it is never a pleasant conversation."

Luisa made a humming sort of noise. Esme knew that

sound. It was her elegant way or dissenting without succumbing to a vulgar snort or a laugh.

"I will tell you this," her mother said. "The Marisol I knew was a bright light. She was always happy while the rest of us liked to waft about complaining of our boredom and disaffection, as you do. She could make the most tedious afternoon a delight, simply by her presence. And when she fell in love with Hugo of Bellaza, it seemed at first that he made her the happiest she'd ever been."

Esme looked at her in surprise and her mother nodded. "It was not long after their engagement, I think, that she started to change. She grew quieter. More careful. After a while, there was no sign of the childhood friend I'd known for so long. She had become Queen Marisol." Luisa looked at Esme then. "And Queen Marisol was the saddest woman I have ever known."

Esme felt something like an earthquake deep inside her.

"Mother," she said, shaking her head. "I'm having his baby—"

Luisa's eyes flashed. "And you owe that baby *you*, Esme. My daughter is a bright light herself. Yet every time I see you, the light grows darker and darker in your gaze. Is this what you wish to pass on to your child?" She made a soft noise. "I would tell you that Marisol most assuredly did *not* want that. Yet that is where she ended up. And if I'm not mistaken, the child she loved to distraction takes after his father. Not her. Not the parent who loved him because he was hers, not because he would one day be king."

Then the music changed and they were interrupted by distant cousins. Luisa squeezed Esme's arm with her own, kissed her on the cheek, then let her go.

And Esme found herself thinking of nothing else but what her mother had said for the rest of the evening. She kept her professional smile in place. She applauded the bride, who looked like she thought she'd won the Cinderella lottery. She smiled at the groom, who looked very pleased with himself. She danced more than once with her husband, who she'd once thought would be her own fairy tale, and tried her best to get the sadness out of her eyes.

Whatever her mother had seen. Whatever that meant.

That night, they stayed in a fine old house near the palace, and made love to each other with a ferocity and a depth that made Esme think she might actually weep.

Particularly afterward, where she laid curled up beside him, and had to accept that whatever she thought was happening, it was a certainty that *he* did not think making love as part of what they were doing. *He* could be telling himself anything.

He might not even find all of this as beautiful and transformative as she did.

"Are you all right?" he asked in the dark, the two of them so close on the new bed. "You seem…"

But he didn't finish what he'd been about to say. He kissed her instead. He threw them straight back into that fire of theirs.

Hadn't he made it clear? He didn't *want* to hear the things she had to say. He didn't *want* to listen to her, because when he did, he had to *feel*.

Esme couldn't seem to get that out of her head. They flew back to Bellaza and she told herself that her spirits should have been lifted as they descended down into the kingdom. The valley was bursting with wildflowers, all preening beneath that bright spring sun overhead. The lakes and the fields glittered with light and color, and the mountains that ringed the small country were white-capped and gleaming.

A perfect picture, she thought. *Too bad that there's nothing real beneath it.*

At the palace, she felt out of sorts and waved off the hovering staff as she took herself out into the gardens.

The palace gardens were nothing like hers had been at the manor house. They were deliberately and ruthlessly orderly. They stayed in their straight lines and even the happy colors of the spring flowers were very carefully arranged and controlled so that no *exuberance* could infect the grounds.

Walking out along the tidy paths made her feel as if her ribs were closing in on her. As if she was being pressed to death on all sides.

Like these gardens were a prison. She felt as if she couldn't breathe.

Esme made her way down to the lake at the far edge of the gardens. It was full and deeply blue now that March was coming to an end, gleaming beneath a sun that seemed to think it was already summer. On the far side of the lake, she could see the city skyline, all those lovely old houses mixed in with newer buildings, all of them arranged along the lakefront.

It wouldn't be long now before there were boats out on the water. Landscape photographers would spend days trying to get the perfect shot to capture the lake and careful gardens with the palace above. It was part of the kingdom's allure. This fairy-tale palace. Stacked above a high mountain lake with its beautiful gardens spread out beneath an endlessly blue sky.

She didn't know why the very idea of that perfect image made her want to cry today.

"You were supposed to be in my office a half hour ago to conduct a postmortem on that wedding and any conversations that came out of it," came Tadeo's voice from behind her, jolting her out of whatever daydream had claimed her. She'd moved along the lakefront, she realized, and had wandered her way out onto one of the docks. It was clear that he must have done the same, though she hadn't heard his footfall on the wooden planks.

"As you can see, I have missed that appointment," was all she said in reply.

What she wanted to say was that she found it rich that when women reported what they'd said and heard at a party it was considered gossip, yet when a man did it, it was *intel*. But she suspected he would find that churlish. And emotional.

She was both, but she wasn't sure she had it in her to fence words the way they usually did.

"Are you all right?" he asked again, the way he had last night, sounding… She wouldn't say *worried*. Or even *concerned*. That was all far too emotional for Tadeo, who liked all the images of his kingdom and his marriage to be aspirational and lovely and had no intention whatsoever of putting the work in on the other side.

"I'm not all right." She turned to look at him. "I'm tired of your rules, Tadeo. I know why you felt you had to set them up, but it's just one more way of distancing ourselves from what was actually going on here. What's been going on here forever."

He frowned. "The rules are the rules."

"If only you were a king, who could make any law he liked on a whim." She laughed, though there was very little mirth in the sound. "Not that that would matter, as we are not talking about the kingdom just now. We're talking about us. You and me."

"I have no desire to talk about you and me." In another mood, she might have found his tone funny. It was quite close to *panicked*, though Tadeo would never allow himself to *panic*.

Still. It was close.

"This is a love story," she told him, looking right at him. "It always has been. And you are trying to treat it like a Royal Proclamation."

"I told you almost a decade ago that love stories are not something I am built for," he growled.

But she remembered it differently. They had started telling each other that they loved each other early on. They'd said it all the time. When he'd come back from that fateful summer and had ended things with her, he'd denied he ever meant it.

The last time she'd told him she loved him she'd been sobbing, on the floor of his town house, and he'd told her he couldn't help that. That it would fade.

It had not faded.

And more importantly, he was a liar.

She had decided that he'd gaslit her at will during that hideous breakup scene. That was the story she'd told herself all throughout the next couple of years. That and he was emotionally stunted. But she'd always ended up on the fact that he was a liar.

Because she had been there.

She knew what they'd had.

She knew what he'd said.

She decided that if he was lying, he was lying to himself first.

And the past seven years proved that. The night of his father's funeral proved that. Everything that had happened since he'd learned about the pregnancy proved it.

It was never that she'd somehow gotten the wrong idea about him, or made him up in her head. She'd been right about him every step of the way.

Maybe, she thought, it was time he understood that.

"Do you know what's funny?" Esme smiled as she said that. She came close to laughing, even. "I know you *so well*, Tadeo. I know that if I say anything about love you will immediately balk, even though everything that's happened between us since you found out I was pregnant has showed me, time and again, that you're as in love with me now as ever."

He looked as if she'd struck him with an ax, but she didn't let that stop her. "That, in fact, the reason you keep coming up with all these walls to put between us is because you're still afraid of that love. But I realized recently that while I know you well enough that I can predict any response you might have and act accordingly in advance—and I do—*you* don't know *me* at all."

For a moment, he looked like she really had smashed something heavy and sharp into the side of his head.

"Of course I know you," he managed to get out after a few tense moments, when she was sure she could hear the sound of his heart. Beating too fast and too hard—or perhaps that was hers. "I don't know what this outburst is about, Esme, but it is the antithesis of our agreement."

She shook her head. "What agreement is that? I don't recall *agreeing* to anything. I went along with you. That's not the same thing."

"It is the same thing," he shot back at her. "I knew this

was a mistake. I knew I shouldn't have let you into my bed again. The reality is that you can't handle it."

Esme did laugh then, directly at him. "Yes, of course. My bad. *I* am the one who can't handle it."

She could see his temper mounting. There was that thunderstorm in his blue eyes, that furious muscle in his jaw. "Do you think I don't know you?" he gritted out. "I know this. Any time there is intimacy between us, *this* is what happens. You start talking about love and it makes you impossible."

"You don't know me at all," Esme corrected him with what she hoped was a calm tone that rankled. Deeply. "For example, did you know that I don't know how to swim?"

"What?" He blinked, as if he was trying to keep up. "What does that have to do with anything? Are you quite well, Esme?"

Meaning, *Have you had a mental break?*

Because, naturally, he would think so.

"I never learned," she told him blithely. "I suppose that should have been a part of my unconventional education. What a tragedy that it was not."

Esme didn't think through what she was doing. Because she knew she was going to do it anyway, whether she thought it through or not. She turned back toward the water and then took off running down what was left of the dock, those last few feet.

Then she launched herself into the air and hit the water, plummeting down beneath the surface of the lake.

And sank.

CHAPTER NINE

For a moment, Tadeo froze in place. In utter disbelief.

There were ripples on the surface of the lake and it was almost as if he was dreaming this, or had imagined it, or—

But in the next second, he was moving. He charged down the dock, threw himself into the air, and dived into this lake he had swum in and boated on the whole of his life. Never had he had the slightest moment of concern about these waters.

Yet everything was different now that Esme had sunk straight down and hadn't come up.

He dived deep, but there was no sign of her. And when he shot back up to the surface for a screaming sort of breath into his aching lungs, something icy and cold gripping him like a terrible fist in his chest—

But he stopped.

Because Esme was there. Floating quite happily and paddling along on the surface of the lake. He could feel his own heart like a drum. He couldn't believe what he was seeing. There was a literal red haze descending upon him, but he blinked it away.

"But you said—"

Tadeo was so furious he couldn't finish.

"I swim like a fish," Esme told him merrily. "See? You don't know me at all. As I have said."

"I thought—" But he stopped himself again, because he refused to tell her that he'd thought she was drowning. That felt like a bridge too far.

You are already in the water, fully clothed, a voice inside reminded him. *Who cares about bridges at this point?*

Still, he said nothing. If he told her she'd scared him... Well. He presumed that had been the point of this exercise and he did not wish to give her the satisfaction of telling her it had been successful.

"I want more," she told him, treading water in all her clothes. Her hair was now plastered to her head, but those luminous eyes of hers were fastened to his. "I don't want rules. I want a marriage. I want our son to grow up and know that he is loved."

"Our son will be the King of Bellaza when I am dead. He will grow up knowing this. He will understand his responsibilities—"

"He will grow up knowing that he is loved," Esme said again, with a certain steel in her voice. "Do you hear me? Better yet, do you hear yourself? Do you think that perhaps some of the challenges you faced in your childhood were due to the fact that you weren't allowed to be a child? Too concerned with responsibilities and your father's death?"

"I'm not listening to this," he growled at her. He swam to the dock and pulled himself up out of the water, then glared balefully back toward the lake. Where his queen made absolutely no move to follow him. Esme was floating on her back with her arms thrown above her head and her belly poking above the waterline, looking as if she could stay there all day. "I'm not going to take lectures on childrearing from a person so unhinged that she would throw herself into a body of water after claiming she couldn't swim for the express purpose of proving a point."

"Is that unhinged?" She lifted her feet out of the water and kicked off the singe shoe she was wearing on her right foot. Her left foot was bare. "And what point were you making, exactly, when you hauled me before you in the palace and explained to me how I must remain mute in private, like a good girl, if I wished to earn a place in your bed?"

"That was never—" But he stopped there, too.

"Do you think I don't know that you set that up so I would fail?" she asked, and though her face was tilted toward the sky, Tadeo felt that question as if she'd stabbed it into his chest like a dagger. "Of course I know." She moved in the water then, so that she was bobbing there, her solemn gaze on his. "But it didn't fail, because I'm capable of all kinds of things, Tadeo. What's a little stretch of quiet? I've been in love with you since the moment we met and you've been terrified of that, and me, and what we are together for the same length of time. To the point you lied about what you felt. And while I've managed to give you pieces of what you want along the way, you've never managed to return it, have you?"

He thought then that he had never felt colder in his life. As if he might start shattering.

"If that is true, it would seem that you've wasted a decade of your life. You should do something about that."

"Behold me doing something about it," she replied.

She swam toward him then and reached up to hold onto the dock, though she made no move to lift herself up or out. It was possible she couldn't, with her belly, but she also didn't ask him to help her.

Instead, she looked up at him and made him feel pinned to the dock where he stood.

"Have you ever asked yourself," she said quietly, those eyes of hers so intense on his, "what you would do if you could live your life on your own terms?"

"Are you mad? I am the king. I live on no terms but my own."

"Can you imagine," she said, as if he hadn't spoken, even more quietly this time, "who you would be if you hadn't let your father's fear transform you?"

Tadeo wasn't even aware of moving back, of staggering away from her as if she'd hauled off and punched him. All he knew was that she asked him that question, and he was gone. He had to put distance between them. He had to *do* something.

Anything.

He didn't know how long it took him to make it back up the hill from the lake. He was soaking wet, dressed in his dripping clothes when he came back to himself somewhere in the palace. He was also dripping on the floor.

He stood there, his head ringing and that question repeating again and again and again, until he became aware of Arturo there beside him.

"Your Majesty appears to be in need of a towel," said the older man, with his typical restraint. And understatement.

"Among other things," Tadeo muttered.

But he allowed the old servant to usher him up the back stairs through the palace, so that no one needed to see the King in his waterlogged state. A glance in the mirrors they passed suggested that his appearance would likely scare off anyone unlucky enough to venture near.

He rather alarmed himself.

His team would faint dead away.

"The Queen is in a similar state," he told Arturo when they reached his rooms. "It would be better if she did not parade through the palace as I suspect she will want to do."

"Say no more, sir," Arturo said.

"You can bring her to my office when she is dried off," Tadeo said darkly.

He showered, then dressed. And found that he was still vibrating with that same fury. Because that's what it was, he assured himself. Sheer, unadulterated fury at her temerity. At her games.

At *her*.

He walked back through the palace, taking his usual route this time. Now that he was dry and looked like himself again. Tadeo walked from his rooms, out of the private wing and down into the public areas, where courtiers bowed and curtsied as he passed and everywhere he turned his head, there were more emblems of the rich history of his country. His family.

His future.

What was important, he told himself sternly, was that a man keep a cool head so that he could better navigate the demands of his position.

As he thought that, it was like he could suddenly hear an echo from the past. From that part of his past he much preferred to keep locked away.

He could remember walking down this same hall, headed to the same office where his father had once sat, always so clear-eyed and reserved.

Tadeo remembered how excited he'd been to share the good news about his meeting with Princess Esme with his father at last. The miraculous news, to his way of thinking—though he cringed when he thought about it now—that he had met Esme of Clarebonne, and it had gone… Better than merely *well*. Much, much better. An entire year of better.

That they were in love.

He could still remember how he'd felt that afternoon. It had been late summer outside, the lake sparkling with all the light, yet no match for how he'd felt inside. How he had been nearly bursting at the seams, so certain that his father would be delighted.

His father had impressed upon him—repeatedly—that Tadeo could make no decision more important than who he chose to marry. As a king, Tadeo would need to rely on his queen and trust her to carry out her own duties in concert with him. Royal marriages required cool heads and careful planning, King Hugo had always told him.

That was why Tadeo's marriage had been planned for him.

Never had Tadeo been so grateful for a good plan.

She is…nothing short of amazing, he had gushed when his father had waved him toward a seat and asked him what he had to say for himself. King Hugo's preferred conversation opener, even with the son he hadn't seen in many months. *She is a marvel. I do not know how it is you and her father managed to set us up so brilliantly, but I couldn't be happier. Neither one of us can believe our luck.*

He wasn't certain when it had occurred to him that his father had not responded in some time. That he only sat there, his gaze seeming cooler and more distant by the moment. Tadeo remembered when the chill in the room had finally penetrated the haze he'd been in.

How he'd felt it roll through him, like he'd suddenly found himself standing outside in a snowstorm.

Am I to understand that you have been conducting an affair with Princess Esme? King Hugo had asked. He had been sitting behind the desk, his hands folded in front of him with his usual tall, straight posture. His blue gaze had been glacial.

I suppose you could call it that, Tadeo had replied. Though he would never have called it that.

You sound besotted, his father had said in the same colorless voice.

Tadeo had laughed at that, because he hadn't been able to help himself. *I suppose I am. Isn't that wonderful?*

In retrospect, he couldn't fathom what he'd been thinking. How had he imagined that his father would have welcomed this news? But he knew the answer to that. It was Esme. It was the way Esme had talked about her parents, their warmth and kindness, their interest in their daughter that never seemed to hinge on her performance as their heir.

He had been seduced by more than simply Esme herself. He had fallen just as hard for all she represented. No doubt he'd imagined that he would come back here and change things, simply because he'd gone and lost his head—but over the princess that had been picked out for him.

Surely that would matter.

His father's strictures about emotion couldn't apply when it was *love*. There was no possible way, Tadeo had thought.

But, *It is not wonderful, it is a disaster*, King Hugo had said, his voice frigid. *Where do you imagine this will go? Have I not told you, over and over again, that the basis of a proper and useful royal marriage is compatibility, not passion? Never passion, Tadeo.*

Yet Tadeo had known better. *Surely there is room for both.*

And he had not dared use the word that actually fit the situation.

Because even as he said it, he could see his father's face grow thunderous. *Passion becomes scandal. It is inevitable. I will have to speak to King Alain myself. There is no possible way that I can countenance this relationship. I cannot put my country in the hands of a man who allows himself to be swept away by pretty girl at a moment's notice. I thought I raised you better than this.*

Tadeo had felt as if his father had swung out and struck him. *I thought you'd be pleased. How often is it that an arranged marriage suits everyone from the start? Much less so well.*

This is not the kind of connection you should be pursuing, his father had said darkly. *What happens when the passion fades? You already know what route your mother took. Is that what you want for this country? Another sex scandal? More reasons to believe that the royal family is an embarrassment to the nation instead of its spine?*

He had gone on like that for days. He had been relentless.

And by the time Tadeo had returned to Boston, he had been resolved to end it, because it was the least he owed the man who had given him everything. The man who had suffered so nobly for all those years in the face of so much betrayal.

How could he do anything else?

The fact that the moment he had set eyes upon Esme had been like a gut punch, that it had made him waver, only underscored what his father had said.

I don't understand, she had said then. *You said that you loved me. You know that I love you. How could there possibly be a better basis for marriage than that?*

The last thing either one of our kingdoms needs is the

volatility of a love story, he had told her, parroting his father. *My people and your people deserve better.*

And he had believed that. He still believed that.

When he had summoned her to Bellaza a couple of years after their breakup, after she had graduated from college and comported herself flawlessly in London, he'd been able to see that she thought that there was a possibility that he regretted the things he'd said to her when they'd broken up.

He had made certain to make it clear that he regretted nothing.

The fact of the matter is that we're competing against a greater narrative than ourselves, he had said. It was the same thing that he'd told his father, while also making it clear that his childish infatuation with Esme had withered on the vine.

His father had believed him. He'd worked with Tadeo for years by then, and Tadeo had made sure that he never slipped like that again.

Esme had only looked at him for a long moment. *I don't know what that means*, she had said. Archly, he'd thought.

She had looked even more beautiful than he remembered, which he had considered more proof she was as dangerous to him as his father had insisted she was. He didn't want a beautiful wife. A pretty one, certainly—as he was only a man. And the people would expect no less. Even a handsome sort of woman would do, as she would be lauded for her practicality from all corners.

Tadeo had been sure that he could do better—for the kingdom, for himself—than a woman who made him feel as if his skin was being peeled off his body every time he looked at her. Who made him feel as if the world would end if he couldn't touch her. It was an outrage.

But that did not change the myth of the two of them and their betrothal, which too many people in both of their kingdoms had started to call *fate*.

How Esme had avoided hearing about this, Tadeo could not have said.

What it means is that our kingdoms have spun themselves a fairy tale, and we star in it, he had told her in as unemotional a voice as possible.

Let me guess, Esme had said. *You don't believe in fairy tales in the same way that you don't believe in love. Or happy marriages. Or anything that might make the monarchy human.*

What I believe, he had said, refusing to give in to her provocations, *is that all royal marriages are treated like fairy tales, but ours has already been written. You were betrothed to me upon your birth. Our subjects have been concocting tales about us ever since. All we have to do is ride that wave.*

Have you taken up surfing? she had asked. *How fascinating. I have never seen the appeal. Standing on objects that move very quickly on the surface of the water? No, thank you.*

He had ignored that. Especially because he had never enjoyed surfing himself, something he had not shared with her.

I would like to formally begin our courtship, he had said instead. *It will be, by necessity, extremely public. I will furnish you with a schedule. We will be seen together for a year, engaged within nine months of that year, and married at the end of that year.*

For a moment, she had only looked at him with those fathomless dark eyes of hers and he'd braced himself. He'd been certain that she would do something he hadn't thought to ward himself against. Like when he'd seen her after the breakup, very briefly, to exchange the things they'd left at each other's places and she hadn't wept. She hadn't shouted at him. She'd only looked at him, a lot like she did then, and had asked, *What do you do with the real you when you put on this mask?*

He had not answered that question.

And that day in the palace, she hadn't asked it again. Or anything like it.

She had laughed. Esme had come to the palace dressed like a Londoner. Which was to say, she had been wearing jeans tucked into boots, a chic little sweater, and minimal jewelry. She'd had her hair up in a glossy ponytail, and she had looked edible.

If he'd had any idea how long that simple meeting would end up haunting him, he was sure he would have sent a letter instead.

And why do you imagine that I would do any of those things with my ex-boyfriend? Esme had asked him. The funny part was that she had really sounded curious. As if he was a puzzle she could not figure out, which was absurd.

Even then, Tadeo had known himself to be entirely transparent in all ways. Just as his father had taught him. Just as his people deserved.

You either love your country or you don't, he had said. Perhaps a bit darkly, because exposure to her was a challenge. He'd made a mental note to up his workouts. *Which is it?*

Of course, she had murmured. *The only love you admit exists.*

Tadeo found himself thinking about all of that ancient history entirely too much as he paced about in the office now, wondering why it was taking her so long to turn up. Maybe she was still in the lake, paddling about like a happy little turtle. Maybe she had no intention of ever coming out of the water.

Either way, he knew the fault would not lie with Arturo. The old man would do his job perfectly, as he had done since before Tadeo was born.

Just as he knew that Esme would go out of her way to make it difficult, because she made everything difficult. She had been an agent of chaos from the start. He was half convinced that she was a Clarebonne spy, planted here to take down Bellaza from within.

She was halfway there.

When the door opened some while later he turned, and was unsurprised to see Esme saunter inside with her hair perfectly dried and set, meaning that she had taken her sweet time. And was challenging his own memories, for she seemed to be dressed a little too similarly to that memory he had of her in his head. The only difference was her belly, looking bigger and rounder now and reminding him that there was far more at stake here than her talk of love, or his memories of the most embarrassing year of his life so far.

Not to mention what had followed that had led them here.

Though when no one but Esme was in the room with him, it was difficult to remember why he found anything about her or the two of them embarrassing in the least.

You are your worst problem, he seethed at himself.

"If you cannot keep a civil tongue in your head about my father, I prefer you never mention him again," he told her coldly. "The man was a saint."

He didn't like the fact that instead of looking taken back at that, Esme simply looked…sad.

For him. That part was clear, and he couldn't make any sense of it.

"Is that what he told you?" she asked.

Tadeo felt his heart catapulting against his ribs again in a manner he could only call alarming. He felt the way he had down on the dock, as if the world was closing in on him. Or as if he was being sucked out and carried away to…somewhere else.

It took effort to pull himself back. Too much effort for his liking.

"This is an indisputable fact," he shot at her. "Everyone knows what he suffered. What he went through. And through it all, he stayed calm and in control of himself. What's not to admire?"

Esme moved farther into the room. He felt some kind of wave move all the way through him, rocking him. He thought that if she touched him, he might actually explode.

But she didn't come in close. She stopped a few feet from him, making him wish he'd positioned himself behind that intimidating desk.

"Have you considered the possibility that your mother wasn't the Whore of Babylon, Tadeo?" she asked. He couldn't help but notice that she seemed perfectly calm. So calm and unruffled it made him want to get his hands on her to mess her up, just a little bit. Just enough. She also wasn't done, and he did not want to hear a single word of this. "Maybe she was in love with a man who acted like an iceberg. Maybe she did what she needed to do to keep from freezing to death."

Tadeo felt everything seem to slosh about, making

him feel something like drunk. Or dizzy. Maybe both. He held his hand up as if she was advancing on him when he could see that she stopped. "Don't you dare—" he thundered at her.

But Esme only nodded. "Welcome to your actual emotions, Tadeo," she said, and she didn't even sound satisfied or smug. Only that same *sad*. "This is called *feeling things*. I know you're not used to it. But you can't keep pretending they don't exist. When all along, they've been right here, just waiting for you to acknowledge them."

She turned her back on him, and there was no way she couldn't hear the way his heart was pounding so hard against his ribs. He thought they might crack into pieces. She kept going, walking across the room and sitting down in one of the chairs that helped form a little seating area by the windows.

"Why don't you tell me when you're ready to admit that you have just as many emotions as anybody else, after all," she invited him. "I know you don't want to. I know you object to being human. But Tadeo. Isn't your heart pounding?"

He'd known it. He'd *known* she could hear it.

Esme nodded, and he realized that a traitorous hand had risen up and was pressing against his chest.

But then again, she already knew.

"That's not a heart attack," she told him gently. "Those are emotions. Tadeo, I can't believe you don't remember how they feel, because I know you knew this once. I was there." She leaned forward in her chair, her gaze seeming to spear straight through him. "That's how you know you're alive."

CHAPTER TEN

Esme hoped that he couldn't tell that she was holding her breath.

She doubted that he could. He looked so *undone*. As she watched, Tadeo seemed to implode, right there before her eyes. Right there on the carpet before that massive, imposing desk that made her think of monoliths and mysterious henges, not monarchs.

If she listened hard, she was fairly sure that she could hear him *exploding*—

But he didn't. Not quite. She watched his nostrils flare. She watched him stand straighter. A moment passed. Then another. And she began to realize that she was watching him wrestle himself under control again.

He was rendering himself unto ice. Esme was watching him make himself into a sculpture that resembled him, but wasn't him. Not the real him. Not the him who *felt* and laughed, danced and loved. Not the him who had been so *alive* and so potent that the real truth was, she'd never recovered from the loss of him.

And it wasn't the first time she'd seen him do this.

"This is what you did in Boston," she said, and felt a kind of trembling deep inside—a terrible recognition. She could remember the sense of dislocation, of betrayal. How could he stand there and look like the man she'd loved and who'd loved her back so deeply and yet somehow... not be him at all any longer? How was that possible? "I watched you do it. You stood there in that living room in your Beacon Hill town house with all that wood and the sunshine pouring in and you turned yourself into an ice sculpture right in front of me."

She remembered the wood floors, old and scarred and beautiful. The sun pouring in like it was any day, even a good day, somewhere else. And all too well did she remember the stranger staring back at her from the face of the man she'd been so in love with, it actually hurt.

It still fucking *hurt*.

"You always defer to the theatrical," Tadeo told her after a moment, and he even sounded like ice now. As if all he had to do was set the temperature gauge inside himself and sooner or later, no matter what, he would freeze. "I'm not a sculpture. There's no ice involved. I am merely making certain that I'm always in control of myself."

He did not have to say, *You should take note of this skill and try it sometime*. It was implied.

"Control is feeling your emotions and choosing not to be governed by them," Esme told him, using her own control then. Not to act like a different person, but to make sure she was *herself*. "It's not pretending you don't have any emotions at all and shoving them away inside of you, so that the very hint of one is a catastrophe."

He stared at her so long she wondered if she needed to worry about frostbite. "You will forgive me if I do not intend to take advice from a woman who threw herself into a lake to make a point."

Esme shrugged. "Similarly, I am not about to be shamed by an automaton. My emotions have never interfered with the duties that I perform. But you can't say the same, can you?"

He stood straighter as if he'd been shot. As if she'd shot him through the heart when, to her recollection, it was the other way around.

"I have never failed to do my duty," Tadeo ground out, outrage in every syllable.

"To your country," Esme agreed. She leaned forward in her chair. "But what about your duties to me? I am your queen. I am your wife. I will shortly be the mother of your child. Don't you think you owe me more than all these rules and regulations you dream up purely so that you won't have to *feel* something?"

He scowled at her, but she counted reactions as victories.

"What complaints can you possibly have to make?" he demanded. He had dressed in an identical suit to the one he'd worn when he'd jumped into the lake, she noticed. His uniform. Always elegantly subdued, contained. "No one is cruel to you. I maintain you in the finest style. I am endlessly courteous to you in public, and recently, in private, we—"

It was possible, Esme thought then, that she was less in control of her emotions than she'd thought.

"First of all," she said, getting to her feet and scowling right back at him, "you seem to have forgotten who I am. It's not simply a case of you not knowing me well, it's that you seem to be laboring under the misconception that you picked me up at a roadside stand on the way to the Cape."

That muscle in his jaw flexed. "I have no such misconception."

"Do you not? Are you sure?" She drew herself up to

her full height and gazed at him with all the centuries of her ancestors in her bones. "I am Princess Esme, of Clarebonne, only child and heir to my father's throne. You cannot keep me in style or at all. I keep myself." She shook her head at him. "I never *needed* you, Tadeo. I *chose* you. Even when you told me that you would court me coldly and marry me bleakly, I still chose you. I'm choosing you today as well."

And maybe she'd needed to remind herself of that, too.

"I do not understand why you insist on making all of this an amateur theatrical hour," Tadeo threw at her darkly.

But his blue eyes were wild and stormy, she could see. Filled with what she knew were feelings, though she was certain he would deny that if she pointed it out.

"I do it to wound you," she told him sweetly. "That could be my only aim, of course. I'm certain that between the two of us, with all our education and life experience, we couldn't possibly come up with another reason why a woman would choose a man."

"And how dare you suggest that I don't know who you are," he continued, and Esme wasn't sure if he was pretending she hadn't spoken or he really hadn't heard her. Another indication that he was not the ice floe he pretended he was. "I have been handed dossiers prepared about you since you were a child. I know that your favorite color is pink. That you apparently like to paint, but only on historic walls. I know that you create relationships with every single person you meet." His eyes blazed blue fire. "And you think that makes you better than other people."

"Not better," Esme corrected him, though her pulse

had picked up. "Just open to other people. It's not the same thing."

"You are caring, compassionate, and kind," he told her in the same tone, but he did not sound particularly complimentary as he thundered this at her from across his office. "These are all reasons that I chose you to be my queen even after the debacle of Boston."

"Was the debacle with us that whole year?" she mused. "Or did it come back with you after you went home that summer?"

Tadeo looked like he wanted to answer that, but didn't. He pushed on. "I'm fully aware of who you are. I simply do not need nor want to immerse myself in the things that you think are necessary for a relationship. I don't even know why you insist upon it. I watched you build relationships with every staff member you've ever had. You treat them like family. What do you need with me?"

Esme blew out a breath, suddenly less interested in this fight. Because it was always a fight, and she always lost. Every time, she lost.

"I don't know how else to tell you that I love you," she said quietly. "Just as I don't know why that's meaningless to you."

Once again, he looked as if he was coming apart at the seams. As if she was piercing his flesh with knives instead of standing across from him and keeping her hands to herself.

"It's not meaningless at all," he bit out, and he sounded...*furious*, she thought. She was taken aback. He sounded something like *livid*. "I just find it psychotic."

"*Psychotic*," she repeated, stunned.

"Look at what love has wrought in this kingdom alone," he seethed at her, not quite shouting. Not quite, but close. "My mother claimed to love my father. So deeply, so desperately, that she then shared that love with every man she encountered. My father claimed he loved her too, so very much so that he enmeshed his kingdom in the dirt and grime of her exploits, tainting our family name."

"Just because they loved badly doesn't make love, itself, bad," she managed to get out, though her throat felt tight.

"What use is love?" he demanded, and he was definitely louder then. "We have something far more enduring. The legacy of both of our kingdoms and how we will usher them into the next era. Why must you always push for more than that?"

"We are *people*, Tadeo. Human beings. We are made of flesh and bone, we bleed, we cry." Even he cried, she thought, though she doubted he would admit it. "Why shouldn't we feel what everyone else feels?"

"I don't want to feel any of this," Tadeo told her starkly then, with all of that stormy fury and an undercurrent of something a lot like grief beneath it. "I tried to tell you this in Boston."

"You were lying," Esme threw at him.

But he only shook his head, and she saw there was something grim in his gaze. "I wasn't lying. I was coming to my senses. As I'm doing now, too."

She remembered this part. That tone. That distance in his eyes.

It took everything she had not to start shaking, right there, the way she had then.

"Don't you see?" Esme realized that she was pleading with him, but she was unable to stop herself. She wasn't sure she really *wanted* to stop herself. "Your parents' relationship isn't you. It doesn't have to be *us*. We can make whatever we want out of our life. Out of this reign of ours." She blew out a breath and took a step closer to him. "You remember what it was like. I know you do. When we would lie in bed, drunk on feeling, imagining how beautiful we could make this life we got to share?"

"I do remember it," he told her, ice and fury. "And I want no part of it."

"Tadeo. You have to—"

"I don't have to do anything," he told her, and there was a terrible note of finality in his voice.

She remembered that, too.

But he was still talking. And it kept getting worse. "It was a terrible idea to bring you into the palace. I will be removing you immediately. You can go back to the manor house, and you will stay there. You will only emerge to perform your official duties."

"Are you putting me in jail, Tadeo?" she asked him, though her throat felt tight. "Again?"

If he heard her, he gave no sign. "When the child is born, he will stay there and make it his primary residence until he's old enough to have his own room in the palace. We will never divorce. You can wander the palace grounds, flinging yourself into lakes and violating the walls of the historic buildings you encounter to your heart's content. You can scream into the wind. You can dance in the rain. I don't care. But Esme." And his blue eyes seemed to tear into her. "You will not do it with me."

"Tadeo," Esme whispered, her heart pounding, something like a headache starting at her temples.

But he was already moving. Across the room and to the door, flinging it open to bark orders down the hall.

And he was the king. What he said happened, immediately.

It was Arturo who collected Esme, apologizing profusely and politely while he herded her back out the family entrance she'd used the day she'd come here to live, and into a waiting car.

"Her Majesty's belongings will follow later today," he assured her.

Esme paused, half in and half out of the car, and caught the loyal old retainer's gaze.

"I hope you take care of him," she said quietly. Intently. "Because you know no one else will."

Arturo inclined his head. "Madam," he said in the same tone, "that is my raison d'etre. You may depend upon it."

Then he closed the car door behind her and tapped on the roof to let the driver know she was ready.

Esme wanted to cry out—scream, maybe—that she was anything but ready. Instead, she let herself sit back. She stared out the window, though she saw nothing but that look on Tadeo's face.

The drive back to the manor house was painful.

But not as painful as when they dropped her off in the drive in front of the house, and she found herself staring at the facade of the building. First because she didn't see it. Then because she did.

"What did you expect?" she asked herself fiercely, her voice a rough scrape that the breeze stole away.

She didn't know what she expected. That it would be left as a monument? That they would simply leave her paints be?

It shouldn't feel like a slap that they hadn't. That the

manor house now looked precisely the way she'd first seen it. Elegant, austere.

A jail. The same jail she'd been sent to on her wedding night. This was like being caught in a time loop. Would it be another seven years before he touched her again?

Could she bear it?

She walked inside, and saw that they had redone the interior, too. It even smelled like fresh paint.

Everything was muted again. All her bright colors were gone, covered up, erased. She felt her pulse begin to get rapid, a lot like she was having a panic attack, and so she forced herself to take deep breaths as she walked down the long, main hall toward the back of the house. So she could see what they'd done to the gardens.

That wasn't a surprise either. But she found herself sobbing all the same, because they'd cut down all her flowers. They'd mulched up her wildflower beds. They hadn't let spring do with this private, unseen, unvisited garden what it would.

Because it didn't send the right *message*.

Esme stood on the terrace and she let the tears come. She held her belly tight, and as she bowed her head, she cried.

It was as if she could see it all spool out, how the years would pass.

He would keep her here. Over time, she would stop… being herself, because there would be no point. He would take her child and call it *duty. Responsibility.* He was very unlikely to have another one with her, even though it was something they had promised each other when they'd signed their wedding documents. Not because a winter masquerading as a man really wanted children, but because of the dynastic implications and thrones in play.

But either way, if they did have a second child, she imagined he would take that child, too, and teach them to be little versions of him. Snow and ice and nothing nice, that was what her children would be made of, and the very idea made her feel sick.

She would be left here. To paint the walls or perhaps creep around them, peeling off the wallpaper, like the book she'd read again and again in college.

A book about a woman driven mad by a world—and a husband—that wanted her to conform, not *live*.

And all the while Esme would know that if she'd just done as he'd asked and had never gone looking for him after his father's funeral, she would have been free of all this by now.

But even as she thought that, everything in her revolted at the idea. She cried a bit more, and then wiped at her eyes, because she couldn't quite countenance this level of self-pity. Despite what Tadeo thought, there was a fine line between feeling her own feelings and theatrical productions of them.

She wiped at her face again, then smoothed her hands over her belly.

"I would rather have you than be done with all this," she told her baby, fiercely. "I would pick you, over and over again."

She felt a quick series of kicks at that and it made her smile right there on that empty terrace, with her destroyed garden in front of her.

And she knew, with a deep down, bedrock certainty, that she was going to be okay.

That no matter what happened and no matter what Tadeo thought he was going to do, Esme was going to be just fine. She would make certain that her baby was too.

This meant that she had no intention whatsoever of allowing Tadeo to raise their child to follow in his chilly footsteps. Duty and responsibility were all very well, and even necessary given the family business, but they weren't everything.

Her child was not going to grow up frozen solid from the inside out.

She took a deep breath and blew it out again. Then she turned and walked back into the manor house, now fully restored to its historic glory, and pale because of it.

Esme had no intention of becoming a series of elegant, empty rooms that were pretty enough to walk through yet left nothing of themselves behind.

She would not stop fighting. She would not succumb to despair.

Not this time.

He could only toss her aside if she let him. Because despite everything, she still knew the truth. She still knew not only who she was, but who *he* was, too. She had always known. She hadn't fallen in love with herself in Boston. She hadn't made up what happened between them.

There was no possibility that she could have loved him this long if he was truly as inaccessible as he wished he was.

The only way for love to fail, she thought, was for it to be given up on.

Until then, it was simply a matter of time.

Esme had a lifetime.

And she intended to start using it.

CHAPTER ELEVEN

THE MATTER OF Esme was finally settled, Tadeo thought. There had been too many years of turmoil, but that was finished now. He had outlined the future for her, he had accepted that no other future was possible, and that was that.

He expected to settle down into the day's work without sparing so much as a thought for errant wives or replaying unpleasant conversations. After all, there were ministers to meet with, dignitaries to soothe and flatter, and the business of the kingdom to occupy him.

Tadeo was sure that the stranglehold Esme had held him with for all this time was gone, now. He was certain that she would simply be another obligation he thought about only when necessary, and—once she was no longer necessary—not at all.

Starting today, he thought with satisfaction, *I am a new man.*

But that was not quite how it went.

He couldn't seem to sit still at his own desk. His mind kept wandering. He kept running over and over all the things that Esme had said to him, and it was as if she was saying them to him all over again. He was having the same reaction. He could hardly catch a damned breath.

After a while, he realized he was wearing a groove into

the rugs in his office, he was pacing so much. He sat in meetings and could not have been asked to repeat what was said to him. He could not concentrate on *messaging* or social media campaigns or the various reactions of the press to the news of Esme's pregnancy when all he could think of was Esme herself.

We can make whatever we want out of our life, she had said, as if that was easy. Or possible. Or permitted. *Out of this reign of ours.*

As if it had always been theirs, to do with as they pleased. It was laughable.

But he was not laughing. *You remember what it was like*, she had said. *I know you do. When we would lie in bed, drunk on feeling, imagining how beautiful we could make this life we got to share?*

He did remember. He remembered too well. That feeling of possibility, of limitless horizons. That scandalous, glorious feeling that the two of them truly could beat all the odds—because they already had. They'd expected to find each other passable at best. Nice enough, even.

Instead, one look and they'd *ignited*.

It had to mean that they could change their whole worlds—Tadeo remembered how deeply and fully he'd believed that. With Esme at his side, there was nothing he couldn't accomplish.

But his father had set him straight. He'd always been so grateful for that. He'd spent all the years he'd had left with his father making up for that lapse. He'd gone out of his way to prove to King Hugo that he had a worthy successor.

And Esme had made him question all of that. *Have you considered the possibility that your mother wasn't the Whore of Babylon?* she had asked.

When Tadeo knew exactly who his mother was. Exactly who everyone knew his mother was. That hadn't changed simply because Esme wanted to be difficult.

Still, he couldn't seem to get her words out of his head. *Maybe she was in love with a man who acted like an iceberg*, Esme had said, and it had punched straight through him. *Maybe she did what she needed to do to keep from freezing to death.*

It occurred to Tadeo then that he'd never considered his father cold, only correct.

But if he wasn't…

Later, he found himself pacing through the palace, and he must have had a fierce enough expression on his face because no one attempted to speak to him. In fact, they stepped out of his way, bowed their heads, and kept their eyes averted.

A lot like he was having the sort of emotional episode he wanted—badly—not to be capable of.

Tadeo found himself in the portrait gallery yet again, looking at the faces of his ancestors as if they could offer him some clues. Looking at his own wedding portrait that he'd always thought had adequately captured what their marriage was. Cordial, but appropriately separate. Cold, certainly, but that had been representative of the relationship they'd had then. The relationship he'd assumed they'd always have.

He'd already realized, since Esme's pregnancy had been revealed, that he'd been ignoring how sad she looked in the portrait. Somehow he'd always believed that she simply looked like a queen. Appropriately solemn—but no.

She looked like she wanted to cry.

Tonight he was horrified to discover that even looking at the painting now made him...

Something in him balked. He didn't want to name it. He didn't want to call this what it was, because that gave it a power—

Sad, something in him whispered, sounding a great deal like Esme herself. *That's the word you're looking for. Sad.*

The last time he could remember using that word to describe his state, he'd been eleven years old. His mother had died under less-than-ideal circumstances—gallivanting about, quite publicly, with a lover on a boat near Crete—but his father had decided to give her the state funeral her position demanded.

A funeral fit for the queen, nay, the woman *she should have been*, the self-righteous television anchor had intoned.

It had been a somber affair. Now, looking back, Tadeo found himself wondering if everyone had been aware that it was all for show on his father's part. Some believed he was simply *that good*, certainly. But surely there had to be others who wondered if, perhaps, King Hugo had been going to a great deal of trouble to prove that he had been the decent spouse. That he was self-sacrificing even to the end, and even in the face of his wife's outrageous behavior.

Someone had to have wondered if, perhaps, he'd been protesting too much. If they did, they did it quietly. The papers had already been calling King Hugo a saint.

But eleven-year-old Tadeo hadn't known anything about *messaging*, or the manipulation of the press.

What he'd known was that his mother was dead. Moreover, that he was highly discouraged from commenting on that or displaying any of the many emotions he felt about that death in public.

Why are you making that face? his father had asked as they had walked soberly and slowly behind Marisol's coffin through the streets of the kingdom. *You are being watched, Tadeo. A certain decorum is expected from a future king and it is best you exhibit it.*

I'm sad, Tadeo had said to his father. Not the King, just…his father. *I'm just sad.*

But Hugo had not spared him a glance. He had continued his slow and precise pace, his back straight and tall, his eyes forever forward. *Don't be so maudlin*, he'd said, in that cold, dismissive way of his that had settled deep into Tadeo's bones. *You are the Crown Prince of Bellaza. You are, by definition, never anything so pedestrian as sad.*

Over the years, Tadeo had decided that his father had been trying to give him a pep talk. That Hugo had been trying to keep Tadeo's spirits up while they saw to such a grim task, and more, while they did so under such intense scrutiny.

It had been a great kindness, Tadeo had decided. He would have argued about it, had anyone dared ask. *Not all kindnesses feel good*, he would have said. *There is no law that insists it must* feel *warm and fuzzy, only that it do what it is meant to do.*

But now…

He thought of his child, his son, still nestled deep inside Esme's belly. He thought of the nights he'd spent smoothing his own hands over her belly, murmuring to the child within.

Tadeo had not met his son yet and yet try as he might, he could not imagine telling that child that he could not be sad at a funeral. His own mother's funeral, no less. Even if he and Esme remained as much at odds as they were now forever, he would not expect *her child* to react stoically to her passing.

Even if Esme behaved in ways Tadeo did not like, how could that possibly dictate the behavior of her own child in the face of her death?

These thoughts tore at him. He felt a kind of fissure open up inside him, yawning wide, and he had the strangest feeling that there would be no closing it again. That there would be no repairing this.

He just didn't know what that meant.

When he heard footsteps, he schooled his expression to the expected neutrality—but was pleased when he saw that it was Arturo. Possibly even relieved.

"It grows late," the most loyal of all the servants in the palace said, and whatever expression Tadeo had on his face, Arturo would never appear to notice it. "Would His Majesty care for dinner in his rooms, perhaps?"

Tadeo didn't move. He couldn't seem to look away from the portrait of his parents now. It was like it was calling to him. "You remember my parents better than I do. You were here when my father was growing up."

Arturo did not change his own expression by so much as the faintest twitch. "It has been my great honor to serve three generations of the Santiago family, Your Majesty."

"All I know are stories." Tadeo ran his hands over his face. "Stories in the papers, stories from my father." He looked at the old man. "What do you remember? What really happened?"

He didn't know, until he said the words out loud, how much seemed to ride on the answer.

For a long moment, he thought the other man wouldn't

reply. Arturo had been in the palace for so long that he was, in many ways, the finest example of royal protocol there was. It was possible he would think that he had no business discussing such matters and therefore would not. It would not matter if the King himself commanded him to do so.

But after a moment he cleared his throat, and when Tadeo looked at him again, he had a curious look on his face.

That fissure inside Tadeo...widened.

"Your father was a strange boy," Arturo said after a moment, which was perhaps the last thing Tadeo would have expected anyone to say about King Hugo. "Oddly still. Decent to all, if robotic. But one does not speculate about such things, not if one wishes to remain in the palace. I watched him grow up and he was always the same."

"He valued constancy," Tadeo said, agreeing.

He realized he was frowning and forced himself to stop.

The older man looked at him, a canny sort of light in his gaze. "Did he value it, or was it all he was capable of?" he asked, in his quiet way.

And something inside Tadeo went terribly still.

He had a sudden flash of memory then. It was something he had overheard his mother say when he was very young.

Tadeo had been playing in a part of the palace where he'd been told many times not to go. He'd heard his mother with her voice raised, which usually meant she was talking to his father. *Just because you can't feel anything doesn't mean you should dictate to the rest of us who have the full spectrum of human emotion*, she had thrown at the King.

In return, he had heard his father's slow, measured tones, but not the words he'd used.

His mother had responded with a wild laugh. *I would never wish to be like you*, she had said. *I would rather die.*

Tadeo had known better than to get caught listening to his elders without their knowledge. He'd ducked back down one of the servants' stairs and had hurried away.

Now, here in the portrait room, Arturo shifted from one foot to the other. "I cannot excuse what your mother did extramaritally," he said, and sounded as if he was being very careful. Almost *judicious*. "But I will tell you that it was done deliberately. To prove a point."

"I don't know what that means," Tadeo managed to get out, though his jaw felt like granite.

"My understanding is that her first affairs were in private," Arturo continued in that same, measured tone. "And the King, may he rest in peace, did not care at all. He only cared when her affairs were public. Because what he cared about was not the infidelity, if you catch my meaning. It was that other people knew of it."

Tadeo felt himself getting…overly warm. As if he was sweating. As if he was *flustered*.

As if a pedestal was crashing to the ground and taking him with it.

It was as if Arturo knew it. As if he could see it too. "What I am trying to tell you, Your Majesty, is that I am not certain that King Hugo—for all his many virtues and may he rest in peace—was *capable* of caring about anything besides the kingdom. Or if he was, I never saw it."

The full import of those words took a moment to settle on Tadeo. When they did, they landed hard. He felt as if the old man had taken a swing at him. And had landed a knockout punch.

"Including me, is what you mean," he said when he was able to speak.

Though his voice sounded unlike his. Too rough. Too raw.

Arturo looked him straight in the eye, which was revolutionary and upsetting itself. "It is my observation that your father went to great lengths to teach you how to tamp down the emotions that he never felt himself, Your Majesty. Not because he truly felt that they would impact on your ability to be a good king, but because he didn't like them."

Tadeo knew, then, what he would say. He knew, and yet he could do nothing to stop what was coming. He could not repair that widening chasm inside him. He could not *breathe*.

"They reminded him too much of your mother," Arturo said, inevitably, and Tadeo let that settle on him too, like so much granite and despair. "King Hugo preferred things tidy and always precisely the same. Do you see what I mean, sir? He never thought of himself as empty. So he emptied out those around him instead, so that they would match."

And Tadeo had no idea how long he stood there, staring in something that wasn't quite as simple as shock at the portrait of his father on the wall.

Yet all he could see was Esme.

All he could *hear* was Esme. All the things she'd said to him over the years, and today. All the accusations she'd laid at his feet that he'd swept away, so certain that *she* was the problem.

Because a man who couldn't feel at all had told him that he felt too much.

And then it was as if Esme was a great swell inside

him, growing like a wave, taking him over, knocking him down—

But Tadeo did not fall.

Instead, he ran. He ran through the halls of his own palace, leaving stunned and shocked courtiers in his wake—and for once he did not care at all. He could not have been less interested in what *message* he was sending.

Tadeo ran until he found one of his vehicles parked out by one of the garages, ignored his guards, and jumped behind the wheel.

He set off for the manor house, driving the roads of the royal estate far too quickly. Time seemed to press in on him, and inside himself, he felt certain that it was running out.

That it might very well be too late already.

The night was dark but clear, and the stars were so bright they felt very nearly blinding. He felt almost as if he was drunk, though he knew full well he was not. The road wound down the hillside, cutting through the fields on the back side of the palace, and Tadeo took one turn so fast that when he saw the headlights coming in the opposite direction on the single-lane road he had no choice but to drive off to the side, narrowly missing a stout, medieval hedge.

The oncoming car stopped. He heard the window roll down.

"Are you all right?" came Esme's clear, concerned voice through the dark.

Tadeo felt that wave wash over him all over again. That chasm in him seemed to stop growing. Time released its pressure.

She didn't even know it was him, he thought. It could

have been anyone. And yet she, the Queen, stopped her vehicle and inquired after his safety when she was the one who was six months pregnant.

The fissure had stopped growing, he realized then, because it had torn down all the armor he'd worn, all the walls he'd built, all the things he'd built his life around because he'd thought that was the *proper* way to do it.

Everything she had said to him was true. Her emotions didn't inhibit her or diminish her. They only made her stronger. They made her better. They made her...*her*.

The bright light that was *her*—far brighter than her headlights that picked up the wide expanse of royal acreage on either side of them.

Tadeo pushed his way out of the car. Esme was getting out of hers, more awkwardly these days with her pregnant belly. She stopped when she saw him, her jaw dropping open a bit.

"Tadeo?" Her voice was little more than a whisper, as if she didn't believe her own eyes.

But finally he thought that he believed his.

There were stars above, and Esme was here, and for the first time in so long—ten whole years—everything made sense.

He hadn't realized how empty he'd felt until now, when he finally felt whole.

When he finally understood the whole story of not just his life, but his father's and his mother's and all the ways they'd led him here.

"I was coming to look for you," Esme said after a moment, sounding...thrown, perhaps. But she rallied. He saw her square her shoulders. "I have something to say to you, Tadeo."

"Say it," he bade her, and he leaned back against the

boot of his car and folded his arms, because if she wanted to talk to him, he would listen.

This time he would listen as if his life depended on it and he would keep his father out of his head while he did.

"The manor house has been desecrated," she told him, very seriously. "It smells like new paint and regret. It's pale and sad and diminished." She moved closer to him and then she pointed her finger directly at his chest. "That's what you want to do to me, Tadeo. And I won't allow it."

She wasn't wrong, and he would have to live with that. But that was for later.

Now, he shook his head. "I doubt you could ever be diminished, Esme."

He did not expect her to scowl at him, much less so ferociously. "Don't patronize me, please. I have no intention of letting you shuffle me off again. I don't know why I put up with it for seven years. I kept thinking that if I was perfect enough, if I was dutiful enough, I would somehow live up to whatever paragon it is you have in your head. I thought that I could prove that even though we were blessed with the chemistry that drew us together, I was also capable of being the perfect queen for you. I think I did that, Tadeo. I think I pulled it off." She pulled in a deep breath. "It still wasn't enough for you."

He said nothing, but she moved closer still. He watched her as her gaze searched his, and could not begin to imagine what expression he wore.

She frowned, so he assumed it was unusual. "On the night of your father's funeral, I only wanted to comfort you. But it turned into something else and I realized the truth. *That* was the real reason you never wanted to be alone with me. Because there was no getting away from it, is there? There's never been any escaping who we are to each other." Another breath, like she was preparing herself. Her chin rose. "And I'm not going to facilitate it anymore."

She was even closer now and Tadeo felt nothing inside him but that great wave and swell that was all her, always her. It was beautiful Esme, the mother of his child. Esme, his queen. Esme, who had knocked his world off its axis by smiling at him outside a Boston restaurant on that fateful first evening.

Esme, the woman who had loved him when he most certainly did not deserve it for the past ten years.

He reached over and pulled a thick lock of her dark hair between his fingers, then rolled it back and forth.

Her breath stuttered slightly. He saw a flash of heat along her cheekbones. "What are you doing?" She frowned, but it looked to him as if summoning it took work. "Why aren't you putting up your usual fight?"

And then, at last, it was Tadeo's turn.

He was determined to get this right.

"Esme," he said, tasting her name on his mouth the way he'd used to do, as if it was some kind of sweet liquor that could only go to his head. "I have been fighting against you since the day we met. You came in like a storm, swept me away, and I never found my footing again."

"You didn't need your footing. You have a crown."

He tugged slightly on the lock of her hair, and she subsided. "I tried my best. I broke up with you in a way calculated to hurt you the most. I insisted on a cold pageant of a wedding, and worse still, a frigid marriage. And you went along with all of those things. You went along with them, and I intended to reward you for that service by divorcing you."

"Yes," Esme agreed, though she looked…not quite *confused*. Something more like *wary*. "You're the worst man I know. I have no idea what I see in you."

"Nor do I," he assured her. "But tonight, if you will allow it, I want to make you a new kind of vow."

He moved in closer then and he took her hands in his, and was cheered when she gripped him in return.

"I was told that love is a fantasy, and emotions are weakness. That my country required me to lock those things away and hide them where they could never be seen, never be felt, and never, ever shown to those around me." He lifted her hands to his mouth and pressed a kiss on her knuckles. "And what has that made me? An ice sculpture, as you say."

Esme's eyes were wide, now. He could see the pulse in her throat going wild.

"Everything I know is inside out," he told her, his voice low and raw, because perhaps that was what truth did when it finally came out. It left marks. "It is possible my father was simply incapable of feeling anything and considered that his greatest virtue. Perhaps he decided that those who did not possess that virtue the way he did—meaning everyone around him—were disappointments. Maybe my mother simply refused to keep the parts of herself locked away as he demanded."

It was his turn to blow out a breath, and he did, then held her hands tighter. "When I came home from Boston that summer and told my father that I'd fallen in love with the woman that everyone expected me to marry—an absolute miracle of epic proportions—he was horrified. I should have realized that was his problem, not mine.

But I had been raised on a steady diet of my mother's scandalous behavior and my father's noble attempts to keep his head up high despite them, and I believed he knew better."

He held her gaze intently, then. "I'm sorry for that. I'm sorry for not defending something so beautiful from the start."

He felt the jolt that went through her, and saw the emotion in her eyes.

But he wasn't finished. "You were the only one I wanted anywhere near me at my father's funeral, but I could never admit that to myself. I was relieved when you found me. And I remember exactly who started that kiss that night. It was me. Filled with all those emotions I would have told you I didn't know how to feel and just drunk enough to hope no one would notice."

"Tadeo, I don't know—" she began.

"I cannot bear the thought of raising our child like that," Tadeo continued, urgently. "I can't imagine turning my son against his mother. I can't imagine pretending that you're not the reason I even know what love is." He let out a rusty sort of laugh. "I fought so hard against it, Esme. I gave that fight my all. And yet every time, no matter how hard I fight, I come straight back to you."

He found he was holding his breath then.

Esme gazed up at him, her hands in his and her eyes wide and solemn, and once again he wondered if he was too late. If he'd taken too long. If he'd lost her, after all.

Then he saw her smile, and it was as if she took all the stars from the sky and aimed them straight at him.

"You do," she said softly. "And I want you to do that. I don't think you ever had a safe space in your life, for all you have palaces and manor houses and servants, and royal compartments that could house a crowd."

"The only fight I'm interested in," Tadeo told her, intensely, "is fighting for you, my Esme. Even if the enemy I must fight is me."

"I have an idea." She moved closer to him and she pressed that heavy stomach of hers against him and looped her arms around his neck as best she could. She gazed up at him, and he felt like they made a perfect circle, there beneath the stars at last. The two of them, their foreheads touching. The baby they'd made pressed in between their bodies. "Why don't we start over?"

"Can we do such a thing?" he asked, but he realized he was smiling.

In private, not for a camera or a political reason.

A real smile, for the first time since Boston.

"You will have to ask the king of this realm," Esme told him, her smile wider. She ran her fingers through his hair. "He is *very* powerful. He can do whatever he likes."

"It sounds like you have an in with him." Tadeo let that smile of his do what it liked. And her too. "I like your chances."

She smiled up at him and then her smile faded as she traced her fingers over his face, as if she was learning his contours all over again.

"So do I," she whispered. "So do I, my love."

He captured her hand and held it to his cheek.

"I love you," he told her, with all the solemnity and intensity of a vow made in cathedrals in the presence of most of Europe. Though it was better now. It was only them. "You were right. I have loved you since the moment we met, and I have loved you badly. All I can hope for is that you will let me spend the rest of our lives making it up to you."

"I don't need you to make anything up to me," Esme told him, and there were tears on her face, but joy in her gaze. "All I need from you is *you*, Tadeo. Because between us, we can do anything, whether it's change the way we rule these kingdoms or love each other the way we deserve."

"I want that," he whispered. "Though I doubt I deserve—"

She put her hands on his mouth and stopped him. "We have wasted too much time to dwell in the past. We have a baby coming, and I want him to know us like this. In love. In harmony." He kissed the fingers on his mouth and she smiled. "We can do it. I *want* to do it, Tadeo. With you or not at all."

And from that day forward, because he was indeed the king of all he surveyed and particularly of this sheltered valley in a remote section of the Pyrenees, Xavier Tadeo Santiago, King of Bellaza, made it so.

CHAPTER TWELVE

LIKE EVERYTHING ELSE he had ever done, which was no surprise to Esme, Tadeo took to love as if it was something upon which he would be tested. And might fail at any point.

They did not sleep apart. Ever. He told her that he loved her as often as possible.

"Someday," she said with a laugh, "you might even say that without sounding as if you're worried that the words might bite you back."

He was lying next to her in their bed that time. And he looked at her, his expression a mix of affront and astonishment.

"Loving is perilous," he said. "For my heart. You will have to excuse me if it takes some getting used to."

But he got used to it.

Because of course he did. The first thing he did was get rid of that monolithic desk from the king's office. He did not explain why, though Esme had her suspicions. It was consigned to some far-off corner of the palace, never to cross the King's eyesight again.

And in its place, Tadeo installed a lovely, wooden desk that caught the sun and gleamed in a way that reminded both of them of that marvelous old town house of his in Beacon Hill.

Before the baby was born, he took Esme back to Clarebonne, so that her people could cheer for her—or that was what he said. But Esme rather thought it was to show her parents that things were better between them now. Thawed.

"Do my eyes still look sad?" Esme asked her mother on one of their walks.

Luisa had her arm laced through her daughter's, and she squeezed it tight. "Not a drop," she said.

Their son was born two weeks late, a squalling, dark-haired slice of perfection, who they both fell in love with immediately. They called him Alain for Esme's father, a man to admire and look up to. And Hugo, for Tadeo's father, as a chance to shine brighter.

But the name they used was Enrique, and Enrique was a delight.

One night after she nursed him, Tadeo held the baby and soothed him to sleep in his arms, looking something like stricken when Esme caught his gaze.

"I had no idea," he said, hoarse.

"About what?" Esme asked.

"That it was supposed to feel like this all along," he whispered. "So huge. Almost painful. But so beautiful, Esme. Incapacitatingly beautiful."

"That is exactly how it's supposed to feel," she told him, coming over to the chair where he sat and kissing him on his temple.

He reached up and smoothed his palm over her cheek. "When I met you, I felt like this and I thought something was wrong. I thought it had to be a mistake. Something to fight and get over." His eyes glistened, and Esme's heart thumped. "I'm so glad you never let me."

Esme leaned down and kissed him on his mouth. "And I never will," she promised him.

She gave birth to their daughter three years later and called her Marisol Luisa, though the family knew her as Soli. She was made of grit and sunshine, and even the older brother she tortured was besotted with her.

Together, the two of them would rule the two kingdoms.

Esme considered it her job to make sure that they never lost themselves in the jobs that waited for them. And when it came to the future Queen Soli of Clarebonne, Esme and her daughter spent as much time as possible with the expert on that topic. Luisa.

On one such visit, when Luisa had come to Bellaza and was walking in the gardens with her granddaughter, engrossed in very serious conversations with the small girl, Esme stood by a window and watched them.

Her parents were not simply grandparents to her children, Enrique and Soli and the three others she'd had after them because she and Tadeo could not seem to think of a good reason *not* to have the big family they'd always wanted as only children. Over the years, she had watched her parents stand in, in many ways, for the parents Tadeo had never had.

They had showed him the love he had always deserved.

And she had watched her husband bloom into the man she'd always known he could be. The man she'd fallen in love with so long ago.

"I pinch myself every day that we get to live like this," he told her one night as they danced at some glimmering ball, surrounded on all sides by the toast of Europe—though Esme had eyes only for Tadeo. "Like everything is magic, no matter what challenges come our way."

She tilted back her head and smiled at him. "I love you too," she said. "And the best part is, the magic only gets better as we go along."

Esme knew that this was true. Because she knew that all the way on the other end of the palace estate there stood a manor house. And maybe one day, when she was gone, her daughters would congregate there and wrinkle up their noses, and restore the place to some former ideal of sophistication and elegance.

Assuming she had failed to raise them right, that was.

But in these years, when they needed a night away from the palace and their boisterous family, Esme and Tadeo would liberate one of the royal vehicles and take off across the back roads in the dark, and they would paint like wild animals and laugh all the while.

They would make love to each other in every single one of the rooms, moving into intensity and joy and holding space for the sorrows of life brought, and the inevitable scars they carried.

But all of that became beautiful, because it was shared.

Because it was allowed to be bright and messy, a visual cacophony of the secrets their hearts carried.

When her children grew older and asked Esme to tell the story of how their parents had met, she told him the truth. With only a few details omitted, to protect their tender sensibilities. She showed them that terrible portrait in the gallery and pointed out how stiff and sad both she and their father looked.

"Because we were," she would say.

And as they gasped and laughed and were scandalized by their father's seemingly tyrannical behavior, Tadeo would laugh too. He would hold Esme on his lap and smile at all the fine young humans they were raising to feel every single thing they felt—but learn how to control it, too.

"Lucky for me," he would always tell them, "your mother loves me well enough that I learned to love myself, and her, and all of you, too."

He also commissioned a new portrait for their fiftieth anniversary, a far better representation of the two of them. The same pose. The same people. But the love they shared poured out of the canvas and lit up the whole of that gallery.

And if this was the happy-ever-after that she got, Esme liked to think, it was worth those ten years of uncertainty. It was worth everything. Given the chance, she would do it again.

In a heartbeat.

That was the kind of thing she told only Tadeo, tangled around him in the bed they shared, where he could respond to her in the only way that mattered. The only way that made both of their hearts beat out the same rhythm.

Because it was perfectly clear to the both of them that they had always been meant to be one, all along.

And now they always would be.

* * * * *

If you loved King's Heir of Hate, *make sure to read*

Sicilian Devil's Prisoner.

*This fantastically dramatic romance
by Caitlin Crews is available now!*

CHAPTER ONE

Birds sang in the thick green trees as they danced through the dense, overgrown gardens outside the magnificent old villa some thirty minutes from the center of Palermo, Sicily. But what Giovanbattista D'Amato—called Jovi by the few who dared address him directly—noticed despite their chatter were the sounds that should not have been there, soft beneath the usual noises he knew so well.

It seemed he had a guest.

When he was not the kind of man who encouraged visitors, especially of the uninvited persuasion. Something that must surely be clear by the untended sprawl of gnarled oleander and fig trees that had grown up around the gates down near the road and made the entrance to the villa seem all the more secretive and, therefore, more provocative.

The villa was perfectly preserved and stunning, as everyone always whispered in shocked tones, *despite everything*. Teenagers and tourists who thought they might poke around a place with such a riveting, tragic past were usually scared off by their own overactive imaginations long before they made it to the villa's front door.

The ghosts that haunted the villa and its quiet slide toward a graceful, genteel ruin knew only too well how to occupy a mind and sneak deep into an unguarded moment.

Jovi knew that better than anyone.

He heard the car out in the front of the villa, on the winding drive that had given way to the demands of changing seasons and the scrubby mountainside that stretched above and below, though nothing could conceal the bones of the estate, a crowning achievement of the Sicilian Baroque period. Neither time nor negligence could dim its glamour in the slightest.

Jovi had certainly tried.

He heard the slam of the car's heavy door, yet he stayed where he was. He sat perfectly still in the shade of the towering oak tree some gardener long-dead had planted here in another lifetime, as if he was contemplating nothing more than the easy mysteries of a warm, Sicilian afternoon.

But that was only the impression others might form if they saw him here, sitting so quietly.

And only those who didn't know him.

Because anyone who knew Giovanbattista D'Amato knew exactly who and what he was. Ice, straight through.

Ice where other men were flesh. Ice in place of organ and bone.

He remained still. He supposed that it was possible that somewhere, back in the dimness of the youth he did not allow himself to recall too closely—or too often, lest he give those ghosts free rein—he had gone ahead and taught himself these skills he used without thought, now.

The ability to sit so still that the birds themselves mistook him for a statue. A stone like any other.

The capacity to wait. To do nothing else. To simply *wait*, without moving. Without breathing too much, lest it make his chest move and differentiate him from the stone walls. To easily parse the various sounds that reached his ears. The birds. The breeze and the trees above. The rustle of small creatures in his gardens, long since surrendered to riots of rogue blossoms and weeds—a rebellion against the meticulously maintained, award-winning planting concepts that had once been synonymous with the villa and its residents.

He identified all of those, set them aside, and listened for the heavy fall of a man's leather shoe inside the graceful, empty rooms of the once-proud villa that rose up behind him.

Jovi did not lock the place. Why should he? Terrible things had already happened here and there was no pretending otherwise. There was nothing to steal that he could not replace, assuming that he could be bothered. To his way of thinking, anyone was welcome to drop in. Unannounced and heavily armed, if they wished.

Though they might wish otherwise. Quickly.

He was not concerned about people entering this place where he lived when he was in Sicily. Because he knew that the difficulty was not in the entering. But in the leaving.

Once someone invaded his space, they would leave it again only if *he* wished it.

His were the only wishes that he would allow to prevail on this sprawling parcel of land, set up on the rugged mountainside, claimed by men who must have imagined it was ever truly possible to escape the chokehold of Sicily.

Jovi knew better.

He heard feet on one side of the duel staircases in their Sicilian Baroque style, all high drama as they marched away from each other and then angled back to meet at the great door.

And as the footsteps drew closer, he heard the faintest sound. Like a rough laugh, checked before it was anything more than a breath.

No need, then, to worry about his response.

He waited instead. And when the footsteps drew even closer, barely making scraping sounds across overgrown flagstones crafted by the finest stonemakers in Sicily and left to the whims of the sun, there was another laugh. This one untethered, likely because its owner thought he was alerting Jovi to his presence.

The way he always did.

"I don't know how you live in this haunted place," came the intruder's familiar, disparaging voice.

Not an intruder, Jovi corrected himself. Not exactly.

He did not bother to turn around. He knew who his uninvited guest was. Had known, in truth, the moment he'd heard that particular heavy cadence of footfalls from inside the villa.

Carlo D'Amato, his cousin. His oldest cousin and his uncle's favorite son. This meant Carlo was also considered the *sotto capo* of what some news organizations liked to call the *D'Amato crime family*, but only because they dared be disrespectful from the distance afforded them through newsprint.

To those who knew better than to show disrespect, they were known as Il Serpente, wily enough to outwit the many criminal investigations that had plagued families like theirs since back in the 1800s. Not to mention the rival criminal organizations who muscled in where they could.

Most shivered at the very thought of Il Serpente, a true

family organization built on blood ties, because blood brokered loyalty. Blood was less likely to be bought.

Jovi was a part of this family, but not the way Carlo was. Because Jovi's father, the traitor Donatello, had betrayed his own brother—bringing dishonor to the family name and very nearly handing them all over to the authorities who stalked them.

This was a stain upon them all. Jovi alone of his father's family had been spared.

So he was *family*, yes. Blood where it counted. More importantly, he was a weapon.

The weapon, perhaps.

"Did you hear me?" Carlo's voice rose in pitch as he swung himself around the chair so he could look down at Jovi from the front. Allowing Jovi to watch, fascinated as always, as this big, powerful man who feared nothing and no one—a fact Carlo liked to broadcast whenever possible—looked more than a little *wary* at the sight of his supposedly lower-ranked cousin.

The way everyone did if they had the misfortune of seeing him.

Because there was rarely any reason to see Jovi that did not involve pain.

Carlo, as ever, could not hold Jovi's gaze. He looked away, and his shoulders hunched, more signs that he was intimidated by the cousin he liked to brag that *he* did not find frightening in the least.

He even spat on the ground, as if Jovi was a superstition in need of clearing. "You're a spooky *stronzo*," he muttered.

Jovi only waited. Carlo knew exactly why Jovi lived here. This was the home Jovi's father had inherited from his own father, as he had been the oldest D'Amato son in his generation. Donatello had been too soft for the family business, however, according to the stories everyone liked to tell. Jovi's grandfather had used to say that he had two heirs.

Donatello for the public family legacy, charming and academic and sophisticated. And the crafty, cunning, and wholly soulless Antonio for the family business, where sophistication was not required but brutality was celebrated.

Antonio had wanted nothing to do with this place after he had meted out bitter family justice upon Donatello, his wife, and his two young girls.

Jovi did not allow himself to think of them in other terms. His father and mother. His sisters.

They had all lost the right to those connections when Donatello betrayed their family.

He rarely permitted himself to think of them at all.

It was his cousin who seemed to enjoy bringing up ancient history whenever he came here, always pointing out the empty, echoing rooms. Always making certain to remind Jovi of the things he opted not to remember. Or, perhaps, reminding Jovi of his roots in the only way he could without risking Jovi's displeasure.

Despite what Carlo liked to tell the rest of Sicily, and likely himself, both Jovi and Carlo knew very well that Carlo would never dare to *actually* insult his cousin. Here, in these private moments, Carlo's cowardice was always clear.

Carlo swallowed. Then took his time looking Jovi's way again. "Patri has a job for you," he said.

This, too, was obvious. Only a directive from Antonio himself could compel Carlo to visit this place of shame and despair, a stain upon the family name. There was no possibility that Carlo would ever come here to spend time with Jovi, to catch up or whatever it was people did when they had all of those social connections Jovi had never been permitted.

Even if Carlo wasn't terrified of Jovi, they would never connect in this way. Jovi shared blood with his family and their ancestors, here in Sicily and across the water in Calabria.

He did not share anything else.

That would require that he be made of something more than ice, and his uncle had made certain that he remained too cold to melt. Ever.

In truth, he preferred it that way.

Sometimes Jovi walked through the crowded squares of Palermo or drove past the beaches in summer. They were always teeming with people having their coffees and their harder drinks. Talking loudly, waving their hands in the air. Clustered together over tiny tables in public spaces or flung about in abandon on the sand, entirely unaware of their surroundings or what sort of monsters might be waiting there, watching.

Looking for a chance to strike.

He could not understand it.

Yet Jovi knew his cousin not only understood these things, but enjoyed them. Carlo maintained his never-ending stream of mistresses despite the carefully selected bride from a Calabrian family he'd married so ostentatiously in the cathedral in Palermo. Despite the vows Jovi had heard him make with his own duplicitous mouth. And the babies his dutiful wife, raised by men just like the one she married, had already provided him—three sons and counting.

Jovi did not make vows. He kept promises.

And he was not given to acts of sadism the way his cousin was.

He was Antonio's favorite form of detached and dispassionate justice, meted out in the face of betrayal, a broken word, or a disrespect too great to be ignored.

Or sometimes simply because Don Antonio felt like serving it to his enemies, with impunity.

Jovi was the final solution to problems that torturers and deviants like his cousin failed to solve.

Carlo knew as well as Jovi did that even Don Antonio took care to aim his best weapon carefully. What mattered was that Jovi was loyal. The son of a known traitor had to demonstrate his honor and devotion, without fail, forever. Even more so than the rest of the family. When he was young, Jovi had done what was asked of him—whatever was asked of him—because he'd had no choice if he wanted to live.

These days, everyone was aware that Don Antonio's orders to Jovi were a lot more polite than they had been. Or than they were to anyone else.

That was the trouble with crafting a perfect weapon. There was always the worry that it could be aimed back at oneself.

Most of the time, Jovi simply waited, letting the ice in him grow thicker by the day, feeling nothing at all.

This was not to say that he was a saint or a monk. He fucked. A lot.

There was no shortage of women who were drawn to him as surely as reckless moths to an indifferent flame. He took what he was given, left them in pieces, and never took the time to learn their names or commit their faces to memory.

Sometimes, in the middle of the night, he would dream

of the boy he barely remembered, a creature of heat and need, flesh and yearning. He dreamed of a bright, wild, intense boy who had delighted his father and made his mother laugh as she pretended to look to the heavens for the intercession of the saints.

But thinking of these things in the light of day was like telling himself fairy tales, anodyne little ditties about obedience, and Jovi could not relate to them. They were not the memories he allowed himself.

Because there was nothing in him that burned. He breathed destruction and delivered pain.

There was not one part of him that was not cold.

Even Carlo, who claimed he feared no man and was the scourge of many, was always wary in Jovi's presence.

Perhaps more than simply *wary*, Jovi thought.

Clearly disliking the quiet, Carlo outlined the situation that his father had sent him to share. It was no different from every other task Jovi had been set over the years. The particulars changed, but the outcome was always more or less the same. There were many men who played these games, who waged these wars in the dark shadows where fallen men created their empires, ripped down others, and were kings in all but name. There were many men who preened in their own power, little realizing that power, like any other commodity, could be bought and sold.

Because there was always more power. There was always someone more desperate to claim it. A circle without end.

These same men never understood that they as good as signed their own death warrants the moment they started throwing their weight around, because there were always higher bidders with deeper pockets. There were always new markets with more motivated sellers.

It was only a matter of time until they were all worth more dead than alive.

"We want him to hurt," Carlo said of the man in question today, some or other arms dealer in Eastern Europe. It didn't matter who he was, only that he'd decided he was more powerful than Il Serpente and could dictate his terms. "Eventually, he'll pay the price for his disrespect but first, a little pain."

Carlo carried himself as if he was a man of supreme beauty, though it was difficult to tell if his mistresses cared at all about his supposed good looks when his wallet was so well-upholstered and infinitely deep. He was not afraid to fight with his own hands—and, indeed, preferred it—a rarity at his level in an organization like theirs.

See again: sadist.

Accordingly, he kept himself in shape as if he anticipated that fight occurring at any time, despite his exalted position as his father's right-hand man.

It had been a long time since Jovi had heard his cousin complain to the rest of their cousins that it was difficult to keep up with his fitness when he was Sicilian, and there were too many delicacies forever on offer. Many a man had fallen into softness thanks to the preferred cuisine around the family tables and the local cafés, called bars.

The most dangerous men in the world are fat and round, Carlo had told Jovi once, his eyes dark with shame, when Jovi had effortlessly outperformed him in the gym.

Then they are not as dangerous as they think, Jovi had replied with his typical equanimity. *The men who fear them are the dangerous ones. The ones who do their bidding and could therefore do someone else's, too.*

Sometimes, like now, he thought his cousin remembered that conversation. There was something about the way Carlo refused to look at him sometimes that assured him it was something Carlo kept close. No doubt dreaming of the day that he would rule this family and give Jovi orders. Or better yet, get rid of Jovi altogether.

Jovi did not bother to inform his cousin that his loyalty was not transferable. He did not need to remind his cousin that his skills far outstripped Carlo's sick little games.

A day of reckoning would come, that was certain. These lessons could wait until then.

"Boris Ardelean is a collection of former Russian nationalities," Carlo told him in that sullen way of his, never quite able to look Jovi in the eye. "A mutt. A Czech national who should shut the fuck up, learn his place, and sell his guns. Instead…"

He shrugged. There were some who would see a shrug like that and lose control of their bowels. A shrug like that, from a man like him, had death written all over it.

Jovi was unaffected.

Carlo continued. "Instead, he thinks he can play games. He thinks he can dictate terms. He thinks he can go around the family to make his own name for himself. But… *Lu rispettu è misuratu, cu lu porta l'avi purtato.*"

"Respect is measured." Jovi agreed with the proverb his cousin was quoting. It was how they all lived. Or in Carlo's case, pretended he lived. "Whoever respects others will be respected in turn."

His cousin nodded. "Don Antonio likes his own name." The meaning was clear. This arms dealer needed a lesson. "Killing him would be too easy. How would he learn? How would he fully understand the depth of his disrespect?"

These were not questions that required an answer.

He stayed where he was, sitting still in his chair and watching as Carlo paced a little, as unable to stand still as he'd been when they'd both been small boys. Five and six and allowed to run wild while all the old women in black smiled at them and called them angels.

Only the fallen kind of angels, Jovi thought now. Fallen deep and hard, lost somewhere far beneath the surface of any lake of fire.

If he was an angel, it was the angel of death.

"This Boris has a daughter," Carlo was telling him. "He's been putting out feelers, seeing if he can marry her off in the old style to create an alliance. My father thinks Boris's only alliance should be with us."

Jovi inclined his head. "I understand."

For a moment, Carlo still stood there, staring down at Jovi, with that same wary look on his face that he often wore in his cousin's presence. To cover his uneasiness and fear, Jovi was certain.

"Other men might ask if she's pretty," Carlo pointed out. "If they might have a little fun, a little pleasure with their work. But not you."

"I do not believe in pleasure," Jovi replied. He didn't even bother to shrug. "In my work or anywhere else. It has no purpose."

Sex, killing—it was all the same to him. Women or men, it made no difference. Sometimes there was set dressing, the better to send a message. Sometimes mementos were required, whether before or after the death depended entirely on the reasons for the death.

He felt nothing about any of these things. He did his job.

Ice was ice wherever it was cold enough.

He could see that Carlo was holding back a sneer. That his cousin dearly wished he could speak frankly to him, though Carlo would never dare. Jovi even knew what he would say, as he'd said as much to others who had foolishly relayed it, imagining Jovi was the sort of man who would make alliances.

He's a freak, Carlo liked to tell the rest of the family. *Him and his freak father. If it was up to me, I never would have let him live.*

"I'm not the one who fears death, cousin," Jovi told him now. "I don't have to dress it up and make it a game."

If he was anyone else, he thought Carlo would have lunged at him. He could see the loathing in his cousin's gaze. But then, of course, Carlo did nothing.

Because, at heart, he was a coward.

He showed this to Jovi every time they came face-to-face. Every single time.

And well did Carlo know it. Because he said nothing further. He only swallowed back whatever he wanted to say—no doubt thinking better of it and hating himself for it—and then turned around again to storm back into the house.

Jovi heard a crash from inside and assumed that Carlo was expressing his displeasure the way he often did, because he ran hot. And if asked, could claim any damage was an accident.

Jovi, obviously, had never asked.

Carlo was a coward, but he was also dangerous. He was sick in the way many men in their profession were sick. Pain was a game to them, not a means to an end—and because of this, they would be their own undoing.

It was written all over them.

It was what made Carlo who he was. His life was a preview of how he would die.

Jovi supposed his was, too. Ice unto ice, frozen into nothing.

This was as inevitable as the death of the daughter of a fool named Boris who thought he could play games with the likes of Antonio D'Amato.

Theirs was a world with very strict rules. They were always the same rules. Death stalked them all, and none of them could escape it. None of them would.

Especially not if it came for them in the form of Jovi, Il Serpente's coldest flame.

He sat still for a while longer, until the sounds of his cousin faded away. Until the roar of Carlo's engine was swallowed up once more by the sunshine and the breeze. The careless birds wheeling overhead.

Only then did he rise and head into the villa filled with ghosts and the shattered remains of whatever glasses Carlo had thrown against the wall, so that Jovi could begin planning the most expedient way to do the thing he did best.

Because unlike his traitor of a father, when Jovi had promised his body, soul, and eternal loyalty to his uncle right here in this villa on the night of the great brotherly reckoning when Jovi had been eight years old—he'd meant it.

Copyright © 2025 Caitlin Crews

Did you fall in love with King's Heir of Hate?
Then you're sure to enjoy these other sensational stories by Caitlin Crews!

Kidnapped for His Revenge
Her Accidental Spanish Heir
Forbidden Greek Mistress
An Heir for Christmas
Sicilian Devil's Prisoner

Available now!

FROM CONVENT TO QUEEN

MILLIE ADAMS

MILLS & BOON

To Presents, which is always the place
for my imagination to run free.

CHAPTER ONE

THERE WERE BLUEBELLS as far as she could see. It was peaceful. So nothing. Nothing like she had ever experienced while growing up in the palace at Cape Blanco. Here, in the wilderness she knew peace. Here at the convent she finally felt like herself.

Fern.

Who felt so different than Fernanda Luisa Camila Esperanza Cortez, Princess of Cape Blanco, the small archipelago on the cusp of the Alboran Sea, crowded with her brothers and their aspirations of power.

They were all handsome and world-renowned for one thing or another. Juan—a great politician and heir apparent. Miguel—a financial genius, who was cold as ice. Julio—an actor, of all things. Rafa—a writer who seemed to delight in his own tortured mind. And Ricardo—who was perhaps the only brother who'd ever engaged her in conversation, but was a terrible rake, a model and a professional cad.

Fern was the youngest, and the only girl. Her lone claim to value of any kind was the marriage contract drawn up by her father with the presumed leader of Asland. The island nation, populated by Vikings hundreds of years ago, had been ruled by a monarchy ever since—until the royal family had been overthrown in a military coup that had promised greater freedom but had ushered in authoritarian rule.

Fern's father had made a bargain with the president that Fern would marry his successor—who had been all but handpicked by the current president—when she was born. The union would ease trade between the countries and offer great military support.

Fern had been opposed. But it had also been a fact of her birth.

Like her green eyes, black hair and small stature.

Something she was born with. She might wish she was six feet tall, but she couldn't change her height. Just as she'd always wished she wasn't promised to be married off to a false president for the pursuit of yet more power.

But three years ago the authoritarian regime had fallen—a revolution led by the long-believed-deceased heir to the throne had upended everything, and restored balance and freedom to Asland.

King Ragnar was as formidable as he was dangerous—according to her father. And the agreement—should he choose to try and apply it under the present circumstances, could put them all in danger.

Which was when—at the age of eighteen—Fern had been sent off to the Isle of Skye to an isolated convent, where she felt like she had found herself for the first time.

Funny how she felt more...*her* in hiding than she ever had when living in the palace at Cape Blanco.

Or at the very least she felt connected to part of herself—her strength—that had never been allowed to blossom before. In the palace she'd learned diplomacy. Watching her brothers spar with one another had taught her well just what *not* to do.

What she had never been allowed to be was soft. It was far too dangerous. But here? Here she could embrace the quiet. The contemplation. The rhythms of nature. She had spent her life locked in quiet wars in the palace in Cape Blanco, and had never known who she was apart from that.

It had been an awful thing, her life in the palace. She'd had all those skills, and yet her word had never been respected. She was as smart and strong as any of her brothers, yet it didn't matter. She was forced into a mold for self-preservation, and then it wasn't even valued.

She despised men.

Men and their pursuit of power.

She had been steeped in it all her life. Her father and her five older brothers wanted nothing more than power. Her oldest brother—the heir to the throne—was as rigid and exacting as their father. And just as much of a liar.

Then there were the spares.

They were no better.

They spent their time in Europe, Africa, Australia, Asia, forging alliances and trying to jockey for power positions within their father's administration by greasing palms the world over.

When you were a small nation, diplomacy was of utmost importance. At least, that's what her father always said.

She didn't feel they excelled at true diplomacy. They were simply very opportunistic, and very practiced liars.

As for her, her entire function had been to become a wife. So she'd learned diplomacy of another kind—but while she'd been taking in her lessons she'd been learning other truths. She had learned that as long as she seemed biddable, as long as she kept her voice soft and expression sympathetic, she could often manipulate a situation better than her father or any of her brothers.

They didn't look for the strength inherent in women.

They didn't look for the steel in the softness.

They were a pack of misogynists.

Her mother had never been considered a full human. She was an accessory to her father, and if she was unhappy with it she never betrayed it to Fern.

Fern often tried to look through her mother's poise and impeccable manners to see if there was anything beneath them. To see if she was sad about the way she was sidelined, ignored and minimized.

Fern wondered if her mother had built a facade so thick and perfect that even she couldn't break out of it now.

All Fern had ever seen ahead for herself was more of the same. She'd met the new president five years ago. A man in his forties with a charismatic demeanor that made Fern want to scream and run away and hide forever.

She'd been sixteen, facing down the prospect that in only two years she'd be marrying a man well old enough to be her father, but even worse—the same sort of man as her father.

She would never be free.

She would never have a life.

And all the things she'd learned—the ways she'd navigated her whole minefield-filled life—wouldn't matter because she would just be playing power games from behind the bars of a cage.

It had been a low moment.

Then Ragnar had taken the throne back in Asland and those plans had fallen apart.

She'd never been so relieved.

This man, whom she'd never met, had saved her.

At least, that was what she'd imagined. Until her father told her that Ragnar intended to marry her still—as the leader of the nation and the rightful beneficiary of the agreement.

She'd been sure her father would bundle her right off and send her into marriage with a total stranger—after all, he'd never cared what she wanted before.

But she'd tried to resist. To protest. She'd always thought it a useless thing to do, but faced with what felt like a certain demise or the futile defiance of her father, she'd decided to raise her voice.

To her surprise, he'd listened. She understood that it was because he agreed—for some reason—with her concerns.

So now she was here. Hidden. Protected. Surrounded by other women, who found meaning in serving others and in sitting in silence. In serving the divine, not man.

It was a whole new way of being. One that Fern had never been exposed to before. At first she'd missed her phone—she had it with her but it barely worked. There was only wired internet available at the convent and only then in Mother Superior's study, and only used to communicate with the diocese and to receive time-sensitive information.

She had missed sleeping in at first too.

At the convent they arose at five to spend time with God. Though Fern had been given license to spend it in whatever type of meditative state she chose.

Eventually she stopped missing the fast pace of the internet and the constant relentless news cycle. Eventually she stopped seeking quick hits of shallow satisfaction from mindlessly browsing online. She started to look forward to the mornings. To the time alone with her thoughts.

She had friends now. She did chores. She took long walks. She read. She didn't perform, because the sisters had taught her that it didn't matter what a person pretended to be; it mattered who they were in their heart.

Here, she felt like her insides finally matched her outsides.

She didn't have to wear makeup or designer clothing to project her father's wealth and importance. She wore linen dresses and aprons. She had one simple pair of boots and a simple pair of flat shoes. She didn't add highlights to her hair or put ruthless straightening products on it anymore. Her curls were dark and wild.

She was wild too.

Perhaps part of the sweetness of the wild was knowing that it could be taken. If her father decided to come and fetch her.

If Ragnar found her.

Freedom was tenuous, and not truly hers, as ever.

If she thought about it too much it filled her with rage. But she was here. In the sun and the quiet and the glory, so she chose not to think of it.

She chose to be at peace, because she had otherwise never been permitted peace.

And in the three years she'd been here her disdain for her father had only grown. What had been a feeling—that he was wrong about most things—had become clear, fully formed thoughts now.

His manners weren't good. They were repulsive because they were lies.

He was rotten inside, and that was what mattered.

A person's heart was what counted, not their appearance.

Maybe he would forget about her here. She often fantasized about that. No one had been to see her in all the time she'd been in Scotland.

She was okay with that.

"Sister Fernanda." She turned at the sound of Mother Superior's voice behind her.

She wasn't a sister, but Mother Superior called her that to reinforce her place here, and the equality of all of them.

"Yes?" She squinted slightly, the sun shining in her face.

"Would you mind going and checking the bees and collecting some honey for supper?"

"Oh, I would love to."

Fern loved the bees. She'd found that she was very interested in all manner of farming practices, but cultivating honey was one of her favorite past times.

She went to the barn and gathered the beekeeping gear and a large jar from the shelf by the beekeeping suit, and walked across the expansive field toward the beehives.

At first, she'd been afraid of the bees. But she just hadn't understood them. She hadn't understood so many things.

She'd had perfect table manners but she hadn't been connected to the land, to the way that it fed humanity as long as humanity fed it back.

Now she knew.

She used her smoke to clear the bees away as she got into the hive and began to collect honeycomb and put it in the jar.

Then she walked back to the barn and took the beekeeper's suit off, holding the jar close to her chest as she walked back toward the convent.

Her stomach growled when she thought about the dinner they'd be able to have. They would have vegetables from the garden—potatoes, carrots and leeks. And there would likely be bread and butter, and now honey.

Though they were not entirely vegetarian at the convent, they ate very little meat, due both to the cost and to Mother Superior's general discomfort with taking life in any form, even if it was animal life.

Fern was so unaccustomed to that level of consideration and compassion. She'd been shocked by it at first.

Now she tried to cultivate it. To bring it into her own heart.

This deep caring about others.

This peace.

Silence had been all around, nothing but the wind through the flowers and grass, and then suddenly, the silence was broken by a rhythmic pounding.

She turned sharply behind her and saw a black horse

with a large figure on the back of it, riding toward her at full speed.

She had never seen anything like this out here before. Had never seen one of the farmers from a neighboring property out riding like he was being chased by an enemy army.

She took a breath. And then began to run.

Without thinking. Without pausing.

Away from him or whatever might be after him. She felt like she'd fallen down into an alternate world—or maybe out of time, though that wasn't an uncommon feeling out here in the wild Highlands.

But this was uncommon.

This fear.

Everything here had always been peace and now she was running.

Why was she running?

And it hit her then, with each beat of her feet pounding the ground. She was running because she'd been sent here to hide.

Because if there was something to run from there was a high chance that the danger was there for her.

So she ran like she would die if she was caught, because perhaps she would be.

She ran like her freedom depended on it, because perhaps it did.

But she wasn't faster than a horse.

She could hear the hoofbeats getting closer and closer, and it confirmed that he was here for her. He was here for her.

Ragnar.

King Ragnar Gunnarson. Once deposed heir of Asland, now the king.

She didn't look back; it would only slow her down. So when she found herself being lifted up off the ground midstride it was a shock. She flailed and tried to escape the ironclad hold she found herself in, as she was positioned on the horse in front of its rider, one muscular arm holding her fast against a rock-hard chest.

He smelled good.

That was the dizzying, nonsensical thought that crowded out all the other ones as she sat there, entirely trapped. He smelled like the forest. Like the sea. Like the wilderness itself.

Whoever this man was, he was a warrior.

Her father and her brothers smelled of expensive colognes.

Not of the wild.

And then it was like whatever haze had fallen over her suddenly lifted. What was she doing, pondering the strength and scent of him and not trying to escape?

Without overthinking it, so that she didn't give her next move away, she arched backward and created space between herself and the rider, and then used that moment, that split second where he loosened his hold, to roll sideways off the horse.

She hit the ground hard, rolling to the side, and then stood up and began to run again. She no longer heard footsteps. She just had to get to the convent.

She just had to—

And then she was being lifted up again, this time, not onto the horse, but simply into the unseated rider's arms.

She looked up at him and her heart leaped into her throat.

He looked like a Viking from the old world. He had long blond hair, and a full beard. His nose was straight and angular, his expression fierce.

This wasn't an agent of Ragnar, King of Asland.

This was the king himself.

His eyes caught hers and held.

Blue.

Shockingly blue.

And then it was all she could see, as her world narrowed and fear and exhaustion rolled over her, claiming her consciousness.

CHAPTER TWO

She had fought him valiantly, and for that she had earned a small amount of his respect. But now she was unconscious and bruised besides for her foolish escape attempt, and that made Ragnar less inclined toward positive feelings for his wayward wife.

He hauled her back up onto the horse, adrenaline still coursing through his veins. He hadn't intended to turn this into a military operation but it certainly felt like a battle.

Why he'd thought it would be different, he couldn't say now.

All he knew was battle.

And this creature...

He held her firmly as he began to maneuver his horse around to head back to where they had come, to where his private plane would take them back to the palace in Asland.

He would have her examined by a doctor as well. He was certain she'd fainted from fear, but there was a small chance she'd hit her head when she'd fallen. Or rather thrown herself off the back of the horse.

Little fool.

It had been a long time since he'd held a woman.

He pushed that thought, and any accompanying desire, aside. There was no time for that. There was a reason he hadn't indulged himself since taking over the throne. He had to stay sharp.

He felt the moment she woke up, her body no longer relaxed. She sat up against him, her body going rigid.

"Do not fling yourself down to the ground again," he warned, against her ear.

She turned just slightly, her expression fierce. "Let me go!"

"We have an agreement."

"I don't have an agreement with you."

"You do, signed by your father."

"I didn't sign it. It has nothing to do with me, except that my father decided my future without consulting me. That isn't an agreement with me. Just with the patriarchy."

"I will see the agreement honored."

"Then you're boring," she shot back.

Boring?

He had been called a great many things, but never boring.

"Yes. Because you're doing the exact thing that all men do. In the pursuit of power you will ignore everyone else."

"I am ignoring nothing, little one. I have a country to run and to stabilize. Your father promised you to the next ruler of my country, and that is now me."

"I don't want to go with you."

"I don't care."

If she was looking to find a man who might be moved

to compassion by sorrow, or helplessness, then she was sadly looking in the wrong place.

All he had ever known was the brutality of survival. He didn't remember the details of his family. Oh, he had been old enough when the royal family had fallen that he should have some memories of them, of his life at the palace before. But they were gone. Erased by whatever trauma had come that day with the deposition of the king and queen.

With their execution.

He had read about it in documents, in news articles. The king and queen had both been slain in their seaside home, but he had no memory of that day at all, or of any of the days before.

It was his nanny who had helped him escape—so he had been told. Though she had passed him on to members of her own family and not stayed with him, and that was where things had gone wrong.

Everything crumbled. Nearly overnight. Any prosperity to be had in the country was gone. And he had been used for labor by the people who had taken him in.

At least there had been food and shelter. Though that had not lasted either.

Softness was not something he had experience with. She would not get it from him now.

"We are flying back to my country tonight."

"How did you find me?" she demanded, the haughty, glittering green gaze that of a princess, however humble her clothing was.

"It was a mistake of your father to tell your brothers where you were. They're fools. Your father is not a fool, though he is a man who looks out for his own interests. I understand that he was afraid I would not be interested in guarding that which he valued. He made an alliance with my enemy, and I imagine he fears me for that reason. He should fear me. But with you in the palace, he should know that he is safe. But I will also expect an alliance in return."

"He isn't going to take kindly to you kidnapping me."

"But I didn't. Because he sold you to me. I will send him the bride price that is in the paperwork."

"A bride price?"

"Did you not know? It is not just eased trade and military alliances."

"Well, that means he decided that he didn't want the payment as much as he wanted to keep me safe."

"That is one way of looking at it, I suppose. The truth is, I think what he was afraid of is that I might seek to uncover some of the more nefarious things he engaged in with my predecessor."

"You can say whatever you want about my father, but Cape Blanco is not a dictatorship, and he did not commit human rights violations, not like the man who ruled your country."

"No," he said. "He didn't. You are correct about that. He was too smart to do it here. Too smart to do anything to his own people. But I'm willing to let bygones be bygones. For the strength of my nation."

If he could, he would see the destruction of every corrupt man. But unfortunately, corrupt men were the pillars of society. It made it difficult. What he had discovered when he had begun his mission for revolution, to reclaim the throne, was that he could not be a purist. There was no place in the world for a purist. Only for strength.

He could only do so much. He couldn't change the entire system. What he could do was save his own country.

And Princess Fernanda was part of that salvation whether she wanted to be or not.

"Are we riding your horse back to Asland?"

"Don't be ridiculous."

They had landed the plane in a covert area in a desolate place in the Highlands, with permission from the Scottish government. He had told them it was a matter of diplomacy, and no one had pressed. As long as he was leaving as quickly as he had come, no details were required.

The cargo area of the plane was open, and gripping Fernanda tightly, he rode the horse up the walkway and straight into the stable area in the cargo hold.

"Why the horse? You could have a fleet of sports cars down here."

"I could." He didn't offer her any explanation.

He didn't owe her one.

She was not so foolish as to think that her happiness, her desires, anything played into the way that the world ran. She was like him. In a fashion. She had grown up in a royal family. And even though he had grown up outside of one, the reality of being a king informed everything he did.

They might have been able to remove him from the palace. To remove him from the throne, but they had never been able to remove the responsibility he had to his country, to his people.

It was part of who he was. The very blood in his veins.

He'd had amnesia, still did. And yet he had always known who he was, with a deep certainty. There had been years when the true meaning of that had been lost to him, but he had never fully lost himself.

When he knew nothing, he knew he was the rightful king of Asland.

When he knew nothing, he knew that his father's blood called him to power.

"Will you tell me anything?" she asked.

"Do not bother me, or I will leave you down here with the horse."

"Well…"

She was clearly weighing her options. Testing him or complying. He didn't want to leave her down here, but he would. If she pushed.

He had no patience for hysterics.

He hadn't really gotten a good look at her yet. But as she stood there in the plain, glaring up at him, her green eyes glittering with rage, he finally got the measure of her. She was small. In height and in build, her figure neat and proportioned well. Her black hair went down to her waist, and was a wild snarl, all curls and now scattered through with pieces of the Highlands, since she had gone rolling in the dirt.

"Manage the horse," he said to three of his men who had come down the stairs. "I'm taking the princess up so that she may rest."

She didn't move when he did, so he gripped her arm up by the shoulder, his hand fitting entirely around it easily. He didn't have to hold her firmly to hold her strong. She moved in angry, halting steps behind him, going up the stairs and into the main seating area of the plane. He had brought a small contingent of his military with him, while leaving his highest-ranking generals behind.

There was a sense of real stability in his country now. Now that all of these freedoms had been restored, now that people were able to live again, there was a sense of calm, and he didn't worry about forces rising up against him. But he wouldn't take chances.

Not at this time.

He ushered her through the main quarters quickly, and took her back to his private office and bedroom area.

Her head whipped around toward the bed, her eyes going wide, as she looked up at him.

"Don't worry. I don't want your body. I want your bloodline."

"Wow. That is not reassuring at all. And seems to suggest you require my body eventually."

"We'll worry about that down the road. For now, I have to concern myself with quickly and publicly marrying you before reaching out to your father."

"I have to agree to the marriage."

"You don't. The plane is about to take off, and then we will be in my country. I could stand in the center of the palace and declare us married and it would be so. You do not have to make vows to me. What I would like is a spectacle for all the world to see, so that there is no move your father can make that wouldn't receive so much public outcry that it wouldn't be worth it for him."

"But you require my obedience."

"You are with me now. You don't have the power. Let me explain this to you. We have an agreement. Your father is on the losing end of this. And I do not wish to make trouble for your country. But what I have done, what I have survived, is simply too high-stakes for me to leave any loose ends. This marriage was meant to happen. I need a wife. I need a queen. I can fight a war, but I do not know how to act on the throne, and I do not know how to…"

"Diplomacy?" she asked, her tone dry.

"Yes," he said. "That. I'm not a negotiator."

"I've noticed."

"You're not in any danger," he said.

"I'm not scared of you. If you care at all about public perception, then I don't think I have to worry about you hurting me. You should find another princess. I'm sure they would line up for the opportunity."

"But it's Cape Blanco that I want an alliance with. I need their trade agreements. Our country was increasingly isolated with that despotic dictator in charge. We were left devastated. And it is up to me to fix it. This is the only way."

"Surely it isn't the only way."

"It is the easiest way. And given that I have done everything up until now the absolute hardest way, a marital alliance seems like a good route to take."

"Marriage. Really. That's the only thing you can think of?"

"You say that as if I should have some sort of respect for the institution. As if it carries some kind of weight. I don't care about marriage. It means nothing to me.

Family means nothing to me. You mean nothing to me. Nothing but a symbol. Get some rest."

And then he turned and left her.

It might seem cold to some. But he knew the truth. She would be better off without him near her.

It took about half of the plane ride for Fern to realize that she didn't have her phone. She didn't have any way of contacting anyone.

She had become so sporadic in her use of it that she hadn't been carrying it with her when she had been out today. She hadn't even touched it. But then the second thing that she realized was that she wasn't really in regular contact with anyone outside of the convent. She didn't have a network of people away from there. Of course, the sisters would do whatever they needed to to save her. She was confident in that. But she didn't know how they would do it.

There was nothing that she could do. She was physically outmatched. The man was more mountain than human. And on top of that, he had a whole team of men on board the plane.

She wasn't scared of him. Not physically. She knew exactly what King Ragnar had done when he had taken control back of his country. He'd dismantled the previous regime, sent the leaders to prison for the rest of their days.

He'd taken back the military—banishing all generals who opposed him.

He'd restored freedom that had been lost, abolished oppressive laws.

What he'd done had been for his people.

Which couldn't be said about the man that her father had intended to marry her off to.

Ragnar was still older than her. Though in his thirties, she suspected. She thought of the way he had looked at her with those cold, ice-blue eyes. He wasn't like the other president. He wasn't like the other man she had been promised to. But it didn't make her any more thrilled about being a spoil of war. Or whatever he had decided that she was.

A chip to be used against her father. To keep him in line. She suddenly felt very small. Impossibly so. Because this had been her fate for as long as she had understood it. She was nothing more than a bargaining chip. She was nothing more than a conduit for something else. And she wanted to be firm. She wanted to be inconsequential. Yet somehow larger in herself.

It was such a strange thing. She could be a political figure. She could be the queen of this country, but that had so much less meaning to her than waking up in the morning and tending a farm. Collecting eggs. Gathering honey.

She suddenly felt bereft about the honey that was lying in what was likely a broken jar, somewhere away from the convent. A waste of what they cultivated.

Emblematic of the last three years of her life.

It meant nothing.

No. It meant something. You learned about yourself. You know who you are.

She bolstered herself with that.

She knew who she was and what she wanted. She knew more about herself now than she ever had, and she knew more about the world. Funnily enough by being removed from it.

She was not in the same position that she would've been if she had been married off to a dictator at eighteen.

What a strange thing, that in many ways Ragnar's timing three years ago had saved her from something, and now he had come to collect.

She wasn't prepared to be a queen.

She didn't want to be trotted out all over the world, onstage, trussed up and living her life for public engagement.

And as the plane began to descend, she had a second thought.

She wasn't prepared to be a wife.

That thought made her face suddenly grow hot, made her stomach clamp tight.

She had intentionally never thought about that.

She had been promised to a man that she didn't want from her birth, so she didn't think about marriage and intimacy, and the fact that she was meant to carry a dictator's baby.

She didn't think about it because it was important. Because it couldn't be borne.

But now that she was here, on the edge of it, she couldn't release the thought.

He wanted to marry her immediately. Like he had said, he could stand in the center of the throne room and simply pronounce them married and they would be.

And then what? Would he want to consummate it like a medieval conqueror? Is that what it would take? To make sure that the marriage took. To make sure that she was trapped with him. Because that was what he would want. For her to be stuck with him. For her father not to want her back. And the truth was, him taking her virginity would go a long way in making her useless to her father. Her father wouldn't be able to simply farm her out to another world leader, would he? She would be damaged goods.

Men really were so boring.

She hated them. Every last one of them. And by the time the plane touched down, and Ragnar opened the door to the bedroom, she was nearly overflowing with hatred. Where was her peace? Where was all that peace that she had found in the convent? Where was the diplomacy that she had learned?

She was ready to fling herself right at him and attack, but the immense impact of him stopped her. It wasn't fear coursing through her veins. No. It was something else entirely.

He was big and broad, masculine in a way that nearly made it impossible to gaze upon him directly.

Perhaps it was simply because the convent was a female place. No men at all. Perhaps that added to the intensity of his impact. Of his...

Beauty.

The word sent a pang of fear through her.

No. She wasn't her mother.

She would not offer a brittle smile while she was broken into pieces. And she would not trade herself for the attentions of a man, simply because she found him beautiful.

"I'm not getting off this plane until we come to an agreement."

"I am perfectly capable of carrying you off the plane, little one."

"But not without the entire world seeing you manhandling me, *pendejo*, so I would assume that it's in your best interest for me to walk off here on my own two feet."

She glared up at him, resilience making her stand straight.

"What is it you wish to negotiate?"

"If I'm to be sentenced, then I want a term limit."

"Marriage is for life, my queen."

"Why?" The image of her mother, a beautiful, frozen emblem who lived in a house full of men who neither loved nor respected her, galvanized her now. "This is simply to cement trade agreements. To help you become the ruler that you want to appear to be. Why do you need me forever for that? You can find a new queen once you get rid of me. One to bear your children. To give you an heir. I don't want it."

"You don't want to be queen?"

"What I want is to be *free*."

"You want freedom from your father?"

"Yes. I will do whatever you ask of me as far as your image, as far as helping you with your present issues. I will not have a child. I will not share your bed. But I will get off this plane on my own, and I will look for all the world like a beaming bride. I am the only one who can give you the public-facing victory that you want. I am the only one that can give you your lavish, public wedding, because I have to look happy to be there. So you have to give me something."

"Two years," he said. "Or until the agreements feel eased. We may have to extend."

"Fine. That is fine with me. But you will not… I will not…"

Those blue eyes looked her up and down. "Do you think I'm about to fall on you like a lust-crazed animal?"

His words were so scathing, and she felt like she had been lit on fire.

"I know how men are. I grew up in a house filled with them. I know how little they respect women. I certainly know how little I've been respected."

"I didn't take you because you're a woman. I took you because you were useful to me. If the agreement was between me and the oldest son, then I would have taken him."

"Oh," she said, not certain of what to say to that.

"But alas, we live in a very traditional society, and you were the offering. But you are a worthy opponent. And I would prefer to have you as an ally." His eyes were sharp and clear as he looked at her. "You're very smart, aren't you?"

No man had ever said anything like that to her before. The nuns recognized that she was intelligent. But her father hadn't. Her brothers hadn't. If her mother had, she would never have said.

She had to resist the urge to feel pleased with her kidnapper.

"I could have been smart, or I could have been defeated growing up in the palace like I did. But my options were limited. It really was one or the other."

"You have a room prepared for you at the palace."

She stared at him. "I was not going to force you into my bed."

She felt her face getting even hotter. "I didn't say that you were." Now she was reassuring her kidnapper? What was the matter with her? "I didn't accuse you of anything, but I wanted to make my stance clear."

"Are you a nun?"

"No. Though maybe I would like the chance to decide if I want to be one. Maybe I want the chance to decide if I want to be a pole dancer. Maybe I just want the chance. The choice."

"What a sweet, modern idea. Choices are rarely actually available. And even when they are, they're generally an illusion."

"That's not true," she said.

"You challenge me?" he asked, clearly shocked.

She was used to men like him, though. It was true that in the space of only a few hours he'd shown her more respect than her father had in years, but that was more of a commentary on her father than on him.

But he didn't intimidate her—maybe he should. But what would he do? Hurt her and start a war? He wanted her for diplomacy and the truth was, he needed her.

In many ways, she'd probably never been safer.

It made her want to laugh except it wasn't funny.

"Yes. I do challenge you, because no one ever has, clearly, and they should. You men love to tell yourself you have no choice when in fact it simply means you take whatever it is you want. Saying there is no choice is an attempt at insulating yourself from argument. You didn't accidentally take the throne back over from an evil dictatorship. You had a choice, and you made your choice."

He laughed. Hard. Low. Rolling. It didn't make her feel amused, no. It chilled her. All the way down to her bones.

"Fernanda—" he used her name for the first time "—I bled for this. I fought my way up from nothing, for this. Perhaps, as you say, there was a choice, but as far as I'm concerned this was a mandate created in my very bones."

She gazed back up at him, and swallowed hard. "That is spoken like a man. You believe that you're the only one in the world who can accomplish this, but you need to use me? I'm just an accessory to your goal, and as long as you say that there's no choice it justifies it?"

"You think that your happiness is more important than that of an entire country?"

"I have spent my entire life being told that I'm inconsequential. I cannot be nothing to my father, a thing to be manipulated and moved around at will, and yet essential to this."

"I never said you were inconsequential, and the truth is your father doesn't believe you are either. If he did, he never would have hidden you away at the convent. He would never have used you as a bargaining chip in the first place. This much you can know for certain. I have certainly never said you had no value. I would not have run you down on my horse if you didn't."

"Perhaps," she said, still making eye contact with him. "And if you had any sense of fairness you would have tried to capture me in a foot race so that we were evenly matched."

He nearly laughed; she was glad that he didn't. Because the sound of his voice, his laughter, was in no way pleasant. "Little one, I was not striving for fairness. I was intending to win. Rules and warfare are for other men. The stakes in this are too high for me to leave anything up to chance. For now, we have an agreement."

"And how am I supposed to know you'll honor it?"

He looked her up and down again, like she was a mere object. "You don't. You can only choose to take my word or not. But at the end of the day, any negotiating we have done is out of the goodness of my heart. You are my captive. And you will take what I give you."

Anger spiked in her blood, and she took a step forward, forcing herself to continue to look into those fathomless blue eyes. "You see how far you get if you have to drag me kicking and screaming off this plane. You see how well your plan works if your bride is a captive for all the world to see."

"You have to trust me," he said. "I have given you my word. I'm not your father. And I am not the man who held this position before me. I am the rightful king, and my only aim was to restore this country to its former glory, and then some. If you cannot trust in the goodness that may or may not lurk in my heart, trust in that. I do not care if it is you or any other woman who is by my side in my later years. I do not care if you are the one to give me an heir. All I care about is this. This moment. This agreement."

Whether she should or not, she believed that. Those callous words that might have wounded her if she cared even a little bit. But it was to her advantage that he didn't have any designs on her. To her advantage that he didn't care about her one way or the other. Specifically.

There had never been a silver lining to being a political pawn. There was now.

He stood tall, and held out his arm, and she looked at him for a moment before realizing what she was intended to do. Then she took a step toward him, and placed her hand over his forearm, and allowed him to escort her from the room.

She kept her word. Part of him had expected that she would fight him, but instead she had done exactly as she had promised.

She had fire in her. It was a surprise. When he had discovered that the bride promised to the ruler of his country had been spirited off to a convent, he had imagined someone pious. Quiet. Prayerful, even. She was not a nun; that much was certain.

Not that he knew anything of the faithful. He had no use for fantasies. No ingrained connection to some spirit in the sky that was supposed to offer health, safety and blessing.

He had never experienced it.

No. When he had been alone in his life, he had been alone. There had been no comforting presence. No divine comfort to be had.

Still, he had thought that it might be a good thing to have a bride who had a more tempered personality.

She was not the one. It was no matter, however, because what he had said to her was true. He did not care how long they remained married. Once he felt secure in his position. Once the trade routes were well established, and they proved to be beneficial to everyone, once he had signed long-standing military treaties, he would have no use for her. He could trade her in for a new wife.

This one could be like another adviser. Not a wife in truth.

He looked down at her as he opened the door to the car that was waiting for them. Her eyes met his, and he felt the impact of her gaze like a freight train driving straight through him.

Apparently his body appreciated the challenge.

It was very like him.

If he wasn't fighting, he didn't know who he was. So in many ways, it wasn't a surprise that this woman who looked at him as if he was not great and terrifying, but was an obstacle to try to overcome, was appealing.

Most people found him frightening. For good reason.

He was barely more civilized than a wild animal. Than the wolves that had once famously roamed Asland. Women who were interested in him were often as hard as he was, experienced and jaded.

Princess Fernanda had a core of steel, but it was different.

She was not jaded.

She still believed that there was some measure of freedom out there for her to possess. Some great joy that she could find if only she were unfettered.

He knew that wasn't the case.

Responsibility would always pull you back, and if you owed yourself to no one and nothing, then it was simply a black hole of nothingness.

No purpose. No point.

And yet she was beautiful.

"Get in the car," he said. She obeyed, but she continued to look at him with those green eyes. He slammed the door shut, and got in on the other side.

"Shall we invite your family to the wedding, Fernanda?"

"Fern," she said.

"Excuse me?"

"I prefer to be called Fern. I don't like my full name. It makes me think of my father being angry with me. It makes me think of my time in the palace. At the convent, I was just Fern. And that's what I would like to be here."

"Isn't that a plant?" But as he said it, he thought that her eyes were rather that color. That cool green found in the depths of the forest. A plant that thrived even in darkness, even without the sun.

"Yes. And I have a greater connection to nature than I do to my family."

"Queen Fern," he said. "It does not have a particular ring to it."

"All the better that it won't be permanent."

"And you imagine when all this is over you will go off into a life of obscurity?"

"Yes," she said. "Why wouldn't I?"

"It is not feasible to expect that you would be queen of a nation and then simply slip off into the darkness."

"I suppose both of these things appeal to the rather erratic things I have been told all of my life. I am forgettable enough to slip into nothing. But important enough that I have to do this first. The paradoxical nature of being the youngest in a royal family. Of being the only daughter."

"I'm the only one," he said. "I wouldn't know."

Silence ruled as the car began to drive away from the airfield, up the winding road that would lead them to the castle on the craggy mountaintop. It overlooked the largest city in the nation. There was only one.

It was a small country, but with a rich history. Or at least, he would have considered it a rich history prior to the coup.

"Of course," she said, "I'm sorry. Your parents were killed."

"Yes," he said. "They were. A strange thing to have your personal tragedy in the history books."

She nodded. "I'm certain."

She looked…almost sorry for him and he did not care for it.

"But that is the problem with being in the position that you and I are in," he continued. "Our lives will never truly be personal. They belong to our countries."

"I can see why you feel that way. Because you're the heir. Because you're the only one left. It's nothing like that in my family. I have five brothers. In many ways, I am so unimportant because of my gender. And yet, in other ways… Had I been a sixth son I would truly have offered him nothing new. At least as a daughter I was able to offer the ability to enter into marriage agreements. He could sell my womb to the highest bidder. And did. But either way, I have never felt singular. Not to my country. I am only useful to my father's political ambitions. If I esteemed those ambitions then perhaps I would feel differently. But I don't. I don't care about what he wants."

"By all accounts Cape Blanco is a thriving country,

particularly for the size that you are. Another Monte Carlo."

"My father is a capitalist. The fact that it is easiest for our country to be wealthy due to tourism is probably what keeps everything so stable. He wants it to be safe and attractive. Anything good that he does is a side effect of it being good for him." She paused for a moment. "That is perhaps uncharitable. He's not an evil dictator. But he did make a deal with one. And was not in any way hesitant to hand his daughter over to him."

"Did you have feelings for him?"

He felt that it was important to ask. If she harbored a connection to his enemy, then she could be a liability. It hadn't occurred to him until that moment, but what he was gathering from this entire conversation was that the marriage had been arranged in her infancy. Which meant she didn't know anything else.

Her face contorted in horror. "I absolutely had no feelings beyond contempt. I'm glad that he's rotting in prison getting everything that he deserves for being a despot."

"Then I find your father quite monstrous."

"Why? Clearly my free will doesn't matter to you. You don't even think I actually have it."

"I didn't say that. What I believe is that there are some things that bear so much weight your internal compass will continually point you back to them. What I believe is that eventually you realize your choices are not limitless, because the things that you believe in, the things that you value, will keep you on a path."

She looked out the window. "I don't even know what my path is supposed to be."

"Perhaps when this is finished you will find it." He found that he meant it. He found that maybe he even cared. Even if just the smallest bit. On the surface he had nothing in common with this woman, this princess who seemed to bemoan her life growing up in a palace. But in other ways, he did understand. Because he had been thrust into a life that did not belong to him, and he had been forced to claw his way back out.

It would be easy to write her off as being spoiled. Selfish.

But she hadn't had a chance to create her own fate. He supposed she was doing it now.

A valiant effort that he could only admire.

The car pulled up to the wrought iron gates that separated the palace from the rest of the world. Security was still extremely high, turning this place into a fortress. But they were such a new government, even if they were a continuation of the old. He took nothing for granted. For now, the people were happy. For now everything felt like a gain. But he knew how quickly the tide could turn. If there was a downturn in the economy, if something went wrong, then his rule would be blamed. There would come a time when what had happened in the past might not be at the forefront of their minds anymore. It had happened once. Only a fool would believe that it could never happen again, that he could be immune.

He turned to look at Fern, whose eyes were wide as she looked up at the imposing black palace.

"I've never seen anything like this," she said.

"Did you not come to the country to visit your intended?"

"No. I met him once. When I was sixteen. He was in his forties. It was at the palace in Cape Blanco. He made my skin crawl. I thank God that I never came here to visit him. Who knows what might've happened."

"Why *thank God*? If He truly wanted to help you He could have removed the problem altogether."

"He did," she said. "Eventually."

Her eyes met his and held, and her lips curved just slightly.

"Out of the frying pan, I'm afraid," he responded.

"But if I move quickly enough to the flames perhaps they won't scorch me."

He let out a hard breath, and when the car came to a stop, opened his door and rounded to her side. He did not allow anyone to open doors for him. He had not acclimated to any sort of royal protocol. It was clear, however, that the princess was accustomed to having the door opened for her. She had not made a move toward the car door one time since they had first approached the vehicle.

These were the sorts of things that betrayed her as royalty. He thought about what she had said. About the paradox of her existence. He could see it. Because there was wealth and high status in every line of her body. The way that she held her chin up high, the straight set of her shoulders. The imperious way that she spoke to him, even when she was at a clear disadvantage.

And yet she had no power.

She stepped out of the car, and he became suddenly very aware that she was not dressed in clothing fit for a princess. Thankfully there was no press awaiting his arrival today. They had no reason to. Another fledgling enterprise in this country—free press. For the last twenty-five years they had been nothing but a mouthpiece for the regime. He encouraged them to print the truth, and along with it their opinion. They were allowed to criticize him, and often did. They also watched many of his movements with great fascination.

When he did announce his engagement to Fern, and their swiftly impending marriage, it would create a firestorm. But thankfully, the fire hadn't started yet.

And when it did, perhaps it would be as Fern said. They would move through it quickly enough to not get scorched.

But in the meantime, she would need to be clothed in a way that befits the future queen.

He took her arm again, and led her to the grand front doors of the palace. It was made entirely of volcanic stone, the interior as dark as the exterior. There were sconces that illuminated the walls, but there was only so much light that could be introduced into such a dark antechamber.

Other parts of the palace had been made brighter with Sheetrock and texture, paint or wallpaper rather than this oppressive stone. But the entry and the throne room were much the same as they had been at the end of the Viking age.

"Medieval," she whispered.

"Yes. Fitting, given that it has been standing since the Middle Ages. Thoren the Bloody was the first ruler to take control of the nation, such as it was at the time."

"You're Vikings."

"Yes. Thoren and his company came here shortly after Iceland was taken away from the Irish monks. This land was barren, and was seen as a safe place for the Vikings to send their women, and to use as a base when they went on raids. The women of course came from all over, as you know the Vikings famously claimed brides wherever they went."

"You mean kidnapped and subjugated women."

"Most marriage was based on kidnapping and subjugation at the time."

She gave him a long, dry look. "Some still is."

He chuckled. He did find it amusing the way that she insisted on fighting him. "True. But you know, we famously have quite easy divorces."

"Do you?" she said, tilting her head. "Are you being serious?"

"Yes. And Viking women could divorce their husbands, as far back as the Middle Ages. They only had to declare it. This is still true. My country honors the old ways. At least we do again."

"And yet you seem to take a dim view on God."

"I would definitely be more inclined to say a prayer to Odin if I had the occasion to say one. But no."

"I imagine losing your family the way that you did… affected that."

"I thought you weren't a nun."

"I'm not."

"You seem awfully concerned about the state of my eternal soul."

"No. Just your…your peace, I suppose. I feel a great amount of peace in knowing that there is something bigger than me out there."

"If that's the case, why hasn't He fixed anything?"

"You're here, aren't you?"

"You can't convince me that I was meant to go through all of that."

They had paused in the entry, and he began to walk again, eager to get out of the conversation.

"How did you escape?"

"Why do you care?"

"If I'm going to help you, I would like to know you."

"You seem to be forgetting, you are my captive."

"No. You seem to be forgetting that we have a deal. And I don't want to be treated like a captive. But a partner." She stopped walking, and was looking at him with a mutinous expression.

He sighed heavily. "I don't remember. I don't remember anything about my life in the palace as a child. I don't remember how I escaped. I barely remember who I was. For years. I knew, but it meant nothing to me. It was like I was in a fog. It wasn't until I was fifteen or so that I decided I needed to make my way back here. That I needed to do something to fix what was broken. And that was when I began to make an army. As quietly as possible. Without tipping off the broader world that I was still alive."

"How did you do that?"

"Very carefully. Now, come to your room."

This time, she obeyed without pushing back. They walked up the spiral staircase, and into the more modern part of the palace. The hallway was well lit, with richly colored wallpaper that caught the light and didn't feel quite so oppressive. He preferred the darkness, personally.

The room that had been prepared for her was sumptuously outfitted. There was a canopy bed, a plush chaise, a bistro table and chairs so that she could take her breakfast in the morning. The bathroom had a glorious tub, and a large shower. His own room was completely Spartan. He didn't wish to get soft.

He still slept on a bedroll on the floor most nights.

It was hunger and a need for things to change that had gotten him here.

He never wanted to lose that hunger.

He was glad, too, that the seaside home his family had been killed in had been burned after the coup. It was why his own survival had escaped notice for so long.

It also meant he could never go back there.

Those memories would never find a foothold.

Her expression was dreamy, soft as she looked around the room. He imagined that she had been without such luxuries at the convent.

As if she had read his thoughts, she turned to him. "I was very happy at the convent. But I would be lying if I said I didn't miss having my own room."

"You shared a room?"

"Yes. With Sister Mary Celeste. Who was lovely, but did snore. And also the bed was a bit…sparse."

"Well, enjoy this. Because when you're off on your own replete with choices, how will you be paying for your life?"

It was perhaps a bit unkind to pose that question to her.

"I don't know. But I suppose I'll figure it out. I'll figure out what it is I want to do. Or maybe I will go back to the convent."

A woman of her beauty devoting herself to the church was a crime that his body rebelled against. He was intent on keeping his hands off of her. He had her for a limited time, and there was work to be done. There was no time for indulging in anything.

But still. He couldn't help but notice her beauty.

It didn't mean that he would act on that notice.

"Thankfully you have some time to consider it. In the meantime, the only thing you have to worry about is preparing to be my wife. I will be making announcements to the press tonight. We will marry on the balcony in front of all citizens who wish to attend. In the meantime I will have someone sent to make you look like a queen."

CHAPTER THREE

IN SPITE OF the fact that the bed was gloriously comfortable, she didn't sleep. She still didn't have a phone or a means of accessing the internet, so she had no idea what ripple effect Ragnar's announcement had in the rest of the world. Or indeed, with her family. Maybe they were drawing up a treaty. Maybe it had started a war. Why would anyone tell her? It wasn't like it was her life.

She had been stewing, also, on what he had said about her needing to support herself after the marriage ended.

She knew that. It was just that she had vague fantasies about waiting tables and living in a small cubby of an apartment while she figured all that out. She could go to Spain, Argentina, Mexico easily. Or to Canada, England or even Australia. Spain seemed the most familiar, potentially. Mexico was very far away. That held its own appeal.

It was difficult to know exactly what her dreams were. Because the biggest thing that had been hanging in front of her was her crushing lack of control over her life. If she had run away from home she would've been tracked down and brought back. There would have been no way for her to escape Cape Blanco. She wasn't anonymous. No one was going to help her get money or documentation that might help her escape. Again, part of the paradox of her existence.

She was in theory a person with power. Privilege.

And yet none of it was accessible to her.

Not when she wanted it. Not when she needed it.

It was why the convent had felt so revelatory.

She had been cared for, and there had been a structure, tasks, but there had been a lot of time for her to sit and think. But of course the things that she liked to do were the kinds of things everybody likes to do. She enjoyed reading. Sitting and drawing, even though she didn't have a talent for it.

Though really, if she could choose any sort of life, it might actually be on a farm. She could go from being a queen to being a farmer. She looked forward to telling Ragnar that was her plan. She hoped that it astonished and baffled him.

In fact she wanted nothing more.

Sparring with him was unlike anything she'd experienced before. There was something in it she couldn't articulate. Something—

The knock on the door interrupted her thoughts, and she was about to ask who it was when the doors swept open, and in came a servant pushing a cart that was laden with pastries and a pot of coffee. And behind that servant came two women, one holding a large kit, the other pushing a rack filled with brightly colored clothes.

She had slept in her dress last night, and she was feeling wrinkled this morning, and just looking at the sumptuous fabrics hanging on the rack made her feel a strange ache she couldn't recall feeling before. She hadn't missed dressing up, at least not consciously. In fact, she thought that she was happy to not have to go through the farce. The clothes were always chosen for her. It was never about her. Never about what she liked.

And of course this time it wouldn't be either.

"Good morning, Your Highness," one of the women said. "While you take your coffee and your breakfast we will begin to show you some options for today. Then we will bring in the wedding gowns."

"Oh?"

"Yes. Obviously you will need something for this morning, but then you will need to change for the wedding."

It wasn't entirely clear to her why she was expected to have more than one outfit. But she didn't complain—she couldn't. The first few dresses were lovely, pastel and made with sumptuous fabric. The kind of thing that would have been chosen for her to wear back home, but...

"You don't like them," the stylist said.

"They're beautiful," she replied.

"Yes. Of course they are. But they don't speak to you. If I may, I wonder if it would be better for you to look at some more saturated colors."

"Oh. Maybe."

She sat down in a chair. She wasn't sure why that happened, but then she realized that she had been ushered there by a handler who was so smooth he was orchestrating her movements without her even truly considering them. Her coffee was poured, pastries served. She began to eat, and as she did, the hairstylist began to arrange tools, and started evaluating her hair.

"I would like for it to stay curly," she said.

"Of course," the stylist said.

There was no *of course* about that at home. They said that her curls were unruly. That they didn't present a good picture of the crown. That they needed to be tamed, just like she did.

But if she was going to forge a different identity, it was going to start now. She could give Ragnar what he wanted. But she would give herself what she wanted as well.

Her hair was fussed with while she ate, and then she was presented with more dresses. And then, as if by magic, even more appeared.

The selections were vivid, and the winning dress was green, with long sleeves that were tight around her wrist and loose up to her shoulder. It fell softly down to her knees, the lovely, natural fibers in the fabric making it swirl delicately when she moved.

The sides of her hair were affixed upward, creating a slightly retro style that showcased her curls. And once they had settled on that, the wedding gowns came in.

A parade of glorious silks and satins. She chose the simplest one. White and closely fitted to her body except for a train which flowed effortlessly behind her as she moved.

It was marked up to be fitted for this afternoon, and then she was put back into the green dress, and ushered out into the hall, and down the stairs.

Maybe she should feel something. Something more than she did. But marriage had never meant anything to her beyond this. An arrangement. Maybe in another life, with another set of circumstances, she would have been able to be romantic about it. But she never had been. She had only ever been able to be practical about the institution at best. And had dreaded it at worst.

She had never imagined marrying for love. But then, she had never imagined being able to marry for her own gain either, and buried somewhere in all of this was the potential for that.

She almost wanted to weep with relief. Reality hit, and hit hard. If she were being married to the president then her life would be over. She would be little more than his prisoner. And it would last for all of her life, a life that was determined by him. She would not have been choosing her own dresses; she was certain of that. Everything would be laid out for her. Chosen for her.

Even though she was being given choices within a set parameter, they were still choices.

This might be a tunnel, but it now had a light at the end of it.

The only other time she'd had light had been at the convent. Now she could take that experience, and she could make it into something even more expansive. Provided she got through all of this. She was guided down a long corridor, and then a large, black door swung open. There he was, sitting behind a desk. He looked up at her, those blue eyes burning bright in the relative darkness of the room. He had a weathered face. But it was no less beautiful for it. Each line spoke to worries he had carried for many, many years.

To the concerns that he had for his people. He was broad and muscular, and she thought then it was all the better for him to carry these burdens on his shoulders.

Do not romanticize him. He's another man using you

for his own interests. Just because you can use him back doesn't make him benevolent.

It was a timely reminder. She looked over her shoulder, but there was no one there. All of the staff were gone. It was only her and Ragnar.

"Good morning," he said, lifting up the stack of papers on his desk and tapping them once, the gesture so clerical. So civilized that it seemed directly at odds with him.

He was dressed all in black. Not in a suit, but in a black sweater, and beneath the desk she could see black wool trousers and black shoes.

She hadn't noticed what he was wearing yesterday. Oddly, it had gotten lost in the kidnap of it all.

"Good morning. I assume that there is some public-facing event happening, or I wouldn't have been dressed like this."

"Correct. We are going to stream an announcement together about our upcoming marriage."

"What exactly are we going to say?"

"I'm going to address the nation. You are going to sit beside me."

"Am I meant to gaze up at you in adoration?"

"That is up to you."

"This is going to look like a political alliance, you realize that, right. I don't think people are going to find it overly romantic."

"I don't need my people to romanticize me. I need them to see me as someone strong and capable. Choosing you as a wife suggests that I am engaged in diplomacy."

"You also want me because I can teach you something

about this life. My father isn't a good man. At least not on a personal level. But he is very good at making his people believe that he only ever has their best interests at heart. He's extremely charming. His manners are beyond reproach."

"Yes, as were my predecessor's. He would lie, and he would smile, and he would slither off into the ether to do vile things. I am exactly as I appear."

"Yes. But you might want to appear slightly more approachable. And you may want to let me speak."

She didn't really want to. It was one of her least favorite parts of royal life. Any of the times that she had been called upon to be part of the face of her country. Not because she didn't love her country—she felt deep affection for it, but she did not enjoy being in front of people. Still, the idea that he had, to present some kind of stony announcements to all the citizens of the country, with her sitting silently beside him like exactly what she was—a trophy representative of the revolution, and not a human being—was not going to do what he hoped.

"I think that we should say you and I have been working together on diplomacy. On easing things between our countries, healing divides. Even my father won't want to come and make trouble if I do that. I think that's been part of the problem. He hasn't known how to extricate himself from what until now had proven to be a very unpopular regime. Now that you're back, and you've had so much success, it's incredibly obvious that he would've been making a mistake marrying me off. I can fix that for him."

"And you want to do that?"

"No. I don't. But what I would like to do is make

sure that my freedom is assured. By doing that, I need to bring my father on board with this arrangement. And I truly believe that we might be able to do that if I say the right things now. If I make it clear that my father supported your revolution, even if quietly."

"It is a lie."

"Of course it is," she said, moving up closer to his desk. "Of course it's a lie. But I was raised in this. This backstabbing, treacherous life. What I learned when I was taught manners and elocution was to look for the truth and meaning between the words. Manners hide all types of sins. They make it so a person can smile at your face while stabbing you in the side. I did not make it this far in royal life without understanding that."

At least here that could matter. At least now she could use it. She felt a small measure of power now, in this moment. To finally be able to use the skills she'd honed and hidden in the palace. She was not the Fern she'd found at the convent now. But she was not the Fern she'd been in Cape Blanco either. It was like the two were coming together, and were stronger for it.

"A trade. We make your father look better than he is, and then he will not be able to interfere negatively with the marriage without damaging the reputation that you've created for him."

"Exactly. You and I have been working together on diplomacy."

She took a step closer, and for some reason her heart began to beat faster. "We began to develop feelings for each other. You are a man who has sworn to protect his country above all else."

"Won't that make our divorce more difficult?"

Her breath hitched. "Yes. It will. But I think it will also make everything seem like a better story. You don't want to present yourself as a man made of ice."

He shifted slightly, then stood up from where he was sitting. She had truly forgotten how large he was. She barely came up to the center of his broad chest. He looked like a relic from another time. One of his Viking ancestors brought forward to this moment. All he was missing was a broadsword.

"I do not mind my enemies thinking that I am made of ice. You will be seen as a vulnerability—you realize that, don't you?"

"Do you have faith that you can protect this country?"

"Of course."

"Then you must have faith that you can protect me. People would prefer if you had a vulnerability. It makes you that much more human. You said yourself, your ancestors initially brought their women here to keep them safe."

"I believe that was more about possession than feelings."

"Why do you think that? Humans have always found a way. Through all of history. We are a testament to that. We've found so many ways to survive. Even when it seemed pointless. As for me, I found a way to dream, even though my future seemed certain. Wouldn't you rather know that a leader had a spark of passion inside of him?"

He turned toward her, and even though there was still space between their bodies she felt enveloped by him. His presence was nearly overwhelming. Magnetic. He looked like a king. Like a man who was born to sit on the throne. The truth was, he was the kind of man that would instill confidence in anyone. Looking at him, it made her want to vow loyalty to him. To hide underneath his protection. Very suddenly, the idea of freedom felt frightening.

Don't falter now.

She took a sharp breath. "Don't be afraid to show them your humanity. It is the lack of true humanity in the man who ruled before you that made him frightening. The ability to turn it on and off. You don't need to be charismatic. Be you. With a hint of a beating heart."

The truth was, he was charismatic. Just not in the way that many would define it. Perhaps *magnetic* was the better word.

"I will let you tell the story of us, then."

He gestured toward two chairs by the fireplace, where there was a stand in place for a camera.

"It is already hooked up to the broadcast channels, and to official online accounts. You and I are set to go on in one minute."

She didn't have time to protest, because he put his hand on her lower back and led her to the chair.

His hand was large, hot against her lower back, and she couldn't recall if she had ever had such close contact with a man as she had with him.

In fact, she had seen no man at all for the last three years, and she would have said that was a boon.

But suddenly she was very aware of him. The press of that palm against her back. And then she turned away from him and sat in the chair.

He sat beside her, and put his hand over the top of her arm, her hand.

His skin against hers electrified her.

And for the first time, she felt something that was truly like fear.

What was this?

But she didn't have time to question herself, because then the light on the camera turned on. He began to speak in Icelandic, and she did not know the language. She was suddenly very nervous, because they hadn't discussed what she was supposed to do.

They spoke English to one another, the common language between them, and that was going to have to be okay now. She imagined it was more likely that the people in this country would understand that, rather than her native Spanish.

She did her best to smile and to respond when she felt like it was appropriate.

"My fiancée will address you in English."

She felt a sweep of relief that he answered the question.

"Yes," she said, looking into the blank, dead eye of the camera. She was so aware of him touching her. And then he moved his thumb across her knuckles, and her heart leaped up high in her throat.

"Yes. I just wished to address all of you and say I am honored to be here. And to be part of this nation, and its new future. I have been working with the king for three years now, easing diplomatic ties between his country and mine. Over that time, he and I began to develop feelings for each other. So though this feels quick, I know, it is actually just a visible bloom on a seed that has been growing for a very long time."

"Our wedding will be this afternoon," he said, still

speaking English. "We will wed on the large terrace at the front of the palace, and whoever wishes to attend may come and watch. This will usher in a new time. A new era. As we continue to work for the betterment of all people in our country. And with Queen Fern by my side I know that I am assured of this future."

The light on the camera went off, whoever was monitoring the broadcast clearly right on cue.

"Perfectly done."

"You don't believe in giving anyone much time to prepare."

"Nothing about you has suggested to me that you need extra time to prepare for anything."

She felt warmth, pleasure, spreading in her chest and she looked away. "Are you talking about the fact that I almost got away from you yesterday?"

"You didn't. But you tried. And then you skillfully renegotiated the terms of this arrangement. Somehow I knew that you would manage to do so again."

"That's a lot of confidence in a woman you only just met."

"When I was putting together my army—such as it was—to reclaim the country, I had to become an excellent judge of character. I couldn't afford to trust the wrong people. If the wrong word went into the wrong ear, the revolution would have been over before it began."

"So you're saying you're an excellent judge of character, and you have judged me to be excellent?"

"In a sense."

His hand was still resting on hers; she drew it back. And without thinking, brushed her fingers over his knuckles.

Those blue eyes met hers, and she felt something spark low inside of her.

Of all the things.

She had been immune to men all this time. Mainly because they had been adversaries to her.

She didn't respect them, didn't like them, so how could she ever want one?

Like marriage, romance had felt very much like it didn't fit into her life in a conventional way.

She wasn't certain that what she was feeling for him now was romance. No. It felt like something altogether more…earthy.

"The wedding will be in three hours," he said.

"Three hours?"

Suddenly, she imagined him pulling her into his arms and kissing her. Weddings had kisses. She felt very suddenly panicked about that.

"What am I supposed to expect with this wedding?"

"It will be quick."

"Okay. Anything else?"

"A traditional Aslandian wedding."

"I don't know what that is."

"Of course not. Because in these last twenty-five years my culture was nearly wiped out. Though I was living with villagers who still held to the old ways. And that's why I feel such a strong connection to those ways now. It is very much a warrior's wedding. There are vows, and then rather than a kiss, the husband cuts through his cloak and gives a piece of it to the wife. Binding both their hands with it to symbolize the union. But she has taken up his cause, and he has offered his protection."

It felt so grave. But it was a relief that she wasn't going to have to kiss him.

"You're not a very romantic people," she said. She said it to make herself feel better.

The space between his brows creased. "Do you not find that romantic? Perhaps it is because my life was marked by betrayal that I find the swearing of loyalty to be the deepest, most romantic concept there is."

"Do you?" Those blue eyes hit her hard. "I mean, do you feel that it's romantic?"

"No. I don't feel it. But I don't feel much of anything. Still, I recognize it for what it is."

"I guess that proves that I'm right, about the lack of romanticism here."

"I suppose that it does. But we will see just how much that is true by how many people come."

"Somehow I have a feeling that the crowd will turn out in force for their king that they thought long dead, especially now that they think he's found love."

He laughed, that cold, chilling laugh again. "It is best they don't know the truth. I might not have died that day, but most of me did. It will be a show. But as long as we put on a good one, I suppose it doesn't matter."

CHAPTER FOUR

HE WAS DRESSED in a military uniform, one that denoted his high rank, and the accompanying cloak, which would be part of the ceremony. He found that he had underestimated his captive. She was extremely clever. Perhaps more clever when it came to these matters than he was. He would have to watch her closely. She had spoken of her father, said that he was manipulative.

It was clear that she understood the mechanics of manipulation.

He would have to keep special watch on her to ensure that she wasn't trying to do it to him.

Though what he had said to her was true. He did not have finer feelings. That made it very difficult for him to be manipulated. Though when he had touched her hand...

Yes. There were other ways to manipulate men. And he was no better than any other man when it came to matters of the flesh.

He had made a bargain with her. He would not take her to bed. And at this point, it was for his own security as well as hers.

She was a very sharp knife in a drawer. A valuable thing, but if you reached around blindly, it could be used against you.

He walked out of his chamber, and down the stairs, toward where they would convene for the wedding, just as the door to her quarters opened. She came out, her hair styled elaborately, with white flowers placed in her dark curls, the wedding gown fitting closely against curves that had only been hinted at in the clothes she had worn so far.

She was so feminine and fragile. The kind of thing he would have to be careful holding in his hand. He had no gentleness in him. He could crush her far too easily.

That is part of her charm. Part of her ability to manipulate. Nothing is fragile about this woman, and you know it.

Yes. He did know that. Because she had fought him and fought him well when he had taken her captive. And when she had discovered that fighting him physically wouldn't work she had fought him with her wits. And now she had convinced him to create this story where they were in love. And he could see the easy merit in it. But he had to wonder if she was seeing something that he didn't.

She looked at him, and a delicate blush colored the top of her cheekbones.

Warmth cascaded through his bloodstream, and he chose not to question it, not to linger on it. Not linger on what she had been thinking or what he felt in response.

"Take my arm," he said.

He needed to become immune to her touch.

She was only a woman. It was only her hand. But he realized as the two of them began to walk toward the balcony that one thing she had done by turning this into a love story was cut him off from his ability to find release. He had been celibate for three years. The idea of being celibate for two more suddenly seemed unbearable.

He could make arrangements, he knew. He could have the women sign nondisclosure agreements. But she had made this very difficult for him.

"Of course, with the story that you have told, you've made it very difficult for either of us to take lovers."

Her fingers curled, her nails scratching him just slightly through the fabric of his military jacket. "Excuse me?"

"Now that you have painted it as a great love story, you have put us both in the position where any love affair we might have could be weaponized."

"I wasn't aware that you were considering having one."

"Two years of celibacy?"

"Ragnar, I have been in a convent for three years."

He might as well have been. Though he didn't wish to tell her that. Because it might give her the idea that she had more power to exploit.

"And before?"

"I was barely eighteen and living in a palace. You could put those pieces together yourself."

But they were then swept out onto the balcony, and he was prevented from following that down the logical road.

There was a sea of people down there, and the cheers when they came out were deafening. Even up there.

His country had turned out to see this. His people.

He felt suddenly overwhelmed. By a wall of something inside of him that was pushing against his chest. Creating pressure behind his eyes.

He had been cut off for all of his life. He had been alone. But these people, they had waited for him. They had needed him. This was why he had made it this far. He would not make a mistake now. He would not fail them.

He would manage this, all of it unerringly, for them. He would give them whatever they needed.

He took that feeling and pushed it down deep, added it to all of the dogged determination that lived inside of him.

This was the right thing.

So long as he remained in control.

The officiant came forward, an Orthodox priest who incorporated new and old ways. And he began to speak the vows for them to repeat. Ragnar realized that Fern would not understand.

"I give myself to you," he repeated in English. "For all of my life, and into the next. I give you my heart. My body. My breath. I give you my sword, to raise against your enemies, for they are now mine. In my home you are always safe. You are the most important battle I will ever fight."

He pulled his knife from its position on his thigh and grabbed the edge of his cloak, cutting the end off, and tearing a strip.

Her eyes were wide, the green more intense as she stared up at him. And he pressed his hand against hers, that strip of cloth held between their palms as he began to wind it around them.

The priest began to speak her vows. She looked at

him, repeating the words as best she could, but clearly not knowing what they meant.

"Now I am bound to you," he translated. "To keep your hearth and home. To forsake the touch of any other, and their children for your name. My bloodline is now yours. Your home is now mine. I forsake all that I was, to become all that you need."

The color drained slightly from her face, and he tightened the cord, even more so cementing the bond.

"And what has been joined can never be torn asunder. Not with any sword wielded by the hands of men. For this bond extends beneath skin. To the soul. Unto heaven, and the underworld."

They turned and he held their arms up, so that the people below could see where they were bound. The cheer rolled through him, and then they turned and walked away, back into the palace.

Her hands were shaking, and she brought one over and began to fiercely undo where they were knotted.

"I… I need to get out of this. I needed to be untied."

"Stop," he said. "Steady yourself. Until we are alone."

He walked with her down the corridor, and into his study, where he closed the door firmly behind them with his free hand, and she continued to attack the knot like she was an ermine caught in a hunter's noose.

He flexed his forearm, and pulled, snapping the bonds. "There."

"Those vows are horrendously misogynistic," she said.

"How exactly?"

"I had to pledge my very blood to you, and you just have to fight for me."

"Unto death, Fern. I am obligated to lay down my life for you."

"You didn't have to pledge your cojones to me, however. I had to promise my womb." Color mounted high on her cheekbones. This time from embarrassment.

"The vows were for show."

"Maybe," she said. "But it feels like a very sacred thing to be taking lightly."

"How can it be both misogynistic and sacred?"

"I think you'll find that doesn't seem to be a conflict in most of humanity."

"You did well. You did exactly what was asked of you. And now we wait for your father to call."

"I'm surprised he hasn't already."

"He did. But I put him off until the last moment. And then expect…"

His phone rang. He went to the desk and picked it up. "King Octavio, it is good to hear from you."

"What have you done?"

"I've married your daughter. And now things will look different between our countries."

"Put her on the phone."

She tilted her chin up. "I have no problem speaking to him."

"English," he said as he handed her the phone.

She shot him a hard glare. "Hola, Papa. As you can see, I was taken from the convent. But I think that you will agree that the solution is a fine one."

"You cannot trust this man," he said.

"I don't trust him. But I do believe that we would be better served working with him rather than against him.

And I did what I had to do to disconnect you from the previous dictator. You're welcome."

"He has not harmed you?"

The expression on her face shifted. "No. He has not. But thank you for asking."

He stole the phone from her then. "I have treated her better than anyone in your household ever did. I will be sending over my demands by the end of the week."

"You have the terms of the agreement," Octavio said in response.

"I will have the terms I lay out. You tried to run from me, Octavio. Men who run from me are always caught. Make no mistake."

He hung the phone up and tossed it down on his desk.

"He won't go against you," Fern said. "He's far too aware of his own need to preserve himself."

"You definitely made an impossible situation for him."

She laughed. "Well. Seeing as he spent the last twenty-one years putting me in impossible situations it feels almost poetic. I never would have thought that I could use any of these things to my own advantage. How nice to be proven wrong."

"A word of caution to you," he said, pausing for a moment and looking into those fathomless green eyes. "I will not be manipulated."

"Then continue to treat me like a partner and I won't need to do it."

He almost admired her. The way that she refused to cower. Refused to say that she wasn't trying to manipulate him, or that she never would.

She was intent on going toe to toe with him. It was difficult to object.

Because in his life, strength could only be admired. And he had to admire hers as well, even if he also had to be wary of it.

"You are not in a position to negotiate."

She smiled. "Neither are you. Now, we have married. What is it that you intend to do next?"

"I have new legislation to review."

"Do you have a parliament or anything like that?"

"No. There has been some talk of implementing one, but until then, I am mainly focusing on restoring functionality to the system."

"Is there anything that I can help with?"

He frowned. "I did not marry you for help with matters of state."

"In a fashion, you did. You said that you wanted me to help you with diplomacy."

"That's different. It is a woman's work."

He said it dismissively. Without thought. And when he looked back at her green eyes, she was giving him a deep glare. "What? Do you object to the characterization?"

"Yes. I do. Because I watched my mother be pushed into the background, disrespected, relegated to the shadows because her work was only a woman's work."

"You don't intend to stay here," he pointed out.

"No. I don't. How…was your parents' marriage? How did they balance things?"

And here was where that great yawning cavern existed. That place that stood empty. Meaningless. His past life before he had left the palace.

"I don't know," he said.

"You don't know it at all?"

"No. I've mentioned already, I don't remember how I escaped. I don't remember the day that the palace was taken. And I don't truly remember my life before."

"Did you…?" She moved closer to him, her scent intoxicating. She was like wildflowers and the forest. Something that he missed sometimes.

There had been few moments in his life when he had been a man without a mission. But when he had been simply a man, it had always been in the wilderness. He had given that up. He was a symbol now, not a person, and it was something he believed in. Felt keenly.

But it did not mean that sometimes the memory of his teenage years did not call to him. The lure of freedom…

She was a witch, perhaps. Her own designs on freedom infecting him. Informing him now, when he should not be thinking of that at all. He should be thinking about ways to continue to move his country forward.

She let out a breath. "We don't have to talk about it."

"It doesn't bother me. How can it? I don't recall it."

"Did you have amnesia? Did you have any idea who you were?"

"Yes. I did, but it only lived in the back of my mind. A very vague understanding. I knew my name, though they did not call me by my name. It was dangerous for anyone to know that I was alive. I understood that. I understood that I was the rightful king, but… I don't remember life here. I don't remember if I was close with my parents. It's all gone. Wiped away by whatever happened that day."

Her voice had grown hushed. There was softness now

on her face that he had never seen directed at him before. "It must've been terrible."

"Happily, I don't know. Maybe it was. But it is not in my memory. I don't need it to be. That's what I've decided. It must be useless information. Everything that I have ever needed to know has been there. Every skill that I have ever needed to have has presented itself to me. This, I am certain, is no different. I misspoke. It is not because it is women's work that I need you to do diplomacy. It is because it is the one thing I don't understand."

"Well. That's better."

He didn't like admitting deficiency in any capacity. But a good leader also knew where his weaknesses were.

He would not hold his country back by being stubborn here.

"Well, that was my first piece of diplomacy accomplished—keeping my father from storming your shores—I will go away and ponder the rest."

"A good plan, my queen."

It seems a shame, to not be the one to remove her wedding dress.

The thought was so unexpected, the feeling that accompanied it so visceral, he had to brace his palms on the desk as she walked away from him.

He had never thought about marriage. Not beyond the potential for it to be useful politically. Not beyond the need to produce a child to carry on his bloodline.

He had not thought about it all those years, even when he was lonely in the woods. It meant very little to him.

He had always known that he wasn't part of any of those warm families in the village where he had grown up. That he was not part of the family in the household he was brought up in. He was different. Separate. Later it had become clear to him that it was a good thing he had always been held separate. Because his life was meant to be in service of others. It was meant to restore this nation. It was his responsibility. Born into his blood.

Marriage, family, love, none of that was part of it.

Still, right then, the place where they had been bound together by his cloak burned.

He had no explanation for that.

CHAPTER FIVE

SHE WAS HIGH on adrenaline. There was no other explanation. She felt like she had the energy of ten pikas trying to dry hay for their den before the winter came.

She was motivated, more than ever, to make use of these two years.

What she had learned from her time in the convent was that no time was wasted. Even when it felt like it was.

Her time at the convent had taught her more about herself than anything else in her life had. But it had been a quiet time. It had been a thoughtful time, where her own mind had been the teacher.

This was different. She had a job that she could do. She had a purpose.

He was right. She thought that she was going to go out into the world after this and just live a normal life. It was what she wanted. But she would need money. She would need education, a career.

Maybe she would start a farm. But she would need to understand what went into running it and keeping it going.

She could take advantage of this time. To learn. To gather what she needed. Because this was the beginning of something. Truly. She had help. She was not going to simply be an accessory to a man for the rest of her life. She was not going to rot away and lose herself the way that her mother had.

No.

That conversation with her father had proven to her that she had power. That she was smart.

She wasn't lesser.

She had won. Today, she had won.

"Excuse me," she said, when she saw the man that she had learned was Ragnar's right-hand adviser. Soren. "I need a computer. And an internet connection. I'm also going to need some idea of what the finances for the country are. And..."

"I will check with the king."

"Well, do that. But I'm not a prisoner."

"Are you not? I seem to recall that you were taken forcefully."

"But Ragnar and I have come to an agreement."

"I will see."

She gripped the front of her dress and swished back to her room.

It really was a lovely dress. She took it off, and went to her wardrobe, taking out a pair of camel-colored pants, and a loose-fitting top. By the time she was finished dressing there was a knock on her door.

"The king says you may have this."

She was presented with a laptop. Brand-new from the look of things.

She clutched it to her chest. "And?"

"He says he will send you information that might be relevant to you."

"How?"

"He established an email address for you."

And with that, Soren was gone.

And she set the computer on her desk and began to hunt through different webpages for information on Asland. Not just recent history, but the history of the past.

The history of what had happened at the palace on the day of the coup.

A coup that had resulted in horror for everyone.

The king and queen had been killed.

She knew that. Logically. But reading about it now that she knew Ragnar made her feel cold.

The young prince was eight years old. He was thought to have been killed along with his parents initially.

She squeezed her eyes shut as she realized that the implication of that was that there had been other victims who were children.

What an awful thing.

It made her feel a sense of deep anger at everyone involved. At her father. Who had formed an alliance with this new government rather than repudiating it. Who had done what was expedient to him at the time, rather than what was right.

There were no details about what had happened with Ragnar, because no one knew. His appearance on the scene had been a surprise to everyone the world over. But DNA results had proven that he was exactly who he said he was.

There was a dinging sound, and she opened up the email program. She smiled just slightly when she saw his name. In an email program. It seemed so weird and modern, civilized, when in practice that man was none of those things.

She clicked on the message.

You will find that the treasury is solvent. There is a budget in place for certain things. Why are you asking about this?

She tapped Reply.

Because, I'm thinking about what I do to accomplish diplomacy. And that might necessitate expenditures.

Another email came in quickly.

This is your budget:

The sum that he provided was more than generous. He had been right about the treasury being solvent.

Amazing, but she supposed that was what happened when a horrendous dictator hoarded everything for himself.

She could see by looking through all the information that a lot of the money had been returned to the people. The treasury was still healthy, and they were able to implement the sorts of programs necessary to keep a country running, but also there had been a real effort to lift the citizens out of the abject poverty they'd been forced into.

She sent him a new email.

I also want a list of countries you would be interested in strengthening ties with.

There was nothing in the body of the returned email. Only a document.

She tapped her chin as she read through it. And she began to formulate a plan. If he wanted to make a statement with their marriage, then they would make a statement.

A national paid holiday for all the citizens, with a celebratory atmosphere. And a party thrown at the palace.

For all of these world leaders that he wanted to strengthen ties with. Yes. She could do this.

She was confident in it.

She created a proposal, an outline for the events and how it would be executed. Of course, she would hire people who were more experienced than she was to oversee the details, but one thing she knew from her father was how to create a spectacle that would engage even the most jaded of guests.

She sent the proposal to Ragnar.

She was surprised when he didn't respond.

And when there was a deafening pounding on the door she nearly jumped out of her skin.

She scuttled away from the laptop, and opened her door. There was Ragnar, standing there holding printed-out paper in his hand, glaring.

"What?"

"A party?"

"Not just any party, reception. For our marriage. To set our intention for how we intend to rule the country together."

"I do not do parties."

"You wanted me for this. You want me to teach you

how to be with people. So you have to let me do what you've asked me to do."

"I don't have to do anything. I can throw you in the dungeon for the next two years—or forever if I like. That I have given you anything is a gift."

Her heart began to pound faster. "You are a beast. A flat-out monster, a feral animal who was raised by wolves. And if you want to be a king, a leader of men, then you have to start behaving like a man."

The tragic thing was, she felt like this was in line with men's behavior. She didn't give that gender very much credit at all. Her own life was a testament to how selfish they could be.

How difficult.

He let out a low growl and slammed her bedroom door shut as he walked inside. This was a huge space, and yet the way that he filled it was almost overwhelming.

Made it so that she couldn't breathe.

How could she be so angry at him and yet also...?

The truth was, she had spent her life exposed to men. But most of them had been her family. And the ones that weren't, were people like the vile dictator her father had been intent on forcing her to marry.

She had never been left alone in any sort of capacity with a man like Ragnar.

A man who was as compelling as he was terrifying.

A man who really might be closer to beast than human.

He was so large. So broad.

All of the men in her family had olive skin, black hair—like her own—and fine features. The kind that could easily put them on the cover of fashion magazines—and several of her brothers had been featured on such magazines. Ragnar was completely different.

He was rough-hewn, as if he had been carved from stone. His blond hair shaved at the sides, longer on the top, pushed back off of his face. His blue eyes were fierce, and his full beard added to his feral look. He didn't wear suits. Even today, he had been dressed in war regalia. And now he was back in the same all-black sweater and pants she had seen him in before.

There was nothing practiced or artful about him. In fact, he was frighteningly authentic and honest. He made her want to hide.

Not because of his broad shoulders and well-muscled arms, but because she was quite certain that he could see through her.

In a way that no one else ever had.

Maybe in a way she had never even seen herself. Not even after three years in a convent pondering her life, her feelings, her motives.

When he looked at her now, he made her throat go dry.

"You could keep me in a dungeon," she said, steeling up all her courage as she moved closer to him. "I understand that. But I don't think you will. You're a very smart man, Ragnar. Everything that I've seen of you so far suggests that. And you know that I'm no use to you if I'm a prisoner. If I'm a prisoner, then you could have taken any woman."

"That isn't true. I have now earned the allegiance of your father."

"You could have more."

Those words landed between them, and something flared in the depths of his icy gaze. Her heart leaped, her stomach going tight. And all at once it didn't feel like they were discussing diplomacy. Not a ball, not relations with Cape Blanco. All at once, it felt like something darker. Something more personal.

Something she truly had no experience with at all.

"Could I?" he asked, tilting his head to the side.

She curled her fingers into fists, her nails digging into her palms. A strange thrill shot through her core, and she had to fight the urge to press her thighs together. She didn't want him to see her react. She didn't want to betray the strange feelings that were rioting through her system, not at least until she could get a grasp on what they were.

"Yes," she said, swallowing hard. "In that I know how to manage all of this. I understand how to do this part. I learned from watching my father. And even though I don't respect him, even though I think he's kind of a terrible person, he is very good at making connections. So good that he even cozied up with an evil dictator. And he'll cozy up to you as well. He has no real morals where that is concerned. I do, though. I just also know…"

He lifted an eyebrow. "How to manipulate people?"

"I don't like to call it that. But I suppose it is. But isn't that actually what diplomacy is? You tweak everything just right until the other party is happy. In this case, we want them to see what you are offering. And why you're making things different. You've had a few years now to settle in, and now you've got married. So it's time to show everyone who you are now. And exactly where this country's going."

"It is a bit of a bait and switch, considering that you're a temporary addition."

"So you're going to have to outshine me," she said.

He chuckled. "Some have said that my personality is lacking."

"You said that you wanted help with that. Well, I can."

He moved to her desk and leaned back against it, and there was something nearly obscene about it, though she couldn't say why. Something about the way he held himself, about those muscular thighs, and how large and battered his hands were, gripping the edge of that desk.

She felt something that she couldn't even define inside of her. Something that was like instinct, as old as time. Something that was part of her, even if she didn't know how to define it.

She was innocent of men. In that way. But right then she felt like she knew. Exactly what she wanted from him. Exactly what she could do to him. And what she would want him to do to her.

Her breath caught. "I'm going to help you," she said.

"That remains to be seen."

He pushed off from the desk, and moved away from her, out toward the room. "We can meet tomorrow at noon."

"I will send you a detailed plan ahead of time."

When he left and closed the door behind him, a breath exited her body on a gust.

Now all she had to do was think of a detailed plan. And not about the way that her hands were shaking.

CHAPTER SIX

It had been difficult to keep his hands off of her when he had been in her room. And the dark thoughts that had taken hold of him had almost made it more difficult, instead of easier.

Part of him wanted to push her. She wanted to use her body to manipulate him then...

Maybe he could show her.

Show her that if it became like that, he would have power over her too.

No.

He was not going to do that.

She was nothing more than another tool that he was using to bolster his country, and he would not allow her to become more than that. He got her itinerary, and didn't read it before he printed it off. But once he did read it, he found himself storming toward the study where she asked to meet him.

"Dancing?"

"People do love a dance," she said, standing up from the chair that she was sitting in. She was dressed in a white dress that fell just past her knees, the fabric diaphanous. Nearly see-through. It flowed when she moved, the bodice molded to her breasts. She looked like a virgin sacrifice. A goddess of old sent from Valhalla. The lust that gripped him was visceral. Beyond reason. It nearly blinded him.

And he felt his ancestors rising up inside of him. If he had a sword by his side he would've brandished it now and roared. Threatened to slay all enemies. Just for her.

"I don't," he said. "And I will not be doing it."

"I can dance with other men, but that will create conversation."

"If I don't dance, there doesn't need to be a dance."

"It's a party," she said. "There will be spectacular food, music and dancing. People enjoy it."

"It is opulence."

"People like opulence. And your people deserve a bit of opulence. Which is why I have suggested that a certain number of citizens should be invited to this."

"I'm not opposed." He was attempting to cool down the fire in his blood. "However, I am opposed to dancing."

"Why?"

He gritted his teeth. "I don't know how to do it."

"Is that all? I am an excellent dancer. Because of course I had to be, because I was being fashioned into a lovely, biddable puppet to best represent my country as the sort of feminine woman that my father wished me to be. I can teach you how to dance."

"Teach me?"

"Yes. Teach you. You wanted me to teach you things, and I can. But you don't get to be picky about what it is I teach you. How can you know what you don't know?"

"This is ridiculous."

She picked up a remote control and pointed it at the corner of the room, and music began to play.

"Don't be silly."

She crossed the space and draped her hand over his shoulder.

On instinct, he put his hand on her waist. And he regretted it instantly. His fingertips burned. The dress was as thin as he had thought it was. He looked closely, he could see the shape of her pert breasts beneath that thin fabric.

It had been his opinion that pursuing sex would be a distraction as he had been reestablishing his country. He saw now that it had been a mistake to deprive himself. Because he was on edge. On edge in a way he certainly wouldn't be if it had been more recently that he had satisfied himself. Surely then he would not be half so taken in by the feel of her beneath his palm.

"Come on," she said. "I'm going to lead, just for the moment. I'm sure that you'll pick it up."

And then she was counting, as she gripped his hand in hers and began to guide him along. Her steps were decisive, perfectly in rhythm. He could hear the rhythm. He could feel it. He was used to the hoofbeats of his horse, the pounding of his heart, establishing the tempo.

He could understand dancing in that sense. But he was distracted. Wholly and completely by the warmth of her body. By the shape of her.

The incendiary beauty when she looked into his eyes. All that green.

The song switched to something faster, and her steps picked up as well.

And soon, he had simply lost hold of himself. The

time, the place, and why he had objected to the dance in the first place. There was nothing but this. But her. But him. There was no world outside these walls and it made him feel like he was something different than he had been all these years.

Perhaps a man and not simply a king.

The music changed again, this time going slow.

He found himself tightening his hold on her, his hand on her waist moving lower as he brought her body in closer to his. Her breasts touched his chest and he felt a shiver move through her body.

She looked up at him, and her cheeks were pink, her eyes sparkling.

She wanted him.

That much was clear. She was responding to his nearness, his touch.

As if you aren't being taken in by her.

For this moment, it didn't matter. As long as he knew what was happening. This was a dancing lesson and he was enjoying having a woman in his arms again. There would be no broader implications. Nothing that reached beyond that.

It was just a moment.

And in the moment it was all that was real.

"You lead," she whispered.

And then she was no longer guiding the steps. He took over, patterning his movements after hers. They moved together, the seamless rhythm shocking him as they hit each step in sync. Another man would be tempted to make a metaphor from it, but he didn't believe in romanticizing things.

He didn't believe in romance at all.

But the heat being generated between them now wasn't romance. What it was, though, was impossible to deny.

They were spinning around the room; he moved as if he were on air, and she was in the clouds with him. Perhaps that was close to romance as he would ever get.

Then he backed her up against the bookcase on the wall, without realizing he had gotten so close.

She gasped, and his body brushed hers. They were still then, only an inch of space between their mouths. He could claim her like this. Make her his wife in truth rather than just in name. He could lower his head and claim her mouth now. Taste her. Consume her.

She wanted him.

She was... She was enticing him.

He let out a hard breath and pushed away from her.

"I think you've proven your point. You are certainly an excellent teacher."

"You're an excellent student," she said, her voice sounding scratchy.

She seemed undone enough that he had to wonder if it was as calculated as he had let himself believe for a moment.

But the truth was, it didn't matter what the truth was. The truth was, he was better off believing that she was a potential adversary, rather than simply believing she was a woman caught up in the moment as he was a man wrapped up in it as well.

"What else do we need to go over?"

"Probably manners."

She moved away from him. He had to hold back a growl.

"Are my manners lacking?"

"They could be a little bit more polished."

"Perhaps you simply don't understand my culture."

"I believe that you have a distinct culture here, don't mistake me. I just also believe that you personally have been out of society for enough time that you probably need a little bit of help. It isn't just about your culture now, it's about global relations anyway."

"I probably had excellent manners at one time. Pity that it's lost along with everything else."

She turned toward the bookcase and touched a blue spine, then looked at him. "You really don't remember anything?"

"No. Nothing."

He didn't feel inclined to elaborate. So he wouldn't.

"Did people have a lot of questions for you when you…when you appeared?"

"No," he said. "I've barely talked to anyone who isn't part of my…"

"Your personal military attaché?"

"That's one way of putting it."

"People will have questions for you. They're going to want to hear your story. Eventually, all of the people in your country are going to want to hear your story. And why wouldn't they? I was reading up on the history of your country. You're part of the history of this country. And people are going to want to know everything."

"They don't need to know everything."

"Well, maybe you can figure out something to tell them. About how you lived, about how you saved them. You're so difficult sometimes."

"I wasn't aware that entertainment was in the job description."

"But you know that it is. Because people want to feel like they know and understand their leaders. I'm sorry if it seems silly to you, but it is true. One of the reasons my father is able to get away with being so slimy behind the scenes is that he is so charismatic when he's on stage. He's a man who understands that he has an audience. And that the audience has to be played too. Understandably, your country has been in survival mode. And so things have been different for you. But somehow, all those years ago, your relatively happy, harmonious country was overthrown. And the horrendous dictator that led the charge was supported by your people at first. People blame their problems on the government. That's just the way it is. Even if the government didn't cause them. Their anger and their desperation allowed them to walk right into authoritarianism."

"Are you implying that charisma on my part might prevent that from happening again, or rather that a monosyllabic answer might send us tumbling back into the Dark Ages?"

"Yes. Yes, I am saying that. People want to feel a connection from you. I know that you care. I know that you lived, to spite everyone. Despite everything. That you survived for these people. They should know it too. They should understand how much you do care."

"Do you really think that people want to hear about the days and weeks and months that we spent camping out in the wilderness, trying to evade detection? Do you think they want to know that I lived as a farmhand? What kind of confidence will that instill in them?"

"Plenty. You are truly a man of the people. You fought for them. You have lived for them so strongly up until this point. And I think that you should talk about it. This is what you have me for. Whether you realize it or not. It isn't just about royal protocol. You need somebody to make you human."

"I don't want to be human. Humans are weak. They are weak and they are susceptible to cold, to fear and to hunger. Exhaustion and hopelessness. A symbol cannot experience any of those things. I would rather that they saw me as a warrior."

"Does it have less to do with how people want to see you and more to do with what you want? Because you don't want to feel those things anymore?"

"If you think that you can trick me into some sort of sharing moment, you will find yourself disappointed."

"If you don't want to share with me, then you don't have to."

"You sound like a kindergarten teacher."

"You're acting a little bit like a kindergartner."

Her gaze went steely. There was something about that challenge that ignited a flame inside of Ragnar. What he wanted to do was close the distance between them and push her up against the bookcase. He wanted to bring his mouth down on hers. She was being insolent. A brat.

One thing he could not recall was the last time a woman—anyone—had challenged him. Not outside of a life-or-death situation, at least. And so it created this bonfire of adrenaline inside of him that left him breathless and trembling with the intensity of it, yet also gave him no immediate relief.

Because what he truly wanted, he could not have.

"I will go to your ball. And I will dance with you," he said, moving toward her, his heart raging now. He felt dangerously close to being out of control, and that was not something he had experienced in a very long time. He didn't like how raw it made him feel. How precarious. How much it reminded him of…

Of something he didn't want to know about.

"But I will not be manipulated into sharing. I will not be manipulated—"

"And why are you so convinced that I am manipulative? What is it that makes you think I'm trying to trick you?"

"I don't know," he said. "Except that I have watched you. I have watched you play your father, and I am not convinced that you aren't playing me."

"And what makes you feel that you would be vulnerable to that?"

He growled and moved toward her, trapping her between his arms, pressed against the bookcase. He glared down at her. "I told you. I'm not sharing my feelings."

She smelled like the field that he had found her in. Like spring, fresh and new. Like the kind of tender hope he himself could not recall ever experiencing. She was devastating to him, and it made him want to beat his chest. It made him want to start a war.

It made him…

She reached up and touched his face, and he drew back. It broke the spell.

"Do not," he said.

"Ragnar," she said, her voice steady. "What are you afraid of?"

He laughed. "I'm not afraid of anything. Are you? But perhaps you should be."

"I'm not impressed by dark muttering. I'm not impressed by the way that you deflect constantly. You've turned it back around to me, when we were talking about you."

"I did not choose to talk about me. You did."

"Maybe I'm not thinking clearly. But it seems to me that there is something," she said gently, slowly. He didn't like it.

"There is nothing," he said.

And he felt like he needed to claim control of the situation. Felt like he had no choice. "The only thing it's bringing up, is this."

And then he closed the distance between them, and claimed her mouth with his.

CHAPTER SEVEN

She had pushed him into this. She couldn't lie to herself. She had wanted it. She couldn't lie to herself about that either.

But she wasn't prepared for it. He claimed her mouth like the conqueror he was.

It was an absolute undeniable conquest. His mouth was hot and firm, forceful. She parted her lips for him, and he claimed yet more ground. Sliding his tongue against hers. The guttural moan that rattled through him sending a sharp shock of pleasure down between her legs.

This was desire. All at once, she understood. She had so deliberately held herself back from it. And who wouldn't? When your whole life already belonged to a man you didn't want, why would you ever let yourself think about sex, about desire or about what being married would mean? She had deliberately shut that part of herself down. And now, here it was, awake, alive with the pleasure that he was creating in her body.

This was the kind of thing that she had feared for all of these years.

And here it was. It wasn't scary. It was glorious. The kiss was hot and slick and created a cascade of sensations that weren't confined only to her mouth. She could feel him everywhere. It was like a brand that heated her entire body. That scorched her from the inside out.

His hands were large, and he moved them down and grabbed hold of her hips as he continued to kiss her, deeper and harder.

Like everything else about him, there was nothing soft or tender.

But she would rather have that. The honesty of this moment. Free of…manipulation.

He was so very afraid of manipulation.

Just as that thought passed through her head, he pulled away from her. And she could breathe again. Except she didn't want oxygen; she wanted him.

And suddenly she was furious. That he had accused her of manipulating him. When he had all this power. All this experience. When she had been left with no choice but to use the cleverness at her disposal in order to turn the situation into anything other than captivity. Lifelong captivity for her.

Why was it wrong for her to try to get whatever she could out of this? Why was it wrong? It made no sense.

His worries were those of a man. Knowing that emotions that he hadn't cared for or honed could be used against him. That his baser appetites could be used against him. While her worries were those of a woman. Knowing that she could be physically forced into whatever a man deemed her lot in life. Whatever he decided.

Because he had been so angry. But as long as it had been his idea, he got to kiss her.

She pulled away as much as she could with the bookcase still at her back. "Who is using manipulation now?"

"That was not manipulation."

"Oh no. I forgot. Forcing your way is an asset. Trying to have some diplomacy is apparently duplicitous."

"I didn't say that."

"Here's a question I have for you. Why shouldn't I use what I have in my arsenal? Why should I lay down to be a conquest for you? In any capacity. I am a human being. And I have hopes and dreams. You can laugh at them all you want. You can say that I have no choices, but I want to see for myself, and I deserve that. I don't deserve to be passed around by men. As they decide what they think is right for my life. I deserve to decide what is right for my life. And if you find that selfish while you remain in total control of everything, then perhaps you need to ask yourself why you don't think a woman deserves the same rights that you do."

She slipped away from him, and he grabbed her arm. "It has nothing to do with you being a woman. And everything to do with the fact that you were what I needed to accomplish my goal."

"Even better. It isn't personal. So it isn't women that don't matter to you. It's everyone."

"I have sacrificed my whole life to liberate my people. I care for the greater good. Not for the individual."

"I don't think you care for anyone or anything. I think you're driven. Driven to win. Driven to dominate. Everything. Including me. You thought you were going to a convent to pluck a helpless woman out of her life and force her into yours. You call manipulation me having a voice. Me pushing back. Only because I'm not what you expected. Only because you expect everyone and everything to fall in line for you. I will help you with your ball. I will do what I said. Beyond that… I will please myself."

She turned away from him, and she stormed out of the study, down the hall and toward her chambers. She was done. Done with all these men. With their designs on her life. She was not a chess piece. Why was it that when men could do something it was a strategy, while she was…manipulative?

She stormed into her room and shut the door behind her loudly. If he could hear, if everyone in the palace could hear, that was fine with her.

What was the point of being a queen if she had to keep her voice down, had to close the door quietly? What was the point of being a queen if she still had no control over anything?

This life…

This was her life for the next two years. Dealing with this man.

She was trembling still. From the kiss.

He was…

Outrageous.

Yes. He was outrageous.

He had given her her first kiss. And it was still echoing inside of her.

Need was warring with anger. And she found that even more outrageous.

How could she want him when he made her so angry? How could she want him when she also wanted to strangle him?

Two years of this. At minimum. That was depending on whether or not he found that things were secure enough by that time.

He had all the control. That bastard. No. She had some control. He wouldn't be worried about manipulation if he didn't think that he could fall prey to it. Like she had said to him directly.

She definitely had power over him. He wanted her.

That was a part of herself that she had ignored. And certainly not something she had ever sought to use as a weapon.

She still didn't want to use it solely as a weapon.

But...

Two years.

She wanted it to mean something. She wanted to count for something. She was learning things. About herself. She was learning by planning this and...

She was innocent. Physically. Maybe there was something that she could learn here about that. About men.

She had been promised to marry a man twice her age. More than twice her age. And then Ragnar had stolen her, and his initial intent had been to make her his wife in truth.

Men had played games with her, and with her sexuality for her entire life.

The idea of having the choice for how she would express it, when she might claim it, made her feel powerful.

Maybe it shouldn't. No, she knew that it shouldn't. Because it should be something that was innate. Something she expected. It never had been.

She had never been able to count on such a luxury.

So maybe now she would. Maybe now, she would take what she wanted.

She could seduce him.

It didn't matter that she didn't have any experience. She had gotten a glimpse of her own power in that library. Had truly tasted it as she had tasted the desire on his tongue.

More to the point, she wanted him. Whether she liked him or not.

Even as the thought filtered through her mind, she let out a long, slow breath.

She did like him. Unfortunately. If she didn't like him, then him calling her manipulative wouldn't have hurt her feelings.

But maybe it was a good thing he had called her that.

It had forced her to take a look at herself. At her whole life.

She didn't feel any guilt for what she had done to give herself just a little bit of agency.

She refused to.

He was just…

Traumatized.

She really didn't want to feel sympathy for him. But it was impossible not to.

He had been traumatized. Absolutely and completely. The little bit that he had told her…

But he couldn't remember anything. Not about his parents, not about his life here in the palace.

He couldn't remember anything.

It must haunt him.

Perhaps it wasn't as haunting as remembering. That did make her feel sympathy for him, even though she didn't especially want to.

He was human. It would be easy to let herself forget that. To tell herself that his humanity didn't matter in the face of all of the ways in which he was difficult. But the truth was, he wasn't entirely different from her.

He had experienced a life that was laid out before him; he had been taken as a child, and treated like an object. His life had not been of his own making.

Maybe she wasn't feeling benevolent; that was pushing it a little bit far. But maybe they could both have something nice in these two years.

Maybe if she asked he could do something for him.

Not just to set herself free. But to free him too.

And something about that made her feel powerful in ways she hadn't expected.

He had managed to avoid her other than the few times he had been pulled into her orbit during the planning of the event. She had asked him to consult on the menu. That had been interesting.

Truth be told, he hadn't expanded his palate much beyond meat and potatoes. And meat had been a luxury for many years. Not always guaranteed.

But she was asking him to try seafood and pastries, hors d'oeuvres and tiny cakes that looked like they would be at home in a bakery window.

In fact, looking at the tray had given him a visceral memory of walking by a bakery in a small town very soon after the coup.

He had pushed it aside, and hadn't allowed himself to make any connections between the past and the food in front of him.

But now it was the night before the ball, and he could no longer outrun her.

"There are three suits for you to choose from," she said.

"I had thought that I would wear a military uniform."

"I appreciate your commitment," she said. "But I think that in the spirit of the evening you should go with a suit."

As if this had been timed, a tailor came through the doors of the study, with a rack full of suits.

Well. She wanted to do this, so she could stay.

He took his shirt off, and turned to the rack of suits. "What is the difference between these?"

He looked back at Fern, who was staring, eyes wide.

"If you do not wish to be involved," he said.

"I'm going to be involved," she responded.

He undid the buckle on his belt, worked it through the loops, and then cast it onto the floor. Then he took his pants off, which left him standing there in his black undergarments. And he could sense her eyes on him.

He looked at her again; her face was bright red, but she wasn't backing down, and certainly wasn't making a move to leave.

Well. It turned out he was not above a little manipulation himself. Not that he was trying to get her to do anything. It was only that he was proving to himself that she wanted him. And that it wasn't simply a tactic on her part. The look on her face made it clear.

"There are three different styles," the tailor said. "A more traditional tuxedo, a suit and then a slightly more modern choice."

"Traditional," he said.

"That is shocking," Fern said.

"Is that a commentary on how predictable you find me, my queen?"

"Perhaps," she said. "But you should know that I'm

not shy about making commentary. I said exactly what I meant."

"Of this I am aware."

"I think you should do the suit," she said. "I think it will feel more natural to you. More black. Less cummerbund."

He lifted a brow. "I'm not even sure what cummerbund is."

The tailor took a strip of shiny fabric off the rack. "It's this."

"No," he said, the rejection easy.

"I thought I might have guessed correctly."

Which was how he found himself being dressed, and his wife watching all the while.

His wife. She wasn't truly his wife.

She was...a complication.

He had been turning over their conversation in the library for days now.

The way that she had spoken about him not liking to be manipulated... Who did?

She spoke to him as if he had some sort of hidden trauma—well, he did. He knew well that he did.

His brain protected him from whatever it was that had befallen him the day of the coup, and beyond that, it had protected him by not allowing him to remember the happier times of his family. Which would have only been painful. He could only miss the idea of them. But not them.

He didn't bemoan the missing memories.

But she made him wonder... No. There would be no wondering.

The suit was fitted expertly to his body, then removed

from him. And before he could dress again, the tailor left to see to his work, and left him, wearing nothing, standing there with Fern.

"Obviously, I couldn't act as if your body was a shock to me. We're meant to be married." She turned away from him.

"Is that why you were staring so intently?"

"No. I was staring intently because you have a nice body."

She looked over her shoulder. "You must know that's true."

"I've never thought about it one way or the other."

"Surely you must know that somehow your lovers respond to it."

"Are you interested in having a dialogue about my previous lovers?"

"Perhaps."

"Whatever game you're playing, I don't like it."

"Must everything be a game?"

"I fear that everything must be."

"And if it wasn't, I suppose then it would be very serious, and would therefore have much further reaching implications."

"Perhaps."

He put his pants back on, buckled the belt. She was still determinedly turned away.

"And what are you wearing to this event?"

"That's going to be a surprise."

"A surprise? Why?"

He wanted to know. And yet at the same time he didn't want her to know that it felt significant to him.

But he was allowing himself to imagine her in a glorious gown.

He hadn't seen her in anything like that since the wedding.

She had been...a vision.

Resplendent.

He had wanted her.

Utterly.

He still did.

This was the trouble with living with a woman. With her being his wife, even in a place the size of the palace. He couldn't truly escape her.

"I didn't know any of my previous lovers," he said. "It was always opportune moments. Towns that we would be passing through."

"Ah. I see. So casual sex is your thing."

"I wouldn't say that. I would say that much like I would try a different pub when we passed through towns, looking for whatever meal we might find, getting something to satisfy my hunger, I would treat sex the same way. It is an appetite, nothing more. There is no need to feel shame about it. There is no need to turn it into something more than it is."

"Spoken like a man."

"Why do you think that's masculine of me?"

"Because you have the physical power. Even with this life that you didn't choose, nobody sold your body away. By promising me to a stranger, my father promised my virginity to a man that I didn't want. By kidnapping me and intending to take me as your wife, you laid a claim on it too. But you don't think about being forced into bed, do you? So, of course, to you it feels simple.

Of course to you it feels like something that shouldn't carry weight, or shame. But for me, it can't be that way."

Her words were sobering in a way he hadn't anticipated. "But I have not forced you into anything," he said, the incendiary kiss burning between them.

"No," she said. "You haven't. But I didn't know that. Not when I ran from you. You think that my wanting choices is silly. You think that my having dreams is silly."

"You said this to me once before."

"And you didn't understand. I can understand why that feels shallow to you. Why can't you understand for me that it feels like everything?"

"I don't have practice trying to understand other people."

"Did you even have friends growing up?"

"No. I was a servant, for all intents and purposes."

She turned around and looked at him, her gaze landing at the center of his chest, and then quickly moving to his eyes. "A servant who was meant to be king?"

"It wasn't so bad as that. It was lonely. But then I had a lot of time to decide who I was going to be."

"Did you have a mentor? Somebody who...came alongside you and told you that you were the chosen one?"

"No. I decided to be the chosen one. I decided that nobody was going to fix the mess. And that it was my blood that made it my responsibility."

"You never thought about running away and leaving this place?"

"No. Because these are my people. I owe them my best attempt. Even if it isn't perfect."

He had never shared any of this with anyone before. It was strange. To talk about something so personal.

He had been a symbol of revolution. And he had found people who agreed with him. When he wanted them to fight alongside of him, and form a coalition to oust the government, he had no longer been lonely, but what they had spoken of was not personal. They had spoken of ideals. They had spoken of government. Of war. They had been prepared to die if need be. But then they had managed to get the military onto their side. And it hadn't been necessary.

They had taken everything down from the inside; by the time he had walked into the throne room, it had been reclaimed.

A bloodless revolution, even though he had been prepared for violence.

This woman… She challenged him. Danced with him. Got him to talk to her.

It was such a strange thing.

And he found that the more he spoke to her, the more he wanted to speak to her.

It was like one of those little cakes. He had tried one, and it only made him want another.

He was studied in self-denial. Much less so in the craving of things.

"And what about you? You grew up entirely in a palace. And yet you were not treated like royalty."

"No," she said. "I told you I have five brothers. And my father could only use me one way.

"My mother was just… I don't know why she married him. It was just because she had aspirations to be queen. If it was political, if her hand was forced the way that my father intended to force mine… I don't know, and I don't know that I ever will. Because I don't know how to talk to her. It's like she's withdrawn from her own life. All she cares about is fashion and manicures. I like those things too, but I also like to speak about other things. I judged her harshly for a very long time. But now I wonder if that's simply how she survives it. But I couldn't do it. I couldn't hollow myself out to be a vehicle for a man's plans."

"You were going to do what he wanted," he said.

"I didn't especially have a choice. You would think that I would've missed the opulence of the palace when I went to the convent. I think my father thought that I would. I think he found it somewhat amusing. Like it would be lowering for me to be sent there, like I would maybe learn a lesson, and be more grateful. But I wept in relief when he left me on the Isle of Skye."

Her eyes filled with tears even speaking of it.

"All I wanted was to be left to my own devices there. And I did find the divine. I did find a connection to myself that I didn't know I could have. I found thoughts that I'd never had before. And strength, much more strength. I thought a few times about running away when I was in the palace, but I really didn't know how to survive away from my family. Or what it would look like. But one of the reasons I ran from you so easily was that by then I knew what independence felt like. I didn't want to go back."

"You don't like being royalty?" Guilt lanced him. It was so unfamiliar he almost had a difficult time identifying it.

"No. I don't. I find it to be…" She stopped speaking.

"I don't actually know what it is to be royal. For me it has always meant existing to do the bidding of someone else. Not even for the good of my people. Maybe I would feel differently if I was the one in charge. But for me, it has meant living a life of gilded subjugation."

"Your father's foolish for not respecting your mind. I understand why you're angry at me, but I fear that you are clever and insightful."

"You fear it? *Well*." There was some satisfaction in that word.

"A brilliant mind is a fearsome thing."

"You were so angry at me that night."

"I'm not accustomed to..." He didn't even know what to call it. Whatever this was.

"Friendship?"

Friendship. He turned the idea over in his mind, and felt that it fit the situation uncomfortably.

And yet, it was possibly closer than many other things. He had shared things with her that he had otherwise never shared with anyone.

He felt compassion for her. Even sadness when she shared some of her life in Cape Blanco.

"Friendship," he said again.

"Yes. Or maybe we're moving toward something like it. Is that so absurd?"

"Not absurd," he said. "Just...unexpected."

"If you let me, if you stop resisting, it really would help you."

"I still don't wish to tell my life story to strangers in a ballroom."

"You don't have to. But it would perhaps be good to have an easy version of events that you can share."

"Ah yes. For my place in the history books."

"You don't care about that, do you?"

"No. All I wanted was to survive for this moment. For this task."

"And do you know what to do now that you have survived?"

The question was pointed. And he still didn't have a shirt on. He wanted to move closer to her, and put her hand right at the center of his chest, where her eyes kept dipping. But he supposed that wouldn't be the act of a friend.

Part of him rebelled against that word. He was a warrior, a conqueror, and he should behave in that way, not like this.

And yet her words, the revelations that she had given him about her life, the way she had been treated, the lack of choice, made him…

Care.

He was used to caring about causes, not about people.

But perhaps it was the next step. What came after survival.

Living, in some capacity.

"We would be having cake at the ball?"

Cake seemed easier than whatever was happening now.

"Yes," she said, scrunching her nose up. "There will be. I noticed that you liked it."

"Oh. That is… Thank you."

CHAPTER EIGHT

HE HAD THANKED HER. He had thanked her for the cake.

She had been thinking about that ever since, along with the vision of his body, covered only by those tight black boxer briefs that he'd been wearing.

She was extremely distracted. Even as she got her hair and makeup done, and was zipped into the gold gown that she had chosen for tonight.

She had been thinking about him far too much.

But it was okay, actually. Because she had made a decision about tonight.

Tonight was important. And she was going to sparkle, build connections and keep him on track for the whole of the celebration, and then she was going to seduce him.

Because she wanted him.

Because she felt they both deserved…

Were they friends?

It was the word that she had come up with when they had spoken.

She wasn't sure she'd ever had friends either. The nuns were the closest thing. And they had been tasked with taking care of her, and also had very little in common with her in some ways.

It had been a contemplative life. But sometimes it had been fun, and sometimes they'd had deep conversation.

Yes. In the three years that she had been there it had definitely been something like friendship.

So maybe this could be too. Maybe they didn't have to be at odds.

Maybe she could learn physical things from him, so that when she went out into the real world, none of it would be shocking. Perhaps it would be easier. She would know how to deal with men. How to be normal.

Preferable to going out into the world as a twenty-one-year-old virgin, she supposed.

She clung to the idea of a life opened up. Of a life where she made her own choices.

And in the meantime, where she could make her present situation all the more pleasant.

Where she could learn about herself.

She had done that thoughtfully, internally on the Isle of Skye.

Maybe it was time to do it physically.

Her makeup had been done expertly, in that way where it took quite a few products and skill to accomplish a natural look.

And her hair had been left curly and wild as she had come to prefer it.

She felt like herself. And that was interesting. To feel at home in her skin in this sort of dress, when that had never been true back in Cape Blanco.

The plan for them was that they would arrive thirty minutes after the guests. Wherein they would be presented to those in attendance. Fashionably late.

Her stomach fluttered. Not because of the entrance they were going to make soon, but because soon she was going to see Ragnar.

It was amazing what that did to her. How it made her feel. How in this short span of time he had gotten beneath her skin. He had found the power to affect her body.

The first time she had seen him, riding on that horse, the thunderous hoofbeats sending terror streaking through her, her reaction to him had been pure adrenaline.

But now? It was still adrenaline, she supposed. But it was something deep. Something more. Something nice.

It was…attraction. Need. This luxurious, wonderful feeling that she had been prepared to never, ever feel, in defiance of the life that her father had laid out for her.

As a way to maintain control.

And now she didn't want that. She didn't need it. Not in that way.

Feeling it was control of a kind. It was a type of power.

As if a door inside of herself had been opened up for the first time, as if she could suddenly feel everything. And it wasn't all contained inside of her. Wasn't a private, secret thing that she could never share with another person. She wanted to share it with him. To make him feel what she did.

Which was maybe a bit of a lofty goal for a woman who had until recently never kissed a man.

But she was hungry. Maybe some people would think that this was Stockholm syndrome. But she didn't think that she was very susceptible.

If so, she might have had different feelings about her father. She certainly didn't.

Time had never made her look more fondly upon him regarding the things he was trying to manipulate her into.

It had never made her warm to the idea of marrying a stranger.

Ragnar was different. Yes, he had taken her captive, but when she said what she wanted he listened. He might initially be dismissive. He didn't know how to deal with people.

He might sometimes be insulting, but he didn't have any friends.

It had nothing to do with respect for her, and she actually believed that now. Now that she had gotten to know him just a little bit better.

Now that you've seen him in his underwear and you've decided that he's so hot you don't want to keep your hands to yourself anymore?

Even if that was the case, she wasn't going to question it. It was an experience that she was hungry for.

She wanted to indulge her appetites. The way that she had seen him indulge himself with those hors d'oeuvres that she had prepared for the party tonight.

Neither of them had had very many nice things in their lives.

Even when he spoke about his past lovers he didn't make it sound fun. He made it sound ruthlessly efficient, like everything else he did. As matter-of-fact as eating a bowl of stew, which was not the way that she wanted to imagine sex.

Maybe she would find that she was the one who was wrong about the whole thing.

Maybe.

But her entire life had been marked by being both sheltered and unprotected. Sheltered from anything that she might want, from the kinds of normal mistakes and experiences that other people were able to have. While also being set up to marry a man who wouldn't treat her well. A man she didn't want.

Any protection that she had received had been about what her father wanted, and not actually about her.

So if she made a mistake now, if she slept with Ragnar, and got hurt, if it made things difficult when it was time for her to leave, that was a consequence that she was willing to accept. Because it was her consequence. Because it was her right to make those mistakes.

He wasn't pressuring her. It was her decision.

She felt his presence when he entered the room, and she turned sharply, just as he stepped fully through the doorway of the antechamber to the ballroom. That black suit that he had tried on the other day now fit his muscular body to perfection.

That broad chest, narrow waist and the thoroughly muscular thighs were still visible, his appearance only just on the correct side of civilized.

His blond hair was slicked back off of his forehead, shaved tightly at the sides. His beard expertly trimmed. His blue eyes were as arresting as they had been the first time she'd seen him. And it was interesting to feel the subtle shift in her response to him. Now when her heartbeat picked up it wasn't fight-or-flight.

It was desire.

She recognized that. Purely. Absolutely.

His eyes skimmed over her curves, and she felt that look like a brand. He was difficult to read. Nearly emotionless. But the heat in his blue gaze didn't lie. The intensity. Especially now that she recognized the difference inside of her, she could see it in his gaze.

It wasn't simply the triumph of a conqueror closing in on his conquest. It was desire. Just like her own. A mirror into the deepest parts of herself, all fathomless blue.

"You know the goddess Freya?"

She shook her head.

"No."

"She is the goddess of love, beauty. Sex. But also war and gold."

"That seems a strange combination of things."

"Not really. For what do we fight wars over except love, sex and gold?"

She had never thought about that before. Gold, yes. Greed. That was the biggest reason she could think of for war. But throughout time, and in small ways, every day she supposed people did wage battle for love and sex. Need, erotic need, was something she was currently fighting a battle inside of herself about.

"Freya rules Fólkvangr. A heavenly field where many soldiers who die in battle go."

"I thought that in Norse mythology they went to Valhalla?"

"Some do. But there is a different path. Some in my culture think that it's soldiers who are loved that go to Freya. Because she saves a space for their wives."

"Oh."

"You look like her. Freya."

She laughed. "That can't be. I'm hardly a Scandinavian beauty."

"Your lack of blond hair doesn't make you less a beauty. Freya herself is brave and bold. Clever. As a goddess must be. There is also sadness in her. I would say that you are definitely Freya. All that gold."

It was the most deeply beautiful thing anyone had ever said to her. And she felt seen in a way that she hadn't expected to be seen by him.

She would've said that they were different. Entirely. But they weren't.

They were two people who had been deeply isolated in different ways throughout their lives.

And the only time in his life when he'd had a family he couldn't even remember.

He was a warrior, yes, but he must've spent a significant amount of time in his own mind. Thinking. Making a declaration like that proved it to her.

"I didn't think you believed in the divine," she commented.

"I never have."

Then he reached his arm out and she took hold of it. He didn't say that he did now. Or that he was changing his way of thinking, and yet it felt like he had paid her a glorious compliment all the same.

Maybe this was just her shifting and twisting the moment to make it into something undeniable. So that when she kissed him after the ball tonight, she could justify it.

I don't have to justify anything.

No. She decided that she didn't. She decided that she

didn't have to have any reason other than the fact that she wanted it.

Because she was entitled to that.

After everything, surely she was entitled to that.

They walked through the double doors of the ballroom, and the scene below took Fern's breath away. The room was full, and decorated gloriously. There were fresh flowers strung across all the surfaces, bright pinks and purples that were set off beautifully by the black walls and gold trimmings.

The light, natural beauty was unexpected in the heavy, medieval surroundings.

And even more wonderfully, the room was filled with people. Some she recognized from events at the palace in Cape Blanco, and abroad. Others she suspected were citizens from this country.

And all heads turned to look at them as they walked out to the top step.

She curtsied, and Ragnar gave a deep bow as they were introduced.

"His Royal Highness, King Ragnar. And his queen, Fernanda."

She could forgive the use of her full name. Here it seemed right.

She was firm with Ragnar, and that was good enough.

The sense of warmth that radiated inside of her when she thought of that surprised her.

It surprised her that it mattered.

That there was something between the two of them that she didn't share with anyone else.

His hand felt warm on her arm as the two of them began to descend the stairs.

She looked at him; his face was stern. Unapproachable, even though she had a feeling he didn't mean to be. She smiled. Doing her best to look easy for the two of them.

Yes, she was doing her best.

Because she actually cared. This wasn't just about blending in. It wasn't just about being the perfect accessory. She was actually trying to help him. She believed in this.

She believed in him.

This country was beautiful. Though she hadn't seen as much of it as she would like to yet. She had fully been realizing how much she had in common with Ragnar, but she also had something in common with the people of this country.

They'd had their choices taken away from them. Their lives had been stolen from them. Their freedom had been stolen from them.

She felt a burning desire to change that. To bring back their sense of identity. To restore their dreams.

If she could do it by smiling now, then she would.

Ragnar bypassed several members of the ruling class and nobility from other countries, and she felt like she needed to offer an apologetic smile as they made their way past. But then she realized. He was moving toward his citizens. His people.

The woman that he approached looked startled, and then she began to bow.

He shook his head. "We will not stand on royal protocol," he said. "We are family. United in our desire to change things for this country. For the better." He stuck his hand out, and the woman took it. He shook it. His expression was grave, but it was real. Authentic. And she felt a surge of pride inside of her.

"I'm Fern," she said. Because she decided that she would give their people that name as well. They went around and introduced themselves to every single citizen of Asland, just like that. There were tears. At one point a woman hugged Fern.

They were so hungry for joy. For a sense that someone cared about them. About how they were doing, and about their futures. The futures of their children.

An older woman clasped Fern's hands in hers and looked up at her with shining eyes. "Queen Fernanda. When you have children it will be such a blessing."

A pang of guilt shot through her. Because she was planning to leave. She was forging these alliances, these relationships, and then she intended to leave. She had this idea of getting on with her life, and she was overwhelmed with the deep realization that this was their life.

They weren't just passing through. And she had to give this all the care that she would if she planned to stay forever.

Children.

If Ragnar had heard any of the exchange, nothing about his expression indicated it. She could see that his people appreciated his strength. That they responded to his demeanor. He seemed sincere because he wasn't putting on a show. Because he was sincere.

It made her chest feel sore.

She had this idea of the way things had to be, and it was based on the actions of someone she didn't even respect.

Ragnar had to be free to be the king that he was.

Still, she had been right to have this.

She did most of the talking when they interacted with diplomats and royals, while Ragnar ate an entire plate of small cakes.

It was perhaps the most delightful thing she had ever seen. Tiny, pastel cakes in his large hands.

He was enjoying them; she could see that, even if his expression remained stubbornly neutral throughout.

The band began to play, and the large dance floor was cleared. "We have to dance first," she said.

He nodded slowly, and then he held his hand out to her.

She curtsied, and then placed her hand in his. He wrapped his fingers around hers, completely engulfing them.

And then he pulled her out to the center of the floor, his arm tight around her waist, his other hand holding hers like she was anchoring him.

"You remember," she whispered.

Of course, when they had practiced dancing, things had not been so easy between them. And what she remembered wasn't just the dancing. His resistance. His angry kiss.

Her heart began to beat as he took the first step in time with the music. As she moved with him.

As he swept her over the dance floor and she kept imagining his mouth on hers, her back pressed against the bookcase. His hard, hot body right on hers.

His hands. Those large hands on her hips.

And she could see the memory reflected in his own gaze. In the blue depths, fire and ice and all that he was.

He was such a complicated man.

A puzzle to be solved. And maybe she would make that the mission of the next two years as well.

To untangle all of the aspects of him. To find the man beneath the warrior. The man beneath all of his pain.

She wondered about his missing memories. Would he ever get them back? Was it more of a blessing if he didn't?

She wondered about all of that while memories of the kiss echoed persistently in her brain.

While he held her close, in time to the music, beneath the keen gaze of their audience.

And finally, halfway through the song, they were joined by the rest of the attendees at the ball. Still, even surrounded by all those people, it felt like they might be the only two in the world.

A dangerous feeling. When they were here to serve. When they were here to be of use to the people of this country. To forge alliances. They weren't the only two people.

She had to remember that.

But tonight would be for the two of them. On that she had decided.

They danced through several songs, and then exhausted themselves making another circuit of the room. Until they had spoken to everyone. She could feel Ragnar losing strength. And it made her think again about his life. About all the things that he had done. And about how few of those things included these kinds of arduous social situations.

Of course it was exhausting. The man would probably rather be on a battlefield.

As soon as the clock struck midnight, it was their cue to leave. And they were officially excused as they had come in.

Once they were out in the antechamber, in the silence, away from everyone, she turned to him. "I don't wish to go back to my room tonight."

"You do not?"

"No. I intend to go back to yours."

CHAPTER NINE

Ragnar had not anticipated this.

He felt like his skull was about to implode. He had not spoken to so many people in all of his life, let alone in the compressed space of a few hours. And yet there was more. Touching her for hours had left him on edge. For a man who had spent so much of his life in relative silence. Isolated. In the woods, it was an overload to his senses. And what she was offering was a chance to take that energy at the center of his guts, and pour it all out.

He had been so en garde about her manipulating him. But she was a goddess. He had that realization when he had seen her tonight.

He did not often think of Freya. He had let go of the idea of deities so long ago.

And yet he could remember a story. Whispered to him before he fell asleep at night.

He couldn't remember who had told him. His mother, a nanny? But when Fern had come in wearing that gold gown, he had thought of Freya.

That soft voice inside of him whispering about the promise of Freya's afterlife.

It is one thing to die in battle. It is another to die for those you love. And any soldier who goes to battle with love in his heart is dying for that love. Freya weeps for her husband. Because she separated from him. She understands the pain of love being lost. And that is why her field is reserved for those who wish to meet again with their heart's desire after death.

Such a strange thing. The memory had been so strong. It was still.

And it made him want to draw closer to Fern.

It certainly made him feel as if he didn't want to resist.

No. He had no desire to resist.

He also couldn't wait. He wrapped his arm around her waist and pressed her body up to his.

It was familiar now. And yet gloriously undiscovered.

He lowered his head and kissed her. The taste of her mouth better than the cake. And he had decided he very much liked cake.

He kissed her. Deep and hard, and with a ferocity he had never before given to a lover. Because he had never felt such an intense, specific need before. It had to be her. It had to be.

He held her face as he kissed her. As he tasted her, his tongue sliding against hers.

And then when they parted, she looked up at him, those green eyes clear. "Yes. Take me to bed."

"I have questions for you first," he said, a strange sensation gripping his stomach. Concern. For her. He no longer felt that he was in danger of being manipulated by her. Because this was not manipulation. It was far too honest. But he required things to also be clear.

"Yes?" She looked uncertain.

"Why is it that you've decided you want me?"

"I don't know that I decided that I wanted you. I simply do."

"You know that I'm not staking a claim on your body by keeping you here as my wife. You are not obligated to give yourself to me."

"I know that."

"You have told me that no one in your life has ever cared for your choices. You told me that you felt like all these men made a claim on your sexuality, me included. I didn't even think of it that way. I…"

She touched his face. "I believe you. I know that you were practically raised by wolves. And I know that… I wasn't a person to you. I was an ideal. A goal. And I would be more offended by that except I also understand that you even see yourself as a person. As a man. You see yourself as a symbol of revolution. As a king, but not as a man."

"True," he said, the words rising rough in his throat. "All true."

"But I see you as a man. And I want for you to feel like a man tonight. I want you to let go of everything. Of your idea of duty, and honor. Take what you want. And I'll take what I want."

"I don't understand."

"There is nothing to understand. I spent the last three years in a convent, and even I know that."

"Sex isn't confusing. Need isn't confusing. It's simply an appetite."

"This isn't an appetite. There's something between us. Even when you were furious at me in the library, you wanted me. Even when I was running from you, when you brought me up on the back of that horse, I felt…

your heat. Part of me wanted to lean into your strength, rather than run away from it—I can't explain it. But we have this time. This marriage. Why can't we enjoy it?"

"You want me," he said. Because everything else she was saying was difficult to hold onto. In his lust-addled brain it was moving through too quickly.

"Yes, Ragnar. I want you. Not because you kidnapped me, and not because we got married. If I had seen you across a crowded ballroom, if you had always been the king of this country, if you had been in the life you should've had, and I had been in mine, I would've wanted you."

She wanted him. She was choosing him. Of all the limited choices that Fern had been able to make in her life, he now counted as one of them. There had been spare few pleasures in his life that he could remember. Only small moments of joy.

But this stood out as one of the greatest. One of the most profound. It was nothing like the potential for satisfying an appetite. It was something deeper. Something that reached through the garden walls around his heart and touched him.

Touched his soul.

He hadn't even thought it was possible. He wasn't even sure that he retained a soul. In much the same way he had lost his faith in anything divine.

But then, he kissed her. And it was like looking into the heavens. An experience beyond anything he had ever had before. She was a virgin.

And yet he might as well have been.

He had always looked at sex as something divorced of any emotional connection. He had honed his skills, because he did not believe in using a person for pleasure without giving it in return. But it was only his body involved. While now everything felt locked in. Everything felt engaged.

And then every pass of her lips over his, of his tongue against hers, felt like something new.

He lifted her up, sweeping her into his arms, the way that he had done on the Isle of Skye when he had plucked her off the ground. Only this time, he did not put her on the back of his horse. This time, he held her against his chest as he carried her down the long corridor, and to the spiral staircase that led to his chambers.

The room was sparse, and he still was not in the habit of sleeping on the bed. When he opened the door, his bedroll was still on the floor beside the large canopy bed, and his eyes went to it, even though he wished she wouldn't notice.

"What is that?"

"I'm not accustomed to sleeping in a bed. I spent most of my life sleeping on the floor. And then on the ground outside."

"Oh but that's…"

"It's all right. I have been saving this bed. I needed a reason to use it. And you have given me that."

She smiled, and it was like something had been lit up inside of him. "That was almost funny."

"I feel almost amused."

With her lips still curved into a smile she wrapped her arms around his neck and kissed him again. He growled, laying her down in the center of the bed. The mattress was soft. And so was she. He looked down at her, at all that glorious gold over her beautiful body. He touched her face, and for a moment, he could only stare in reverence at all of her beauty.

She truly was glorious.

Not a conquest. Even better than that, she was giving herself to him. Joyfully.

She had chosen him.

That reality echoed inside of him, stronger than any heartbeat. Stronger than anything.

If this was joy, then he could understand why people threw away their duty, their honor, their everything to pursue it.

He himself was unfamiliar with the feeling. He had felt something like it when they had finally managed to reclaim the country, but even then it had not been pure joy. Because on the other side of the victory lay a long road ahead.

While this was all about the moment. Not a race to the finish line, not the beginning of the next step. He intended to take his time with her. To devour her. To luxuriate in this.

"What do you know about sex?" he asked.

"I have not spent these past years in the woods like you. I think I know quite a bit about it."

"Yes? You think?"

"I'm not ignorant."

"You were in a convent."

"Not because of any great pious thoughts on my part. I was in a convent because I was being hidden away. But I wasn't reading the catechism."

"Were you reading manuals about sex?"

"No. In fact, I deliberately didn't think about it. It's

why it took me some time to realize that I was attracted to you."

"Is that so?"

"Well. That and you being my kidnapper."

He chuckled. "I can see how that might be a barrier."

"I told you. I felt like I had been given away. It made it so that my fantasies weren't even mine. Because if I thought too much about sex, if I thought too much about any of that, then I would have to think about it with…him."

"And of course you didn't want that."

"No. Of course I didn't. So yes, I know about it. I know plenty, but I wouldn't say that I'm…"

"I'll teach you."

He lowered his head and kissed her neck and she arched beneath him, grasping his shoulders.

He growled, and she gasped. He raised his head and looked at her. "Did I frighten you?"

She shook her head. "No. I… I like it."

"I am not a civilized man. Perhaps if you had chosen differently, you would not get a man who growls."

"If he doesn't growl then I don't want him."

Then she kissed him, and he kissed her back, luxuriating in the feel of her soft mouth on his.

Then, the warrior in her came out. He could feel her nerves leaving her body, could feel all the resolute determination within her as she kissed him, his face, his neck.

As if she was the one mounting a seduction.

"Let me," he said.

Even though he knew that she wouldn't. Because she had to fight him; it was what made her feel alive. He knew that much.

One warrior recognized another.

He pulled away from her, stripped off his jacket and then unbuttoned his shirt. Then he cast both onto the floor, before getting off the bed momentarily to take off the rest of his clothes. Her eyes went around, her focus going immediately to his cock.

She bit her lip, her reaction much more so one of interest than of nerves.

She rose up on her knees, her dress pooled around her like a golden puddle, her hair falling forward. Divine. Pagan. All at once.

She leaned in, and pressed a kiss to his hip.

A short grunt rose up in the back of his throat.

"I told you—"

"And I told you that this was my choice. So let me have what I want."

She leaned in, sliding her tongue along the length of his arousal. And then she parted her lips, taking him in, a feminine gasp escaping her lips as she released him a moment later. And then she went back, teasing him, tormenting him, lavishing him with attention.

He gripped her hair, watching as her mouth slid up and down on his rod, watching as she took her pleasure by giving him pleasure.

She made whimpering sounds, sweet, tormented noises that told him she was delighting in this as much as he was.

"Good girl," he growled.

Her cheeks went pink as she continued to suck him, and he felt himself reaching the end of his composure. The end of his control.

"Enough, my Freya. Or I will deny you the loss of your virginity by losing myself."

Her lips curved into a smile, those wicked lips, swollen now with need. "So you liked it?"

"If I liked it any more, then this would be over."

"I've never done it before."

"I assumed. But not because it wasn't good. Only because… You are mine, aren't you? Entirely? You have never kissed another man, never touched another man. You've never even wanted one, have you?"

It was suddenly imperative that he know that. That he be absolutely certain that her need was for him, and for him alone.

"Yes," she whispered. "You are the only one."

"Good."

Everything in life that had once been his had been taken from him. In some way, it healed him to know that she had come to him, and she was his. It was that simple.

And in two years if she went her own way, and went to another man, he would still have been her first.

And right now, she was his. It was all that mattered.

She reached behind her back, as if she were reaching for the zipper of her dress. "No," he growled. "That's my task to complete."

He lifted her up, and repositioned her so that she was sitting on the edge of the bed. Then he gripped one of the straps of her dress and pushed it down, so that it fell, loosening her bodice. He did the same to the other side. The diaphanous fabric was still covering her breasts, but had exposed more of her ample cleavage.

He left her just like that, her hair a wild tangle, the image she made that of a feral, gorgeous creature.

Then he got down on his knees, and pushed up the hem of that skirt, exposing her slim ankles, her calves. Pushing the skirt up until he could see her thighs, until he saw the sheer panties that she had on beneath the dress. He could see the shadow of dark curls beneath the diaphanous fabric, and his body throbbed in anticipation of having her.

But no. He would not claim her like that. He would not sink himself into her without preamble no matter how badly he wanted it. He had to bring her to pleasure first. He had to give her everything. And then some.

He hooked his fingers into the sides of her underwear, and pulled them down her legs, opening her thighs so that he could see her glistening folds.

She was art, this woman. And he would worship at her altar, above any other.

How could such pagan beauty exist? Someone so strong, resilient, regal and yet hewn from the earth.

He would never have thought that a princess would appeal to him like this. He would've thought that he was the kind of man so lost to the civilized world that he could not want a woman like her, and yet. It was as though she had been brought forth from the forest just for him.

He leaned in, inhaling the scent of her arousal before he pressed a kiss to her inner thigh.

She gasped, and he pressed forward, licking her right where she was wet and needy for him.

She gasped, her hands going around his hair as he began to devour her.

How long had it been since he had tasted a woman? It didn't even matter what the answer was. Because no woman had ever been her. No woman had ever appealed to him in this way.

No one had ever reached the heart of him. But she did.

Like she had reached up into the sky and brought the stars down among them. Like she had made magic between them with nothing more than the wave of her hand.

He kissed her there. Teased her, tormented her, and then he pushed a finger deep inside of her tight passage, stretching her, trying to prepare her for what came next. But what came next didn't matter. What mattered the most was what was happening now. What mattered the most was him giving her all the pleasure that she could ever receive.

He pressed a second finger inside of her, and she moved her hands to his shoulders, her fingernails digging into his skin.

He sucked her clit deep into his mouth, as he continued to thrust his fingers within her, and she gasped his name, tightening her thighs on either side of his face as she came explosively against his mouth.

He kept going. Because there was no reason for him to stop. Because there was no reason she couldn't have more.

Because she had been given so little in her life, because people had shown so little care for her feelings. For what she wanted, and him among them. He owed her penance. He owed her pleasure.

And he would forfeit his own desires for this, any moment.

Every day.

Her back arched up off the bed again, a second orgasm tearing through her as she curled her hands around the bedspread.

"Yes," he growled, lifting his head and kissing her thigh again.

"Beautiful."

He looked up at her, and she touched his face, her eyes gone dark, like the deepest part of the forest.

"Ragnar..."

"You are mine," he said. "This body is mine. But only to do as it pleases you. That is my calling. It is my right. To claim you, but in the way that makes you scream my name."

She was trembling when he stood, his body so hard it hurt now, and reached around to undo the zipper on her dress. She reached out and gripped his shaft, squeezing as he let her dress fall around her waist, exposing her breasts.

They were beautiful. So much lovelier than he had even imagined they might be.

"They would've written songs about you," he said. "Back in the conquering days."

"Would they have also stolen me from my home and brought me to a strange land?"

"That is what I did. I can hardly expect the barbarians of old to behave any differently."

"But the song is supposed to be the consolation?"

"The song is attribute. An offering. To a goddess."

"Oh."

He reached out and took her hand, had her stand, and her dress fell to the floor. She was completely naked in front of him, wearing nothing but her gold shoes now. He knelt down, and began to undo the buckles.

She watched intently as he did. "Because two things can be true," he said. "I can claim you, but you can claim me. I might be the king. But I will be on my knees before you."

"And will you take me?"

"Yes." He stood, and wrapped his arm around her, brought her up against his body so that they were pressed together, totally naked, holding onto each other. And he kissed her just like that, luxuriating in the feel of it. The decadence of being there, being naked, and having time.

To kiss her all over. To take her as he wished.

As she wished.

"No, my lady," he said, picking her up and wrapping her legs around his waist and then climbing onto the bed, laying her on her back at the center of the mattress. "I will have you."

He put his hand between her thighs, pushed two fingers in her again as he felt how wet and ready she was.

Then he kissed her mouth, her neck, lowered his head to take one nipple into his mouth and sucked hard.

She arched up off the mattress and then he positioned himself at the entrance of her body, and thrust deep inside of her in one smooth stroke.

"Ragnar," she cried, her internal muscles pulsing, tightening around him. She did not seem to be in pain. Rather she seemed to be having the aftershocks of another release. He began to move, not allowing that trembling to subside as he staked his claim over and over again.

Her wet heat drove him to the edge. Made him feel more beast than man, but for a better reason than ever before. Not because he was being stripped of every comfort, every bit of humanity, but because he was acting only on instinct. Only on need.

He could feel her getting close. Another orgasm building within her. And his own was about to steal every last bit of his control. He put his hand between them, brushing his thumb over her clit as he continued to thrust inside of her.

A short cry escaped her mouth, and he drove himself into her quickly, chasing his own satisfaction. And when it hit, with all the force of a pack of wolves, gripped him around his throat and left him gasping for air, he cried out her name: "Fern."

His Fern.

"Mine," he growled, resting his forehead against hers.

They held each other for a long moment after.

Then he moved away from her, and tucked her against his side. He pushed her hair away from her face. He had never done this before.

Never held a woman in the aftermath of pleasure.

"Why is there sadness in Freya?"

Her voice was soft, in the silence of the room.

"She's sad because her husband left her. He's roaming the earth, and she's waiting for him back home. But he isn't there."

"My husband is here," she said, putting her hand over his.

He felt as if he had been stabbed, clean through the chest.

The sweetness, the softness of her words nearly unmanning him.

"Yes," he said. "I am. I will never leave this place."

In truth, in the future, he would be more like Freya.

Tasked with guarding a particular place, and unable to follow her as she went on to make her choices. To live her life.

But she could be unburdened of all of this. She could be free.

And he would rejoice for her.

He hadn't cared at first. Not at all. He hadn't seen her as a person, just as she had said. She had been an ideal. A symbol. Something that he had thought might be useful.

But not a person.

She had in this short space of time become the person that he knew best. She had become someone who mattered. And he couldn't remember the last time a person had mattered to him. An idea, yes. People as a group, yes. But not a person. One that he wanted to know. To touch, to kiss, to keep with him.

"I guess I'll always know where to find you," she whispered. Then she leaned in and kissed his hand.

"Yes," he said. "You will."

CHAPTER TEN

Fern woke in the early hours of the morning, and it took her some time to remember what had happened the night before. She had slept with Ragnar.

That was when she became aware of her body. Of her surroundings. She ached in interesting places. And she was lying in a bed different than her own. But she was alone.

She frowned, she looked around and then sat up. Then she peered down over the edge of the mattress and saw that he was there. On the floor, on that awful bedroll.

Her chest tightened.

It wasn't as simple for him as leaving that life behind. It had left an indelible mark on him. He couldn't even fully enjoy comfortable things.

She wanted to tear down the walls of the castle, to unmake the world and remake it for him. If only she were a goddess. If only she had that kind of power. If only things were different.

She had said to him that if she had seen him at a ball, and she had been free to approach him, and he had been free to approach her, then they would've ended up together. They would have too.

But they didn't have the option of finding each other

in that ideal space. They didn't have the option for being those people. They were Ragnar and Fern. And they were shaped by the things that had happened to them. Deeply. In ways that were not quite so simple to fix.

If they were, this man wouldn't be sleeping on the floor when he lived in a whole palace.

She couldn't make that pain go away for him. But she could join him where he was.

She climbed out of bed, and lowered herself down onto the floor, taking the blanket with her as she lay alongside of him, only able to claim just a small sliver of the bedroll. He startled, sitting up like he was ready for battle. And then he looked down at her.

"What are you doing?"

"I wasn't going to leave you down here to sleep by yourself."

"You don't need to sleep on the floor with me."

"Then why are you sleeping on the floor?"

"It is none of your concern."

"It is my concern, though. You are my concern."

"And why is that? Because you're going to leave this place. You're going to leave me."

That life, the one that she had envisioned for herself after this, felt different now. It didn't seem as clear. It didn't seem as sharp.

"But two years are not nothing," she said. "Think of the three years you've been back here. Think of all that has changed. Think of all the more that will be changed by the time our agreement comes to an end. Maybe you'll be sleeping in a bed."

He sat up. "Maybe."

She sat up with him, grabbing hold of his bicep. He

had gotten dressed, which she didn't like. "I'm all into this. For the time that we have."

"You do not have to sleep on the floor."

"You could sleep in the bed."

"I don't like to sleep too deeply. In case something happens."

Her heart hurt. "Were you potentially under attack when you were waiting to take the country back?"

"No. Earlier. That was when things were truly dangerous."

"You talked about it before. It was your nanny that helped you escape?"

"That's my understanding. Because I don't remember. But I was told later by the family that cared for me."

"Your nanny didn't continue to take care of you?"

"No. She was afraid that she would be too easy to track down. She left me with some distant relatives."

"And they knew that you were the heir to the throne but they treated you like a servant?"

"They always told me it was for my own good. As I said, my identity was never hidden from me. And I knew. I knew my name. I knew that I was the king. With both of my parents dead, I knew. But it meant nothing to me. So it seemed perfectly reasonable that they had me sleep in the barn. I used to guard the animals."

"Oh God, you've been without a bed for all this time?"

"Yes. It became something of a habit."

He sounded completely remote. Emotionless.

"Doesn't it make you angry? Shouldn't someone have taken you and treated you like family?"

He shook his head. "I already told you. Family doesn't mean anything to me because I don't remember mine.

How can I miss what I don't understand? And it was what I needed to make change. I left that situation when I was fifteen. I got work washing dishes in a restaurant. That was when I first heard rumblings of desires for revolution. Those people didn't know who I was, but I paid attention to every word. Gradually, I realized that the national mood was for a change in leadership. And I realized that I was the person who could bring about change. But I had to. Because a new leader would have to prove himself. It wouldn't be so simple as taking things over. But for me it would be."

"It took you seventeen years from that point?"

"Yes. Because you can't go around announcing that you are the long-lost heir."

"I don't suppose you can."

"No. You have to be very careful about who you talk to. About who you reveal your plans to. I started with the other man I washed dishes with. Soren."

"And he's your right-hand man now."

"Yes. We began to build an army. Using a whisper network. We were like Robin Hood's band of thieves. Or like Vikings of old. We had a few bases of operation. One deep in the woods, which you have no doubt picked up on. And another in the city. In the capital. Very close to the palace. That was how we began to infiltrate the military. And all during that time I educated myself. On government, on the economy. On leadership. I read about the way that my father ran the country. And I tried to figure out the mistakes that I thought he had made. How he had gone wrong. Because something must've been wrong, or those people would not have happily supported a coup." He lowered his head slightly. "Even then I could not remember him. He was words on the page to me, nothing more."

She nodded slowly. "So most of your life you've devoted to this."

"Yes. It was much better than being a servant boy with no family and no future."

"Still. It sounds like a very hard existence."

"The only kind of existence available to anyone in Asland for the last twenty-five years has been a hard existence. Mine is not unique. That's why when I meet my people I tell them not to give me deference of any kind. I'm not unique. We have all suffered. And we must all move forward together."

"But can you heal?"

Her heart was pounding heavily, painfully.

"I've never thought about it."

"Can you sleep in a bed. Can you enjoy cake? Can you let yourself rest? Sleep? You're in a castle surrounded by guards."

"This is the same palace that my parents were killed in, Fern. I can no more sleep deeply here than I can anywhere."

The horror of that truth washed over her. Of course he didn't feel safe here. It had proven to be unsafe. It was the same palace where his family had been killed, but it was also the same palace he had reclaimed all those years later. He knew every weakness. He had exploited those weaknesses. And he had been the victim of those weaknesses. Why would he ever feel safe?

She hated it. That life had been so appalling to him.

"It is so important to you," he said softly. "To try to make everything okay. You wish to erase the bad things in your own life as well—that is what you see ahead of you when you think about a life filled with choices, is it not?"

"I guess so."

"But they have happened. These bad things. We cannot make ourselves unchanged by them."

It was so like what she had been thinking when she had first seen him down there on the floor. That it didn't matter if they would have found each other without all the trauma. Because the trauma was real. Because it had shaped them into who they were.

But it was just hard to accept that they might need it. She was sure that wasn't true. Nobody deserved to be treated the way that he had. And she felt certain that she didn't deserve what had happened to her—even though in the end she had been safe.

"You're a warrior," he said.

"Excuse me?"

"You are like me, Fernanda. You are a warrior. A great strategist. I've seen it."

"You said that I was manipulative."

"I take it back. Because I see you differently now. You had to be strong and smart, you had to learn how to operate in a way that keeps you safe, but also advances your cause. You are a warrior like me. A true warrior does not fear battle scars. A warrior understands that it is part of battle."

"I never wanted to be in battle."

"It doesn't matter sometimes. In fact, it doesn't matter most of the time. We are not asked what life we would like to live. We are given this life. We are given our fate. But we have to decide what to do with it. But we do not run from it."

"And where do we start making choices?"

"We are making them. Now. Do you think you really have not been making choices all this time? You have been. The way that you learned to be, and the way that you acted, that was a choice. What you did with your time at the convent, that was a choice. The way that you used all that you had learned from your father to get me to grant you your eventual freedom. That was a choice. What we did last night. And what we are doing now."

She looked down at her hands.

"We are stronger for what we've been through. Stronger for the battles that we have fought. Don't you see?"

She took a shuddering breath. "Yes."

"Now. Today, I think we should go out into the country."

"The country?"

"Not just the country. Our country. I wish to speak to the people."

"Okay. Then that's what we'll do."

And as she got herself ready, she could only think about what he had said. When they were in the car that was carrying them toward the town square, she was still pondering it.

"Yes?"

"Nothing. I'm just thinking." She looked out the window, at the view of the city. People going to work. Smiling. Laughing. All of those people had a particular set of circumstances that they were given. Fair and unfair.

And they were making what they could of those circumstances. In that sense, she could understand what he had been saying to her all this time. About choice being an illusion. No one had infinite choices. They had the circumstances they were given. People that they were responsible for.

Just as he was. Responsible for this entire country.

"You were thinking very loudly."

"I'm not trying to."

"You might as well tell me."

"It's silly. And in fact, I imagine that you think I'm a silly girl entirely. You're right. What I wanted was to be normal. Or whatever I thought of as normal. I wanted to be able to leave my father's house, and become somebody that I wasn't raised to be. Become somebody who hadn't lived the first eighteen years of her life cloistered in a palace, promised to marry a man that she didn't care about. Someone who hadn't been treated like she didn't matter, even while she was surrounded by luxury. I wanted to live like I had sprung fully formed from the convent, and go on my merry way. But I can't be separate from those experiences. I can't be someone who didn't have them. And you're also right, that I can't make…any choice that I want. I have a shared responsibility with you now. For these people."

"I do not think you're silly," he said. "Most people want to be happy."

"You don't?"

"It's not something I've ever considered. Whether or not I was happy."

"That makes me even sillier. You realize that, right? I have been thinking to myself that we actually have quite a bit in common. That we both spent so much of our lives lonely, but I never had to worry about my survival. When I saw you sleeping on the floor like that, I realized…you never feel safe, do you?"

"That isn't true. I am entirely able to defend myself, and that makes me feel safe. But no, sleeping deeply doesn't entirely appeal to me."

Their conversation was ended because their car parked against the curb at the town square, and they got out. "Is this what we're doing? We're just…"

Their security detail was with them. Soren first and foremost. And now she knew and understood that he was Ragnar's lifelong, trusted friend. Even if he wouldn't call him a friend. That was a very male thing. Quite literally spent seventeen years in the company of someone, and waged a literal war with him, but still not quite think of him as a friend.

"Let us speak to our people."

It didn't take long for them to be lost in a crowd. A crush of people that were excited to meet them. There were photos being taken, flashes on cameras and cell phones being shoved in their faces. Through it all, Ragnar remained completely calm.

Fern clung to him like she was afraid she was going to lose her grip, and be separated from him. The idea of being separated from him frightened her.

But he held her tightly, and while people did get close to them, they never made physical contact, because Ragnar's demeanor discouraged them from getting too close.

There was a benefit to having a husband who looked like a Viking warrior of old.

They finished with the crowd of people there at the city center, and then got back in their car, and began to drive toward a nearby village. She hadn't seen this much of the country yet.

The buildings were an interesting mix of clean, modern lines, and old structures. There were black churches, standing stark against the countryside.

"There are so many trees here," she commented. "Iceland doesn't have trees."

"Yes. The legend is that the Vikings cut down all the trees in Iceland and they never grew again. Personally, I don't believe that. They are a renewable resource after all."

"And what do you think it is?"

"Giants? Trolls?"

"I didn't think that you believed in the divine."

"I don't. However, that does not mean that I don't believe in trolls and giants."

She blinked. "It doesn't?"

"Of course not. Anyone descended from Norsemen believes in trolls and giants. You are foolish not to."

"I didn't realize."

There was never as big of a crowd as the first one they drew in the capital city, but people were friendly, and greeted them with enthusiasm everywhere they went. They stopped in a pub, where they had fish and chips and cider. She had never done anything like this. She had never walked around in and among people. She had either been cloistered in a palace, or cloistered in a convent.

Maybe this was what her life would be like when she went to make her own way. Maybe she would live in a village, and she would simply talk to people.

Except of course they would all know who she was. Well, maybe not all. Just because they were well-known in this part of Europe didn't mean they would be well-known everywhere.

"We have been invited to stay in one of the oldest hotels in the country," he said.

"We have?"

"Yes," he said. He gestured toward the end of the street. "That large stone building there. It was once a place where royalty stayed. And I suppose it can be again."

"I would like that."

And they would of course get the same room, and it would be...

Just thinking about it made her warm.

When they arrived at the room, she took her phone out, and began to look at headlines on a news site. And was shocked to discover that they were the focus of many of them.

"Look at this," she said, bringing her phone over to him. "There are...hundreds and hundreds of pictures of today."

"You seem alarmed."

"I didn't realize..."

"You are very popular," he said. "After the ball we received glowing press about you."

"I didn't see it."

"Why not?"

"I was distracted by the sex."

"Ah. I was also distracted by that. But I received communication about your popularity early this morning."

"And you didn't share it with me?"

"I didn't have a chance to. But now I am."

"It isn't only me that's popular," she said. "You are too. A king of the people. Unlike the evil dictator before you. And unlike..." She frowned. "Unlike your father."

She turned the screen of her phone off, almost like she was trying to protect him.

"I know," he said.

"What?"

"I already know that my father was not considered a man of the people. I told you that I spent seventeen years trying to figure out how to be the leader that this country needed. Part of that was finding out what had made it ripe for revolution in the first place."

"You don't have any memories of your father, only these...pieces written by other people?"

"I spent a fair amount of time talking to people who remembered him. He was seen as decadent. Out of touch." He frowned. "It feels foolish to have to ask. To not know."

"I should've asked about that before I went and threw a ball."

"Nothing about your ball seemed decadent or out of touch. My father would never have welcomed the citizens of the country. At least, that is my understanding. He certainly never would've walked through the town square."

"You're trying to counteract his reputation."

"Yes. I would be foolish not to."

Yet again, she saw that inability for him to feel certainty. For him to feel like anything was fixed or secure.

Because in his experience, it wasn't.

"You're your own man," she said. "All of these articles recognize it."

She looked around the room, properly, for the first time since they had arrived. It was lovely. Filled with cultural charm. That modern, Scandinavian type of design, mixed with more ornate old-world art and wallpaper.

But she didn't care about the surroundings. She only cared about him.

"I am whatever the people need me to be."

"Is it so impossible for you to let yourself be human?"

"Yes. It is."

"Let yourself be a man, Ragnar."

"I have to be better than that. I'm a king."

"Not in here. If I can give you one thing over the next two years, I want to give you that. With me, you don't have to be a king. With me, you can simply be a man."

Driven by the impulse that was making her heart beat faster, she reached around and unzipped the dress that she was wearing. Let it fall away from her body. Let it fall all the way to the floor. "I don't need you to be a symbol of anything. I only need you to be a man."

CHAPTER ELEVEN

HIS EYES WENT DARK. And she could see that he wasn't going to argue. Wasn't going to resist.

Instead he crossed the space between them and pulled her into his arms. "What is it you want exactly?"

"You," she said, moving her hand down to cup his arousal. "I don't need you to be on guard. I only need you to be Ragnar."

She could see him fighting a battle inside of himself. She could see that he wanted what she was offering. That he wanted to surrender to her. To his need.

She could also see that he was desperate to hang onto that guarded component of himself.

It wasn't just a sense of self-protection. It was more than that. It wasn't only about being there for his country. The way that he had depersonalized himself was essential to his survival, and she could see that in the tortured lines of his face.

She craved his surrender. But she did not crave his destruction.

He was strong. He had cultivated that strength over years of being the man his country needed. Of being the man those around him needed. A myth. A legend.

And yet there was more to it.

She sensed it now; she just couldn't figure out exactly what it was.

But he was a man with razor wire around his heart, and she had identified that from the beginning.

When he had accused her of manipulating him, it had been coming from a place of self-preservation. But why?

Yes, there were so many reasons in his past, but she didn't think that they were the reasons that he had given her.

She didn't think he was lying. But she did think that he was an incomplete man. A man missing pieces of his past, a man who didn't know how to embrace the future. Not apart from duty and honor.

Slowly, she reached out and put her hand on his chest. A short growl escaped his lips, and then she reached up and touched his face. Stroked his cheekbone, down his jaw. "You don't have to fight a war right now. Just be mine."

She was wearing a pair of purple high heels, and matching underwear, and she watched as his gaze darkened. As desire propelled him forward.

"Ragnar," she said. "All you have to be with me is you."

It was as if he lost control entirely then. His growl was deeper, more feral, more sustained as he reached out and wrapped his arms around her, drawing her up against him and kissing her with all the ferocity of a man on the front lines of the battlefield.

He claimed her. Forced her lips open then thrust his tongue deep. There was an honesty to this that soothed something inside of her.

But perhaps it had always been that way with him.

Because he might be a man who didn't know himself, he might be a man who didn't know how to explain all of the things he'd been through or all of the things that he believed in, thought and felt, but he was a man of integrity. A man who did exactly what he said he was going to do. A man to be proud of.

She had never been proud of any of the men she had ever known. She found them selfish. Manipulative. Diabolical.

Men who sowed lies and acted like they might grow something other than a poisoned crop.

But not Ragnar.

He was a man who had survived. A man who had fought, all for the good of others, and never for the good of himself. It made her want to worship him. To give him everything. All of herself.

It made her want to fling herself upon his altar and worship.

So she did. With her lips, her tongue. She offered him supplication in the form of her neck exposed for him, to kiss, to bite. In the form of kisses that she spread across his chest, as she worked to remove his clothes, as she dropped to her knees and took him deep into her mouth.

As she gave him all of the evidence of her longing.

All of her desire.

She needed him.

And she wanted him to know that.

Thinking about the isolation that he had lived in filled her with despair.

Who had ever been here for this man? If anyone ever had, he couldn't even remember it. So she had to build new memories for him. Feelings of warmth. Of connection. Of family.

You can't leave him.

She pushed that thought aside. She continued to pleasure him with her mouth, her tongue, her hands.

As she drove him to the brink, took him to the edge.

As she gave to him, wholly and completely.

"Fern," he growled, his hands in her hair. He was trying to stop her from finishing it this way.

But she would not be stopped.

He had said it himself. She was a warrior. Maybe of another variety than him, but made from the same mettle all the same.

And so she continued. Sucking him in deep until his hips arched forward, until he surrendered. Until he gave her the victory that she craved, on a hoarse cry, spilling himself down her throat.

And now she knew what it was like to win in battle. Because this time, she truly had.

He let out a long, ragged breath, releasing his hold.

She stood up, and took his hand, leading him over to the bed. She stripped off all of her remaining clothes, and got beneath the blankets beside him, stroking his chest with her fingertips.

"There will be more," he said, an iron promise in his voice.

"I know. But there doesn't need to be right this second."

"You are a handful," he said.

"Yes. I've been told that. Every tutor that I ever had despaired of me. Because my mind was always several steps ahead, and I thought most of what I was being taught was stupid. I'm all for diplomacy, as you know. But what I'm not all for is empty manners that might be pretty on the surface, but serve nothing and no one beneath."

"No. You don't strike me as someone who takes kindly to dishonesty."

"I'm not. That's why I got irritated when you said I was manipulative."

"You are not dishonest," he said. "I misspoke. It was only that I thought you might get me to change in some way, and for a while I was resisting that."

"And are you still resisting it?"

He looked up at the ceiling. "I suppose I've never had to change around other people. I was tasked with growing myself into a leader, and I did. Inflexibility was a hallmark of the good that I was doing, and so change feels like the mortal enemy of that. But you are right. It was a different time. Different than when I was growing up. And my job is now different. What I wanted was for you to teach me how to put on a performance. I didn't want you to truly change me. But I'm learning things from you, Fern. Whether I set out to do so or not."

"Oh, that must bother you so."

"It doesn't bother me. Not anymore. Not now, anyway. Perhaps tomorrow it will."

"I do think that we both grew up quite lonely. I was surrounded by people, but they didn't know me. They didn't care for me. Not as I was."

"They only saw what they could make you into."

"Yes. But still, I... You grew up with no one. Did no one ever care if you were hungry? Cold?"

He shook his head. "No."

"I wonder if that's why you don't know how to show any sort of care or compassion to yourself. Because nobody ever showed it to you. No one taught you that it mattered. If you were comfortable. If you felt good or bad or scared or upset…"

"I've never been afraid."

"Never?"

"No. To tell you the truth, I have always assumed that whatever happened that day in the palace frightened me so much it was like a fire had been held to the part of myself that once was able to feel fear, and scalded away all of the nerve endings. Left it completely dead. I have felt vigilance. A deep sense of protectiveness for my people. But not fear. Not for my own self. Not for much of anything. It is a gift."

"Is it? Even when it prevents you from feeling everything else?"

"I don't feel anything else. Or rather, I don't miss what I don't feel. How can you, when you have no idea what to expect?"

That must be because he didn't have any context for himself. He didn't remember the first eight years of his life, and she couldn't imagine what that would do to somebody. How badly that might impact you.

There were things that she wished she couldn't remember from her childhood. But it was different to having a whole swath of yourself entirely erased.

"Just because you don't know it doesn't mean it isn't important. Like eating cake. You might not have known that you were missing out, but you were."

"And yet, it isn't an important thing. If I had never had it, I would not miss it."

"But doesn't it bother you? Knowing that there is so much out there that you haven't experienced?"

"No. It does bother you, though, doesn't it?"

There was deep compassion in his eyes, nothing dismissive. It was entirely different from all the times before when they had talked about what she wanted from life. And the great irony was, she didn't feel like she wanted it any longer. Not in the same way.

Yes, there were things that she was curious about. There was the potential for a life that she might enjoy out there, but it was only a possibility. It wasn't real. Not in the same way that he was. Not in the same way that this was.

"I think it bothered me so much because I felt like I didn't get to choose," she said.

The truth of that rang inside of her like a bell. So clear, so bright. "I felt like because I didn't have a say in my own future that it seemed unfair. That there was such a big wide world out there and I would never get to explore it. I don't feel that same urgency now."

She didn't feel like the walls were closing in. She didn't feel like every step was laid out before her before she ever got a chance to choose it.

She wanted to stay with him. He had agreed to let her go.

Maybe she was just a contrarian.

She didn't think so.

It was like what he'd said. Initially, she had been determined to come out of this without changing. Then she had begun to open herself up to the idea of living while she was here.

But living meant changing. It meant growing in understanding. Of herself, of what she wanted. Of who she was.

It meant being affected.

She had been fighting that for so much of her life. Resisting allowing her father to alter who she was. To dent her spirit in any way.

He was right; she had been resisting being changed or affected by her trauma. But it had happened. That part of her life was real.

Just the same as she could allow herself to be changed by this. And she had. She could change what she wanted. It didn't make her a failure. It didn't mean that she was losing a fight.

She wasn't giving in.

Not to anything other than what she wanted. What she was moving toward. There was something good in that. Something powerful in it. In feeling. In wanting. In accepting.

"After this the world will be yours."

She wanted to correct him. She wanted to tell him that she was going to stay. But the words got stuck in her throat. He was changing. He had admitted to that. He had even said that he didn't hate the idea of it anymore. That was the beginning of something.

But she was afraid. Afraid to push him too hard too fast. Though what she thought he might do, she couldn't say. He had been intent on taking her as a wife forever.

Forever.

Was that really what she wanted?

She felt something, something big and fierce in the center of her chest, and when she looked at him it was nearly painful.

When she touched him, it felt like coming home. In a way that home had never been.

She didn't have words. Not to speak, not even to form inside of herself to try to create an understanding. So she leaned over and she kissed him, letting the blankets fall away, so that her bare skin could press up against his.

He wrapped his arm around her waist, brought her over the top of him, cupping her face as he kissed her with all of the pent-up desire inside of him.

She sat up, and looked down at him, her hair enveloping them both in a dark, tangled curtain.

She felt alive. She felt free. She felt like she belonged to him, and it was nothing like being owned. Because she felt as if he belonged to her too. As if she was the only person who might totally understand. Even if she didn't today, maybe someday she would. She wanted to.

She wanted to change around him. Wanted to re-form herself in his arms.

She couldn't make him want the same.

But she felt...

She bent down and kissed him, and he growled, gripping her hips and moving her down so that her wet heat came into contact with the blunt head of his arousal. She gasped. And then she arched her hips backward, taking him in deep from her position on top of him. She moaned as he filled her, slowly, completely. And then she began to writhe above him. A claiming of her own.

Mine.

Mine.

Mine.

Yes.

She gripped his shoulders, letting her head fall back as she established a rhythm that drove them both mad.

She carried them both to the brink.

This man. He was something. He was everything.

She moaned, shuddering as her orgasm claimed her unexpectedly. And then he growled, reversing their positions so that he was on top of her, driving into her. His powerful hold was like chains, but she never wanted to break free of them.

It was the beauty of him. The paradox of him.

A conqueror, who never made her feel conquered.

Who only made her feel stronger. More herself. More alive.

She had never seen it coming. She had never seen it as a possibility.

Would she give up everything for him?

No. She wouldn't. Because staying with him would mean giving up nothing.

He would be a partner. A lover. Her husband.

My husband is with me.

She thought of Freya, that goddess up in her heavenly plane, forever mourning the husband who was lost to her.

Fern had a husband. And he was not lost to her.

She needed to keep him. She needed to hold onto him. She needed to have him. Forever.

Yes.

There was a whole world out there. Filled with many things. But in this room, with this man, she had found something that she hadn't even truly known existed.

She had found things out about herself. When she had been in that ballroom she had realized...her purpose was to help other people. It wasn't to go away and hoard her freedom, but to try to make life better for others.

For him, for their citizens.

She had been searching for a home all this time, and it was here. Not simply because it was a beautiful country, not simply because she wanted to help the people in it. But because of Ragnar.

It was his home. Branded on his soul. His blood was infused with it.

And she...she loved him. The totality of him. Which meant loving this place. Which meant being part of his mission.

He had been right all along. You couldn't outrun your destiny. What was meant for you could not be denied. Couldn't be turned away from.

They were what had always been meant to be.

A wave of desire rose up inside of her, and she wanted to fight against it because she was still breathless from her last orgasm, but she couldn't keep it from washing over her. She cried out his name.

She loved him.

It was a revelation.

It was glory.

Pain and pleasure and power and more than she had ever even dreamed of desiring.

She had imagined a life where she went off by herself and made all of her own decisions, but that was an illusion of freedom.

It was an illusion of happiness.

She hadn't been able to imagine caring about other people, thinking about other people, and being happy. Because living her life, living the way that she had in the palace in Cape Blanco, her family had made her miserable. And so she had imagined herself alone.

Oh, it was so much more work to care about another person. But she wanted to do that work. With him.

His face was set in stone as he continued to thrust inside of her, as he continued to chase his own release.

She could tell now that he was playing a game with himself. Prolonging it all. Holding himself back.

She smiled. She lifted her head and kissed his neck, kissed down to his collarbone. She felt his large body shudder, felt him pulse deep inside of her.

"Yes," she whispered into his ear. "Take me, Ragnar. I'm yours."

And that was when he let go.

His battle cry echoed off the walls as he surrendered to his need, as he spent himself deep inside of her.

And he gave himself over to the great and powerful need built up between them. And he pushed her over again. The unexpected force of her third climax making her cling to him so hard she was certain she drew blood.

He was breathing hard, and he moved away from her, lying on his back. He was breathing like he had been running. Like…

She looked at him; his eyes were glassy.

"Ragnar?"

She put her hand on his chest; she could feel his heart beating. "Are you okay?"

He growled, and gripped her around the wrist, flinging his body over the top of her again, but this time, it was as if he was shielding her.

"Ragnar," she said.

He rose up over her, looking somewhere back behind

her, but there was nothing there but a wall. "Touch her and die."

She put her hands flat on his chest, held them there. "Ragnar. No one is here. Nothing is happening. I swear to you. Nothing is happening."

And then, he made a terrible, strangled sound. Like that of a man being tortured. Physically, mentally.

Wherever he was, it was a dark place. Wherever he was, it might as well be hell.

"No."

He moved away from her then, his body shaking. He got off the bed, then he stood, like a man waiting to be taken to the executioner.

"Ragnar," she said again. "Please. Whatever is happening…"

And then it was like the fog had lifted. It was like he could see again. Like he was with her. He made a terrible sound. Like a wounded animal. One that had been gutted. And he fell to his knees, his head in his hands. "I remember," he said.

"Oh, Ragnar." She got out of bed and she went over to him. She knelt beside him, and she wrapped her arms around his shoulders. "What did you remember?"

He lifted his head, his blue eyes hunted, haunted. "It was my father. My father was the one that betrayed us all."

CHAPTER TWELVE

It had been like a thunderclap.

It had been nothing like he had ever expected. He hadn't thought much about regaining his past memories, not truly. Because he had always felt like it was a protection to him that he didn't remember. But he had thought that it was because it would be a terrible thing to remember the details of the deaths of his parents. Instead, it was the death of something else.

It was the death of every idea he had ever had about himself and his bloodline.

Yes, his father had been deemed somewhat selfish. A man who craved opulence. A man who loved the finer things in life, but he had never been accused of being a coward. A murderer. He had…

A sick, cold feeling slithered through his veins. As if his blood had turned to ice.

"He handed me over to a guard. To be killed."

"What?"

"He…he killed my mother. He killed her in front of me. He couldn't kill me."

"Ragnar. Slow down. Why…?"

"I think… I think he was working with them. I think he knew that they were going to take over, and the only way for him to save himself was to promise to leave and to never come back. But he also promised us. As...as some sort of sign that he... That he was sincere. That he was never going to reclaim his throne. He killed my mother. He killed her."

"No. He... That can't be right."

"It is," he said, knowing now exactly what had stolen his memory from him. Exactly.

Thankfully, his memory was that of a boy. He could remember hiding in the corner. His father raising a large knife. And he could remember his mother falling, her body obscured by the bed.

But it was unmistakable, what he had witnessed.

There were guards. Military men. "Take him. Dispose of him."

"It wasn't my nanny," he said, the realization rocking him to his core.

"What do you mean?"

"It wasn't my nanny who saved me. It was the soldier that my father gave me to. He took me away. He brought me to those people."

"Why did they tell you that it was a nanny?"

"I don't know. It must've been to protect him. It must've been. He must not have been able to kill a child. My father was too much of a coward to do it. He should've done it. He should have raised his sword and struck me down the way he did my mother."

"I still can't understand. Where is your father?"

"I don't know. For all I know they might have killed him anyway, but he tried to get out of his own death in the most cowardly way possible. He betrayed us. He betrayed the country. He would see his own son killed."

"Oh…"

He put his hand on his forehead. Because then there were more memories. More and more.

His mother. Reading to him. It wasn't a nanny in his memory, telling him about Freya.

There is another way to be a warrior. One who leads with love.

"My mother," he said, his voice rough. "She was my best friend. She was the most important person in my life., I… My father, he was my hero. I saw him as a man who was strong. The kind of king that I wanted to be when I grew up.

"But my mother… She was the one who cared for me. She read to me every night. I felt so safe. I always felt so safe. The palace was my home, the seaside escape was a dream and I trusted them both."

"Of course you can't trust now. Of course everything feels like manipulation. Of course it all feels like a lie."

He looked at Fern, who looked devastated. Her green eyes were filled with tears, her complexion pale.

He had nothing to say to comfort her. Not when he felt entirely undone by the realization.

"It wasn't real. None of it. My father didn't love us. We were never the family that we appeared to be. Not if one day he could decide to raise his own hand against his wife." He pressed his hand to his stomach. "I had no memories. I had filled those blank spaces with an idea, with an ideal. And none of it is true. My father was complicit in what happened to this country, to our family. He saved his own skin. But at the cost of everyone else. Everyone else. My mother, me, the citizens of

Asland. Then he burned it so that no one would know he survived. I am... I am shot through with tainted blood."

"No," she said. "Don't say that. You aren't. You are brave. You are a man who has spent your entire life fighting against what happened to you. Because maybe you did tell yourself a new story. And maybe you didn't remember, but I believe that your body knew. And has known all this time. You are a good man. You brought yourself up from nothing to save this country, and your father never would've done that. He would've laid down and died in the dirt. A man so cowardly that he would kill his own wife, and give his son over to be killed... He would never do what you did."

"I don't know that," he said.

He felt like an imposter. Suddenly it all felt like a lie. He had been meant to come back and rule this country. And yes, he had known that he would be a different sort of ruler to his father, but in many ways he had felt like he was restoring the rightful bloodline, but his father had sold it away. He had sold them.

He had betrayed them, and left them. He had sacrificed everything for his own gain.

Yes, he had lost the throne, but he had... What he was out there living?

The very idea made him feel sick. That his own father was out there watching all of this, watching the return of his son, watching him discover that he had not succeeded. From the comfort of...whatever new existence he had fashioned for himself.

"I will find him," Ragnar said. "And I will have him killed."

"Ragnar. I understand that you want revenge. But the

work that you're doing here in this country is so important. And revenge…"

She stopped.

"What? What is it that you have to say to me?"

"Nothing. You saw your father kill your mother. I'm not going to tell you to take the high road. I can't say what would benefit your soul, not today. Not knowing that he did that. Not knowing that he passed you off to a soldier to be killed."

She was still sitting with him, on the floor, as she had been that morning that she joined him after they'd first made love.

"Of course you don't like to be too comfortable. The only time you ever were it all turned out to be a lie."

She was stroking his face, and he couldn't bear it. He couldn't bear any tenderness with the vile memory still echoing in his head.

"Leave me," he said.

"No. I don't want to leave you. You've been dealing with all of this by yourself for all this time and—"

"You didn't ask for this," he said. "You were supposed to escape. Escape toxic families, and all of the other baggage that you grew up with, and here you have found that my family was worse than yours could ever be. It sounds as if your father is a sniveling coward. But one who would never ever get blood on his own hands. My father was dripping with it. I despise him. I… I am unclean. His blood is in my veins."

"I don't know what to say," she said. But she still didn't leave. She put her hands on his face. "I don't know what to say because this is monumentally fucked up. Because there is no guideline or handbook for how to help somebody through this, but I'm here. I'm here. I'm not going to leave you."

"You should."

She looked at him, her green eyes measured. "We have an agreement. I promised you that I would stay married to you for at least two years, and I will keep that promise, King Ragnar. I will stay your queen. Because you can trust me. You can trust that I will do what I said, that I'm everything I appeared to be. I'm not lying to you. And I would never, ever betray you. I swear it."

Her vows came from deep inside of her, and she understood them. They were nothing like the vows they had spoken to each other at the wedding, in a language that she didn't comprehend.

She was promising to stay with him and… He had no idea how he was going to feel in five minutes, let alone over the next two years.

At the moment everything felt degraded. Destroyed.

He had been inside of her, and everything had felt good. For a moment, everything had felt so good it was like all of the walls inside of him had ceased to exist. And that was when the memories had come.

It was why he couldn't afford to be too comfortable.

It had been a warning.

And he had let himself down by letting everything fall away when he was with her.

He had no one to blame for all of this but himself.

The truth is the truth, whether you know it or not.

Yes. That was true. He couldn't deny it.

But he also couldn't reconcile the terrible burden of knowing these things either.

It made him want to drain the blood from his veins.

It made him want to claw into his own skull and remove part of his brain. The part that knew these things.

He wanted to go back to the way things were.

He wanted to go back to not knowing them.

Then go back.

You don't have to be open like this. You don't need her. You don't need anyone. And you sure as hell don't need these memories.

Yes. He needed to get a grip on himself. He needed to go back to when he didn't know.

He could rule the country that way.

He never had to think about this. He never had to acknowledge it. Yes, it would mean never finding his revenge, and there was something unsatisfying about that. But he would be a better king, a better man, if he didn't have to face the reality of this.

He would go back. He would go back. He just needed to erect the barriers around his soul again.

That was like a memory too. This act of building up a wall inside of himself. Around those thoughts. Around everything that had happened.

He had done this once before, and he would do it again. He never had to think about this again. Not ever.

He never had to think about it again.

He stood up. "I will sleep in the other room tonight."

"Please don't."

"I must. It is for the best. Tomorrow we will go home."

And with that, the conversation was over.

In that he was determined.

CHAPTER THIRTEEN

HE WAS COMPLETELY inaccessible to her now. Whatever had been building between them had shattered the night that his memories had returned. And she didn't know what to do. She didn't know how to reach him.

But he had shut the door so firmly it was impossible for her to even have a conversation with him.

It didn't make her inclined to go to his bed, and he hadn't asked. The one night she had woken up, her heart in her throat, she had gone in and peered into his chamber, and had seen him sleeping on the floor.

A prisoner of the past.

And yet he wouldn't even acknowledge it.

And this was where she decided to do something that she would never normally do.

She decided to call her brother.

Ricardo was the least awful of her brothers. The middle of them, and extraordinarily handsome. He was also very well-connected. A bona fide man-whore who slept with anything that moved, had extracted information from each and every one of his partners.

He was the most terrible gossip in all the world, and all of that information tended to keep him in the lifestyle that he had become accustomed to.

He wasn't the least bit trustworthy.

Which was exactly why she wanted to talk to him.

"Hola," she said, speaking quickly to him in Spanish.

"Fernanda? I'm surprised to hear from you."

"Not that you bothered to check in with me."

"You become a whole queen. What a boon."

"I guess."

"Are you going to invite me to come and visit?"

"That depends. I don't know that I want state secrets to end up splashed all over the global news."

"You wound me," he said, but he didn't sound the least bit wounded.

"Well, I imagine that you'll recover. But I do have something to ask you."

"A favor? You haven't even spoken to me casually in ages."

"I was sequestered in a convent, not that any of you ever asked."

He sighed heavily. "I'm sorry. I find it best never to ask about what our father is up to. There are certain things I don't want to know, because I don't want it to be incumbent upon me to keep any secrets for him."

"That I can understand."

"What is it you need?" he said, sounding much softer.

"I need to know if there are any rumors out there about the former king of Asland."

"Oh," her brother said. "That is some ancient history."

"I know. It's not exactly the lifestyles of the rich and viral. Which I know is much more your specialty."

"That is true. But I know some people that I could ask. What exactly do you want to know?"

"I've just been made aware that there is some reason to believe that the king could still be alive."

"And what do you think will be accomplished if you do find him?"

"He should pay. For what he did," she said.

"I see. Well, I'll see what I can find out. You know all you need to do is drip honey into the right year and usually you can find a trail."

"I trust you."

"You probably shouldn't," he said.

"Maybe not. But...for what it's worth, we were both raised in a family with our father. So we've both suffered."

There was silence on the other end of the phone. "Yes. Though you suffered the most. You didn't have the freedom to leave. Not like we did."

"Well, our oldest brother certainly doesn't have the freedom to do whatever he wants."

"No. That is true."

"It's reserved for those of us who are expendable," Fern said.

"But you were never expendable, Fern. You were something different to him. An asset in a completely different way. And I would never say that it was better. I managed to disappear into the crowd. And there is something to be said for that."

"I've escaped now."

"Into an arranged marriage."

"There's nothing arranged about it," she said. "I... I want to stay with him. But I have to figure out how to help him. I have to figure out how to help fix this."

"I am not very good at giving advice. I'm certainly

not anyone whose life should be admired. What I can say is that you cannot help someone who does not wish to be helped. You could deliver his father to him trussed up like a Christmas goose and if he did not want to accept the gift, he wouldn't. If he did not wish for that to heal him, it would not. Our father doesn't wish to be a good person, Fernanda. There is no amount of offering salvation to him that would make him take it, because he does not believe he needs it. If your husband does not believe he needs healing, then there is nothing that will ever make him accept it."

"Is that why you never come home? There's nothing you can do to fix any of it."

"Nothing. And so I go and I live my life. Out here in the world where there are no arbitrary rules like the ones our father made. You could do the same."

She would have thought of this as the brightest, shiniest apple only a few weeks earlier. Now, she wasn't so sure. Yes, a man like her father was somewhere beyond saving.

But it was different.

"The choice has to come into it somewhere, Ricardo, and I don't just mean the choice to be healed. Ragnar didn't choose this pain. And he had no one to help him through it. He has no idea how to handle it still. That doesn't make him bad. And it doesn't make him broken. It only means it might take a little bit of work."

"But as far as I know, you did not choose to do this work, my sister."

"No. I did. I am choosing this."

"You could also choose to meet me in the French Riviera."

"I appreciate the offer. But that isn't going to work for me."

Love was something she hadn't seen when she was growing up in the palace at Cape Blanco. What she had seen was her mother surrendering all of herself, her father imposing his will on everyone and her brothers becoming islands unto themselves in order to survive it.

She had never really thought about what love looked like. It wasn't manipulation. And it wasn't sitting down and letting another person suck everything out of you.

It wasn't passive. It wasn't malevolent.

Love, she thought, was expensive. It had a cost. It took work.

Sacrifice.

Because yes, she could cut ties with everyone and everything; she could go to the French Riviera with Ricardo. She could have lavish parties, and drink her troubles away. She could live alone. Or she could dig in and do the work here. Wasn't he worth it?

This man who had been betrayed.

This man who had gone through life with no one.

Wasn't she worth it?

Wasn't she worth all this hard work?

She was beginning to understand that the most important things in life were hard. And freedom was making the choice to do the hard thing.

The thing that held weight. Had real value. Yes, she had dreams about a little farm. But that was just… It was a dream from an old version of herself. Who hadn't truly known everything that she was capable of. Who had thought that she could only hear herself, find herself in the quiet.

But she knew different now. She knew that she could stand strong, be the person that he needed and in turn the person that she needed.

"The next time we have a party, I'll call you."

"Thank you," he said. "In the meantime, I'll see what I can find."

And while she waited, she would have to decide what she was going to do about her husband.

Would she be like Freya? Waiting and waiting?

No. She was a goddess. And if she was a goddess, then she was going to go and make something happen.

It was late, and she wasn't quite certain where she might find him.

She had a feeling he wasn't in the palace, even if she couldn't say why. She put on a coat, and went outside into the harsh weather. The season was changing, and the harsh climate here was growing teeth.

So of course he would be out here. Of course he would be out here punishing himself.

Sleeping in the stable. As he had done when he was a boy.

She tore across the grounds, and went into the stable, where she saw him, standing by the stable with his horse.

His horse.

The horse meant something to him. Something important. He hadn't told her. He had come to get her on a horse, which was ridiculous.

"Why did you ride the horse to come and get me?"

He looked at her, his blue eyes shadowed.

"Please," she said. "Talk to me."

"For a number of years he was the only constant in my life. My most trusted...friend."

"See, you have had friends. Soren. Your horse. Me."

"We are not friends, Fernanda."

His use of her name hurt.

"You said that we were."

"Things have changed. I am reminded of who I need to be."

"Please, Ragnar. I don't want things to be like this between us."

"They cannot be another way. I cannot be a different man. I can't… I have to be the king."

There was such a weight to those words. Especially with what he knew now. He had to be the king. He had to be beyond reproach. He couldn't have any weaknesses. Because now he was comparing himself to his father even if he didn't think he was.

"You are not your father."

"I don't wish to speak about that."

"It's important that you realize that."

"I have not spoken to you since we came back. Do you not realize that it was intentional? I am not asking for your advice on anything. I'm not asking for you to heal me."

Her brother's words echoed in her head.

"But maybe you should. Maybe you should ask for some help. Goddammit, Ragnar. Maybe you could be happy."

"Happiness has never been important to me. What is important is fulfilling my duty."

"And what about me?"

"You were never anything but a means to an end."

"Liar," she whispered. "I am Freya. And that means something, it matters. It means—"

"*Nothing.* Nothing but fractured memory in my fractured brain. It meant nothing."

He moved away from the stable, and stormed outside, into the wind. She followed. "I didn't take you for a coward."

"I am nothing like a coward," he said, the wind was blowing at his back, the cloak that he was wearing catching the breeze. And she could see that it was the one he had worn to their wedding. With the strip torn off.

"You made vows to me," she said. She pointed at his cloak. "You promised yourself to me."

"And I already told you. It is not binding, as it is not a promise I made to any deity that I believe in."

"And that's how life works for you, isn't it? You think that you can set your own reality with what you believe, and acknowledge and don't believe, and don't remember. But it isn't true. You don't get to decide. You don't get to decide what's real. You cannot fashion a new truth just to suit yourself. We made those vows. And I don't care if it's to a God you believe in. I believed what I said."

"You didn't," he said. "If I recall correctly you told me it was the most misogynistic thing that you had ever heard."

"Not those vows. The promise that I made to you that night in the hotel. I gave myself to you, and I meant it. And you don't get to control how I feel. You don't get to control what I want."

"I don't have to give you anything in return either."

He began to walk away and she reached out and grabbed the edge of his cloak. He stopped walking, even though she knew full well that he didn't have to. He gripped the edge of his cloak, and tugged it toward himself, bringing her along with it. And then he kissed her. Fern sensed the storm that was beginning to rage around them. She felt raindrops against her face, the wind picking up.

"Is this what you want?" He separated from her, his eyes wild.

"I want you," she said. "Real and raw and difficult. I want you."

"You may regret that."

His kiss was ferocious. Overwhelming. His lips bruised her, and she leaned in for more.

He was trying to frighten her, and she was trying to prove that she was strong enough to stay.

He needed to believe that there was poison in his veins. He needed to believe that something was broken irrevocably, because he was trying to protect himself. And now he was trying to prove that he was stronger than this thing between them, but she knew better.

She was stronger.

Because she had made her choice.

He gazed down at her, his blue eyes visible even in the darkness.

"My husband is far away from me," she said, touching his face. "And I miss him."

The growl that reverberated through his body was feral. Unlike anything she had ever heard. And that was when she found herself being laid down on the ground, cold and wet; he didn't care, and neither did she.

He tore at her dress, and she tore at his clothes, until his cock was free, until he thrust inside of her. There was no game being played. There was no tally being kept of who was satisfying who, and who had the upper hand.

It was a mutual claiming.

A mutual race toward either heaven or hell—which, it was difficult to divine.

He claimed her, over and over again, and she gave him back as good as he gave. Thrust for thrust. Until she cried out his name in time with the first rumble of thunder that rolled through the air.

And he clutched her hips and came, silent in defiance of the magnitude of it all.

"I love you," she whispered, touching his face. The rain poured down, droplets sliding through the creases by his eyes, nature shedding tears for him that he could not shed for himself.

"I love you," she said again. "I'm staying. I'm choosing to stay with you. It's not going to be two years. It's going to be forever."

He pulled away from her, snarling like a wounded beast. "No," he said.

"Yes," she responded. "You need me. You need me, and I need you. And I want to see this through."

"You need to leave, Fernanda."

He pulled away from her and stood up, and she clambered to her own feet, brushing at the wet spot on the back of her dress, shaking, trembling still from the aftermath of the pleasure that had been followed up by so much pain.

"That isn't how life works when you share it with another person, Ragnar. You are not my king. You are my husband."

"And it was only meant to be temporary."

"Bullshit. When you ran that horse across the Isle of Skye and stole me from the convent you didn't intend for any of this to be temporary. I asked for it to be, and now I have changed my mind."

"And I haven't changed mine. In fact, I aim to give you your choice, Fernanda. You will take my plane, and it will fly you anywhere in the world. Anywhere you wish to go. But you cannot stay here."

"What about your...your diplomacy?" she spat.

"I don't care about it. I don't care about this game. I don't care about anything except being the king I need to be, and I cannot do it with you here."

"You're scared. You are so afraid of your feelings."

"And maybe you would be too," he roared. "Maybe you would be too if the center of your feelings contained an image of your mother's dead body on the floor. A realization that your father is a monster. I knew love. And it betrayed me, brutally. I will never love again."

"Then I'm sorry for you," she said. "Because when I fell in love with you I found my strength for the first time. I could have left, Ragnar. At any time. And I could've decided to keep to our original agreement, but I have decided that loving, and living, and feeling all of this pain is worth something."

"If you ever have to look into the sightless, lifeless eyes of your own mother, then you can speak to me about pain. If you know what it is to grow up with nothing and no one, and more comfortable with the floor for a bed than a mattress, then you can speak to me of pain. You are a spoiled, selfish princess, Fernanda, and you not getting to go to whichever party you fancy, or marry whichever man you find handsome, is not actually the struggle that you think it is."

A few weeks ago that would have hurt her. Maybe

even shamed her. But she was not going to let this frightened fool of a man hurt her. She wasn't going to let him minimize what she had learned. What she knew now.

"I don't know the exact pain that you've gone through. But I know what it means to be lonely. I am sorry. I am so sorry that you were hurt the way that you were hurt, and I want to help you. And if you won't let me help you, just let me love you."

"Just like your mother? You would like to love me until your eyes grow dim? Until you lose every bit of yourself. Until you forget that you were ever a warrior? Because you know that is what loving someone broken brings. If it doesn't bring about your own death."

"You're not your father."

"No. And I can never afford to be. You…you make me weak. And I cannot afford it. The plane will leave in the morning. I've said my piece. This is done. It's over. You have your freedom."

"And what about my choices?"

"You are free to choose anything. Except me."

CHAPTER FOURTEEN

THE NEXT MORNING he watched the plane leave, watched as Fern left. He had demanded it. And she had obeyed. And yet, even as he got what he wanted, he felt as if his chest was being split open.

He was…destroyed in a way he hadn't thought possible.

He was ashamed of himself. Of the way that he had taken her last night. Of the way that he had taken a proclamation of love and thrown it back in her face, but he had no idea what else he was supposed to do with it.

Because it was far too terrifying. Far too powerful.

And so he had lied to her when he'd said that he couldn't feel fear. The moment that she had said she was going to stay with him…he had felt fear like he had never known before.

Deep, unending, primal fear.

But what did life look like without her? He could do this. He could continue to rule the country exactly as he had started. But now he…he knew.

Now he knew that there was something sweeter, something happier available for him if only he wanted it.

How ridiculous that he had thought that he could be

with her for two years, and simply replace her with another wife.

He would never want another woman. Not as long as he lived. How would anyone ever be like Fern?

Freya.

His goddess.

There is another way to be a warrior...

His mother's voice echoed in his head, and he pushed it away.

Because it was far too painful.

It was far too…

It was a reminder of what love really is.

Of the fact that it didn't have to be defined by loss.

No. He refused.

He stormed around the castle, and found it far too comfortable for his liking. Every piece of furniture so soft and inviting. Everything inside of him was breaking apart. It took hours for him to be able to sit. For him to even contemplate eating.

And then his phone rang.

It was from a number he didn't recognize.

He answered. "Hello?"

"Hola. My name is Ricardo. You have just sent my sister to me."

"Fern."

"Yes. Fernanda is with me. She also tasked me with something. And even though I'm furious at you because my sister has come to me broken, she says that I still have to tell you this. I have found your father."

He felt like he had been hit in the chest with a brick. "Explain."

"I found your father. He's living in a small village in

Spain. New name, new identity. Lots of money. I can have him brought to you."

"How?"

"I have my ways. But he can be taken captive, and brought to you if you like."

"Yes. I would very much like that."

He felt numb. His father was going to face justice.

And while nothing that happened would ever be made right, it would be... Something could be healed.

What about you?

There was something that still felt profoundly broken in him. And even as he prepared to receive the man that he hated more than any other, he felt no real triumph.

Because nothing in the past could truly be fixed.

And he had no idea what he wanted in his future.

It was world news. The former king of Asland had been found, living a secret life in Spain, and had been taken into custody. Imprisoned for crimes against his people, and also for murder.

She had been proud. Because he hadn't simply killed his father. He had allowed justice to prevail. He would now be sharing a cell with the other man who had destroyed the country.

It was fitting.

And she still felt devastated. Lonely.

She still missed him.

She still wanted him.

But she could be glad that some part of him had found... Perhaps justice would put him on a path to healing.

Perhaps it would placate something in him.

She was sitting by the pool at her brother's villa. She was more than one margarita into the day, and she was realizing that she needed to get herself together. She wasn't going to sit in her heavenly plane mourning a man who wouldn't come to her for the rest of her life.

She could at least be happy that this had given her a small chance to get to know Ricardo a little bit better. But she had also gotten to know his current boyfriend, and she liked him very much, and if Ricardo did his typical thing and blew it all up then she was going to be cross with him. She had told him that last night after dinner and he had only laughed.

"So I should attempt heartbreak like you?"

"You should not be an idiot like my husband. If you have a good thing you should keep it."

He hadn't been amused by that.

She took another sip of her margarita and looked out at the pool.

"You should slow down on those," said her brother, meandering near her lounge chair.

"Why? It's more fun than thinking."

"I agree. But you are much smarter than I am. You also engineered justice that was long overdue. Not something I would've done."

"You did help."

"I did. Though I confess it was not initially out of the goodness of my heart. Just guilt."

"Some would suggest that your capacity for guilt means that you do have a good heart."

"I don't know about that."

"Vincenzo certainly seems to think you have a good heart."

"That's not what he likes."

"I disagree."

"Excuse me."

They both turned to see Vincenzo standing in the doorway. For a second, she was worried that he had overheard them.

"You seem to have a visitor," he said.

She and Ricardo exchanged glances. "I'm not expecting anyone," he said.

"I believe it's your sister's husband. I recognize him from all the recent news."

Her heart leaped up into her throat. She could scarcely believe it.

And then there he was, as if he had been summoned. Entirely incongruous in this sun-drenched setting, an ice-cold Viking, and her in a bikini.

She stood up slowly. "What are you doing here?"

"I'm here to thank you. And your brother. For what you have done not just for me but for my country."

Of course. He would be noble in the face of all of this. She didn't want nobility. She didn't want a consolation prize.

What she wanted was him. But she needed that to be love. Not just desire.

"I did it for my sister," Ricardo said, colder than Ragnar at this point, which was impressive, honestly.

He gestured to Vincenzo, and the two of them went into the house. Leaving her and Ragnar alone.

"I contacted Ricardo about finding your father before I was sent away."

"Does that mean you wouldn't have done it?"

"I would have. It was the right thing to do. I knew that he would be able to help. He's very well-connected."

"I thought your whole family was worthless?"

"Not all of them. Something I'm discovering is that we were all raised by our father. And we have all made mistakes as a result of that. But not all of my brothers are proud of those mistakes."

"That is healing, I imagine."

"And what about you?" She looked at him directly. "Do you feel healed? Now that you know the truth?"

He shook his head slowly. "It was the right thing. But you know, a narcissist will always tell you that he did what he had to. He is incapable of being a villain in his own mind. There is nothing satisfying in talking to my father. He expressed pride that I lived. And in many ways I feel takes credit for it. There is no remorse. There is no satisfaction. It is only a tragedy, and we all must live in the aftermath. The only tragedy for him is that the end of his triumph is here. But there is no real…feeling."

"I'm sorry. I am sorry about all of it."

"Fern I… I need you to forgive me. There is so much about being human that I don't understand."

His words were soft, slow. It was all very unlike him. Her heart sped up, and then slowed down. "What do you mean?"

"You are right. I saw myself and you as symbols. And I began to make progress, but that progress felt too intense, and so I pulled away. That progress was what knocked the walls down inside of me and brought my memories back. It's why I ran from you. Why I turned away so resolutely. Because being with you made me feel safe for the first time in years. And that was what brought those memories out. I... I built a wall around them when I was a child. I didn't want to know that my father did that. I didn't want to remember what had happened to my mother. Or that he wanted me gone. It was easier. To survive. As long as I believed that the villain had come from outside of our family. I couldn't handle the truth."

"Few people could. It's a monstrous thing to have to face. It's... Few people could've survived what you did. You did what you had to do."

"Yes, I did. But somewhere along the line, I was okay. I just didn't feel like I was. I forgot that I was doing more than surviving. It's the only thing I know how to do. I do not know how to live, Fern. Except... I kept remembering that my mother is the one that told me the story about Freya."

"And what did she tell you?"

"The reason that some warriors don't go to Valhalla is because they choose a different path. They fight for love and not glory. They fight for love most of all, above honor, above country. She cared about that. It was what she wanted me to know. Because I think... my father wanted his own glory. He spoke of Valhalla. My mother... She wanted me to love. And all of these years took that away from me. That understanding. That story. You brought it back."

"I did?"

"Yes. You did."

"I still love you, you know," she said. "It didn't go away just because you weren't ready."

"Oh, Fern." He moved forward and touched her face.

"I am grateful for that. I am so much more than grateful. Because I want to change. I want to learn to live. But I'm going to need you to do it. I... I think I love you. For all that it's worth, coming from a man who has spent his life building walls around his heart."

She moved forward, and gripped his hand. "That means even more."

It was like their wedding, except there was no cloth binding their hands together. It was only them. Only their choice. Only their love.

"Would you come with me?" he said. "Please."

"Yes," she said.

He took her hand, and led her through the house. Her brother and Vincenzo were sitting on a chaise, and watched as they went past.

"I'm going with him," she said. "Thank you," she said. "For everything."

"I expect an invitation to a party," Ricardo said. "And," he added, "if you break my sister's heart, King Ragnar, there is no corner of this earth that will be able to conceal you. Remember, I found your father."

"I'm not my father," Ragnar said. "I stand and fight my battles."

"Even if you're a little late," Ricardo pointed out.

And Ragnar surprised her by laughing. Really laughing. Perhaps the first real laugh she had ever heard from the man. "Yes," he agreed. "I was a little late indeed."

He opened the front door for her, and for a moment she thought she was hallucinating. Because there was a horse. His horse, in fact, right outside.

"You brought your horse?"

"Yes. I bring him to every important battle. I would never trust myself if I left him behind."

"Are you superstitious?"

"Yes. I told you. I believe in trolls and giants. And luck."

He mounted his horse, and extended his hand. She accepted, and he pulled her up onto the steed, nestled right at his front. It was so very different to that first time. Where he had run her down in the field. This time, she was going very much willingly.

"I also believe in Freya," he whispered against her ear. "And I worship at her altar. And will, for the rest of my life."

He didn't need to say it. She knew that it was true.

He was driven by love. Whether he knew it or not, he always had been. The love for his people, the love for a mother that he had lost.

And now, his love for her. He had never been a man who felt too little. Only a man who felt too much.

But now all that feeling had somewhere to go.

Now, he wasn't alone anymore.

She looked back at him, into those brilliant blue eyes.

Blue, as far she could see. Wild, untamed.

And in his eyes, she saw the future. Their future. Their love, their marriage, their children.

Forever.

And in his arms, she finally felt like herself.

Fern.

His chosen queen, who had absolutely chosen him back.

* * * * *

If you couldn't put From Convent to Queen *down, then be sure to check out these other desire-fueled stories from Millie Adams!*

His Highness's Diamond Decree
After-Hours Heir
Dragos's Broken Vows
Promoted to Boss's Wife
Heir of Scandal

Available now!

MILLS & BOON®

Coming next month

BODYGUARD'S ROYAL TEMPTATION
Abby Green

She felt incredibly delicate and yet he sensed a latent strength.

He had a feeling he shouldn't underestimate her. After all she'd managed to ditch her bodyguards and avoid her brother.

He looked down at her and she lifted her face. She smiled. It made something inside Ares ache. Why was she so smiley? So perky? She was a princess way out of her depth. She could have been unconscious somewhere now if it hadn't been for him. But again, he had that sense that perhaps she would have surprised him by managing to get out of that predicament. She was using a false name to avoid detection.

Then his gaze went to her mouth. It opened slightly and he had a glimpse of pink tongue. White teeth. A fire started raging in his blood. He'd never been more tempted by a woman. By a woman who was so far out of his bounds that –

Before Ares could formulate another word, she'd reached up and pressed her mouth to his, a chaste and surprisingly sweet gesture. But any thought of *sweet* fast dissolved as *sweet* morphed into burning hot *heat* and intense need. Ares couldn't resist.

Continue reading

BODYGUARD'S ROYAL TEMPTATION
Abby Green

Available next month
millsandboon.co.uk

Copyright ©2026 Abby Green

COMING SOON!

We really hope you enjoyed reading this book. If you're looking for more romance be sure to head to the shops when new books are available on

Thursday 26th March

To see which titles are coming soon, please visit
millsandboon.co.uk/nextmonth

MILLS & BOON

FOUR BRAND NEW BOOKS FROM
MILLS & BOON MODERN

Indulge in desire, drama, and breathtaking romance – where passion knows no bounds!

OUT NOW

Eight Modern stories published every month, find them all at:

millsandboon.co.uk

TWO BRAND NEW BOOKS FROM
Love Always

Be prepared to be swept away to incredible worldwide destinations along with our strong, relatable heroines and intensely desirable heroes.

OUT NOW

Four Love Always stories published every month, find them all at:

millsandboon.co.uk

OUT NOW!

Available at
millsandboon.co.uk

MILLS & BOON

LET'S TALK
Romance

For exclusive extracts, competitions and special offers, find us online:

- **f** MillsandBoon
- **X** @MillsandBoon
- **○** @MillsandBoonUK
- **♪** @MillsandBoonUK

Get in touch on 01413 063 232

For all the latest titles coming soon, visit
millsandboon.co.uk/nextmonth